W9-DJG-770

THE CURIOUS HEART
OF AILSA RAE

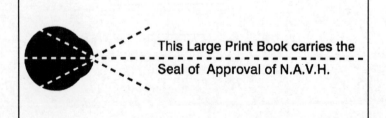

This Large Print Book carries the
Seal of Approval of N.A.V.H.

THE CURIOUS HEART
OF AILSA RAE

STEPHANIE BUTLAND

THORNDIKE PRESS
A part of Gale, a Cengage Company

Copyright © 2018 by Stephanie Butland.
Thorndike Press, a part of Gale, a Cengage Company.

ALL RIGHTS RESERVED
This is a work of fiction. All of the characters, organizations, and events portrayed in this novel are either products of the author's imagination or are used fictitiously.
Thorndike Press® Large Print Women's Fiction.
The text of this Large Print edition is unabridged.
Other aspects of the book may vary from the original edition.
Set in 16 pt. Plantin.

LIBRARY OF CONGRESS CIP DATA ON FILE.
CATALOGUING IN PUBLICATION FOR THIS BOOK
IS AVAILABLE FROM THE LIBRARY OF CONGRESS

ISBN-13: 978-1-4328-7395-0 (hardcover alk. paper)

Published in 2020 by arrangement with Macmillan Publishing Group, LLC/St. Martin's Publishing Group

Printed in Mexico
Print Number: 01   Print Year: 2020

*For Ned and Joy, with gratitude for their
warm and honest hearts*

■ ■ ■ ■

Part One:
October 2017
Night's Candles
are Burnt Out

■ ■ ■ ■

6 October, 2017

Hard to Bear

It's 3 a.m. here in cardio-thoracic.

All I can do for now is doze, and think, and doze again. My heart is getting weaker, my body bluer. People I haven't seen for a while are starting to drop in. (Good to see you, Emily, Jacob, Christa. I'm looking forward to the Martinis.) We all pretend we're not getting ready to say goodbye. It seems easiest. But my mother cries when she thinks I'm sleeping, so maybe here, now, is time to admit that I might really be on the way out.

I should be grateful. A baby born with Hypoplastic Left Heart Syndrome a few years before I was would have died within days. I've had twenty-eight years and I've managed to do quite a lot of living in them. (Also, I've had WAY more operations than you everyday folk. I totally win on that.) OK, so I still live at home and I've never had a job and I'm blue around the edges because there's never quite enough oxygen in my system. But —

Actually, but nothing. If you're here

9

tonight for the usual BlueHeart cheerfulness-in-the-teeth-of-disaster, you need to find another blogger.

My heart is failing. I imagine I can feel it floundering in my chest. Sometimes it's as though I'm holding my breath, waiting to see if another beat will come. I've been in hospital for four months, almost non-stop, because it's no longer tenable for me to be at home. I'm on a drip pumping electrolytes into my blood and I've an oxygen tube taped to my face. I'm constantly cared for by people who are trying to keep me well enough to receive a transplanted heart if one shows up. I monitor every flicker and echo of pain or tiredness in my body and try to work out if it means that things are getting worse. And yes, I'm alive, and yes, I could still be saved, but tonight it's a struggle to think that being saved is possible. Or even likely. And I'm not sure I have the energy to keep waiting.

And I should be angrier, but there's no room for anger (remember, my heart is a chamber smaller than yours) because, tonight, I'm scared.

It's only a question of time until I get too weak to survive a transplant, and then it's a waste of a heart to give it to me. Someone a bit fitter, and who would get more use from it, will bump me from the top of the list and I'm into the Palliative Care Zone. (It's not actually called that. And it's a good, kind, caring place, but it's not where I want to be. Maybe when I'm ninety-eight. To be honest, tonight, I'd take forty-eight. Anything but twenty-eight.)

I hope I feel more optimistic when the sun comes up. If it does. It's Edinburgh. It's October. The odds are about the same as me getting a new heart.

My mother doesn't worry about odds. She says, 'We only need the one heart. Just the one.' She says it in a way that makes me think that when she leaves the ward she's away to carve one out of some poor stranger's body herself. And anyway, odds feel strange, because even if my survival chances are, say, 20 per cent, whatever happens to me will happen 100 per cent. As in, I could be 100 per cent dead this time next week.

Night night,
BlueHeart xxx

P.S. I would really, really like for one of you to get yourself a couple of goldfish, or kittens, or puppies, or even horses, and call them Cardio and Thoracic. My preference would be for puppies. Because I love the thought that, if I don't make it to Christmas, somewhere there will be someone walking in the winter countryside, letting their enthusiastic wee spaniels off the lead, and then howling 'Cardio! Thoracic!' as they disappear over the brow of a hill intent on catching some poor terrified sheep. That's what I call a legacy.

9 OCTOBER, 2017

Ailsa is alone when it happens.

'We think we have your heart.' Bryony, the transplant coordinator, is smiling from ear to ear, for once. Given that her usual message is No News Yet, that's hardly surprising.

Ailsa feels her hands fly to her chest, as though to protect what's in there, hold it before it dies. She makes herself move them to her lap. They are shaking. So is her voice.

'A new heart?' And then she feels the patched-up heart she has summon up the life to expand with hope: with permission.

Her head is a scramble of thoughts, the practical and the terrible. She needs to be nil by mouth, so when did she last eat? Where is her mum? If she's getting a heart, that means someone, somewhere has died.

Ailsa's mother rushes in behind Bryony, breathless, bringing cold air and cigarette smoke with her. They fight the stuffiness of the room for a second before being absorbed. 'They told me at the nurses' station to get along here fast. What's happened?' She steps across the room; her hand is in her daughter's. All Ailsa can do is nod at her, squeeze her fingers, because her throat has tightened and her mouth is drier than usual. She wants to say: I wish you had been here when Bryony came in. You deserved to hear it with me. But that's silly, and unimportant, and anyway, you don't get to choose these things. You get to accept them.

'We need to have you prepped and in theatre in three hours,' Bryony says. 'Hold onto your hats.' She flips open the file in her hand, picks up Ailsa's notes from the bottom of the bed, and so it begins.

Or ends, depending on which way you look at it.

9 October, 2017

I'm Going to the Theatre!

It's here! The heart is here! So it's going to be a while until you hear from me. (Don't panic. For the next couple of weeks, no news equals good news.)

I'm about to wrestle myself into my surgical stockings and say something that is Definitely Not Goodbye to my mother. I'm not going to tell you how I'm feeling, about the risks, about what's about to happen, or about the donor family, or about anything to do with Mum, because if I even look at those feelings I don't know what will happen to me, but I know it won't be good.

I wrote this poll a month ago and I've been saving it. Posting it before today felt like tempting fate. But now, the dice have rolled. So here is the first poll of my New-Heart life. I'll see you on the other side, my friends. Thank you for the voting, and the comments, and for cheering me on here.

What should I do when I'm well?

15

1. Climb something high. Not a ladder. A little mountain, or a big hill. A Munro, maybe. Somewhere I can see for miles and there are clouds and craggy bits and the odd sheep. Sometimes when I'm really poorly I close my eyes and think about those views.
2. Get a shock. I'll jump into cold water or go on a roller coaster. I'll watch some awful horror film or bungee jump off the Forth Bridge. My new heart will not be scared of anything. The heart I have now, on the other hand, took ill when I typed 'roller coaster'.
3. Learn to dance. I've wanted to tango since I first watched *Strictly Ballroom*.
4. Switch my phone off. For hours. I'll be fully equipped. No one will need to be worried about me. Don't get me wrong, phones are great. But before I had to come into hospital, I did actually have to be glued to mine, in case of an incoming heart.
5. Queue for something. I might go to London and stand for six whole hours waiting to get ground passes for Wimbledon. I'd be the only person who was in it for the queueing rather than the tennis. The important thing is — I'll trust my heart to keep me upright for as

long as it takes.

I thought there would be a thousand things I wanted to do when I could, and my list would be full of Eiffel Towers and Taj Mahals. But those things feel too abstract right now. I don't even have a passport.

I suppose what it all comes down to, really, is one thing: I'll do what I feel like doing. I won't worry about whether I can, what might go wrong, or what the implications are. I'll be impulsive. Unmanaged. (As far as anyone on anti-rejection meds can be impulsive and unmanaged.) I'll be normal.

My question is — which of these will make me feel most alive?

1 Climb a high thing
2 Get a fright
3 Dance, dance, dance
4 Switch off my phone
5 Queue

I'll leave the poll open for a week, and look at it when I'm back from transplant-land. Because, mark my words, I'm coming back.

See you on the other side.

BlueHeart xxx

32 shares
256 comments

Results:
1 Climb a high thing   25%
2 Get a fright   19%
3 Dance, dance, dance   36%
4 Switch off my phone   14%
5 Queue   6%

12 OCTOBER, 2017

Consciousness, it seems, is liquid behind glass: moving, ungraspable. Closing her eyes doesn't stop the fairground-ride heave of it, but it makes it easier to bear. She sleeps again.

'How do you feel?' people ask, what feels like every fifteen seconds or so. 'Ailsa? Ailsa? Can you hear me? How do you feel?'

She wants to say: I feel as though I've been kicked in the heart by a horse. I want to get out of here. Pass my shoes. Pass my eyeliner. Get me a five-year diary.

But her tongue is too tired to move and her teeth are heavy and gummed together, impossible to separate. Something hurts her throat. A tube? She tells her arm to move, to find out if there is a tube going into her mouth. Her arm ignores her.

She opens her eyes. Her vision fills with faces, smiling or questioning, and just the thought of trying to focus on them, to remember who the eyes belong to or to try to make sense of the words coming out of them, seems more impossible than flying. Flying, in fact, feels like something she can remember, something that she could do: if she could just untether herself from the blankets and the noises, she could float. She thinks she was floating, a little while ago.

Her fingers, back to babyhood, grasp involuntarily when other fingers touch her palm.

And she goes back to sleep, for what feels like no time at all, and when she wakes, it's the same thing, over.

15 OCTOBER, 2017

'Fucking hell, Ailsa,' her mother, Hayley, says, the first time she opens her eyes and doesn't immediately feel them drawing themselves closed again, as though her lids have been replaced by bulldog clips. 'I thought you were never coming back.' Hayley's smile is bright but she's paper-pale; her eyes have the horribly familiar I've-been-crying-but-if-you-ask-me-I'll-deny-it look. Ailsa can only see her mother's face, her hair and the scarf around her neck, which is one of Hayley's favourites, a yellow-gold silk rectangle that Ailsa chose for her the Christmas before last.

'Is it . . . ?' she asks. Her voice is whatever the opposite of silk is, harsh and scraping.

'It's all good,' Hayley says. 'Six days since the operation. You were out for the count for the first forty hours, and you've been drifting up and down ever since.'

Ailsa nods, or at least thinks about nodding, but it doesn't seem that her head moves. Her hair feels damp against the pillow. 'Mum,' she gets out.

'I'm here, hen. I've been here all the time.' Her mother's tears are coming now, and she starts to talk, quickly, as though her voice will drown them out. 'I told people not to come but they didnae take the blindest bit of notice. It's been like Waverley Station in here some days. There's a stack of cards for you, and chocolate, and somebody brought gin, but you'll not be wanting that for a while, I should think —'

'Mum,' Ailsa says again. They are here. Finally, after all the years of illness — breathlessness, pain, caution — all the health checks and operations, all the conversations about the eventual need for transplant, all the ways their lives have been trimmed away at the edges because of all the things that Ailsa couldn't do, they are here, in the wished-for place. She feels as though she's going to cry; doesn't dare, because if she heaves a breath, who knows what will happen to her new heart? But Hayley is at her side, and she takes Ailsa's hand, and then she reaches over and presses her lips to her daughter's forehead, and it's all there, every hurt and fear they've shared, every hope.

Ah, here's the nurse. Hayley steps away, and there are lights and tappings and questions. Someone wets her lips. There's no tube.

'Did I have a tube?' Ailsa asks.

'For the first couple of days,' Hayley says.

'My throat hurts.' It's a ludicrous thing to say, because every single part of her, inside and out, hurts. Her ankles seem weighted, her legs are stiff. The downward force of the bedclothes on her toes feels unbearable. Her stomach is surely full of some dark, thick liquid, tar or sour yoghurt, and if she moves, she knows it will spew from her. Her neck is pinched into place by tight muscles, her head sharp with pain, her eyes suddenly allergic to light. And as for her chest . . . She can't even think about her chest. It feels — well, it feels exactly the way she had imagined it would feel if the sternum had been separated, her heart removed, another attached in its place, and then the bones wired back into position and the flesh sewn together again over the top.

Except that the imagination isn't really equal to the reality. There is pain, yes, but confusion too. A memory drifts in: some reading Ailsa did about early transplant experimentation, the head of one dog attached to the body of another. That's her.

She's that dog. Her heart — the heart — knows something has happened, but it doesn't know what, and that sense of confusion is moving through her body with every pulse and beat. Her chest, her bones, are crying out: that wasn't meant to happen. I didn't sign up for that. I am solid. I am not to be opened. I am designed to be sealed, to keep what is inside me safe. You can't just put another heart in here.

'Don't try to move, Ailsa,' Hayley says, and she puts her palm against Ailsa's forehead. 'Breathe. You're safe now. You've done it.'

But breathing feels like the worst kind of moving. Every stitch feels as though it's stretching to the point of snapping whenever she inhales. She tries to breathe more shallowly, but the monitors give her away.

'I feel as though I might break open.' Her words barely scratch the air, but she's heard. There's quiet laughter from her mother and the nurse. It's Nuala, the roses in the perfume she wears sweet enough to cut through antiseptic and cleansing gel. She thinks about saying that she's not joking, but that would be a waste of what little power she seems to have. So she closes her eyes.

'Everything is just as it should be,' a voice

says, in the night. Although Ailsa knows it's a nurse — can even tell it's Frankie, from the clipped clarity of the Highlands in his voice — in the darkness, she hears Lennox, beloved and oh so missed, who waited for a saviour who never came. She thinks about how she has lost six days, or rather traded them for something like a normal life. She was weeks from death. Now she has almost as good a chance as anyone else of seeing sixty. Well, fifty, at least. It's as though she has been given permission to look out of a window that has always been forbidden to her before: she cannot believe how far away the horizon is, how beautiful the view.

The next morning, Ailsa sits up, and eats a banana, and Hayley beams. She throws it up again.

'Ah well,' her mother says, 'you cannae win them all.'

1 November, 2017

A New Friend

Yesterday, Mum and I packed up my hospital room and got into my honorary-auntie's car and brought my new heart home. I've had a couple of day trips and popped in here — hospital is not prison, though they do sometimes tie you to machines so you can't really leave — but this was Official Discharge. Which is way nicer than it sounds. I'll be back at the hospital three times a week for the next wee while, and I'm not out of the woods yet, but there is cause to be pleased.

The moment we got back to the flat, we all three looked at each other and sighed, and it did feel a bit as though we had been holding our breath for — I don't know how long. We were going to get a takeaway, but I took my meds and went to bed, and Mum and Auntie T drank wine and kept waking me up with their laughing. It was a good sound. (They shared a flat in their uni days and sometimes I think they've forgotten that they're not there anymore.)

So, I'm home. The hospital residency

part of my BlueHeart/NewHeart life is done.

Now let the living commence.

Thank you for hanging on in there with me! (And for never, ever making me eat jelly when I asked you to vote on menu choices.) Especially during all those compelling posts about my strange post-operative body and how weird it is to be growing a beard. The facial hair remover is working just fine. And the nurse assures me that it's a temporary side-effect of the drug regime, and won't be forever, and neither will the moon-face and the extremely erratic bowels. Here's hoping. There's still a likelihood of a vote on cures for constipation.

While I was out for the count, you all voted. Dancing and climbing a high thing came out on top. (Do you see what I did there?) And those are absolutely in my plan. But not for a wee while, because of all the getting better there is still to do.

Some getting better is easy(ish). Get enough sleep. Take enough exercise, within reason. Eat the right things. (That one needs a bit of work, to tell you the truth. The major side effect of steroids seems to be an insatiable need for cake.)

And some getting better is different. It's

hard to explain. All I can say is — I wonder whether this new heart is having to learn me like I'm having to learn it.

I know it's not logical. I know it's not science. But we also know that science used to think that deoxygenated blood was actually blue. It isn't. Veins look blue (I looked blue) because of light hitting the skin over them and scattering into the wavelength that we see as blue. So there you go. Just because something looks true today doesn't mean it will still be true tomorrow.

I just — I don't trust this heart. Maybe it's because it's a new-to-me muscle, untried, untested, and so I'm not going to use it to do any seriously heavy lifting until I know what it's capable of. I don't know anything about the person this heart came from. Mum and I talk about them, most days, even if it's just to say, 'Thank goodness for them' and 'I wish they knew what they did'. I do wonder how their heart feels, in this new body.

I was thinking about that this morning, as I was walking, walking, because whatever happens in Edinburgh, rain or sleet or wind or sun or all of them at the same time, I am going to walk every day. At the moment it's ten minutes, five there and five back. Next week I'll up it to fifteen. (Fifteen minutes in Edinburgh can be hard going. Edinburgh used to be a volcano, geology fans.) And I was thinking — maybe I should make friends with this heart. And making friends starts with a name.

I've chosen two, but I'm leaving the final decision to you.

I'm giving you three days.

APPLE: Plump, red and good for keeping the doctor away. What better name for a heart?

AMBER: An amber traffic light means take care, and I need to take care of this heart in all sorts of ways or it will end badly for us both. Amber balances emotion and clears stress.

102 comments

Results:
APPLE: 64%
AMBER: 36%

2 NOVEMBER, 2016

This Time Last Year

'I win the Most Colourful Hands contest,' Lennox says. They've got into the habit of starting Ailsa's visits with a comparison, though she wishes they hadn't, now that Lennox is getting more jaundiced by the day.

'You win this round,' Ailsa says. 'I'm the winner overall, and you know it, because I've got years on you.' Her nailbeds are always bluish, and sometimes the skin on her fingertips has the same unhappy hue. She takes her hand from where it's been lying next to his on the hospital bedclothes, side by side, so that they could compare. Lennox moves his hand too, and their palms kiss, part.

He's diminishing, as well as yellowing, his athlete's body lacking exercise, his appetite gone. She tries not to show that she's noticed. He shuffles along the bed so that she can perch next to him, puts his left arm around her to keep her steady.

'How's life? Tell me things that aren't to do with hospital.'

Ailsa laughs. 'I've been watching *West Side Story*,' she says.

'OK. Tell me things that aren't to do with hospitals or *West Side Story*.'

'You're an ungrateful sod,' she says, and looks down at his right hand on the blanket, but her eyes slide away from its pallor and the cannula taped to it. She's understanding, more and more, what it's like for her mother, her friends, when she's ill enough to be hospitalised and they come to see her. She wants to do to Lennox all the things she hates when people do them to her. She wants to tell him it will be all right, that he's brave. She wants to squeeze him and say she loves him. Hell, she wants to have sex with him, just to see if it will make either of them feel better. The usual rules for ex-boyfriends and girlfriends cannot possibly apply here.

'I know,' he says, and he rests his head against hers. 'What's what with the blog?'

'Oh.' Ailsa jumps with the surprise of remembering it. 'I've got to ten thousand hits.'

'Fantastic.' And though he's tired there's

genuine pleasure in his voice. 'That's amazing for, what, six months? I hope you're proud of yourself.'

'Seven. I started it when I went on the transplant list,' she says. 'But it's weird. I mean, some people leave comments, and share things, so I know people are reading it, but it's a bit — one way. I've been trying to think of a way to make it more . . .'

'Interactive?' Lennox asks.

'Yes.' Ailsa snuggles closer, breathes him in — he's been wearing the same aftershave for almost as long as she's known him, and he still smells of it, even though he gives off the strange, sweet scent of his illness too. 'Whatever I think, or do, or want, is irrelevant, because it all comes down to getting a heart. Or not. I want to show people that.'

'And you want to keep it anonymous?'

'I think that's best. Folk can hear all about my ups and downs so long as they have no idea who I am.'

Lennox shifts his weight so that he can move towards her, and hold her with both arms. 'I know exactly what you're getting at,' he says. 'We've got to hang in and hope. And it's shit. It's out of our control. So you need — how about some sort of poll?'

Ailsa still fits against him so comfortably,

so well. 'You mean if I ask people to decide things any normal person would decide for themselves, I'm making that point, aren't I?'

Lennox laughs, holds her at arm's length, then kisses her, his mouth a little sour. 'Genius, Rae,' he says, and his smile has never changed, not since the first day they talked to each other when they were sixteen and working on an after-school project in a church hall. 'This time next year that blog of yours will be winning awards.'

■ ■ ■ ■

PART TWO:
FEBRUARY 2018
MORE CARE TO STAY
THAN WILL TO GO

■ ■ ■ ■

Part Two

3 February, 2018

Behind the Mask

Today, Apple is dealing with out-of-the-ordinary excitement.

Mum works most days, now that she's not on permanent Heart Alert, and so I've the flat to myself most of the time. I write a post, maybe wade in to some discussion about transplants or waiting lists online. I think about jobs I might apply for, once I reach the magic six-month milestone where Apple and I should know each other well enough for me to be able to protect her in the wide world, and her to be able to meet the odd germ and bug without losing her beautiful rhythm. (To be fair to Apple: it wouldn't be her fault. I'm going to be on anti-rejection meds forever.)

When I got back from my walk today — eight thousand steps (yes!) — and fired up the laptop, I thought I was going to be in for everyday ordinariness.

But it turns out you lovely people have nominated this blog for the Best Patient Experience Blog in the UK Health Blogger awards.

Wow.

Thank you. (No, YOU'RE crying.)

This is a big big BIG deal. On the off-chance that this is the only blog you read, let me tell you — there are more blogs than there are stars in the sky (probably). Being chosen is a huge honour and I cannot tell you how much it means to me.

The fact that I'm here at all is fifteen sorts of miracle, and that's before you get to the transplant. If you're a regular here you'll know that, until the 1980s, Hypoplastic Left Heart Syndrome meant a baby dying while its mother watched. I had three operations before I was four years old and even if there hadn't been a healthy heart to replace my patched one, living until I was twenty-eight would have been considered not bad going.

I'm alive, thanks to a freak set of circumstances, which includes someone else's misfortune. And I think of that every day.

It still seems strange to me that others would even read this blog, let alone come back, and vote on the non-heart related elements of this life that's not my own. I did think that my coping might help others with their coping, and that any HLHS folk, a little behind me on what we've learned to call the patient pathway, might benefit from my experience, and avoid — or at least be a little bit prepared for — some of the things that have knocked me for six. I hoped (still hope) this blog would help the families and friends of HLHS patients to understand what it's like. Being ill is a pain. Being ill and explaining yourself is exhausting. If I have helped, I'm glad.

So — thank you. Truly. With BlueHeart bells on.

I can't go to the awards ceremony. I'll tell you why another time. If I can manage it. The organisers were kind and I'm recording a video just in case I win.

And I really want to. But — if I do — I won't be BlueHeart anymore. I'll be me, un-anonymised, and if I were to show my face there, then of course I have to show it here too, and be me, the real person, in real life. (The one who, coincidentally, isn't blue anymore.) And that's scary. Here's something I didn't expect. Since Apple arrived in my life, I'm not completely sure who I am.

You know what's coming, don't you?

Voting closes in two days.

Should I make the video, and come out from behind BlueHeart?

YES — This is a new phase in your life,

and it's good to make it different.

NO — Protect yourself, physically and emotionally, for a wee bit longer. Send a message. Hide your face.

Until next time,
BlueHeart xxx

2 shares
10 comments

Results:
Yes   87%
No   13%

6 February, 2018

'Do you want me to make some of those cards to hold up? What do you call them?'

Ailsa laughs. 'Idiot boards? No, I think I'll be OK. I know what I want to say.'

They have spent an hour working out the best place to make the film, with a non-distracting background and good light. Now, Ailsa is sitting on the armchair near the window in their living room, and Hayley is perching on the coffee table with the iPad. A mini microphone trails its cable from the audio socket to the floor at Ailsa's feet. She picks it up and holds it in her lap.

'You've only got my head and shoulders in, aye?'

'Down to here,' Hayley says, drawing a line with her finger across her own chest, from armpit to armpit.

'Good.' The test run, filmed from further away, was depressing. Ailsa knows she's gained weight — has to know, because she

41

has to weigh herself every morning, alert for the gain of three kilos overnight that could be a sign of rejection — but hadn't realised that, if she's filmed when she's sitting, there are three rolls of fat where her waist should be. Still, as Hayley says, she could have been a worm's picnic by now. She shouldn't be bothered about her appearance.

'Ready when you are, hen.'

'OK. Press the button.'

Deep breath. Big smile!

Hayley gives a thumbs-up and then watches the screen. If she was looking at Ailsa directly, she'd cry, and Ailsa would cry too. At least that's what happened the second time they practised this.

'Hello. My name is Ailsa Rae, though you might know me as BlueHeart. I'm honoured and overwhelmed to have won this award. Thank you to everyone who has voted for me — and, even more, thank you to everyone who has read my blog, and voted in my polls.

'Waiting for a transplant makes you feel powerless. My blog showed this in the best way I could think of. I had a life-saving operation two days after I was born, another before I was two years old. My childhood was almost normal, but I lived on the edges

42

of what everyone else took for granted. I tried to do all that I wanted to, but by the time I finished my degree, which took a year longer than most people because I had a wee spell or two in hospital, it was obvious that my heart was failing. So I spent almost four years becoming more and more unwell, until I went on the donor register. And then I got lucky.

'This is bittersweet for me, because the person who helped me with the blog in its early days died less than a year ago, waiting for his own transplant. He should be here. He should be —' Hayley makes a gesture towards the iPad, ready to stop recording, but Ailsa takes a breath, deep — and oh, what it is to feel how good that feels — and steadies herself. 'He died. I wish he was alive. If more people were on the organ donor register, if more people made their wishes known to their loved ones before they died, he might be alive.

'Thank you for voting for me. My name is Ailsa Rae. I'm the recipient of a transplanted heart. Please, when you die, when someone you love dies, help to let someone else live.'

10 FEBRUARY, 2018

Today is about Lennox, and enduring the day that would have been his birthday. His mother's email invitation had been clear: this would be a celebration of all their good memories. Easy in theory, but as the taxi brings Ailsa and Hayley closer and closer to the Douglas family home, Ailsa is light-headed and lower-belly nauseous in a way that's different to the feeling her meds sometime give her. She's thinking about all the things she usually forces her mind and new heart far away from: rediscovered love, hanging-on hope, the grief that has pinned her to the ground since Lennox died, staring blankly up into aching grey.

'Ready?' Hayley asks, when they step out of the taxi and onto the pavement. They're a little late getting here, something Ailsa is starting to think might have been strategic on her mother's part.

'I don't know.'

'Take your time, hen,' Hayley says, and she reaches into her bag, pulling out a packet of Marlboro cigarettes and a Zippo lighter that's probably older than Ailsa. 'I'll just fortify myself a bit.'

The house is away from the bustle of Portobello, and past the end of the Promenade. It's a serene-looking place, a huge bungalow with bay windows that look out towards the sea in front, though Ruthie said they bought it more for the garden stretched out behind, which had once been an orchard. It looks well cared for, the front garden neat, the paths without weeds, the gate a shining, flawless black. Ailsa thinks of all the time that such maintenance must take, and how it must fill the grieving days.

She takes a breath. Another. Reminds herself that at least some of the pain must have been cut from her body with her old heart. Apple doesn't really know what it was like to love Lennox, and then to lose him. But it seems she has been paying attention, learning: Ailsa's chest is stretched tight with love and loss.

She hasn't been here since the day of Lennox's funeral, which was a day so grim that just that glance of memory makes her want to cry. Then, she wore black. It's harder to know how to dress for a memorial/

birthday party. That black dress doesn't fit anymore, anyway. She's disoriented by the sight of herself in the mirror, these days. All those chins.

But she is, after all, alive.

Hayley grinds out her cigarette with the heel of her purple patent DM, and Ailsa remembers her red pair, which she loved, but had to get rid of when red became her unlucky colour.

Figures are moving at the windows. It's three o'clock but the sky is already dusking; the lights are on indoors. Ailsa opens the gate, looks at the path. Her foot seems unwilling to step onto it.

'Remind me what the sisters are called?' Hayley asks. People think that Ailsa's mother never forgets a face but actually she revises, learns, practises. She says that when Ailsa was a baby, knowing the names of the nurses made sure they were on their side.

'The eldest is Lucy and the younger one is Libby. Lucy's bairn is Louisa. They all begin with L.'

Hayley puts a hand around her daughter's waist, squeezes, and Ailsa feels something simple and close between them. It used to be there all the time.

Someone is waving from the front window. There's no escaping now. Quietly, Ailsa says, 'It doesn't seem possible. That he's not here.' And that's nowhere near expressing what she's feeling, but it's all she dares say. More, and she'll break, even if her mother is holding her.

'I know,' Hayley says. 'I havenae seen Ruthie and Dennis since you left hospital.' There's a pause, and Ailsa reaches for her mother's hand, holds it hard. They are both remembering Lennox's parents' determination to support them, even though they were grieving for Lennox, even though their visits to Ailsa's bedside felt like silent, aching punishments for them all.

She fixes her best smile, and searches for a good memory of Lennox. The first: him holding her palm flat against his bare chest, saying, 'I would give this to you in a heartbeat, if I could. I would fly it, from me to you.' Another: they are seventeen, standing on the beach at Portobello, then he took off for the sea, rushing in, trainers and jeans and all, up to his thighs, and then he looked back and yelled, 'It's lovely! Come in!' And now more memories are chasing in: the two of them sitting in the hospital garden, trying to teach themselves chess with the board and pieces from the day room. The knights were missing; they'd used two mints fished from Ailsa's handbag for white knights, two dark fallen petals for black.

There will be no more memories now.

'Ailsa! And Hayley! Thank you for coming!' Ruthie — thinner, greyer than last time they saw her — embraces them both at once, clutching their shoulders. Behind her ambles Dennis, smiling but smaller-seeming, who goes down on one knee, stretches his arms wide, makes sure he has Ailsa's full attention before he starts singing.

'Something's got hold of my heart, tearing my soul and my senses apa-a-art.'

'Oh, for heaven's sake, Dennis,' Ruthie says, half impatience, half humouring. And then, to Ailsa, 'He's like a five-year-old. If it's funny once, it's funny forever.'

'It's OK. I think it's funny.' Dennis stands to embrace her. She puts her head, sideways, against the top of his chest. He pats her back, between her shoulder blades. He told her once that she was like another daughter to him. Ailsa wonders if he's like a father to her.

She wouldn't know.

But he's been a steady presence in her life for as long as she's known Lennox. He holds her at arm's length, looks her up and down.

'You look well, chicken,' he says. 'Nothing

48

wrong with a bit of meat on your bones.' He pats his own stomach.

'Dennis! Enough! Ailsa, I'm sorry.' Ruthie looks mortified.

Ailsa catches Dennis's eye and winks. If he's going to try to be kind to her, today, however clumsily, she's going to try to help him out a bit.

'It's fine, Ruthie,' Ailsa says. 'It's the steroids. I'm starting to get rid of it, but I was fighting a losing battle for a while.' Ailsa hears herself, catches her mother's eye, and Hayley winces in sympathy. Talk of losing battles isn't really the thing, here, now. 'At least the beard's under control.'

'Well, you've a lot to be grateful for,' Ruthie says. 'You're a lucky young woman, and we're glad for you.'

'She has that,' Hayley says, 'and we both know it.'

Dennis reaches for Hayley now, embraces her. 'My wee Highlander. Fierce as ever.'

'Drinks are in the kitchen,' Ruthie says, and it's as though each word is spelled out from a script she's learned, for a play called *How to Get Through This Day.* Hayley follows her along the corridor.

Dennis smiles at Ailsa, though his eyes seem too sad for smiling today. He gestures her forward. 'I'll be getting a rollicking for

49

that comment later, don't you worry about that. Let's get a drink. I'd guess you could do with one as much as I could.'

There must be about forty people scattered through the kitchen, living room and conservatory. Ailsa spots Libby and Lucy, some of the staff from the hospital, and a couple of friends of Lennox's from university; scattered now, all well established in their lives, they'll have come a long way to be here. There's the head of the school where Lennox taught PE, and another teacher colleague, the one he called 'Rockets', though Ailsa cannot remember why. She's stabbed by the bright pain of knowing that she can't ask him.

Everyone seems to have made the effort to dress and talk cheerfully, although there's the forced feeling that Ailsa remembers from a Christmas she had to spend in hospital, when it seemed that if anyone stopped smiling the whole elaborate happiness-shaped celebration would collapse and kill them all.

Ailsa almost chooses wine, but decides against it, because she needs to hold on tight to herself if she's going to get through this afternoon. And wine will add to the meat on her bones. Diet lemonade in hand, she scans the crowd for someone she'd like to talk to. After years of breathlessness she still cannot believe that she has as many words as she wants at her disposal. She can let them bounce or fall from her mouth, unmeasured, uncounted, for as long as she likes.

But first, she steps out of the door of the conservatory, and goes to sit on one of two benches in the corner of the garden, on either side of an apple tree that's in a vast zinc pot. The air is cold, but the trunk seems to have warmth, and she puts her palm against it, looks up. Apple stirs. This is Lennox's tree, his ashes buried in the pot. Of course it's going to be warm.

Ailsa looks up into the branches and sees the tatters of dark green card and string on the bare branches. Soon there will be nubs of a different green clustering, waiting. She tries to think about those, instead of that day. At the funeral everyone was invited to write something on a label, a memory of Lennox, that would be tied to the tree. There wasn't a memory she could so much as glance at, then, without knowing that she'd shatter, so she'd written something else. Three words: 'Please come back.'

'Could I join you?' Lucy has emerged from the house, a drowsing Louisa heavy in her arms.

'Of course.'

'I didnae want to disturb' — she settles the toddler's curly head against her shoulder, and leans back on the bench — 'but it's getting a bit hot in there. A bit noisy.'

Ailsa takes her hand away from the tree trunk and rests it in her lap. It's as though she's been caught in an intimate act. Being close to death had been easy when she was with Lennox. With anyone else, she doesn't know how or when she'll cause offence.

'He thought the world of you,' Lucy says, her voice a sad, low note of loss. 'How have you been?'

Ailsa nods. 'I've been . . .' But she can't complete the sentence. She almost says, 'lost' — it's the word that surprises her by springing to mind — but she can't say that she's lost when she's alive and well, and sitting next to a sister who used to have a kind, clever younger brother and now has, instead, an apple tree with the disintegrating remains of memories hanging from it. She's not sure she should be here, in this garden — or even in the world. Apple could have gone to a more deserving person. If she'd died sooner, would that change whatever equation the universe was using, and could Lennox have lived? She can't say that to Louisa. 'I thought the world of him, too.'

The February chill and encroaching dark drives them inside, and Ailsa is immediately drawn into conversation by Craig, one of the critical care nurses who looked after Lennox in his last days. They are soon joined by Suze, an old friend of the Douglas family. Craig asks questions about what Lennox was like, before he was ill, and between them Suze and Ailsa pull together a patchwork of anecdotes that has all three of them laughing. Suze's memory goes back further than Ailsa's. She remembers Lennox, ten years old, coming home with a dog that he'd untied from outside a shop, claiming that the owner had given it to him as a present; she talks about the swimming competitions he won; how his parents despaired of him ever sitting down for long enough to do his homework. Ailsa's stories only really start at sixteen, when she and Lennox both got involved in a project to provide activities for underprivileged kids. Lennox was one of the students who arranged games, Ailsa and some others helped with homework, and slowly they noticed, then got to know each other. By the end of the six weeks of the project, they were holding hands on the way to the bus stop. She doesn't tell Craig and Suze that part. It's just for her.

And then, suddenly, Ailsa is exhausted. She sees what Craig was doing, how kindly and cleverly he was taking their minds from the loss that is still too great to think about as a whole. She excuses herself and finds Hayley talking to Dennis. She hears 'beta blockers' as she approaches, and smiles to herself, because anyone who knows that Hayley is a pharmacist seems unable to resist talking to her about their drug regime. Ailsa catches her eye and tugs at her left earlobe, an old signal for 'I've had enough', useful at visiting times when she was in hospital or on any day out when she wasn't. Hayley nods, extracts herself from Dennis's monologue — 'It's your GP you need to be talking to, Dennis, but there's no reason why those two drugs shouldn't be compatible, so the indigestion is likely something else.'

They start to make their goodbyes. Ruthie talks about meeting up with Hayley, doing something to 'get her out of the house'. Libby says she'll call, because the family is talking about fundraising in Lennox's name, and Ailsa says she'll help. Making arrangements to see Lennox's family again makes it easier to leave.

Or almost leave.

Hayley's hand is on the front door when

Ruthie calls them back. 'Oh, before you go! You remember those swatches you looked through with me at the hospital? Well, I took your advice — I think it was you, Ailsa, who said the blue would be too dark, and the grey with the silver stripe would go with anything?'

'I think so,' Ailsa says, although she doesn't recall. She does remember long afternoons of sleeping, on and off, Ruthie keeping her mother company, and the two of them talking about curtains with an inappropriate desperation — as though they were using their words to hold up a roof in the rain. Which, of course, they were: Lennox was dead, Ailsa was dying.

Ruthie leads them along a passageway, and opens the last door on the left. They are in the study: there's a desk, a chair. And oh, look, there's the rug Ailsa and Lennox had sex on once, when they were supposed to be revising for their Highers. Libby had just left to meet a friend and Lennox said they had ten minutes before his mum got home. Focus on the curtains, Ailsa.

'Lovely,' Hayley says, 'they're just the ticket, aren't they?'

Ailsa nods, although they look very much like curtains to her. She likes the blinds in their flat, which are bamboo, a little bit tatty at the edges, the cord to pull them up and down knotted in so many places that it looks like a string of beads.

This house feels dark and quiet. Ailsa wants to be out in the air. Hayley squeezes her elbow.

'Well . . .' she begins.

'Ah, just before you go,' Ruthie says, and she sets off back along the central corridor, making a 'this way' motion with her arm. Hayley raises her eyebrows at Ailsa and Ailsa shrugs, but they follow.

Ruthie opens a door, and ushers them into the room ahead of her. She follows them in and, as they stand there, says, 'I thought you might like to see Lennox's room.'

It's not, mercifully, a shrine, because Lennox never properly lived here, apart from during university holidays. The family had moved from Tollcross to Portobello when Lennox was nineteen. So at least there's that.

The room is neat and plain. There is navy bedding on the double bed, matching curtains, pale walls, an oak wardrobe and chest of drawers, and a white desk with a black swivel chair pulled neatly up under it. Ailsa recognises the wardrobe from his bedroom at the Douglas's Tollcross house, but the rest of the furniture is new. She stops herself, just in time, from wondering what might be in the wardrobe. She doesn't know whether she wants it to contain Lennox's pressed shirts, or home a variety of old board games and boxes of photographs, or be empty.

Above the desk there's a noticeboard with ticket stubs (rugby matches, cricket internationals, football finals); airline boarding passes; tickets to Buddhist temples and city museums; postcards and railway maps. It's a jigsaw of the life Lennox lived after university, his travelling years and his school-holiday sporting pilgrimages once he started teaching. On a shelf above sit framed photographs. There's one from his graduation, and another from Libby's, two years before; they could have been taken in the same week, as he looks almost identical in both, broad-chested and smiling.

It's designed to make Ailsa miss him with each iota of her soul. She can feel every cell of her body contract, as though it is trying to make a fist of itself.

At Lucy's wedding, he's squinting into the sun, tanned, bearded. Ailsa half remembers that he'd come back from Thailand to be there. The fourth photograph is smaller, poorer quality, and the most painfully recognisable of the lot: Lennox is raising his arms, half grinning and half grimacing, as he crosses the finish line at his first and only marathon, in London, in 2015. He did it in four hours and twenty minutes. His slow recovery time was the first clue to the fact that all was not well.

Ailsa doesn't know what to do, or what's expected of her. She doesn't want to look at Ruthie, in case she's crying, or in case she's waiting for Ailsa to cry. Which she will. She's a tear storm waiting to break. Hayley's hand is on the small of her back.

She closes her eyes and takes a deep breath.

It's a curious thing, that although Apple never knew Lennox, she's understood, this afternoon, where to hurt for him, where to almost burst with the sheer volume of missing him.

And then, out of nowhere, Ailsa can smell Lennox's aftershave — Driftwood, it was called. He was first given it as an eighteenth birthday gift from his sisters. He used to say that wherever he went in the world it would always make him think of home. He said he was connected by it. And that's what Ailsa feels as she breathes it in now — sage, patchouli, mandarin. Connection.

She didn't notice it when she came into the room. It seems impossible that the scent is even here. The rest of the house smells of tasteful plug-in air-freshener and Ruthie's perfume, which is a melancholy one, jasmine and forest floor. They are too far from the sea for it to make its presence so strongly felt. And yet, the smell of the aftershave is all around her.

'I think we really need to be going,' Hayley says. 'This is all — a lot for Ailsa. But thank you.' She touches her daughter's elbow. Ailsa opens her eyes, and the Driftwood has gone.

Ruthie is sitting on the bed. 'I'll just stay here, for a minute or two,' she says, her voice quiet, 'if you don't mind.'

'Of course not,' Hayley says.

'Do you want me to send Dennis?' Ailsa lays her hand on Ruthie's shoulder, lightly, not wanting to disturb her, in case Lennox's mother is inhaling the aftershave now and she breaks the spell.

Ruthie shakes her head, the smallest shiver, and Hayley and Ailsa leave, closing the door behind them, making their way out of the house as quietly as they can, as though they are trying not to disturb a sleeping child. They don't speak until they are through the front door, down the path, and around the curve of the road, out of sight of the house. And then Hayley stops,

59

holds out her arms, and Ailsa half hugs, half grips her. It's a little while until she feels steady enough to let go.

'Fuck, Ailsa, I'm sorry. You look like you've seen a ghost,' Hayley says. She's pale, too.

'I wasn't expecting that.' She wanted to remember Lennox, and would never, ever want this day to pass as though he had been nothing. That didn't mean she wanted the bedroom, the photos, the ghost-scent that surely must have been a trick of her imagination.

'Of course you weren't. Me neither.'

'I think she thought she was being nice,' Ailsa says.

'Well, you know what they say. Nothing says "nice" like "come and stand in my dead son's room in silence for no good reason".' A beat. And then they're laughing, the sound mirthless and barking, still holding hands.

And then they're silent, and it's dark, and it's cold.

'I could murder a drink,' Hayley says. 'Do you fancy? Before we go home? I've only had tea. I'm fair drowning in the stuff.'

'I'd really like that, Mum.' It's only five thirty, but it feels later.

Hayley lights up, inhales, exhales a

straight, tall plume of smoke into the still air above her. Ailsa steps away from the smoke, or at least that's how it looks — but really it's to preserve the last little bits of Lennox's aftershave in her nostrils. The smell of the sea is blowing in to them now, overlaying what might be left. Ailsa used to wear floral perfumes — her aunt, Tamsin, said she smelled like a flower-arranging lesson — but now that she isn't always trying to cover the smells of the hospital, or mask the aroma of illness that she seemed to exude, she doesn't much bother with perfume at all.

Hayley smokes two cigarettes as they walk in silence down the road, not quite lighting the second from the end of the first, but almost. They join the end of Portobello High Street and keep going, silent, with their backs to the sea, until they come to a pub.

Hayley strides to the bar, then hesitates. 'Did you have much to drink back there?'

'I just had lemonade.'

'Good,' Hayley says, then turns to the barman, 'A bottle of Pinot Grigio,' she says, 'two glasses, and two bags of the least pretentious crisps that you've got. Nothing fishy.'

The barman nods, as though this is a

request he gets most days. 'Have a seat. I'll bring them over.'

'Thanks.'

There's a table tucked to the side of a stripped-back slate fireplace, with armchairs on either side of it. They sit quietly until the wine arrives. Ailsa checks her phone, taking her time over it, although there are no new emails, nothing to look at except her website stats, which have been falling fairly constantly since she left hospital. Well, there's not so much drama when she's definitely going to be alive tomorrow. (Not definitely. But not dead of a cold, still heart.) The winners of the blog awards will be announced later. Apple is thrumming the blood around her body a little faster, in anticipation.

The barman puts down two vast glasses and pours an inch of wine into the bottom of each. Hayley tops the glasses up to something nearer halfway, then says to Ailsa, 'That's your lot, OK?'

'OK.' Her mother has always had double standards where alcohol and smoking are concerned. Hayley drinks and smokes to balance out the stress of raising an ill child single-handedly; Ailsa needs to look after herself. It's not logical, but it's obvious. It annoys her, too, most of the time. But maybe not right now.

The barman's back with the crisps, which are sea-salted; he smiles at the topped-up glasses and waits for Hayley's thumbs-up for the crisps ('Not sure why it needs to come from the sea, but they'll do').

'Cheers,' Hayley says, clinking glasses with Ailsa, and then, 'here's to Lennox. And to you.'

Clink, clink. 'Here's to us,' Ailsa says. All of the tension that's kept her going through this afternoon has dissipated on the walk, and now she's tired. 'Let's talk about something that isn't —' She angles her head back in the direction of the Douglas's house. Then, hearing how she sounds, 'I mean . . .'

'Motion carried,' Hayley says. 'We need tae think about something else or we'll break our hearts all over again.' She puts her glass down, opens the first bag of crisps, and holds them out to her daughter.

'I shouldn't.' She takes some of the proffered crisps, even though she's eaten enough today, really.

'Why not? Dinnae let Dennis get to you. Women chucked themselves in front of horses to put an end to that sort of thing.'

'It's not that,' Ailsa says. 'I really do need to be healthier.'

Hayley nods. 'Well, I'll no disagree with

63

that. It can't hurt. What are you going to do?'

Ailsa shrugs, and takes a sip from her glass, because she knows what will come when she answers. 'I'll do a bit of research, then I'll — I'll ask the blog.' The wine is crisp and cool, like the frosty air on the day she and Apple were discharged from hospital.

Hayley's glass makes a stiletto-clack when she puts it down, and she says, 'Oh, Ailsa. I can see you're no happy and the steroids weren't helping you, but why would anyone else decide what you should put into your body?'

'It's not that . . .'

'I mean,' wine, crisps, wave of the hand, 'would you really let people you don't know tell you not to eat cheese? Does that not strike you as mad?'

Ailsa laughs. She can't help it. Hayley does too. 'People get it, Mum. I'm maybe winning an award for it.'

Hayley nods. 'You're winning an award for being clever, and brave, and making your point. But you have a new heart now, hen. Your point's made. You can decide. Stand up for yourself, and what you want.'

Ailsa sighs. 'I know. But how do I know what I want? It's weird. It's like — before I got — Apple — it all seemed clear.'

'What did you think you wanted?'

'All the things we talked about. An ordinary job. A boyfriend who was a bit rubbish . . .'

Hayley laughs. 'They're all rubbish, hen. Have I not mentioned your father?'

Nothing ventured, nothing gained. 'That's one of the things, though.'

'How do you mean?' Hayley's face is serious now.

'When I thought I was going to die, life was too short to really think about a dad I'd never met.'

'Biological father,' Hayley says; it's an automatic reaction to the term 'dad' or 'father' being applied to the man who left before Ailsa was born.

'Biological father. But now I think — maybe — I mean — I don't know, Mum. I'm not saying that I want to see him or anything . . .'

'Glad tae hear it.'

'Right,' Ailsa says. 'I mean we had plans before, did we not? If I got a transplant I was going to get a job, and you — you were going to move out . . .'

'Oh, aye. Me and your aunt Tamsin, reliving our youth. Getting a few tattoos, notching up a few threesomes and some

STDs . . .'

'Oh my God, Mum.' Hayley's hooting with laughter and refilling her glass. Ailsa suspects that they are both reacting to the strain of the afternoon: Ailsa by saying the unsayable about her biological father, Hayley by saying everything that comes into her head.

'Dinnae worry, hen. We haven't learned a lot but we've learned about contraception. Well, Tamsin has. I think I've healed over, it's been that long.'

'MUM.'

'OK, OK,' Hayley says, 'but aye, we did say I'd go and stay with Tamsin after six months, didn't we? Give you your space, give me and Tamsin our misspent youth back.'

'We did — we said you'd move out . . .' And Ailsa has thought that it's what she wants, on her long quiet afternoons in the flat, her mother at work. She's lain in the bath thinking about what she might re-paint and who she'll invite over, and what it will feel like to be living the life she should be living at twenty-eight. Even her least moti-vated uni friends don't live with their parents anymore. She takes a breath. 'I think — I think it will be time. By then. I'm so much better and it's only been four months.'

Hayley looks away from Ailsa, back towards the bar. 'I know, hen. It's — it's hard, though. I feel like I felt when you were tiny. I feel like you're learning everything. I want to make sure you're OK. And then, you cannae really find a job until you hit the six-month mark, so there'll be a lot to get used tae.'

'I know,' Ailsa says, and she tries to make sure that the impatience she feels doesn't come out in her voice, because she's not trying to upset her mother. 'But I'm only going to be OK if I can have a go at standing on my own feet. It's not that I don't want — It's not you. It's me.'

'Ah, so you're breaking up with me now?' Hayley's eyebrows are raised and she's smiling, but it's not really a smile.

Ailsa tries to smile back, but her attempt is just as poor. Try again. 'I need to find out what it's like, now. Being me. And being — there — this afternoon — thinking about Lennox — it makes you think . . .'

Hayley nods. 'But just because he didnae have the chance — it doesnae mean you have to do everything.' Ailsa thinks that's it, but then her mother adds, 'We've never really been without each other,' and there's the smallest catch in her voice, as though a tablet has caught in her throat on the way down.

'And we won't be,' Ailsa says, trying again to put all the gentleness she can into her voice, even though it drives her mad when doctors think words spoken softly make bad news better. 'I don't even care if you don't move to Tamsin's. You can go next door, if you like. Or I could. Rent a room. Nearly everyone I know who has a mortgage is struggling to pay it. I just — I need to find out what I'm about. Now I'm not dying anymore.'

Hayley still flinches at the D-word. 'If that's what you want, we'll talk about it some more,' she says, and drinks the last of the wine in her glass. Then she smiles, touches Ailsa's hand. 'You could be independent with me there, you know. I wouldnae vet your boyfriends or tell you to turn your music down. I never have.'

'I know, Mum. I just want to be — normal. Like any twenty-eight-year-old.'

Hayley laughs, and Ailsa knows what's in that laugh: the memory of when *she* was twenty-eight, and had a five-year-old with a serious heart condition, and was living in a flat in what was then a less-than-desirable part of Edinburgh. But she doesn't say so. It looks as though it might be an effort.

'When you're ready we'll walk along and find a taxi, aye? And by the time we get home you'll have won that award, for sure.'

Ailsa nods. 'Thanks, Mum.' She couldn't love her mother more. But she needs to give Apple a proper life. She puts her hand to her chest. If she presses her palm to her sternum hard enough she can feel the muscle of her heart move. Or at least she thinks she can, and sometimes that's all that matters.

When they step outside, Ailsa takes a deep breath, but now all she can smell is wine, salt, smoke.

11 February, 2018

I WON! And . . . I Need to Lose

Hello, my friends,

Wow. Thank you. Thank you, thank you.

I am officially the UK's Best Health Blogger when it comes to patient experience.

I can't tell you what this means to me. I tried.

Click here to watch the video I made.

Yesterday was a hard, sad day for me, and so this boost really means more than you know.

Here's something you do know, though, if you've watched the video: you know what I look like. You know my name is Ailsa.

You can probably tell from the shape of my face I'm a wee bit chubby.

You know, if you've been here before, that steroids and taking life gently mean I've been putting weight on.

I've gained twenty-six pounds in the almost-four months since I had the transplant, and most of that seems to be in the Space Hopper area. (Don't panic. If my heart was rejecting then I would be gaining about two pounds a day, and it would mostly be retained fluid, so I'd have big squooshy ankles and fourteen chins. And my mother would have me at the hospital before you could say black pudding sandwich.)

In fairness, it's tough not to gain weight after a transplant. I'm going to be taking steroids as well as immunosuppressants for the rest of my life. In time the dosage will reduce, but for now, I'm hungry all the damn time. I've been using cream to get rid of my beard, so I can't even blame the weight on that.

I have to be honest, though, because this is an honest place. I could be hungry and eat an apple or some porridge. But I'd rather have a doughnut or some proper salt and sauce, chip-shop chips. There's a great cafe not so far from here, which is quiet enough in the late afternoons for me to feel safe in, in the infection-avoidance stakes; my mother and I like the flapjacks. Because I have to be a bit careful of crowded places, my friends often come round, and they don't come empty-handed.

Four months feels like long enough to understand what steroids do, eat myself better, and indulge in yay-I'm-not-dead macaroons.

I have to get fit. I have to lose weight.

Getting fit is under control (I think): Apple and I are being disciplined about walking every day, and as dancing won — you lovely folk, you — I've got my first tango class next week. I'm all set.

But I need your help with the weight thing. I've never dieted before — weight has always been the least of my worries, and anyway, when you're in hospital/being not well at home a lot, you spend a lot of time in pyjamas, onesies and other elasticated things, so the odd pound on or off is neither here nor there. I've done a bit of googling and narrowed things down, so now it's over to you.

You know what to do. Polls close in a week. That gives me time to sort myself (and my cupboards) out and start the new regime.

Which diet?

— Paleo: eat like a hypothetical cave lady. No processed foods, no wheat, no dairy (gulp).

— 5:2: eat sod-all for two days a week and feast on whatever your heart desires the rest of the time. (OK, I might not have researched that one very thoroughly, but I think that's the gist.)

72

— Don't be silly, Ailsa, diets don't work. Adopt a healthy lifestyle: lay off the biscuits, keep moving, and be patient.
— Go to Weight Watchers, or Slimming World, or Fat Fighters. Have a list of what you can eat and what you can't, and get weighed every week.

4 shares
39 comments

Results:
Paleo: 32%
5:2: 17%
Change lifestyle: 29%
Weekly weigh-in: 22%

14 FEBRUARY, 2017

This Time Last Year

'Hey, BlueHeart. I made you some red hearts.' Lennox holds out a piece of paper, pulled carefully from a notebook, covered in tiny hearts drawn in red biro. 'Happy Valentine's Day.'

Ailsa finds a smile. 'I thought we weren't doing this.' There's an intensity to the way they are and it frightens her. Because it isn't that kind of love; it can't be. She feels the same way about Lennox now as she did when they first got to know each other, walking back to the bus stop when they'd finished their volunteering stint after school on Wednesday afternoons. She looks forward to seeing him in exactly the same way: with thrill and dread. She wants to touch him. When they look at each other, there's a crackle of unseen light in the air.

But they've both moved on. It's eight years since their first-year-at-university split, and though they are both single now, Ailsa's wary of what's happening here. She feels like a plant in a greenhouse, being cultivated out of season: her emotions are reaching and growing, forced to unnatural spread in this confined, overheated hospital space. Would she feel this feverish need for Lennox if the two of them were walking on Portobello Sands, out in the cold air, their whole lives — the normal span of their whole lives — ahead of them? Probably not. Does that matter? She doesn't know.

'We're not. I just thought — you know.'

'Yes, I know.' She kisses him, a friendly thank-you except the corner of their mouths touch and their faces hesitate, close to each other, waiting to see what happens next. After a (normal) heartbeat, Lennox leans back onto his pillows. She takes a breath and waits until she doesn't mind. 'I didn't bring you anything. I didn't think there was room.'

Lennox laughs, and looks around. 'You've a point, to be fair.' Lennox's birthday, the previous week, had brought cards and gifts from far and wide — not just family and friends, but the kids Lennox teaches (taught) at a primary school near Glasgow. Every surface is covered with home-made cards, most showing Lennox kicking footballs or holding trophies. He had cried as he'd looked through them on the day they'd arrived. 'Do you want to help me get through some of this chocolate? I'm not doing very well with it. And Ma brings shortbread all the time. They're not going to find my liver in all the fat, when the new one comes.'

'Go on, then,' Ailsa says. Lennox shuffles along the bed and she perches next to him, kicking off her shoes and stretching her legs out next to his. 'This time next year, you'll have better things to be doing on Valentine's Day than eating chocolate in a hospital bed with me.'

Lennox offers a box of dark chocolate truffles. 'If I'm fixed, eating chocolates in bed with you on Valentine's Day is the best thing I can think of.'

14 FEBRUARY, 2018

They don't see her; she could be a ghost in the doorway. It's just as well, because she needs a minute to let Apple calm and slow after the stairs. And she's early, too early, because that seemed safer than running the risk of being late.

So she waits, and watches. In the centre of the room, on a dance floor surrounded by tables and chairs, a man holds out his hand to a woman. She rests her palm on his, and their fingers close. She pivots her body towards him. Something in both of them changes; they become taut, tall, ready. His arm curves around her back, and she places her other hand on his shoulder. For a second, they sway, and then he steps forward, she steps back, and they are dancing, a fast fizzing series of steps that makes Ailsa catch her breath as she watches.

The couple is moving — they have to be a couple, surely; you couldn't move with such intimacy otherwise? — as though each body is the echo of the other. He steps to one side and she pivots in the space he makes; she flickers a foot up and under his leg, and then they are travelling again. He's taking bigger steps now, almost striding, and she is matching him, walking back-back-back, until they reach the edge of the dance floor and stop, suddenly, precisely, looking intently into each other's faces, and Ailsa thinks suddenly of Lennox, the grey of his eyes. She pulls her thoughts back to here, now. Valentine's Day is a day to be wary. It's just a Wednesday in February, in the room above the Dragon's Nest pub, and she and Apple are going to learn to tango.

The woman nods and laughs and steps away, and then the two of them start replaying something they did, in slow-motion, counting and talking, looking at their feet. Ailsa realises that someone is standing beside her. She looks around to see a woman of about her own age, slender and straight as a daffodil. She feels herself pull her shoulders back, just looking at her.

'You must be Ailsa? I'm Edie Gardiner. I'm glad you came. That's my sister, Eliza. She was supposed to be setting up the music, but you cannot stop her from dancing.' Edie's smile seems wider than her face. She has the same hazelnut hair, springy with curls, as her sister.

'Thank you for answering all my questions.' On Edie and Eliza's website Ailsa had found details of the weekly tango class: 'All you need to do is grab some shoes with a non-rubber sole, come along and give tango a try!' But it wasn't quite as simple for Ailsa. Nothing is.

'We were happy to help,' Edie says, 'and like I said, we're used to all this, since Fiona had her chemo last year. Hand sanitiser before we start, and we'll be sure to keep anyone who's not well out of your way.'

'Thank you.' It sounds so straightforward, put like that. Maybe other things that feel impossible now will be doable too, when the time comes. Getting on a bus or a train, working in a pub or a cafe where people come and go, finding a worthwhile purpose for this precious life, given to her rather than someone else.

Edie steps past Ailsa into the room, goes to a CD player on the bar. At the press of a button the room fills with music. The beat and thrum invites her blood to find its rhythm, join in. She's here. She's going to tango. She's doing one of the things she promised herself — when all she could do was watch her stats on a monitor and hope

— that she would.

There are about twenty others in the class today, all chatting and laughing as they arrive. Everyone else has brought shoes to change into. Ailsa has just worn the only semi-suitable pair she has, smooth-soled mid-heels that she wore for graduation and which have been needed only occasionally in the six years since. She thinks of them as her glamorous shoes, but compared to the ones the other women are putting on — silver-strapped, sparkling, either high or really high — they may as well be wellies. But otherwise these dancers seem ordinary, the oldest probably in his seventies, the youngest maybe twenty-five, some overweight, some tired-looking, some the kind of person who might smile at you as they pass in the street. Ailsa could feel at home here.

And then the class begins. There's almost time to remember what a terrible idea this is, how broken her body is and how out-of-practice she is at anything but the bare minimum.

But Apple seems to know what she's doing, so Ailsa, in a split-second beat, decides to trust her.

She's got her this far, at least.

They are urged to find their balance, find

their centre, feel as though they are suspended by the tops of their heads, an idea that makes Ailsa queasy. But when she does it she feels herself grow taller, and there's a tension through her body that she equates, somewhere deep, with being alive.

When they have all walked forwards, walked backwards, pulled the soles of their feet along the floor, turned by following arm then shoulder then hip, the class proper begins. Eliza and her partner Guy take Ailsa and Murray, who is also new, or at least newish, to one side and work with them. Edie and Simeon teach the others, and Ailsa is aware of the sound of instructions being called, laughter, occasional applause.

Guy takes Ailsa's left hand, gently, and puts it on his collarbone. He holds her right hand, smiles encouragingly, and says, 'Tango is easy. All we're going to do is walk. You never step on the same foot twice. Push your hand against my hand, and let it tell you what to do.'

There's no time to think about how strange it is to be held close by a man she's just met. Ailsa pushes her palm against Guy's and he pushes back, showing how he can angle her body, how all she has to do is wait to see which way she's being guided. And then they're walking — and it really is walking, and Ailsa can walk, even backwards. There have been times in her life when she's felt that all she's been doing is going backwards. He nods as they move, breathes 'good' under his breath, and finds a rhythm in the music that is slow enough for Ailsa to be able to feel his movement, understand what he wants her to do, and do it. He gives her instructions as they move: to lean in to him, to keep her foot in contact with the floor as she moves it. And somewhere in her belly, she feels something new. She doesn't have time to identify what it is, but she notices that it's there, and she likes it.

■ ■ ■ ■

PART THREE:
MARCH 2018
ALL THESE WOES
SHALL SERVE

■ ■ ■ ■

1 March, 2018

Adulthood

Last night I dreamed that Apple froze in my chest because I let myself get too cold, and I was paralysed but I wasn't dead. And if you think that sounds horrific — you're right. Apple was very much alive, and trying to hammer her way out of my mouth when I woke up.

I still feel a bit disoriented. I'm sitting by the window, just me and my mug of Lady Grey, and watching the world go by. It's mostly students coming and going, because there's a hall of residence just a wee bit further down the street.

I feel old today, and tired. My mother thinks it's Paleo and all my problems could be solved with a nice fat cheese sandwich. After I'd got over the first three days of the diet, though — and it's moderated, as my consultant said I had to add an extra dose of carbs, so I have a side of rice with dinner — I quite like Paleo life. I feel as though I have more energy and a clearer head. Most days. Not today.

Here's something I wasn't expecting

about having Apple in my life. I thought about all the things I would do — you know this, because we talked about climbing high things, giving myself a shock and dancing. I hadn't realised that being an adult, with a full real adulthood in front of them, instead of a twenty-eight-year-old with the physical capability and life expectancy of an ailing cat, would mean I would have more things to think about.

When I was dying I was special and I was protected. Blue was my superpower because it meant I never had to think about any of the stuff that no-immediate-expectation-of-death people are dealing with day in day out. When you might be dead next week, what you're doing with your life isn't really an issue. Thinking about how to pay the bills, contribute to the world, or reduce your carbon footprint, or whether you want to live on your own, or wondering about your biological father — there's no time for that. It's just about the next breath.

I might be going to London for the day, in a couple of weeks' time, and though that's going to be quite exciting if it comes off, it is LITERALLY the only thing I have in my diary apart from hospital appointments. That's not how normal adults live.

(I'll tell you if it happens. Look out for a blog post to help me decide what to wear.)

Another week of my diet and I might have gone down a dress size. It might be time to go out and treat myself to some grown-up pants, or whatever it is you adults wear.

Until then — can you help me out? What's important? What's my priority right now?

Apple and I don't have a clue about this stuff. We need a plan that's more than 'count yourself lucky if you're still here on Friday'. And I need to be able to think about it without getting stuck in the mire of 'I've missed out on everything fun and I'll never catch up'.

I know you're going to want to say 'take it easy' and 'be gentle with yourself' and all that, but I've been doing that for a good long while and I'm — bored.

I'm giving you until Friday to vote. And then I can start — adulting. As well as living.

SORT OUT YOUR BODY: If it's working, everything else will follow.

APPLY FOR JOBS: It doesn't have to be THE job. And it's only six weeks until you hit the magic six-month post-transplant mark and can get out there — it's not that long.

STOP THINKING ABOUT YOURSELF: Do something for someone else. Volunteer or fundraise or just do something that isn't about your cold blue heart.

GET OUT MORE: See your friends even if you don't feel like making the effort. Remember those people you promised to meet up with but haven't yet? Put dates in your diary and stick to them. Go to the pub after tango instead of scurrying home.

1 share
27 comments

Results:
BODY   20%
JOB   30%
THINKING   12%
GET OUT   38%

Ailsa had thought that wearing a unicorn-horn headband and clip-on tail around London was going to make for points and stares, but she gets off the train, crosses King's Cross station, and gets into a taxi to the radio station without attracting a second look. Betsy, who meets her at reception and takes her to the green room, doesn't comment either — it's as though most of her days are spent herding mythical creatures around the place. Ailsa doesn't know whether to be relieved or disappointed. So far, it isn't making for a good blog story. She takes a photo of her pass while she waits in the green room. And then she texts her mother, letting her know that she's arrived safely, didn't take a tube, didn't touch a lamp-post, wasn't coughed on by anyone.

The invitation to appear on a radio show had come via Ailsa's blog and as a consequence of her award win. When she'd called the researcher, she'd been offered the option of taking part from the radio studio in Edinburgh, but she said she'd be happy to go in person. Apple seemed very keen on London. Mr Mokbel, her consultant, had given his consent at her appointment on Thursday.

Hayley insisted on taking her to the train, and they hugged a fierce goodbye. It was strange, still, to do this with something close to casualness, without the possibility of The Final Goodbye casting a shade over them. Ailsa said, 'Don't worry' into her mother's neck — the rainy-day scarf, blues and greys and a tiny hole at the edge where it caught on a hospital corner somewhere — and Hayley nodded, and squeezed a bit tighter. They need to talk, when Ailsa gets home.

Black coffee is Paleo-diet-friendly, so Ailsa pours herself a cup. It's only fractionally better than hospital coffee, which always seems to have a smell of illness about it. Ailsa thinks about getting her notebook out but instead sits back and looks through the glass walls of the room she's in, watching the purposeful striding of people moving from desk to desk. Their hands flap and fly, and she tries to imagine what they are talking about. She'll be like this, one day soon: a woman with a job, a purpose, waving her hands and being interesting for something other than her heart.

The door opens. 'Ailsa, this is Sebastian,' Betsy says, 'the other studio guest this morning.' She has tidied her ponytail and her smile is lipsticked. 'Sebastian, Ailsa. She's a blogger.'

Thunk-a-thunk. Apple is definitely louder than her old heart.

A man in dark glasses throws himself into the corner of one of the sofas, dropping a canvas satchel on the floor. He raises a hand towards Ailsa, drops it again. 'Hey. Everyone calls me Seb.' His voice is the voice of a baritone hero from Rodgers and Hammerstein, smooth and promising.

'Hey,' Ailsa says. 'Everyone calls me Ailsa.' The inability to shorten it was one of the reasons her mother chose it. She doesn't say so. The silence becomes the norm.

Sebastian — Seb — picks up a magazine, and then puts it down again. His denim jacket, battered and black, makes a creak against the pretend-leather of the sofa when he moves. He's wearing a dark pink scarf. (It's definitely not red, thank goodness. Ailsa does not need a bad omen today.) His short, sandy hair is ruffled from where he's run his hand through it, and his cheeks and chin are stubbled. Because of the sunglasses,

91

she can't tell where he's looking, or if he's looking at her.

She decides to take out her notebook after all, and sits forward to pull it from her bag. She brought her satchel, too, the beloved battered turquoise leather one that Lennox gave her for her eighteenth birthday, before satchels were fashionable, because he said it suited her. As she moves, the headband flops forward, over her face. She pushes it back.

'Nice horn,' Seb says.

'I'm a unicorn,' Ailsa replies.

'I was warned. It added a note of the surreal to my Saturday.' He smiles a slow smile, one that surfaces rather than breaking. She's waiting for him to take his sunglasses off, but he doesn't. Instead he stands up and turns towards the coffee, pours half a cup, sniffs it, and puts it in the bin. He sitsprawls again.

'Good call,' Ailsa says. 'It's grim. The coffee.'

'Life's too short,' Seb replies.

'That's for sure.'

Ailsa has met some handsome men in her life. Recently, though, most of them have been sticking the business end of a stethoscope onto her chest and then looking at the ceiling as they listened. Before that, there were plenty of fellow university students who attracted a second glance — though most of the second glances that came Ailsa's way were double-takes at her pallor or the walking stick she sometimes used.

At this moment, Ailsa is sure that she hasn't met anyone quite as startlingly good-looking as Seb.

'I'm not going to ask why you're a unicorn,' he says. 'I'm going to preserve the mystery for a little bit longer. Wondering might keep me awake during this —' He gestures, a flex of elbow and forearm that conveys precisely how little he thinks of the radio show he's about to be part of.

'It's a blog thing,' Ailsa says. 'My blog decided. It — I ask it questions.'

'Not that much longer, then.'

Ailsa wishes she could see his eyes; it would be easier to tell if he was joking. He seemed to be serious, but that might just be — Oh, sod it. Life might not be as short as it used to be, but it's still short.

'Are you joking? Or were you being rude? I can't tell because you've got your sunglasses on.'

That's definitely a smile. 'I was joking. I have to protect my eyes a little bit. Because of the transplant.'

'What transplant?' Ailsa asks. The shock of hearing the word from someone else's mouth is palpable; her scalp shivers.

'I had my cornea replaced,' Seb says.

Ouch. Her eyelids squeeze together for a second. Apple winces, too. 'I'm sorry, I didn't realise. I'm usually the only one with the transplant defence.'

'So that's what the horn's for.'

Ailsa feels her own smile stretching across her face now. 'Yup, that's right. When you've had a heart transplant you need unicorn protection for at least a year. True fact.'

And now Betsy's here again, to take them to the studio. Seb steps back to let Ailsa leave the green room first. It feels as though he's watching her as she moves, but with the Ray-Bans, it's hard to tell.

KAT: And that was 'Hip to Be Square' from Huey Lewis and the News, another transplant-themed song, suggested by Pippa in Rochester. Thanks, Pippa, we see what you did there. Although one of my guests did point out to me, while that was playing, that a hip replacement is not really a transplant. We stand corrected. Now, back to our studio guests: we have Ailsa Rae, known as BlueHeart to the thousands of fans who have flocked to her blog every day for the last two-and-a-half years, to find out whether she would get the heart she so desperately needed. And Sebastian Morley, the actor whose eye infection led to a cornea transplant to save his sight. Hello, again, guys.

SEB: Hello, Kat.

AILSA: Hi.

KAT: Earlier in the show we dealt with the vexed question of why Ailsa is dressed as a unicorn, and we've tweeted a photo and the link to her blog. Ailsa, isn't letting your blog run your life a little — disempowering? Or would you say it's a natural extension of the society we're all living in, where we're more concerned about our online presences than our real lives?

AILSA: Well, I can only speak for myself, I don't think I'm responsible for what all of the Internet is doing!

SEB: Fair point, I think, Kat!

KAT: Listeners, I'm holding up my

hands. It's two against one here. I admit it: Ailsa is not responsible for everything the Internet does.

AILSA: That's a relief. But seriously — I wasn't trying to make a point about living in the twenty-first century, or anything like that. I was thinking about . . . well, I was thinking about myself, my own situation.

KAT: So, tell us more about the blog. Your award-winning blog, we should say. How did winning that award feel?

AILSA: Well, pretty amazing. I've written blog posts in hospital and at home in my flat. I tend to do it when I'm on my own. I see the statistics and the comments, so I know that my readers are there, but I don't know that I ever really thought I had an impact on them.

KAT: Why do you think you won?

AILSA: *(laughs)* I have no idea. I suppose because people can relate to what I'm writing about. A lot of people are touched by heart problems, and a lot are waiting for, or have had, transplants of one sort or another. Plus, I blog about dealing with chronic health problems — nothing to do with your heart — things like tiredness and coping with day-to-day life, that all sorts of people can relate to. I suppose my blog is in the middle of one of those — oh, what are they called, those circles that interlock . . . ?

SEB: Venn diagrams?

AILSA: Thank you. Venn diagrams.

KAT: Maths not your strong point, Ailsa?

AILSA: I've got a Higher in maths. I've just never been on the radio and I'm maybe a wee bit nervous. The way someone might be in a heart clinic. Memory problems can be a short-term side effect of one of the drugs I take to stop the new heart rejecting.

KAT: I'm holding up my hands. I seem to be doing a lot of that this morning, folks! I apologise, Ailsa. Go on.

AILSA: The blog polls started, really, as a reaction to the way I felt when I was told the only way to extend my life was through a transplant.

KAT: And when was that?

AILSA: When I was twenty-five. I hadn't been very well for a while, just gradually getting more breathless —

KAT: Was that when you turned blue?

AILSA: I was always blue. It was a consequence of the kind of heart repair I had. It was a fenestration —

KAT: Hey, it's the weekend! We don't need the nuts and bolts of heart repair. Why were you blue? In layman's terms.

SEB: No, hold on a minute, Kat. You can't just say 'blue' and move on. What are we talking? Smurf? Avatar? Cookie Monster?

AILSA: *(laughing)* Not exactly. Closest to Avatar, I suppose. More like — more like the colour of bleached denim. If you see someone with cyanosis, you probably wouldn't say, 'Oh, look, a smurf in human form.' It would be more like —

they would seem pallid. Very unhealthy-looking. And their lips would have a tinge you'd get from — from eating blueberries, maybe, and your nail beds too.

SEB: So the colour your teeth go when you've been drinking a smoothie with blueberries in?

AILSA: Exactly.

KAT: So now we've established exactly the kind of blue you were, Ailsa, when did that start?

AILSA: It was always there. It's a sign that you're not getting enough oxygen, and although I could function for a long time, quite normally —

KAT: You mentioned that you went to university . . . ?

AILSA: Yes. But it had to be in Edinburgh, because living away from home would have been too complicated. And I didn't really do all of the things other students do. I could keep up with the work, but not really the social life. I used to do what we called after-parties. People used to come to my flat in the morning and I'd make tea and toast, and they'd tell me what I'd missed. One year I was too sick to go to the ball so we had an anti-ball where my friends came round in pyjamas and we watched films and ate pizza. You do your best, don't you? Whatever your circumstances.

KAT: And you live with your mum, is that right? That's got to cramp your style.

AILSA: Not if your style is constant tiredness and inability to breathe. My mother has been amazing. I'm OK, Mum, I've taken my medication!

KAT: And we were talking about the polls. The point being that you had no power? You were just waiting to get a heart?

AILSA: Yes. It just seemed mad to me that I was expected to live like a normal person — to decide what to do with my life, where to go, what to wear — when the biggest single factor in my life's course was completely out of my control.

The only way to cope with that, for me, was to give up any idea of control at all.

KAT: Because things happen for a reason?

AILSA: No. Three weeks ago, I went to mark the twenty-ninth birthday of someone I loved very much. It wasn't a party, it was a memorial, because he died last year. He was every sort of decent, lovely man you could imagine. He caught Hepatitis B when he was travelling, and no one realised what it was until it was too far advanced, and by the time he was treated the only option was a liver transplant, and he didn't get the liver. He died. Tell me that happened for a reason.

SEB: I hate it when people say that. Things happen. That's it.

AILSA: Exactly. Thanks.

KAT: Let's talk about the blog some more. You didn't ask your blog whether you should go ahead with your transplant?

AILSA: No. The need for a transplant

has always been a given. It's a serious thing, Kat — it really was life or death for me.

KAT: Granted. But — you're sitting here in a unicorn headband — look out for the photo on Twitter, folks! I've got the poll here. The options you gave were: Number one — Dress down, it's the radio! T-shirt, jeans, your cowboy boots; Number two — Dress up, it's national radio! Dress, heels, serious eyeliner; Number three — The space-hopper costume you bought for a 1970s party three years ago and haven't worn since (for some reason); Number four — Unicorn headband and tail.

AILSA: I was convinced it was going to be the space hopper costume. But fortunately, most people are good people, even if they do like a bit of mischief . . .

SEB: I had a go on a space hopper once. It was hilarious.

KAT: But my point, Ailsa, is that you didn't give anyone the option of, say, turning up here naked? Or wearing — I don't know, full body armour, or a hijab?

AILSA: I think what you're saying, Kat, is that I create the choices, which is true. But it doesn't negate the point.

KAT: Which is . . . ?

AILSA: If you're waiting for a transplant, the course of your life is, basically, the toss of a coin.

KAT: I would have thought there would be — I don't know — robot hearts by now.

AILSA: Well, there are some man-made and mechanised options. But when you've had a few heart operations, then the area around your heart is already under strain, so your body is less likely to cope with something like that.

KAT: Interesting. Seb, how about you? How do you feel about your transplant?

SEB: I feel grateful. It sounds glib, but you don't really know what you've got until it's gone, or at least going, and the thought of losing my sight — maybe losing an eye — was awful. But a cornea transplant isn't anything like as big a deal as a heart.

KAT: I'm sure listeners who've allowed loved ones to donate corneas won't agree . . .

SEB: I don't mean — emotionally. I mean medically. I could have lived successfully without an eye. No one does well without a heart.

KAT: But you still have a part of someone else's body in your body. And you wouldn't have that unless they'd died.

SEB: I'm not saying I'm not grateful, Kat. The first thing I did when I came out of hospital was get myself on the organ donor register.

AILSA: It's not an easy idea. I'm grateful to my donor and at the same time I find it really hard to think about him or her. It's a difficult thing, to be alive, because and only because someone else is dead.

SEB: Or to be able to see because someone else isn't here to use their eyes.

KAT: What would you say to those donors and their families, if you could?

SEB: Again, it's hard not to sound glib.

AILSA: I can write to my donor's family a year after I have my transplant — though I will never know who they are, the transplant coordinator will pass the letter on. It's an important thing to do, I think, but it won't be easy. I agree with Seb. We say 'thank you' a hundred times a week, for coffee or change or to someone who puts us through to a helpdesk. Using the same words for this feels invalid.

KAT: Yes, because these people are heroes, aren't they? To donate your organs is an extraordinary thing.

SEB: Absolutely.

KAT: And you agree, Ailsa?

AILSA: Well, yes and no.

KAT: Interesting. I would have thought that you, of all people, would appreciate the heroism of donors. I wonder how your donor feels about that? Well, he or she is dead. I wonder how their family would feel?

AILSA: I'm not saying I'm not grateful. But hundreds of people are on a waiting list for a donor of one sort or another, and hundreds of people die every day. If it was the norm for organs to be donated, then many more people would live on. When you've watched people you love die for the want of a liver, it — it changes your perspective.

KAT: So you want to take the choice away from grieving families?

AILSA: That's not what I'm saying. I'm saying we need a — a cultural shift in how we do this. We need to be a bit less emotional about it. After all, when you're dead, your organs are no use to you. The law is starting to change, and I don't think it's a moment too soon.

KAT: Well, as you can hear, it's an emotive topic we're discussing this afternoon. We'll go to our next track, and then we'll be talking *StarDance* gossip with Sebastian Morley. I see you've been learning to dance, Ailsa?

AILSA: I've been to a few tango classes. I love it. Do you dance, Seb?

SEB: It depends who you ask. One of the judges thought I was a disaster.

KAT: *(laughter)* We're sitting in the studio with a very puzzled-looking unicorn. I would have thought that even unicorns would know who Sebastian Morley is. Jermaine from Solihull has suggested 'My Heart Will Go On' by Celine Dion. Nice one, Jermaine. If you're out and about in London later, look out for a unicorn, because she might just push you under a bus to get a lung for one of her mates. We'll be back after news, sport and weather.

'Kat's an arsehole,' Seb says. 'I've been interviewed by her before. Don't worry about it.'

The show over, Betsy has taken Seb and Ailsa back to the reception desk. One revolving door later and they are standing outside on the pavement, in feeble March sunshine, smiling uncertainly at each other like two people who have accidentally made eye contact at a bus stop. Ailsa looks at her hands, sees them shake.

'I'm not worried about it.' And she isn't, exactly. But, 'She wanted simple answers to things that are complicated. Of course I'm grateful. It's not as straightforward as she makes out, though, you know?'

Seb smiles. 'Tell me about it. She once asked me about why I'd taken the job on *Last Orders*. Honest answer? I'd just bought a flat. I didn't have any other long-term offers. The money was good. But you can't say that. She didn't want to know that actors are people looking for work, just like anyone else, and unless you're — I dunno — David Tennant, you take what you can get. You take a job because you're offered it, don't you?'

'I suppose you do,' Ailsa says.

There must be something in the way she says it. Seb turns towards her, for the first time since they left the building. 'I don't know what you do. Apart from not be blue. And blog. In an award-winning way. While dressed as a unicorn.' He laughs. 'Which is quite a lot.'

Ailsa laughs too, and feels something — tension, hurt — leave her. Apple unclenches. 'It's more than I knew about you. I can't work until I get my six-month all-clear. I should be less vulnerable to infection after that.'

'What do you want to do?'

Another laugh, but one with a twitch in it. 'I wish I knew. I've never had a job. I've not really done the things that make you employable. Anything.'

'I'll sell you my Duke of Edinburgh badge if that will help,' Seb says.

She likes that he doesn't smile when he's joking. 'I get one automatically. For being from Edinburgh. You don't have to do any camping or anything.'

'Really?'

'No,' Ailsa says. There's a beat before he looks at her.

'Bloody unicorns,' he says, 'you're all lying bastards.'

And now she's laughing, properly. Everything that she's brought to this morning, the tension and the worry, breaking up and rushing out at the ridiculousness of what's happening right now. Seb is watching her, or seems to be. He's smiling. 'I didn't think it was that funny,' he says.

Ailsa takes a deep breath, now the last of the laughter has bubbled out of her. Oh, the feeling of it; the sense that she can actually be full of all the air she needs, whenever she wants to be, and a deep breath is enough. 'I don't know why it was.'

'Thanks,' Seb says, with a laugh of his own in his voice. Then, 'I've never been to Edinburgh. Only Glasgow.'

'Well,' Ailsa says, 'that's basically the same thing.'

'Really?'

'No.' That smile of his is really something.

'I like how you talk,' Seb says. 'Say "Kat was an arsehole on the radio on Saturday".'

'I'm not a performing monkey.' It's slightly better than 'Can I look at your scar', Ailsa supposes — not that anyone has done that, but she'd had an awful moment in the studio when she wondered if Kat was about to ask.

'No,' Seb says, 'but you are dressed as a unicorn. Please?'

'OK. Kat was an arsehole on the radio on Saturday.'

He is retying his scarf, but as soon as she starts to speak, he stops, one hand mid-air, tassels dropping from the spaces between his fingers; his face attentive. 'Thank you,' he says. 'It's the rs, I think. I've never had to do a Scottish accent for anything.'

'It's an Edinburgh accent, not a Scottish accent. And not really a very strong one.'

'Sorry,' Seb says, 'I didn't mean to offend

your . . . fuck, I don't know, what did I offend?'

Ailsa's breath is white in the grey London air; her nose tip feels cold. 'I'm not offended. But during the last hour I've been a representative for all of the Internet, all bloggers, and everyone who's ever had a transplant. I can't start representing all of Scotland too. I'm out of . . .'

'Representativeness?'

'Aye, representativeness.' Although thinking about it, Ailsa has never been representative of anything in her life: she's been the special, the different, the outsider. Apart from when she's been sitting in a clinic waiting room.

'You see? "Aye, representativeness." Beautiful.'

Ailsa smiles, shrugs. 'If you say so.'

Seb starts to walk away from the main entrance; Ailsa walks beside him. 'Are you going back north today?'

'Yes. I've a train booked at four. From King's Cross.' It's just gone three.

Seb looks at his watch, at her. 'I can go that way.'

'I was going to take a cab,' Ailsa says. 'I can't do public transport. I've a depressed immune system.'

'Music to my ears,' Seb says. 'We can

111

share. You should have time to get a decent coffee at the station. And I can show you my eye on the way.'

Ailsa almost says no. Seb's known her for an hour and a half; he doesn't get to organise the next hour of her life for her. But she hesitates, and while she does so she imagines the question, posed to the blog: Should I agree to a short taxi ride with a handsome (and famous, though I hadn't heard of him) man who has just offered to show me his transplanted cornea? Yes, 100%, No, 0%, is her best guess. Maybe: Yes, 99%, No, 1%, if her mother is voting.

'OK,' she says. She needs to Google him as soon as she gets on the train.

Seb is already flagging down a cab, anyway. One stops within seconds, as though he's magnetic, the car automatically drawn to him. He says something to the driver through the window, and then holds the door open for her. She climbs in and fastens her seat belt. Seb sits opposite her on the fold-down seat and laughs.

'Seat belt? Really?'

'Really. I haven't survived four heart operations to die in a taxi, thank you.' She knows she sounds tart; doesn't care. People take life for granted.

He leans forward and takes off his sunglasses. 'OK. Well, I'm going to take the risk. Look. It's the left one. My left, your right. Can you see the stitches?' Their knees are touching; Ailsa moves hers tight together, so that his can stretch out to the sides. And now she's looking into his eyes. They are the colour that his hair, the colouring of his skin, suggests. It's the green of an imagined meadow. She has to remind herself that she's supposed to be looking at a piece of medical artistry, not behaving as though she is on a first date.

At first, moving her gaze from eye to eye, she can see nothing different about Seb's left eye. And then there it is, like a constellation suddenly making itself apparent in the sky: stitches zig-zagging around the green of his iris. She forgets, just for a second, about pain and panic and transplant. Here is a visible miracle.

16 November, 2017

EYE, EYE: Sexy Seb Pulls Out of *Star-Dance* in Infection Shock

Sebastian Morley, the twenty-seven-year-old heartthrob we were all rooting for to win *StarDance* this year, has had to leave the show, breaking all of our hearts.

The actor, who we fell for as barman Milo Bradshaw in BBC soap *Last Orders,* which he left earlier this year, was top of the judges' leaderboard — and way ahead in the public vote. He had bravely danced a cha-cha with foxy dance partner Fenella Albright, despite being in pain from his swollen, bloodshot eye. Head judge, Bob, quipped that Seb might have a sore eye but there was nothing wrong with his feet.

Earlier, Seb had brushed off worries, joking, 'I'll be blind with panic on the dance floor anyway!'

The sexy star had been top of the leaderboard for two weeks running, with a steamy salsa followed by a romantic American Smooth. Next week would have seen him dance the tango.

Seb's partner Fenella was seen leaving

Moorfields Eye Hospital in London in tears yesterday afternoon, accompanied by his sister Catherine.

Sebastian Morley: Career in Brief

Although he's only twenty-seven, we feel as though we've known Seb forever. It's ten years since he shot to fame. He was runner-up in the reality TV competition *Wherefore Art Thou?,* missing out on the role of Romeo in a six-month West End run of *Romeo and Juliet* by a handful of votes. He'd been the favourite to win — and with his serious green eyes, floppy blond hair, chiselled cheekbones and cheeky grin, we were all ready to be his Juliet! The winner, Xander Maxted-Morton, was booed on his first night in the role when he forgot a line, and Seb's fans picketed the theatre with placards declaring: 'Seb is our Romeo'. Morley came to the theatre to ask them to stop the protest — which only made us love him more. He landed the role of restaurant owner Max Rainbow in Channel 4's Shoreditch-based drama, *Beards and Skittles,* before spending six years in *Last Orders.* He left the soap in February 2017. He was planning to 'have some fun' on *StarDance* before

making his next career move. That eye
infection doesn't look like much fun,
though . . .

19 November, 2017

More to Seb's Problems Than Meets the Eye

We thought things couldn't get worse for sexy Seb Morley, after an eye infection put a stop to his *StarDance* moves. But we were wrong.

Morley's parents left Moorfields Eye Hospital late on Monday night, looking worried. So it looks as though Seb could have a serious problem — he could even lose his sight.

A small band of dedicated Seb fans have set up a vigil outside the hospital, holding candles and sitting quietly on the pavement near to the entrance. Sarah Blake, from Coventry, said, 'We want Seb to know that he has people who really care about him, on his bad days as well as his good ones . . . We have candles because we hope that he can see our light.'

Morley's agent says, 'Seb is still being treated. When there is any news we will issue a further statement. Until then, his family would appreciate some peace, and space.'

Fenella, Seb's dance partner, has been spotted going into the hospital, and so have fellow *StarDance* stars chef Ziggy McIvor and retired swimming champion Vee Bellamy.

2 February, 2018

Actor Morley Thanks Donor and Doctor Following Successful Cornea Transplant

Two months after Sebastian Morley, celebrity soap star, was forced to pull out of *StarDance* with an eye infection, he's stepped back into the spotlight.

Speaking at a press conference at Moorfields Eye Hospital, where he was treated, he said, 'Following the inflammation that led me to dropping out of *StarDance* last year, my eyeball ruptured and it was possible that I would lose my eye. However, last month I was lucky enough to receive a cornea transplant, which has saved that eye. I can never adequately express my gratitude to the person who was prepared to be a donor when they died — or to their family, who made a difficult decision to honour those wishes at a terrible time.'

Despite cries of 'Give us a look, Seb' from the waiting press, he declined to take off his dark glasses, joking, 'It's more than my life's worth to take these off when my surgeon's standing next to me!'

Dr Ali Ahmed, who performed the operation, said, 'Corneal transplantation, like any eye surgery, has high stakes. Sight is precious and, once lost, can be difficult to regain. I am delighted that Mr Morley's surgery had such a positive outcome.'

Asked about his future plans, Seb replied, 'For now I need to give my eye a chance to heal. That means staying away from a busy schedule for the time being. But I'll be back.'

Seb's *StarDance* partner, award-winning Latin dance star Fenella Albright, was with him at the press conference. He declined to answer questions about their relationship, although he did tell one reporter, 'I'm not much of a prospect, am I? One of my eyes is held together with stitches and I'm going to be out of work for the best part of a year!'

From: Seb
Sent: 19 March, 2018
To: Ailsa
Subject: Good to meet you

Dear BlueHeart,
I woke up this morning and thought, this time last week I was in a cab with the only person I've ever met who puts a seatbelt on in a cab. It was good to meet you. I thought you did a great job. Dealing with arses isn't easy.

Don't tell anyone this — especially not journalists — because it's kind of embarrassing, but you're the first unicorn I've ever met.

All the best,
Seb (Morley)

From: Ailsa
To: Seb

Dear Seb,
Thank you for your email. It was nice to meet you too. Unicorns are everywhere, if you look for them.

BlueHeart (Ailsa)

From: Seb
To: Ailsa

Dear Ailsa (BlueHeart),
I'll keep an eye out.

Is it as hard to avoid heart sayings as it is eye ones?

I've already had an eye out. I don't want to be doing it again.

Seb

From: Ailsa
To: Seb

Dear Seb,
Well, your heart has to be in it, or you can soon lose heart, and then you'll never get to the heart of the matter. For most people a heart does equal love, I can see that, but for me the sight of a heart balloon reminds me of the sort of nightmares that you have when you're on really heavy medication. And, I don't like red.

Ailsa

From: Seb
To: Ailsa

Dear Ailsa,
I had a look around your blog. It's very heart-wrenching in places. (Sorry.) If I wasn't reading it on my phone in a restaurant I might have shed a tear.

The idea of crying freaks me out. I'm worried that I'll rub my eye and the cornea will come off on my fingers. I had to wear brown contact lenses for a part once. They were really thin and even though there were only three days of filming, I got through eleven pairs of contact lenses. It was a really low-budget thing. The director went mental.

I'm having some more stitches out tomorrow. They take them a few at a time.

I think I'll be able to see the unicorns better then.

Seb x

From: Ailsa
To: Seb

Dear Seb,
Good luck for tomorrow. I'm still thinking about your eye, and how delicate the

123

stitching is. Eyes are beautiful anyway; yours seemed to have a starburst sewn into it. Thank you for showing me. It reminded me of blown-up images from under microscopes, and you cannot believe how amazing a bit of twig or a skin cell can be.

I wonder if the stitches around my heart are as tidy?

Ailsa

From: Seb
Sent: 21 March, 2018
To: Ailsa
Subject: Eyes and Edinburgh

Dear Ailsa,
All well with the stitches.

I was going to take a photo to send you, but I'm supposed to be careful of bright light. Which is mad because the first thing they do when you go for a check-up is shine what feels like a stage light in it. One rule for the doctor, one for the patient.

And I have a better idea. (Better than the photo, I mean.) I've been asked to come to Edinburgh to talk about a job, so I thought I could show you in person.

If you're around. If you want to. I

know how busy unicorns are.

It's next Wednesday. I'll be free from about 4.30.

Here's hoping,
Seb x

From: Ailsa
To: Seb

Dear Seb,

I had been trying to pluck up the courage, actually, to ask you to do an interview for my blog. I've been doing a body-part bingo thing for the last couple of years. I'm trying to interview people who need transplants and people who have had them. I haven't spoken to anyone who has either had, or needs, a corneal transplant yet.

It's not exactly incisive journalism but all I'm really trying to do is to make information accessible to people.

I could buy you a half-decent coffee (or other beverage — we don't just drink whisky and Irn-Bru up here) and look at your eye.

I should probably warn you that unicorns don't tend to go outdoors much in Edinburgh — the climate's a wee bit chilly for them. I'll probably be disguised as a human being.

Ailsa

From: Seb
To: Ailsa

Dear Ailsa,
I'd love to.

I like talking better in real life. It's easy to be misinterpreted otherwise.

Your post last week made me laugh, about missing bread and trying to hallucinate a pizza from ratatouille. Once when I was doing StarDance, Fenella and I went out for a pizza. She went on and on about how many calories there were in it. The whole bloody meal. And she still ate everything on the plate. Next morning she had a costume fitting so I texted her and asked if her dress fitted over her arse. There was a very frosty rehearsal afterwards.

Seb x

From: Ailsa
To: Seb

Dear Seb,
Just a bit of advice. As a general rule for living, 'do not ask people whether they

126

are too fat for their clothes in any context' is pretty foolproof. And that's from someone who doesn't watch a lot of TV, so I don't know much about Fenella. (Though I did look you up after last weekend, so I know more than I did.)

I've tango on Wednesdays so I need to leave by 6.30 p.m., but that should give us plenty of time. Let's meet in the Northbridge Brasserie at 5. It's just around the corner from the station if you need to catch a train afterwards.

Ailsa

From: Seb
To: Ailsa

Dear Ailsa,
You don't watch a lot of TV? Wow. So you're a kind of entertainment vegan? (Joke.)

Fenella had a ribcage you could play a tune on. So it's not like one pizza was going to do any serious damage. I thought she'd laugh. She didn't.

See you Wednesday. It will be good to catch up in person.

Seb x

From: Ailsa
To: Seb

Dear Seb,
You forget, I used to be dying. And most TV is based on the idea that it's going to go on, and on, and on. What's the point in watching something when you have no idea how it's going to work out? At least if you read a book, or watch a film, you've got a fair chance of getting to the end.

See you then,
Ailsa

P.S. Entertainment vegan made me laugh.

25 March, 2018

'How's your day looking, hen?'

'I'll be out when you get home.' Ailsa is boiling eggs for breakfast while Hayley makes a sandwich for her lunch. Because she works as a locum pharmacist, there's no routine to her days — sometimes even her nights, if she's covering a shift at a 24-hour pharmacy. So there's not routine to home life, either. They might be adapting more easily if there was.

'But your hospital appointment's this morning, aye?'

'Half eleven.' At least Hayley has stopped trying to come along. Maybe this time Ailsa will drop in on the heart unit and say hello to the staff who fought so hard for her. Even as she thinks it, she knows she won't. Just the sight of the artwork on the walls is enough to make her tearful with remembrance, making the old feelings bloom and the old places ache with fear and exhaustion.

'You've your biopsy today?'

'Yes.'

'I could have come with you, you know.'

'I know, Mum. It's OK. I can manage.' Ailsa's voice is, she knows, unfairly sharp. A heart biopsy is not a pleasant thing. Because the heart doesn't have its own blood supply, the only way to check it for health is to take a piece of it, so this morning Ailsa will have a catheter with a snipper on the end fed down her nose to Apple, and a little bit of heart muscle will be cut away. There was a time when she could only do it with Hayley holding her hand, tight. The thought of it still makes her feel sick. She's not sure she'll be able to do it on her own. But she'll try.

'Suit yourself. So where are you later? Are you for dancing?'

'I'm interviewing Seb first.'

Is it Ailsa's imagination, or does her mother stiffen at Seb's name? 'Don't overdo it. And make sure you eat, aye? A potato willna kill you, whatever your book says.'

Oh, a potato. Or some toast. Or a huge chunk of cheese. Or all of those things. The diet is working, for sure, but the novelty has worn off. Still, she needs to be healthy, to do Apple justice, and that means getting to

130

a healthy weight. Be strong, Ailsa.

'Mum. I'm fine. I promise. And anyway, I'll have to manage when you . . .'

Hayley looks up, pretend shock on her face. 'When I die? I think we've a few years yet.'

Ailsa laughs, reaches for her mother's arm for a second. 'We talked about you moving out. Or me. I want to talk about it again. Not now.'

'There's no hurry, for sure,' Hayley says, matter-of fact and almost dismissive.

'Well, no,' Ailsa says, wrong-footed suddenly, as though she's a child again, tricked into looking away while someone gives her an injection. 'But — it's important to me, Mum.'

'Me going tae work is important. Nobody's going anywhere, if I'm not earning.'

Apple clenches, something like a warning, and Ailsa heeds her. 'I know, Mum. I'm just saying — can we talk about it? Properly? Please? Maybe with Tamsin?'

Hayley nods. 'Aye, that makes sense. I've talked to your Auntie T a bit, but if we all sit down . . .' She sighs. 'I worry, though.'

'I know you do.' And they look straight at each other, the way they haven't, lately. Hayley's eyes are brown, and so is her hair, straight as needles and soft as blankets. She never wears make-up and her skin pinches around her lips, at the corners of her eyes, but her smile, when she has reason to use it, is as bright as the best June morning. People say Ailsa has her mother's smile, and she's glad. In most other respects she's different: plump-faced — even when the steroids aren't rounding her cheeks — blue-eyed, dark-blonde. But their smiles, side by side, are reflections of each other. The old intimacy, the say-anything spirit of late hospital nights, is back for a second. So although Ailsa hadn't planned to ask this right now, in this moment it seems right. 'And I want to talk about my biological father a bit. Sometime. I've been thinking I should maybe see if he's still alive, at least.'

She may as well not have bothered. Hayley looks as though she hasn't heard a word. She tucks her sandwich into her bag, puts on her coat, flicks her hair out over her collar, all of her movements brisk and crisp. Then she touches her daughter on the shoulder, and Ailsa turns for her embrace.

'Dinnae overdo it, hen. Have a good day. Take it easy after the hospital's done. And call me afterwards, aye?'

'Will it not wait until tonight? You're busy. I'll call you if there's anything not right.'

Hayley smiles, without the light. 'I just

132

like to know you're OK, Ailsa. It doesnae mean you willnae get what you want. It just means I care.'

And then she's gone.

25 MARCH, 2017

This Time Last Year

As soon as Ailsa comes into Lennox's hospital room, she takes off her shoes and climbs into the narrow bed beside him. Some days he sits up and curls an arm around her. Some days — like today — he doesn't move, and so she lies her body next to his. They don't compare hands anymore, because Lennox's deepening yellow skin is no longer funny. Aftershave can't disguise the sour-sweet smell of illness exhaled by his skin. She breathes it in anyway, her head on his chest.

'BlueHeart.' His voice is still his, though. If she closes her eyes, he's seventeen, the best-looking boy on the football team, and her boyfriend. And she loves him with every bit of her broken blue heart.

'Sleep if you want to,' she says. Since they were told that there was no hope of his being saved, Lennox has sunk more into silence and slumber. Ailsa doesn't know if it's the rising tide of illness, or whether it's easier to lie with his eyes closed than to look at the faces of his family.

'I don't think I want to,' he says. 'You wanted to interview me, didn't you?'

The thought of him talking about the need for a transplant, now that the chance has gone, is something she's not strong enough for. Not yet.

'Not today,' she says.

'OK. Help me sit up?'

She gets off the bed and he uses her arm to lever himself upright. She moves the pillows, presses the buttons on the bed so it inches upward, settles him back. His chest is sinking into itself, his body starting to retreat. She pours a glass of water. Her mother will have to bear this, soon, when it's too late for her. Don't cry, Ailsa. Don't cry.

'I want you to help me with something. I've asked my dad but he — it was too much.'

'OK,' Ailsa says. 'What?'

'I need to make a will,' he says. 'I want everything sorted. I don't want them to have extra hassle when I go. It's not fair.'

The tears are there; there's no stopping them. 'None of this is fair. But yes, of

135

course.' She sighs. 'I should do the same. My mum won't do anything about it either. She just says this time next year we'll be tearing it up, so it's a waste of time and heartache.'

He's put out his hand and is wiping at her tears with his thumb, his face a sad reflection of her own. 'Let's get someone in, outside visiting hours, and we can do it together.'

Ailsa nods. 'That's a good idea.' And it is. She's glad the two of them can share this, understand the practicalities of being likely-dying. But she feels, too, what her mother must feel when she talks about this, biting down her impulse to change the subject, tell him he doesn't need to talk about it today, chase death away with a kiss.

She doesn't have a lot to leave — she makes a habit of keeping everything at home tidy and neat, everything out-of-date or equivocal thrown away, so her mother won't have so much as an old T-shirt or out-of-date scribbles in a notebook to upset her, if Ailsa dies. But a set of instructions, of who to give which memento to, will surely help Hayley, if the time comes.

'Will you ask Craig on your way out? He'll be able to sort it.'

Ailsa glances at the nurses' station, sees

the familiar face of one of Lennox's regular nurses. 'Sure I will.'

'Thanks, Ails,' Lennox says, and his eyes are closing as he drifts into sleep. It's hard not to imagine death every time he does this. She bends close to kiss his forehead before she goes, and just as she gets close, there's the smile she sees less and less of these days, and he says, 'I'd leave you my heart, you know, if I could.'

25 MARCH, 2018

Ailsa arrives at the Northbridge Brasserie first. It's a grand place, forming part of the Scotsman Hotel, with all of the Victorian baronial gothic that that implies. The interior is marble and stone, with everything carved or moulded or . . . something. It's a bit too touristy for the everyday Edinburgh-dweller but, on the odd occasion Ailsa has been here, she's liked it. It's the sort of place that makes you wonder why you don't own a cloak. There's time to order tea before Seb arrives.

When he does come through the door, she's barely stood before he sees her and strides over. He is breathless, his skin clammy when he presses his cheek to Ailsa's. She scans him: brown wool coat, blue shirt, black jeans, bright blue trainers. All good.

'Ailsa,' that slow stretch of smiling, 'good to see you. Sorry I'm late. My meeting went on. I thought it would be quicker to walk but I got lost. I was worried I'd missed you.'

'No bother,' Ailsa says. 'I don't mind waiting.' She almost adds, I've had plenty of practice, but stops herself. Waiting for Apple isn't the only way to frame her life anymore.

'On the map it looks as though you're in the right place,' he says, unbuttoning his coat, which is tweedy, leather-buttoned, a newer version of something Aunt Tamsin would coo over in a vintage shop, 'but then you turn out to be on the wrong level. I've never tried to find my way around a multi-storey city before.'

Ailsa laughs. 'You should try giving directions.'

'No thanks,' Seb says. He slides his coat from his shoulders and drapes it over the spare chair at the table Ailsa's chosen.

'Shall we have a drink?' Seb is sitting back now, raising a hand to a waiter, the picture of confidence that is the opposite of what Ailsa can manage. 'What are you drinking? I don't want to distract you from cave food. Do you want anything to eat? You're going to have a boring Easter, aren't you?'

There's a second before she realises he's talking about chocolate. She'd thought he'd read her mind — the fact that her friends would all be coupled-up or going out over the Easter weekend, while she'll be with her mum and her auntie, listening to them reminisce and trying to find a moment to bring up what they were going to do about her, or Hayley, moving out. Another pair of friends has moved out of Edinburgh for the sake of a mortgage they can afford. She got an invitation to her ex-boyfriend Jacob's wedding this week. She's being left further and further behind. And Apple has a real sense of urgency about this; Ailsa wonders whether she's been twenty-eight before, and she knows how things should be.

She laughs. 'I'll cope,' she says. 'And I've ordered some tea. I ate before I came out.'

Seb orders a cheese plate and some wine. Then he leans back, looks around, and says, 'I thought Edinburgh would be — plainer. You've got to love a city that thinks nothing is finished until it's got a turret on top. Inside, as well. Look at all that — what is it? Plasterwork? On the ceiling.'

Ah, the tea's here. Something else for Ailsa to look at, rather than the elaborate ceiling, which makes her feel dizzy, or Seb, who is dizzying in a different way, not least because she can't tell exactly what he's looking at behind his shades. Not now he's stopped looking up, anyway.

She turns down the milk and asks for lemon. Seb waits until the waiter has gone, then says, 'You're nowhere near the size you make people think on your blog, you know. You just look — comfy — in real life.'

'Thanks,' Ailsa says, though she's not sure 'comfy' is the word she wants to spring to Seb's mind when he looks at her. 'It's how you feel, though, is it not?'

'It is,' and he smiles as though she's said something clever. 'I like the way you sound.'

'You'll have been ecstatic having a day in Edinburgh, then.' She's tempted to dial up her accent. Equally, she wants to tone it down. With the result that she suddenly can't remember how to speak at all.

'Sort of. But Roz — from my meeting — has lived all over the place, though she's from Edinburgh, so she hasn't really got the sound so much. And some people I can't make out. You're just right.'

'Everyone in Edinburgh might not have been from Edinburgh, you know. It's not — an enclave.'

Seb dips his head, as though submitting, then leans forward. 'Before the food gets here. Stitch inspection.' He raises his Ray-Bans, and Ailsa leans in to see, raising her glasses too. She's startled, again, by the clear warm green of his eyes, in this light like a summer-day sea; and then she looks at what she's supposed to be focussing on, and

141

notices how the stitches are no longer a star but a series of zig-zags, broken here and there where individual stitches have been removed. She looks for pin-pricks of darkness where the holes must have been, but she can't see them.

They are almost nose-to-nose, air eddying between them as they breathe.

Ailsa sits back, puts her glasses back on, and Seb does the same. It's too uncomfortable, to be so close to someone. 'Thank you,' she says.

'Your eyes are a lovely colour,' Seb replies, although it's not really a reply.

'They're just blue.'

'You can't say "just blue". That's like saying "it's just raining". There's a thousand sorts of rain.'

Ailsa laughs, looks over his shoulder — what a relief to look away from those sunglasses, and whatever is going on in the eyes behind them — towards the door, with its steady veil of drizzle beyond. 'There is in Edinburgh, that's for sure. Did you bring a brolly?'

Seb shrugs. 'Nah. I'll get wet. In the scheme of things I think I can handle it.'

Seb's cheese and wine arrive, along with the lemon, fanned out in slices on a small white dish. Ailsa pours her tea. She isn't used to thinking of weather as something to be disregarded. A cold can be a bad thing for someone with a heart condition; fatal, for someone taking immunosuppressants. There's an umbrella in her bag, a hood on her coat.

'How was your meeting?'

'Good, I think,' Seb says. 'Now I wait and see. Metaphorically speaking. I don't want to think about it. Distract me. How was your day? What did you do?'

'Fine,' Ailsa says, because it would be weird to say what her days really are: odd, tiring, lonely. Not what she expected them to be. And she's certainly not going to offer that up to someone who only wants to hear about it as a way of not thinking about themselves. 'I'm thinking about what to do. But I don't know the best way to be' — a moment, a sip of tea, a search for the word — 'worthwhile.' It's only as she says it that she realises how much she means it, and her voice sounds tearful. Seb doesn't seem to notice. He probably thinks it's more charming Edinburgh nuance.

'You're clever, though.' It's not a question.

'Yes.' Cleverness is about all Ailsa has, now that heart problems have gone. 'I've got a degree in history. But not a lot else to offer.'

'So you can do whatever you want to. I mean — if you're clever, you can turn your hand to something. Get qualified. I think I got three GCSEs. I failed most things, except showing off.'

'Were you . . .' Ailsa hesitates. She's thinking of Lennox's sister, who is still angry now about the un-spotted dyslexia that slowed her down, although she's made it up in spades since. Is it acceptable to ask someone if they have that kind of difficulty? Probably not.

'I wasn't anything,' Seb says, 'though everyone tried to find something: dyslexia, dyspraxia, ADHD. In the end we all agreed I was just a lazy little bugger who liked showing off.' Ailsa laughs. 'The funny thing is, my parents are teachers. What I didn't do at school I had to do at home. In theory. Phone confiscated, studying where they could see me, all that. Carrots. Sticks. Nothing worked. I didn't care. I just wanted to be an actor. No parent wants to hear that one.'

'I suppose not,' Ailsa says. Thinks: *Not as much as they don't want to hear — heart operation or bust.*

'I got maths and English GCSEs, and an

A* in drama, of course, and the agreement was that I would take a year to start working towards a drama career and then we — the family — would reconsider. Which meant, give him a year to realise how hard it is out there and then talk some sense into him. Then I saw the ad for open auditions for Wherefore Art Thou?' He grins. 'My folks are lovely, but it's funny how they've rewritten history. "We always knew he'd end up on the stage", and all that.'

Ailsa laughs. 'Do you not mind?'

Seb shakes his head. 'First rule of this business: don't mind. You've got people telling you, on a daily basis, that you're too fat, too thin, your face is the wrong shape, you haven't got chemistry, or the other guy is better than you. And that's just auditions. If you're stupid enough to look at the tabloids, it's a million times worse.'

Ailsa thinks of herself, after the radio show and the comments that followed it, slating her for ingratitude. She had lain in bed, tired from the travelling, and trying, fiercely, not to mind; failing. She almost says so — or says something, to agree — but her experience is nothing compared to his. It would be like talking about being in a school play to him.

Seb is constructing a careful tower of

oatcake, pickle, cheese, quince jelly. As he eats, Ailsa says, 'I can see that,' then, 'I've never had a job before. So even the — the marking-time jobs — I don't think I'm much of a prospect.'

Seb puts his head on one side, gives her a look that says I-agree-but-I-don't-agree. 'I'd say there's more to you than meets the eye. Even the normal eye.'

'Hark at me,' Ailsa says, 'complaining about all sorts of things that aren't problems.'

Seb looks at her, seriously, for a moment. 'It's not my business,' he says, 'but when I was first playing Max on TV, I used to go to work and think everyone was better than me, and go home convinced I was a failure. And most kids auditioning for drama school would break each other's legs to do what I was doing.'

Ailsa might be holding her breath. There's a familiarity to what he's saying, and as he talks she feels something in her start to unclench. It's as though Apple is listening too, stretching out to hear. She doesn't want him to stop.

'I used to make a massive effort, you know, always be cheerful, always go out for drinks if anyone was going. Not be offended if people were bitchy. And then one day I was in make-up, and Tom Foster was in the chair next to me, and he caught my eye in the mirror and said, 'Remember, son, just because you've got what you want doesn't mean you have to be happy all the fucking time.'

'Yes,' Ailsa says. 'God — yes.' She almost asks who Tom Foster is, but she knows it doesn't matter. This isn't a story about Tom Foster. It's about Seb. And her. It's about — ordinary. Seb is describing the feeling she's had since she left hospital with her four-beats-to-the-bar heart and a shining life ahead, the meaning she's been grasping for.

Seb takes some more cheese and then gestures, a sorry-my-mouth's-full wave of the hand. Ailsa smiles, waits. She could try to say something but she'd rather just sit here, feeling whatever it is that she's feeling. Understood, maybe.

'I read your blog and I know that was about you, what's inside you,' Seb continues and Ailsa puts her hand to her chest. She can't help it; here is the place where Apple is keeping time for her forever. He takes a mouthful of wine. 'But it made me think about when I started and the way it was — outside me. Some of the people in that show were bastards to me. They had worked their

147

way into TV the hard way and they thought I'd cheated by doing *Wherefore Art Thou?* They were waiting for me to fall on my face. I was determined to show them. I knew all my lines, I did as I was told. And then Tom said what he said, and when I left make-up there were a couple of people who stopped talking as I went past. They had obviously been talking about me. Usually I would have ignored them, or been cheerful and pretended I hadn't noticed, but instead I smiled and flipped them the bird. It felt fantastic. Fuckers. They both got killed off in a car accident last year. They're still waiting for their next jobs.'

Seb leans back, catches the waiter's eye, points to his glass, gives a thumbs-up, returns to his cheese. Ailsa's tea is almost untouched; the slice of lemon has sunk. She wishes she'd written down what he'd said, or been recording their conversation from the beginning. He's looking at her, waiting for her to speak. He hasn't said anything about gratitude or living or what she ought to do. But his story has sent a pulse of recognition through her, top to toe.

Seb's fresh glass of wine arrives. 'Are you OK? Ailsa?'

'What you said,' she says, 'about not having to be happy because you've got what

148

you're supposed to want. Thank you. I feel as though you understand.'

A moment of quiet. A beat of two hearts.

'Do you like tango?'

'I love it,' Ailsa says.

Seb nods. 'I didn't get to do tango on *StarDance,*' he says. 'I would have done, if my eye hadn't . . .' He makes a gesture with his hand, from fist to fully extended fingers in a second. 'Fenella and I had started rehearsing. I loved it. Very sexy.'

'Yes, I can see how it could be,' Ailsa says, although all she's learned, really, is to stop apologising when she does something wrong. Sometimes there's a twitch of something else, a step that works. Not sexy, but something that might be related to it. Eventually.

'Are you learning with the Gardiner sisters?'

'Yes,' Ailsa says, 'they're lovely. Very patient.' But this is a man who is in Edinburgh for the first time, and got lost on his way to Waverley station. 'How do you know them?'

'I don't, really. Only the name, because they did really well on a talent thing. Roz mentioned they're from Edinburgh at our meeting today.'

Ailsa points to herself. 'Entertainment

vegan, remember? I just googled "Tango class Edinburgh" and away I went.'

Seb nods, smiles and pushes his chair to one side a little, so that he can prop an ankle on the opposite knee. Everything he does with his body looks right. No wonder he can dance. Or does his body look right because he dances?

'Do you want to do this interview before I have any more wine?'

'Yes, please.' Ah, familiar territory. She flips her notebook to the list of questions, opens up the recorder on her phone, and gets down to business.

27 March, 2018

The Eye Has It

The eye is a funny old thing, isn't it? Just a squishy ball of vitreous whatever that allows us to see, and yet we make it so important in such a lot of other ways. I think it's closest to the heart in that respect. A heart is nothing but a pump, really, but you wouldn't think that on Valentine's Day. Well, the eye is the window to the soul; sunshine in February is a sight for sore eyes; if you're lucky, you're the apple of someone's eye.

But, you know I like to be unsentimental about the body. If I wasn't, all of my love and a good deal of my spirit would have been taken out of me with my old, broken pump. So let's talk about the cornea. It's a transparent, dome-shaped disc on the front of the eye, which bends the light as it enters the body, and is crucial in allowing us to see.

I've interviewed someone who received a corneal transplant in December. He's going to remain anonymous, so we'll call him Green Eyes. The unedited transcript is below (though I haven't tried to capture the noise I made when I knocked half a cup of cold tea over, and I've not bothered with the clearing-up and apologising. You can imagine that for yourselves, if you want to).

AILSA: Thank you for talking to me about your cornea transplant.

GREEN EYES: No worries. We kind of complement each other. Green eyes, blue heart.

AILSA: Well, yes. Though my heart isn't blue anymore. Metaphorically speaking.

GREEN EYES: Sounds like we might need a bottle of wine to unpick that statement.

AILSA: Tell us a little bit about you, apart from your cornea, Green Eyes.

GREEN EYES: OK. I'm a busy person. I like people and going out. I like good food, though I can't cook to save my life. I live in London. God, I sound really shallow. Shall I say that I read a lot of books?

AILSA: Only if it's true.

GREEN EYES: I must do something apart from eat and go out . . . I go to the gym but that's not really a hobby. I like music.

AILSA: What sort of music?

GREEN EYES: All sorts. Bluegrass, though, especially. And Northern soul. I buy vinyl if I can.

AILSA: OK.

GREEN EYES: Do I sound less shallow now?

AILSA: Yes, on the music. No, on the vinyl. And what do you do for a living?

GREEN EYES: Not a lot, at the moment. I'm an actor but I am, literally, avoiding the spotlight until my eye heals. It's weird.

AILSA: So you can't work at all?

GREEN EYES: In theory, I could. I'm — exploring possibilities at the moment.

But between keeping my eye away from too much light, and having to avoid close-ups because there's stitching in my eye, plus not wanting to get anything in there — there's a limit to what I can do. On camera, at least.

AILSA: You could play people who never take their sunglasses off, maybe? Or pirates?

GREEN EYES: You should be my agent.

AILSA: So — why did you need a cornea transplant?

GREEN EYES: I had a sore, itchy eye that wouldn't go away. I assumed I must have just scratched it or something, but after a week I saw a doctor, and I got antibiotic eye drops for what looked like an infection. It almost went away, but didn't, quite. I should admit that I got a bit lazy — I was really busy — so I stopped putting the drops in regularly and I didn't go back to the doctor, even though things hadn't completely cleared up. And then, over the space of forty-eight hours, the soreness and itchiness went mental, and when I went to the hospital, it turned out I had been wrongly diagnosed. I actually had something called Acanthamoeba keratitis.

AILSA: You had a houseplant in your eye?

GREEN EYES: *(laughs)* I'd never heard of it either. Acanthamoeba is an amoeba that lives in water and doesn't usually cause problems, but if it gets into the right conditions, it turns nasty. It's like one of those people who you really like, and then they get drunk and turn out to be fascists or racists.

AILSA: So your cornea was the right place for it to get . . . racist? Why?

GREEN EYES: One of those things, really. I used to wear contact lenses and I didn't wash my hands every time I put them in or took them out. I wasn't supposed to sleep with my lenses in but there were times when I did. I took my eyes for granted, basically.

AILSA: But there was also a wrong diagnosis.

GREEN EYES: It is quite hard to diagnose. And I created the conditions. I bought the drinks. I was a dick. Can I say 'dick' on your blog?

AILSA: Well, I do prefer to use the correct medical terminology, but . . .

GREEN EYES: I respect that. I was a penis. A stupid penis. Because if I'd done as I was supposed to, and gone back to the doctor, then it wouldn't have got as bad as it did.

(*Note for authenticity: this is when I spilled the tea. It was absolutely nothing to do with someone I don't know very well saying 'penis' a lot, quite loudly, and people looking around, and me pretending to have a drink to cover my embarrassment. Nothing at all.*)

AILSA: What happened next?

GREEN EYES: Long story short: I was admitted to eye hospital and told that I needed a cornea transplant.

AILSA: So if you hadn't had a transplanted cornea . . . ?

GREEN EYES: I might have lost my sight. Or even my eye. There aren't a lot of roles for glass-eyed actors, as far as I know.

AILSA: You'd make a good Bond villain.

GREEN EYES: I'll take that as a compliment. Again, you should be my agent.

AILSA: What's the most common thing that people say to you about this?

GREEN EYES: I don't think there's anything specific. They go, 'Eyes? Yeuch' and they wince.

AILSA: And what do you say in response?

GREEN EYES: I say, I know, I used to be squeamish about my eyes, until I realised what a wreck I'd be without one of them.

AILSA: And you got a transplant. What were the chances?

GREEN EYES: Well, pretty good, I guess, because corneas can be stored, so

157

there isn't the time pressure there is with other organs. And there isn't a blood supply direct to the cornea, so blood-type matching isn't critical.

AILSA: So your cornea can't be rejected?

GREEN EYES: Yes, it can. But the likelihood is less.

AILSA: How long until you're back to normal?

GREEN EYES: The stitches come out, gradually, over a year. There's a question over whether my sight will go back to what it was before, but the fact that I can see a bit at this stage is a good sign. I'm fine. Fine. I'm wearing prescription sunglasses most of the time, because my eye is sensitive to light while it heals, and it is a little bit painful and easily tired. That's not a problem, but I have to think twice before everything I do. I have to — I don't know how to explain it — I have to, sort of, measure everything and decide whether it's worth doing or not.

AILSA: I was like that before I had my transplant. I had two questions — first: Can I manage it?; and second: Can I be bothered to recover from it? There are quite a lot of equations in illness, I think, and this is one of the straightforward ones. Does effort plus impact equal value?

GREEN EYES: Exactly! I don't know why you're interviewing me. You put things much better than I can.

AILSA: I haven't been at the sharp end of a cornea transplant.

GREEN EYES: You actually don't feel a thing. Well — pushing and pulling. Like at the dentist, but with eyes. You see, you're wincing now.

AILSA: Sorry. I don't like the dentist. I have no problem with people pushing and pulling my eyeballs, honest. Last question — has this experience changed your perspective on transplants, Green Eyes?

GREEN EYES: Yes. Yes. I'm ashamed to say that I hadn't really given transplants, or organ donation, a thought before. Now I'm on the organ donor register, and I'm going to start giving blood as soon as I'm medically fit. We need to be less squeamish about all this. Actively say if you don't want your organs donated. Otherwise, be useful.

AILSA: You'll get no argument from me on that.

GREEN EYES: Also, I don't think next of kin should be allowed to overrule the dead person's decision.

AILSA: I don't think grief is a good place to make decisions from.

GREEN EYES: You see? So well put.

AILSA: Thank you. And thank you for answering. I know it's not always great to look back.

GREEN EYES: I'd be happy to look anywhere.

AILSA: God, sorry.

GREEN EYES: Don't take it to heart.

AILSA: One-all. I think we're done.

If you'd like to know more about eye conditions and eye health, start *here.*
Register to be an organ donor *here.*
Make sure your family knows your wishes, and will respect them.
And remember, eyes are just eyes. There's nothing to wince about.

Here's a question, then. Would you donate your corneas? (Let's assume, for the sake of this poll, that your corneas are worth having.) You've got until 30 March. Though it shouldn't take you that long to get to the right answer.

YES — I'd donate them, along with anything else that's useful.
NO — I wouldn't, and I wouldn't donate anything else either, and that's a decision I am entitled to, Ailsa, whatever you think.
NO — I wouldn't, though you can have my liver and my heart and all my other useful bits.

4 shares
19 comments

Results:
YES   83%
NO (and nothing else)   1%
NO (but anything else)   16%

From: Ailsa
Sent: 27 March, 2018
To: Seb
Subject: Interview is up!

Dear Seb,
Thank you for doing the interview. You'll find it on the blog, *here.*

I've kept it anonymous, as you said. I hope it's neutral enough to keep you out of trouble. If not, just say — it's easily altered.

Ailsa

P.S. Tango was good, though I still feel as though I'll never get the hang of it. At least I've stopped looking at my feet. And it's so nice to feel a wee bit fitter every time I go.

From: Seb
To: Ailsa

Dear Ailsa,
Great interview! It's nice to read it word for word, with no editing or opinion. That might be the first time I've ever read something and thought 'yep'. Usually, I spend the rest of the day wondering whether I really said stuff, or how I

managed to come across the way I've been described. Sometimes I think people write the articles before they meet me.

And I think I'm safe on the anonymity front. Wilkie (agent) did say that theoretically I could be sued if StarDance decide I brought the eye problem on myself, but to be honest they got enough publicity out of it to make it worth their while.

I scrolled back a few posts. It looks like you got some stick after the radio. Hope you're OK now and it's settled down.

You should have said when we met. I'm the king of getting slagged off in the press. I could have given you all of my handy hints.

May the unicorns be with you,

Seb x

From: Ailsa
To: Seb

Dear Seb,
I'm fine. Of course the reason I'm fine is that I believe I'm right, which is also what the people who've been having a pop think. That's food for thought. We had better things to talk about than the

bottom third of the Internet when we met.

I'm happy to hear any handy hints, though; there's only so much a unicorn can do to protect me, on the web (they're hopeless at typing).

How is your eye?

Ailsa

From: Seb
To: Ailsa

My eye's fine, thanks. I think my sight's getting a bit clearer.

Here are my tips:

1. If people are arses, fuckwits or in any way abusive, block them straight away. Don't engage. You won't win and by replying you only give them more ammunition.
2. Only look at your emails/go on social media when you're feeling up to it. Or get someone else to look at them for you and tell you what you need to respond to.
3. Remember that although people think they know you, they don't, really. They know the you that they've imagined from what's out

165

there. You're separate to that.

4. Make sure you have a different email, different provider, for friends/family/personal stuff to your blog one. That way you can reply to an email from your bank without having to trawl through things with subject lines like I HOPE YOU GET ADIS YU UGLY PRIK. That was one of mine, when I was playing a gay character, and I've left the spelling mistakes in because I think you'll enjoy them.

Take care,
Seb x

From: Ailsa
To: Seb

Thanks, that's really great advice. It's all common sense, really, and yet I wasn't doing 1, 2 or 4. I think I'm not too bad at 3.

So from now on please email me at blueheartdancing@gmail.com and I'll stick with blue@myblueblueheart .blogspot.co.uk for everyone I don't know in real life.

You take care too. Did your Edinburgh

thing come off?

Ailsa

From: Seb
To: Ailsa

It did! You'll be hearing more about it soon.

OK, you'll be hearing about it in the next three seconds. But shush.

I'm going to be in a show at the Fringe. I want to do something a bit low-key, a bit small, to get me back into it. I was going to have a year off but all I'm doing here is feeling sorry for myself and/or drinking too much. I was meeting a director and looking at a venue in Edinburgh. It was pretty relaxed, as auditions go, because we've worked together before. I think really she just wanted me to see the place so I knew what I was getting into — a fifty-seat venue, basically a room above a pub, no frills. She called me the next day and said it was all mine if I wanted it. I did.

Seb x

From: Ailsa
To: Seb

Congratulations! I'm really pleased for you. I thought after we were talking that you were maybe playing down how much you missed working. Time off when you're ill is a terrible idea. I know, I've had years of it. The worst is when you're sort of OK but you still can't do everything you want to; it's the worst of all worlds. (Although, better than dead/blind, etc., so you don't really feel you can complain.)

Ailsa

You can complain. I need to hook you up with Tom Foster.

X

■ ■ ■ ■

PART FOUR:
EARLY APRIL 2018
MORE LIGHT AND
LIGHT IT GROWS

■ ■ ■ ■

7 April, 2018

It's Time for the Party Bus!

Next week will mark the six-month anniversary of the transplantation of Apple into my body, and her achey, worn-out, predecessor finally being allowed to give up its ghost. (The ghost comes back in the night, sometimes, like the first wife in *Blithe Spirit,* usually when I'm thinking about the past, and Apple loses her rhythm and I get breathless. But we take deep breaths and we manage.)

I feel a bit odd about the marking of days, sometimes. Birthdays are fine, of course, but birthdays of the people we've lost, or anniversaries of their death, are things I don't know what to do with. You can't ignore them, because it feels wrong, but every day is an anniversary of their loss — first Hogmanay without them, every time you go to text them about a funny thing you've seen. They all hurt.

But I'm going to mark the hell out of reaching the six-month point. There's a celebration planned for tomorrow (I don't know what it is) and I am having a day off

171

from Paleo. (I've lost eight pounds since I started, and it's just as well, because there are times when the only thing that keeps me out of the doughnut aisle is watching the number on the scale drop. I'm doing this for good reasons — to give Apple the best chance — but it's hard going.)

I am going to be GLAD. I'm going to love every moment.

Here's what I get, as presents, or maybe prizes:

1. Time off from hospital. Because Apple and I are getting along OK, I can go to have her checked out once a week, instead of twice a week.

2. The tiniest bit of medical relaxing. I can have serious conversations about reducing dosages of medications. Although I will never be truly well — a transplant is always a palliative treatment, a patch over a broken thing — I can, I think, start to think of myself as well, instead of worrying that I will get found out and turned away every time I try to get on the wellness train.

3. Rejoining the world. I've done it a bit — I've been dancing; I've eaten out in quiet places; I've walked through the city as I've been collecting my daily steps —

but now, so long as I'm not stupid, me and Apple and our hand sanitiser are going to get out there.
4. Going on a bus. I've planned my route. I'm going to start in Fountainbridge and take the Number 1 (which seems appropriate) to the end of the line (not appropriate) in Leith. Then a 21 out to Edinburgh Park. I'll travel this seven-hill city from one end to the other. I'll see the grungy bits and the grand bits. I'll look at the river, and peer down into graveyards and up to the tops of blocks of flats. I'll pass the football ground that I can hear singing and cheering on a Saturday afternoon. I'll sit at the top deck, at the front. And I'll know how special it is, though everyone else on the route will behave as though a bus is the most everyday thing that they have, like a fridge or a bed or a suitcase. Or a heart.
5. Finding a job. Being out in the world.

I can do all of these things quite easily (I hope). But as this milestone has loomed, I've been thinking about the bigger picture a bit more than I might have done before.

Here's the thing: Apple has tricked me into feeling like I have a long life — but I probably don't. That is, immunosuppressants are slowly, surely, damaging my kidneys and my liver. If I'm not careful — and who is 100 per cent careful, 100 per cent of the time, apart from the people we never see or know because they never engage with the world? — I could die of a cold, because my permanently depressed immune system can't fight something you would shake off in a heartbeat. I've a higher chance of cancer. And who knows what wear and tear my body is already carrying, after its years of struggle?

So I'm going to make some decisions about how I spend this life.

Just over six months ago, I felt as though I'd done the best I could with the hand I was dealt. When I look back in ten years I want to be able to say the same thing.

What do I do next? I'm going to make a long-term plan. I've been mulling options. I'm not so sure that any of them are right. I'm giving you a week.

POLITICS — Get in there and work for the people, Ailsa. You don't have to want to be First Minister. You don't even have to join a party. You can work for the people you represent.
VOLUNTEERING — Do any old thing to

pay your bills, and throw your real energy into some sort of volunteering. A career can come later.

LAW — If you're looking for people to champion, this is the job for you.

ACTIVISM — You might not want to be all about transplants now, but that could change, Ailsa. It's early days. Don't close the door on this one.

TEACHING — Broaden the next generation's horizons. It's the best possible thing you can do for the world.

FIND A CAUSE — And work for it in any capacity. A charity has to have a well-run office, it has to pay its bills. Being meaningful could be managing spreadsheets.

SOMETHING ELSE — (leave a comment) Things I have considered and dismissed: any sort of medicine, counselling, extensive travelling, or anything that might give Apple a hard time.

17 shares
45 comments

Results:
POLITICS   5%
VOLUNTEERING 18%
LAW   19%

ACTIVISM 16%
TEACHING 18%
FIND A CAUSE 15%
SOMETHING ELSE 9%

Ailsa knew there was going to be a six-month celebration. She didn't expect it to be, literally, a party bus. But at three o'clock, Hayley calls her to the living room — she's just been choosing a lipstick, a thrill that never seems to get old — and directs her to the window.

She looks into the street and there it is: open-topped, ballooned and beribboned, and — best of all — the top deck filled with laughing, smiling friends. There's Emily, Jacob, Pritti and Tim, and Christa, who have stuck with her through thick and thin since they met during their first university term. She sees some familiar faces from the hospital staff, grinning too broadly for Ailsa to feel guilty about not going back to see them. Aunt Tamsin. Oh, and Ruthie and Dennis, with their bravest faces. There's even Edie, Eliza, Venetia and Murray, from tango. So that's why everyone stopped talking when she walked in last week.

Ailsa feels her hands at her mouth, covering the great happy O it's making.

Hayley, beside her, puts an arm around her shoulder and squeezes. 'I laughed when I saw your blog title yesterday. It made me wonder if you'd guessed.'

'No!' And Ailsa can feel the tears rising — she's already more emotional than usual, between her mother starting to pack and the way that the pain of missing Lennox has been flexing again, an old muscle starting to be reused.

But Hayley says, 'Come on, they're waiting,' and before she knows it, she's up on the top deck and the bus is lurching them off around Edinburgh. There's a collective 'ooh' as everyone gasps and finds something to hold onto. And then the sound system crackles into life with 'Don't Go Breaking My Heart', and Tamsin laughs, and Hayley and Dennis start a duet. Oh, life is good today.

They're waiting at the lights near Holyrood when Emily tops up Ailsa's glass with Prosecco. 'Here's to new hearts, and taking buses, and not getting a hangover because we're drinking this outside.'

'I'll drink to that.'

Emily shakes her head, laughs. 'Do you

remember the Bacardi hangover?'

'Worst hangover of my life.' Not unlike coming round from surgery, actually. 'I cannot believe we fell for Jacob saying you didn't get so hungover if you had a drink outside.'

Ah, toffee vodka being passed from hand to hand as she and Emily and Jacob sat cross-legged in the quad after the bar closed, in that first term, when Ailsa Rae and Emily Field were inseparable and everything was new, even this city that had always been her home. Although she had her backstory, the blue of her skin and the slowness of her walk, everyone else she met had a story to tell too. The first weeks were late nights of drinking and talking as they understood who they were, and who they belonged with; then it settled down, into the part that Ailsa loved best, the taken-for-granted friendships and the assumptions that they would be there for each other. On her first admission to hospital that term, her mother had arrived, breathless and scared, after a dash from work, to find Emily, Pritti and Tim sitting around her bed, tapping away on laptops or reading textbooks while Ailsa slept, oxygen tubes in place in her nostrils. That term had muted, and then dissolved, the pain of being without Lennox. He'd gone travelling the summer before starting uni; when he came back, tanned and tired-looking, Ailsa saw the beginning of an inevitable growing-apart for them. She wasn't going to be travelling. She wasn't even going to be leaving home. She would be the equivalent of an ailing parent, holding him back, tying him down. So she ended it, and oh, how her old heart ached. Her new friends gave her, at first, something else to think about, and then others to love. It wasn't the same, but it was something.

In the years since leaving university — though Ailsa was a year behind, having to spread her final year over two — they've seen less of each other. Jacob lives in France now, with his fiancée; Pritti and Tim are close-ish in Stirling, but both work full-time, and are doing up their flat at weekends. Emily and Christa are Edinburgh-based still, and Ailsa makes a point of seeing them every couple of weeks, but it's not often that they are all together like this. And anyway, for the two years between being upgraded to urgent on the transplant list to the time that she came out of hospital, her real-world self had stood still, waited. In the meantime, her friends have found out what they want to do, and where they want to be; they've closed doors, and turned away from what they know isn't for them. Ailsa's time has been spent wanting to be well — or, rather, first wanting Lennox to be well, and herself too, though for a while after he died she would have turned down a heart if she could, for the sake of no longer having to make her way through the swamp of grief she found herself in.

Jacob lurches up to Ailsa and Emily, sitting on the front seat, and plonks himself down opposite. 'Your dancing friends are nice,' he says. Then, scrutinising her, 'You look weird when you're pink.'

'I know,' Ailsa says. She's on what is possibly her fifth glass of Prosecco. Life's grand. Anything goes. 'I think that every morning. It's like the wrong person's in the mirror.'

'What are you doing next?' Jacob has thickened through the body and cut his hair; he's abandoned festival T-shirts for crisply pressed shirts, open at the neck. His smile is the same, lopsided and quick. He probably won't look much different when he's forty; by fifty, he'll have added a touch of grey and jowl. It's hard to believe that they were ever lovers. Though maybe the Ailsa who squashed into Jacob's single bed with him, laughing and shushing as the student in the next room turned up his music, is the one she should think of as herself, rather than the greyscale version who sat with Lennox and watched him fade.

'She's replaced her heart,' says Emily. 'Is that not enough for you?'

Ailsa laughs. 'I can get myself a job now,' she says. 'I'm still living in my flat. My mother's moving out, though.'

'Your mother rocks,' Emily says. 'I was talking to her earlier. She's —' Her free hand punches the air, as though Hayley is a band and Emily its greatest fan.

'She is,' Ailsa says. 'But I want to look for my dad. And that's not gone down so well with her.'

Emily shrugs. 'You've got to do what's right for you.'

'I used to think because he didn't care about me I don't care about him,' Ailsa says, 'but things aren't that simple.'

'How old were they?'

'Younger than us. Early twenties.'

Emily nods. 'Young enough to not really know what you're about. I don't know that I do now.'

'Maybe he just didn't want to be with my mother forever,' Ailsa says.

'Like you, you mean?' Hayley's hurt is wrapped in laughter.

Emily catches Ailsa's eye, an 'oh shit' look.

Ailsa takes a breath and turns around in

her seat. The trouble with buses is that you can't see who's sitting behind you. 'I just meant — maybe the heart thing was an excuse. I'm not saying that's OK, but it's — possible — that he might want to know about me now.'

'Let's say that's the Prosecco talking, hen.' Hayley's voice is aiming for lightness, but with a strong undertow of hurt.

'I didn't mean . . .'

'It's forgotten.'

Emily's eyes widen; Apple flutters, winces. It doesn't sound forgotten.

And then Christa saves the day, moving up the aisle to join them. 'If you really want a job, I can get you a trial. We always need people at the coffee shop. Just let me know when you're ready.'

20 April, 2017

This Time Last Year

'Ailsa.' Her name is coming from a long way away. 'Ailsa, you have to wake up. I've had a phone call. We have to get to the hospital. Ailsa.'

Being shaken awake, when Ailsa is this tired, her old heart struggling so hard, only means news of a death or a dying: a heart having become available, or Lennox. She struggles to the surface, and looks at her mother's face. She sees that it's the dying that she doesn't want.

'Lennox?'

'I've called a cab,' Hayley says. 'Just put your coat and shoes on over those. Let's wait outside.' Ailsa is wearing white-and-cherry-striped pyjamas. Lennox says she looks like a candy cane in them.

It's gone midnight, so they get to the hospital quickly, the city roads quiet and clear, as though Edinburgh is holding its breath for Lennox too, wishing this moment away. Ailsa thinks about Lennox's will, his wish that his body go to medical research and that the money left over from the sale of his flat be used to do something good. She had asked what that 'good' should be. Lennox had said, 'I'll let them decide. It'll give them something to talk about, after I've gone. It might help.' Right now, in the dark and chill, Ailsa doubts it. Nothing will ever ease this pain.

Lucy meets them at the door to the unit, her eyes red. 'He's sleeping,' she says. And then she shakes her head and says, 'This time last year we thought he was maybe getting flu.'

Ailsa and Hayley nod and keep walking.

Ruthie and Dennis stand either side of the bed, Libby at the foot, and a nurse stands back, watching. Lucy follows Ailsa in; Hayley stays at the door, just inside. Ruthie puts an arm out to Ailsa, inviting her to stand next to her.

'He probably won't wake up again,' she says, and her voice has the calm and watchful tone that Ailsa hears so often from her mother, in their own worst moments of bad news and fear.

Ruthie hugs her close, and although Ailsa wants to hug back, it's as though she is a solid mass of fear and sadness, fused to rigidity, a pillar of hopelessness. Ruthie bends in closer, as though her body understands what's happening to Ailsa, and then straightens. Dennis is weeping, a long, slow keen of a sound that is almost music.

Come on, Ailsa. You can be supportive.

She stretches a hand over to Dennis, who nods, and reaches for her fingertips but then puts his face in his hands instead. Lucy, next to him, wraps her arms around him.

So she takes Ruthie's hand — the one that hasn't begun smoothing Lennox's hair back, over and over, or patting the sheet covering his chest into place — and she holds it, tight. There's nothing to be said, but she tries: 'We're all here.'

Ruthie nods. 'He probably won't wake up again,' she repeats, her voice shivering with cracks this time. Ailsa realises Ruthie is telling herself this, over and over, trying to learn what seems to be an impossible fact.

But Lennox is Lennox still, with more staying power than anyone expected, and the sort of strength of will and body that has stretched this death to the point where everyone is breaking. He opens his eyes, the whites like yolks now, and he raises the hand closest to Ailsa, pivoting it from the wrist, his fingers shaking from the effort. It takes a moment for her to understand the question, but then she gets it, and she sits down next to the bed, fits her palm to his, and lets their fingers interlace in answer.

'You win,' she says, and there's something like a smile around the edges of his lips as he closes his eyes. In another hour he's gone.

18 APRIL, 2018

'We've booked the party bus for Guy's fortieth!' Eliza says to Ailsa when she arrives at the following Wednesday's tango class. 'We thought it was fantastic. I'm amazed you didn't mention The Thing, though. I cannot keep a thing to myself when I've had a drink. Or did you not know about it then?'

'I'm so glad you came,' Ailsa says, and means it. In her imagination, people who don't have heart problems have days full of non-stop, heedless adventure, and she was touched by how many people were there to celebrate. 'What thing?'

'You know! The Thing.' Eliza winks. 'I assumed you knew. Because of the radio. Knowing Sebastian.' She says his name as though her mouth is full of glitter.

'Well,' Ailsa begins, though she's not sure where she's going.

But then Edie joins the conversation:

'Eliza! Don't talk about The Thing. It's a secret.'

Though there can't be more than two years between them, Edie always seems older with a capital O: she's definitely in charge. The sisters look almost identical — they have the same dark, curling hair and brown-gold eyes, the same peachy pale skin that makes them seem to glow with health. Although the health could also be — well, health. They make Ailsa think of the pairs of horses that once might have pulled the carriages of the gentry down George Street: fast, perfectly matched, and head-turningly beautiful. She doesn't say so.

'OK,' Eliza says with a grin to Ailsa, and then walks off, halloo-ing to the others as they arrive.

Ah, here are Murray and Venetia, with a couple of the others who Ailsa is only on nodding terms with, in a happy bubble of chatter. They sit down and change their shoes, saying hello and smiling. Ailsa has bought some shoes for tango, so she can join in the changing ritual. They aren't the real thing — £60 seems like a lot to spend when she doesn't have a job — but they are smooth-soled and feel safe and tight on her feet. When she bends to buckle them, she feels a twinkle of excitement.

Although Ailsa is still a beginner, she can tell that she's learning. Each dance sequence lasts for three short tunes, and for the first time, Ailsa gets through two of them without a single mistake, and there's only one slight misstep on the third, which Guy gives her the chance to step her way out of, and she does, rather than stopping and dropping her hands in despair, as she would have done the week before. More and more, she feels what she thinks of as 'the tango feeling' — a lower-belly tingle of anticipation, a spark going up her taut spine, her hands waiting for the pressure from her partner that will tell her feet what to do next. And the more she feels the tango feeling, the more she wants it. She and Apple agree on this. Ailsa thinks that Apple must be new to tango too, because they're learning at the same rate, tiring at the same time.

During the break, Edie and Eliza are talking to a woman Ailsa didn't notice joining the class. The not-noticing is not surprising, because she's spent the last hour looking at the place where her hand sat on Guy's collarbone, trying to read the movements of his torso and translate them into the language that her feet are starting to speak.

'They're plotting something.' Venetia sounds certain, and Ailsa laughs, because that's exactly what it looks like. The three heads nod and the conspiratorial knot unties; Edie and Eliza look around, smiling, and Edie steps forward, walking to the middle of the wooden dance floor. Even the way she walks is measured, precise, elegant, her head so high and straight, on her neck, her vertebrae as precisely stacked as the bricks of a tall Edinburgh chimney.

'Just before we start the milonga,' she says, 'Eliza and I would like to introduce you to someone who would like our help. I'm going to let her explain. This is Rosalind Derbyshire.'

Rosalind must be about thirty-five, tall and straight, in black trousers, black T-shirt, black boots, with Monroe-blonde hair in a truly messy rather than artfully messy ponytail. The red nail polish on her fingernails is chipped, her smile is bright and full of slightly unruly teeth, and her voice is loud and warm.

'Hello,' she says, 'I'm Roz. I'm a theatre director and I'm going to be putting on *Romeo and Juliet* here, in this space, during the Fringe.'

There's a groan, hastily stifled, and then a stricken voice from one of the dancers: 'I wasn't groaning at you — it's just the thought of the Fringe.'

Roz laughs, and she pulls a chair from under a table and sits, making herself friendly. 'I've lived in Edinburgh for a lot of my life,' she says. 'Tell me about it. But this year I'm going to enjoy it, instead of avoiding it, even though it means I can't rent out my flat for August.'

Everyone laughs at this. The Fringe festival brings out a mix of feelings in Edinburgh residents. Ailsa has always loved it — the buzz and bustle, the personalised weather forecast on the news and the feeling that she is, for once in her life, where everything is happening, simply by virtue of being where she always is. The girl who could never take part could sit in a cafe and get infected with excitement. She could go to shows at 2 a.m. with her friends, because she could manage being out for an hour, and support fellow students who were brave enough to try out their jokes or their acting or their poetry. She could become a red blood cell being pulsed around the city. Hayley, on the other hand, complains for what feels like every second of every day of the Fringe. She can't get a coffee without queueing for half an hour; she has to allow an extra twenty minutes to get anywhere; she's rushed off her feet at work with people wanting the morning-after pill and rehydration remedies because they can't control themselves.

Roz starts to lay out her plan. Ailsa leans forward to listen — although every word is clear — and feels the others do the same.

A production of *Romeo and Juliet,* in this room, that seats about fifty. Ailsa's brain is Rubiks-cubing as she tries to remember what, exactly, Seb said in his email. Though every spare space in the city will be having some play or comedian or dance crammed into it.

'The show will take place on this area,' Roz continues, indicating the dance floor, 'and the audience will sit around, just as you are. We'll get some extra seating in, around the edges. There will be a show every night except Monday for the first three weeks of August. It will run from six to eight thirty, and be followed, I hope, by dancing — cast, audience, and anyone downstairs in the bar who fancies giving it a go.' She stands and walks the edge of the wooden dance floor, her cowboy boots clack-clacking as she moves, marking the boundary. 'This will be the stage, our Verona, and the show will have a dance element to it, so I've been talking to Edie and Eliza for a while — and I'm here to ask you to help me out.'

Ailsa takes a breath, on purpose, because she's holding it, by accident.

Roz continues, 'For those of you who don't know the play, it's about two feuding families. They only see the error of their ways when a child from each family, Romeo and Juliet, the star-crossed lovers, fall for each other and eventually die. So there's love in the middle of hate. There's tension between the families, tension between love and duty, tension between what feels right and what is right. Which makes it' — she smiles that great smile again, looks around the room, slowly, seeming to take in each of them in turn — 'a play about the tango.'

There's a gentle exhalation around the room, a sense of 'of course that's the answer'. Ailsa saw the play once with Emily. There was no tango on that stage. The main thing that Ailsa recalls is a lot of wailing. But there was definitely tension. And tension is the thing that makes the tango work.

'I'm going to be using professional actors, and with the exception of the leads, they're mostly from Edinburgh and around,' Roz says.

It has to be Seb's thing. He was really interested in her dancing. Although he would be, anyway, because of *StarDance*. But when you add the winking from Eliza,

194

and the feeling of conspiracy —

'I'm here to ask you to help me with some parts of the play. First, there's a party scene, where the lovers first meet, and I'd like you to help with that, by coming up to dance. I have a cast of eight and that's not what I call a party.'

'How much do we get paid?' Murray says it with a laugh but there's an answering murmur from the rest of the group.

'Nothing,' Roz says. 'I'm hoping that you'll volunteer. I'm not paying myself or my actors either. Like most things on the Fringe, I've no budget and I'll be working on goodwill and hope. The money the show makes will cover the flyers, the advertising, the insurance and travel expenses for my actors who live out of town. Rehearsals need food and water; so do performances. It all adds up. I've been drinking in this pub since I was seventeen, and I've talked them into letting me have the space. I'm sharing receipts with them because they'll need to man the bar up here on show nights. If this goes well for them, next year they've got a venue with a track record. We're doing modern dress and next to no props, and we'll work with the lighting in the room. I'll rope in a designer for the set for free, but even a minimal set costs money. Edie and

Eliza have introduced me to a milonga trio who love to play more than they love to be paid. It's the magic of theatre, I'm afraid. For actors, this show is a chance to get seen. For me, it's an opportunity to explore ideas. For you — it's a chance to do something a bit different, to take to the stage, if you've ever fancied it, to be part of something that might, if the stars align, be talked about all over the place in August, and for all the right reasons.' A pause. 'No one will be out of pocket, so if you have travel costs, I'll cover them. We'll have a party on the last night, and if there are any profits, they will just about cover the cost of that. If not, it's on me.'

Roz looks around the room, waiting for more questions, and when none come, she continues, 'I'll plant some of you in the audience each night to join the cast for the party. They'll come into the audience to ask you to dance, so the rest of the audience will feel as though they are really there, seeing Romeo and Juliet fall in love, not just watching a play. And there's another thing, too . . .' She raises her left hand, and Edie and Eliza, who moved away when Roz started talking, and have sat themselves at opposite edges of the room, are suddenly on their feet, yelling at each other.

'WHAT ARE YOU LOOKING AT?' Edie slams her fist on the table.

Eliza points at her sister, her finger a weapon fired from the shoulder. 'NOTHING! WHAT ARE YOU LOOKING AT?'

Ailsa jumps — *thump-a-thump* — and Venetia shouts, 'Fuck!'. There's a titter of nervous laughter, silence.

Roz waits, smiling, until everyone has looked back to her. 'And I want you to add some — colour. There's quite a lot of fighting in *Romeo and Juliet.* And there's a lot of egging-on from the ones who aren't fighting. People who can stand up and yell when I need them to. Who will make the audience feel as though they're in the thick of a feud. We want to scare them, panic them, make them root for Romeo and Juliet. We're going to make the people who come to this show feel this story, as though it's their own life.'

Feeling not seeing. Oh yes. Ailsa's in.

She's been wishing for an ordinary life, and somehow, this extraordinary thing feels as though it will help. Because surely even the most everyday of people, the ones Ailsa has envied, all of her life, for their average health and their undramatic existences, must have spikes of excitement, moments where they step out of the everyday and do something that makes their story? The thought of dancing here, not as a learner but as a performer, makes her quake and thrill. And if it is the show that Seb's going to be in — she doesn't have time to decide what that means before Eliza chips in.

'We're not going to do formal choreography. We're going to dance the way that we dance at milonga: leaders will lead and followers will follow. It's not about being a great dancer, it's about being confident in what you can do. If you lead in the dance, you need to be a clear leader, and if you follow, you must be able to understand what your partner is asking. And if you get into a — muddle, you need to be able to tango yourself out of it. That's all. Everyone who is here tonight would be able to participate, assuming that they keep coming to class between now and August.'

Murray laughs. 'You mean I'll know my left from my right by then?'

'You'll be amazed,' Edie says. 'Just think about how much more you know than you did when you walked through the door two weeks ago.'

Roz adds, 'Edie and Eliza are going to do some work with my actors too, so we'll all be clear on how we're dancing.'

'Any questions?' Edie asks, and there's a

slow shaking of heads, as the learner-dancers and maybe-performers look to each other. Ailsa realises that, although she's felt like an outsider, she really is part of this club. Apple warms up a notch.

'OK,' Roz says, 'well, the Tango Sisters here are going to send an email, once the show has been announced, explaining the details.' She smiles, stands, shakes out one leg and then the other, as though she is about to dance herself. 'I'm away downstairs for a drink. If you think of anything else you want to know, feel free to come and ask.' She's walking towards the steps when she turns, as though she's forgotten the tiniest of details, and says, 'Please don't share this until after it's announced in the press tomorrow. But my Juliet is Meredith Katz and Romeo will be played by Sebastian Morley.'

Roz is as good as her word, at the bar in easy eyeline of the dancers as they come down the stairs after a slightly shorter, slightly more excitable than usual, milonga. Ailsa is first to leave. She is about to walk past when Roz waves her over.

'You're Ailsa, right? Do you want a drink?'

'No, thank you, I have to get away fairly soon.' The 10 p.m.-at-the-latest medication slot had seemed like a good idea when she'd never been able to stay awake much beyond then. She might need to start to edge it earlier, or later, or just get organised and bring snacks and meds with her. Too much information for this conversation, though. 'I have to — do something.'

'Seb told me about you,' Roz says. There's a high stool, empty, next to hers, and she pushes it out with her foot. Ailsa drops her satchel and shoe bag onto the floor and gets onto it, a half hop with the wrong leg, the least dignified move possible. She wonders what it was that Seb said to Roz that made her recognisable. Her glasses, maybe. Her only really unusual feature is on the inside.

'Really?' Ailsa says. She's not sure that she ever had a view on what actors talk about, but she really didn't think it would be her.

'He was quite taken with your unicorn get-up, I think,' Roz says. 'Did he tell you about this? The show?'

'No, he didn't,' Ailsa says. 'Well, he said he was here to talk about a show, last time I saw him, that was all. We don't know each other that well.'

Although, if she's honest, she would have liked him to have taken her into his confidence.

She hasn't felt like this — as though her

relationship with someone is an equation where the variables keep changing — for a long, long time. She thought it was a teenage thing. Maybe Apple is a teenage heart. The thought of that — of a seventeen-year-old dying, of her mother letting all of the good, working parts of her go onto other, older bodies — makes the world wobble. She holds onto the bar.

Roz nods. 'I've known Seb a long time.'

'We're not in touch all the time. Just the odd email.'

'It's nice that you're part of this group, though.' Roz smiles. 'Synchronicitous.'

'I suppose.' There was a moment, after Roz's announcement, when Ailsa had wondered whether Seb had told Roz about her going to tango, and Roz had been inspired, seen the direction for her production . . . But that would have been the sort of thing that would happen in a film, not in real life. Ah, the everyday. It's not all it whispered it was going to be, when she was in hospital.

'What do you think people thought? The other dancers?'

'I think people like the thought of dancing with Seb. Especially after *StarDance*.'

'Of course they do! Our wounded hero. I'm going to have Juliet on the sidelines for most of the party scene, probably, but

Romeo as a bit of a tart. There's a — distractible — side to him, I think.' She looks at Ailsa; she seems to be expecting something.

'I don't know it that well,' Ailsa says, her shoulders shrugging in apology, 'only from school. I saw it a couple of years ago with a friend. But I remember thinking that he changed his mind awful quick, about Rosaline, and if I were Juliet, I'd have maybe given it a week to just see how it went.' She wonders, as she says it, whether she would have done. Or whether the declaration of love would have swept her away as easily. The thought of being loved brings back Lennox. Even in those last days, the smell of his aftershave, clean and flinty, always there, if you searched your inhaled breath for it, separated it from the smells of hospital and illness and sadness. She might not have consented to a wedding in less than twenty-four hours from a first meeting, like Juliet, but she would have been ready to fall for Romeo. She realises, with a shock, that she is ready to fall, again. Might be falling.

Roz laughs. 'Quite! Give it a week, Juliet!' Then, just as Ailsa is about to say goodbye, 'Seb said you didn't know who he was. He's not used to that. It made me laugh.'

And oh, look, here he is, bright in her

memory, sliding up his sunglasses, squinting, opening his eyes wide to show her the place where the stitches are.

'Between Meredith and Seb, we'll sell out in a heartbeat.'

A heartbeat. Or the blink of an eye.

Ailsa checks her phone as she waits for a bus to take her home. She should be back just in time for her meds; if she's a bit late, it won't kill her. (She tries not to think about how, if her heart does reject — or is rejected, she's never sure which way around it goes — it will kill her. It's like not thinking about being cold, if you're cold.)

She has missed three calls, all from the same number, which she doesn't recognise. There's still a moment of panic — what if the calls were a heart, how could she forget to check — and then she laughs at herself, before she dials her voicemail. It's probably Christa's boss, calling to arrange for her to come in for her trial shift.

Ailsa stands on the street, catching pale pools of moonlight on the toes of her silver plimsolls, which are starting to look the worse for wear now they are doing more miles than they're used to. Funny how the more beaten-up her satchel gets, the more she likes it, but the shoes are going to have to go.

There are two messages from Libby. She actually speaks the word 're': 'Hello, Ailsa, this is Libby Douglas, at eight-pee-em on Wednesday. Hoping you can give me a call re Lennox's fundraiser.' Then, thirty minutes later: 'Hello again, Ailsa, Libby Douglas. I'm going to be away from tomorrow noon for two days, so if you could contact me before then, I'd be grateful.' She doesn't sound as though she'd be grateful. She sounds as though she'd be matter-of-fact. Ailsa reminds herself that it's not personal.

Tempted as she is to leave the call until 11.55 ay-em tomorrow, Ailsa calls as she waits for the bus. The phone rings twice and then is answered with a crisp, 'Libby Douglas.'

'Libby, hello, it's Ailsa here. Ailsa Rae. I'm returning your call. I was just — dancing.' As Ailsa says it she smiles at the sound of it: normal, adult behaviour, to be dancing on a Wednesday evening.

'Ailsa. It's about our first fundraiser, for Lennox's trust.'

'Yes?' Ailsa thinks about everything that she imagined she'd do, before her new Apple-heart arrived, when there was only sleep and weakness and thinking and trying not to think. She is doing nothing. Tango doesn't count. The latest blog poll has been interesting on this: she didn't know how much she needed an answer until she'd asked the question.

'We're thinking of getting a calendar together, as our first project. People who've had transplants, looking happy and healthy, you know the sort of thing. I want people to stop thinking of organ donation in the abstract and for them to see the human side of it. It's much more effective.'

Ailsa has a terrible thought. 'Not naked?'

'Did you say naked?' Libby, unexpectedly, laughs, and when she does she sounds like Lennox. The echo of him takes Ailsa right in the gut, a punch of hurt. Sometimes he's gone from her; sometimes he's seventeen, grinning and holding out a hand, saying, 'C'mon, we'll stop if you get tired.' She looks up to the gloom of the city sky, thinks of Lennox laughing as a good thing, a part of the world that surrounds her, part of what has propelled her here, even if he will only ever now be in her past. She puts her fingertip to the hollow behind her ear, so that she can feel her blood beat. Breathes deep. She can find good in the thought of him.

'Yes, I did. It's quite a popular thing, isn't

it? And when you said "healthy" and "human" . . .'

'Heavens, no. We want something that people will have on their kitchen wall, all year. Nobody wants to look at someone with a scar.' There are many ways to wrestle that sentence to the ground and beat it to a pulp, but by the time Ailsa has opened her mouth to begin, Libby has moved on. 'I'm lining up a photographer. It all needs to be done professionally, of course. Will you do it? Be photographed?'

'Yes, of course.' Ailsa suspects that as far as Libby is concerned, she's sitting on her ungrateful backside while the transplant unit continues to do all it can for people like her, like Lennox.

'Good. I'll email you the date next week, and if you can confirm that you've got my email and you've saved the date, that would be helpful.'

'No problem.'

'There's one more thing, Ailsa.'

'Yes?' She waits to be asked to set up a sales link on her blog, or to write about the calendar, but she's wrong.

'I thought it would be good if we could get your radio friend to do it. The one with the eye.'

'You mean Sebastian Morley?'

'Yes, I mean Sebastian Morley. Will you ask him?'

'He's not my friend.' Ailsa realises that she's not being fair: he was lovely after the interview, came to see her, he agreed to be interviewed, and if those aren't things a friend would do then — She tries again: 'I hardly know him.'

The faintest of sighs down the line. 'Then you've nothing to lose, have you?'

Guardian Online News

19 April, 2018

Morley Is Romeo at Last in Edinburgh Fringe Debut

Sebastian Morley, the actor who was forced to pull out of *StarDance* last year with a serious eye infection, has announced that he is to take the role of Romeo in an Edinburgh Festival Fringe production of William Shakespeare's *Romeo and Juliet.* Following a corneal transplant in January this year, he has stayed out of the spotlight, but says he is ready to return to acting — although treading the boards will be a new experience for him, as he's worked exclusively on TV since shooting to fame in 2007.

The small-venue, modern-dress production will 'take its cues from the tango, which is a dance that connects partners both at body and at heart, and asks them to be absorbed in each other to the absence of everything else,' said respected director Roz Derbyshire when announcing the show. She won a Critic's Choice Award for her direction of the 2016 surprise hit *The Pickwick Papers,* which was staged in the British Library.

'When we first discussed the show, I could see Seb's hunger to take part, and when I heard him give Romeo's speech about his love for Rosaline, I felt the goose pimples rising on my arms. This will be a sparky, sexy production and I'm happy to have Seb as one of two great actors at the heart of it.'

'Being the runner-up in *Wherefore Art Thou?* launched my career,' says Seb, 'but, if I'm honest, it also made me feel as though I wasn't good enough to do Shakespeare. I haven't acted on a stage in ten years and I haven't had to learn this many lines in one go in my life. So it's a big challenge for me. This is one of the most famous parts in theatre. I'm ready to do it. It will be hard work but, at the end of the day, I became an actor because I love acting. This is a pure sort of acting and I can't wait to get stuck in.'

Meredith Katz will play Juliet. The American actress is best known for playing Dottie the au-pair in *Parents Two, Kids Three.* This is her first UK stage role, though she won a Tony Best Featured Actress award for her portrayal of Honey in *Who's Afraid of Virginia Woolf?* in an acclaimed Broadway production in 2013.

Derbyshire and Morley met when Roz was one of the mentors on *Wherefore Art Thou?*, working with the wannabes on their acting tasks each week. She was visibly disappointed when Morley lost out to Xander Maxted-Morton.

The production will take place above the Dragon's Nest pub, in Newington, as part of the Edinburgh Festival Fringe. Tickets will go on sale on 1 May, and are expected to sell out for the run. Members of local dance school Two to Tango will support the production.

From: Ailsa
Sent: 19 April, 2018
To: Seb
Subject: Romeo and Coffee

Dear Seb,
The news is out! And Roz came to talk to the tango group.

I have news too: I've got a trial shift at a coffee shop tomorrow. Well, not really a shift — 2 till 4. Followed by a chat with my mum and my Auntie Tamsin (who's my mum's best friend) about the move. I feel as though my life is moving forward at last.

I hope all's well with you. How's the eye?

Ailsa

From: Seb
To: Ailsa

Dear Ailsa,
That's really good about the coffee shop. And I hope the chat goes well.

Roz was really pleased with how it went. Had you guessed?

I'll be in Edinburgh a lot more, in July and August anyway. (Roz spells it 'Embra'. Is that a thing?) It would be nice to spend some time with you. If you're not working all the hours after your coffee-making trial. (You'll ace it.) And we can dance.

My eye's not great, as it goes. Nothing to be worried about, exactly, but the light sensitivity's not getting a lot better, and I still can't read for more than about ten minutes, or do more than watch about half an hour of TV. I tried to see a film at the cinema the other day. Disaster. I only lasted twenty minutes and it was raining, so my popcorn got wet on the way home. My surgeon says we're going to keep an eye on it. I thought it would be better by now, though.

I'm getting papped again, so I suppose that's a good sign.

Are you OK?

Take care,
Seb x

From: Ailsa
To: Seb

Dear Seb,
I don't know what I could do if I couldn't use my eyes for more than twenty minutes. There's only so long you can walk and dance for.

Did your surgeon use the words 'keep an eye on it'? One of my consultants used to say 'pump' instead of 'heart'. As in: 'you have to put your pump into it'. I'm not sure what the point was but it made me laugh.

I'm OK. I think my mum moving out is what we agreed before my operation, but now it's here it's a bit weird for us both. I've offered to move out, and I wouldn't mind, but she insists that we should try it the way we planned. But we can't seem to talk about it without it getting argumentative. So since Tamsin's involved anyway, she's going to — well, mediate, I suppose, though we haven't put it that way. Wish me luck.

Is papped good?

Don't lose pump.

Ailsa x

From: Seb
To: Ailsa

You always make me laugh! The pump, not the thing about your mum. I think it's always hard with parents — even without life-and-death hell as a back-story. When I moved out, it was gradual, because I was away filming a lot of the

213

time. Then I was offered a flat-share, but by that time I was only going back at weekends anyway. My folks don't like London or travelling, so they don't often come to things. I went to see them at their place in Hampshire at the weekend. I told them about R&J and they said things like but your sister was always cleverer than you, as though they think I've cheated the system. My cheerful face got a lot of practice.

Papped is good in that it means your career might not have lain down and died after all. But it's not really very nice. I try not to look at the stories, but it's not always easy.

I might give this new cornea a name. Then I could give it pep talks.

For now I'm watching The Lego Movie, twenty minutes at a time.

It would be better if we fitted together like Lego. Cornea transplants in two clicks. We could have a zip up the front, and all of our internal organs would be attached to each other with whatever it is that makes Lego click into place. Easy.

From: Ailsa
To: Seb

I now have a vision of you staring at yourself in the mirror in the morning, going, 'Pull yourself together, Alphonse. It's only light.'

And yes to Lego! That would work for sure. As long as surgeons didn't have Lego hands.

Ailsa

From: Seb
To: Ailsa

Good point.

In fairness I should have said that my folks were great when my eye first happened.

I wanted to ask you a favour. Are you feeling generous?

Seb x

From: Ailsa
To: Seb

I need to ask you a favour too. I've been wondering whether I should — but please say no if you don't want to.

215

Do you want to go first?

Ailsa

From: Seb
Sent: 20 April, 2018
To: Ailsa
Subject: The favour

No, unicorns first. It's bad luck otherwise.

From: Ailsa
To: Seb

OK. Lennox, who I was close to — he was my first boyfriend, at school, and we always stayed in touch — died last year waiting for a liver transplant. His family is setting up a trust and they want to do a lot of things to raise money and awareness and support research. They haven't told me all the details but they are good, clever, kind people and I trust them.

They've decided to do a 2019 calendar. They want to photograph people who've had transplants looking — well, glad to be alive. They asked me to do it and I said yes — and then they asked me to see if you would do it.

I almost said I wouldn't ask you, because we don't know each other that well, and anyway, people must be asking you for things all the time. But then I thought you might actually want to do it. So — would you be willing to be photographed for a fundraising calendar? The woman who's organising it will make sure that it's well done, and it will be a professional photographer, properly produced, etc.

Please don't feel you have to say yes. I said I would ask you but I also said I had no idea what you would say. You're not putting me in any sort of difficulty if you refuse.

Ailsa

From: Seb
To: Ailsa

Is it a nude calendar?

From: Ailsa
To: Seb

That's what I said! No.

From: Seb
To: Ailsa

Pity. I've seen a lot more of the gym since I've been 'resting' and it would be good to have my six-pack immortalised.

We definitely know each other well enough for you to ask me about this.

Of course I will. I'd usually say if it fits with my schedule, but that's not going to be difficult at the moment. My agent took the doctor's orders about rest very seriously. I only heard about R&J because Roz contacted me directly to sound me out. And I'm starting to realise that most of my social life is getting pissed after work, which isn't much cop if you're not working. It comes to something when the social highlight of your week is your niece's third birthday party.

Put me in touch with whoever's organising it. They might need to sign some sort of disclaimer/agreement about how the photo will be used. I'll check with Wilkie (agent). And thanks for asking.

Seb x

From: Ailsa
To: Seb

Thank you. I was really in two minds about it.

I'll put you in touch with Libby Douglas. She's organising it. She'll probably come over as a wee bit rude. Don't worry about it, she's like that with everybody.

I thought you would go to showbiz parties left, right and centre.

Your turn — what can I do for you?

Ailsa

From: Seb
To: Ailsa

OK. Here goes. There's a bit of background. Don't feel you have to say yes. But don't say no straight away either. OK?

I haven't been on the stage since *Wherefore Art Thou?* (and that wasn't proper stage work — not three hours in one go, just bits and pieces). Learning lines for TV is different to the stage — you've only got a scene or two at a time, with time to cram in between, and if you forget something, you just go again. I'm looking at Romeo and Juliet and I'm thinking: I'll never, ever learn all of these. Romeo's a chatty sod and if I read for more than fifteen minutes, my eye starts going mad.

Meredith (Juliet) has done loads of stage work and from what I know of the rest of the cast, they have too. I don't want to hold them back. I don't want to look like an idiot. And, between you and me, I'm worried that I've bitten off more than I can chew.

Basically, I really want to be off the book when I get to rehearsals, because apart from looking an idiot, I don't think I'll be able to read a script and work. And I can't see how that's ever going to happen without some help.

So — and I know this is a big ask — I wondered if you might come down and help me to learn my lines? A mate of mine, Yusef, has a flat about ten minutes' walk away from me, and he's on tour until June in The Wind in the Willows. You could stay there. I couldn't pay you but I could cover your train fare, and we could have a good time when we're not working.

What do you say?

Seb

P.S. Showbiz parties aren't all they're cracked up to be. I haven't been to one since I threw up over a tray of canapés (and the poor sod holding them) at a premiere. I think it was food poisoning but nobody wants to believe that.

From: Ailsa
To: Seb

Hello,
Sorry for the delay. I had to look up 'off the book'.

The first line of that message made me think you were going to request a kidney. Which, of course, you could have had, no question, as can anybody who asks nicely.

Am I really the best person to help you with this? There must be someone closer? (Physically and someone you know better?) Other actors?

Ailsa

P.S. That's better than my collapsing-at-a-lecture-falling-down-the-stairs story. I blacked out — not enough blood to the brain. It happened a lot back then, but not always at the top of a flight of stairs. People who didn't know me thought I was drunk too. It was 11 a.m. Though it was the morning after a big night for a fair few people in the room.

From: Seb
To: Ailsa

I could find people to give me a day or two, yes, but I'd rather get it all done in one go, and I think that will take a couple of weeks. I need to go over it and over it until it goes in.

And the trouble with actors is that they want to act. And discuss. And interpret. It's really interesting but I don't want to do that yet, I just need to know the words.

Most of my friends are people I've worked with. They all have their ideas about what I'm like and that might get in the way. And I know we don't know each other that well, but I feel as though we know each other well enough for this. I mean — we get on. Every time I see you I feel as though we could have talked for another three hours. You're easy to be with.

From: Ailsa
To: Seb

Let me think about it. When? For how long?

From: Seb
To: Ailsa

A couple of weeks if you can spare them? Somewhere around mid-May? Say, come on Sunday 13th and leave on Friday 25th? Plus, obviously, if you want a morning off to look at bits of history, or whatever, that would be OK. And there's plenty of caveman food available in London, though it will have to come from a shop, not a forest.

(I realise that now you might be working, this is a question I shouldn't even ask.)

From: Ailsa
To: Seb

Ah, I've always wanted to visit London's famous Whatever Theme Park.

Let me have a think about it, and see how the trial goes and what they say. And I'll have to check at the clinic —

I'm still on weekly visits. Can I email you on Monday, after I've been to the hospital?

From: Seb
To: Ailsa

Thanks for even thinking about it. And I hope the trial goes well.

One more thing — I wouldn't want to tell Roz. Most directors don't want you to learn your lines beforehand because they want to shape the way you say them and think about them. Well, that's not so much the lines, it's the character. They don't want you to fix on the way the character is until you've worked on it together. I suppose it's like muscle memory. If you've already learned lines in a certain way and it's not the way the director wants them to be delivered, you have to unlearn. This is part of why I don't want to work with an actor. I need to know the words, so when we go into rehearsal, I'm not struggling to read them.

From: Ailsa
To: Seb

I'm not big into lying to people. Could you not tell her?

From: Seb
To: Ailsa

I could. But I'm scared she'd change her mind — not because I was learning the lines but because she'd be worried I wasn't really up to taking part. The thought of doing this play is about all that's keeping me sane.

Tamsin has always claimed she is half woman half witch and Ailsa has always half believed her. It's partly based on the way she looks — wild russet frizzy hair, big brass jewellery, purple eyeshadow — and partly her bright, raucous laugh. But mostly, it's her ability to make things happen that seems uncanny. Tamsin has always been able to find the right colouring book, rustle up a lift, turn up with takeaway dinner at the hospital at exactly the point when another baked potato baked eight hours ago feels like the final straw.

Ailsa doesn't remember much of her early years, fortunately, because when she reflects on it it's grim. One procedure within forty-eight hours of birth, another operation at five months, and a third when she was four, all to make her three-chambered heart into an organ that could more or less replicate what a normal heart could do. She knows, from all the reminiscences she's heard, that Tamsin was there with her mother for every struggling beat of her heart.

What Ailsa thinks about when she thinks about her illness is not the surgeries and recoveries on her plum-sized heart, but the slow decline that her condition has brought to her life. At seven and eight, she was roughly equivalent to the kids in her class with asthma, not really up to anything vigorous but pretty ordinary otherwise. As she got older, she started to notice that she was always kept off school for a little bit longer than her classmates if she had a cold. When she went on a residential school trip to Aberdeen for three nights, her mum came to school to have a meeting with her teacher about what support she might need. By twelve, the edges of her lips and her nail-beds were a noticeable blue-grey. Over the years the colour deepened and spread, so she was always pallid. By the time she met Lennox, she was spending her breath the way she'd spend money that she knew was going to run out before she'd bought everything she needed. And her budget became less and less limiting her more and more, until it was almost nothing.

And Tamsin was always there: lifts, laughs, sympathy and sanity.

It hasn't all been one-way. Tamsin lived with them for a summer when Ailsa was in her early teens. Her marriage had broken down, and there were months of the living room piled with boxes, the bathroom full of make-up and scrubs and creams for everything, crying in the night. Hayley is often roped in to helping Tamsin at vintage fairs, especially as Christmas approaches, and Ailsa has spent more Sunday afternoons than she cares to remember polishing up old silver forks and spoons that Tamsin will fashion into jewellery.

But this evening, there's no doubt that Tamsin is the one helping Ailsa and Hayley out. They aren't exactly not speaking; it's more that they are so aware of the tension between them that every word is weighty. So when Hayley had said, 'How about we sit down, the three of us, and work out how this move is going to work?' Ailsa had agreed without hesitation.

Tamsin pours wine for all three of them, without asking if Ailsa is drinking. It's not even six o'clock, and it's not Ailsa's day for having a drink. Paleo is hard. But worth it, she reminds herself. And thrashing out the details of the move will be the same.

'How did your trial go? Was it today?'

'It was a lot harder than I thought,' Ailsa

says. 'I mean, I know how coffee shops work, but when you're the one behind the counter, it all seems much more complicated. But the people were lovely. And I liked being busy. The time flew.' The only place where time has flown for Ailsa lately has been at tango.

'Are they going to give you a start?'

'I don't know. I hope so,' Ailsa says, and she means it, because she never would have thought that taking orders and smiling at strangers would be as much fun as it turned out to be. 'But they asked about start dates.' She lets herself smile, and she lets herself hope.

'Well, we know what that means! We're celebrating, then!' Tamsin says and they clink glasses.

Hayley, who's been quiet — she's heard the news already, by text — says, 'Who'd have thought, a year ago? You've done well, hen. I'm proud of you.' And there's just a flicker of the old them — a moment of connection, a sense of being all each other has — before Hayley adds, 'I didnae think you were drinking today.'

'I wasn't,' Ailsa would normally try to even her tone but she lets the petulance out, 'but now I am.'

Tamsin looks from Ailsa to Hayley and

back again. 'I think it's high time we got this all sorted,' she says, sounding firm. 'On the agenda is: timescale, money, practicalities. We maybe need to add "feelings". But let's get the feelings out of the way first.'

'I don't know that I'm ready for that,' Hayley says.

'No time like the present, eh, Ailsa,' Tamsin says, making Ailsa complicit, whether she wants to be or not — and she doesn't want to be, not at all. 'And anyway, you may as well both get it said, because you could cut the atmosphere in here with a knife.' She tilts an eyebrow at Ailsa. 'C'mon, sweetheart. Say what you want to say.'

Apple beats steady and strong. 'I just want to be normal, Mum. I want to live on my own. It's nothing to do with you. I don't want rid of you. And if we hadn't spoken about you moving out before, I never would have assumed. But that's what we said. And it is what I want. But if you don't think you want to or it's not the right thing, we can think of something else. The last thing I want to do is hurt you. But I do want to be me. Even if that does mean' — she thinks of her biological father, but doesn't dare risk mentioning him directly — 'making what you think of as mistakes.'

Hayley nods. 'I know what we said we

would do and I dinnae think it's a bad idea. It just feels soon tae me. You've dealt with a lot and I'm so proud of you, Ailsa, I really am. But that doesnae mean you're ready for this.'

'You might be the one that's not ready.'

'Ailsa, that's harsh,' Tamsin says gently.

But a moment afterwards, Hayley says quietly, 'It could well be. I cannae quite get used tae the idea that you can manage without me, hen.'

Ailsa closes her eyes against the pain in this, the years of care and hope and fierceness for her that she hears in her mother's voice. 'I don't want to manage without you,' she says, and she can hear tears in her voice, pleading. 'I just want to live on my own. I want to see who I am now I have' — she puts her hand over Apple — 'this. Please.'

Tamsin puts a hand over each of their hands. 'I think we need to try this for six months,' she says, 'and then review. You're both thinking with your hearts and that's not what hearts are for.'

20 April, 2018

Adventure?

I thought, when Apple arrived, that I would be brave.

When you're ill, people tell you you're brave the whole time. This is ridiculous. It's not bravery that means spending months in hospital and having a laugh with the nurses and submitting to blood tests, via-the-nose biopsies, CPR and God knows what else. It's the absence of choice. There's nothing brave about letting people do all sorts of medical hoo-ha that stops you from becoming dead.

Anyway. I always thought I was going to be brave, and fierce, and it turns out that I am average. Ordinary. (I wanted that too, so I can't complain.)

And now I've been offered something that is an opportunity to be brave. I could go to London for two weeks, to help someone out with something. (No, I'm not saying any more than that. Some things are private.) Part of me thinks that it would be a brilliant thing to do: a true adventure. And part of me wants to say no, because

— well, because it wouldn't be home. I've never been away from home for more than a week (apart from being in hospital, which doesn't count). A week was as long as Mum would take off work when I was growing up — locum pharmacists are more in demand than usual in school holidays. I did a couple of study trips within the UK when I was at university, but they were three or four days, and I never took a course that would take me abroad, because it would have been too complicated to organise (before you even get to insurance). I've had holidays at my grandparents' in the north of Scotland, and Mum, my auntie and I went to Wales once. The rain was different in Wales. Not as good as Scottish rain.

Nearly two weeks in London might not seem like a big deal. But it is for me. Whenever I think of it, my stomach gets a blank space in the middle of it that might be dread.

I'd be well looked after and, of course, London has hospitals.

I'm going to keep this open until Monday. If the clinic says I can, should I go to London for two weeks to help someone out with something? (The something is not illegal.)

233

YES, Ailsa. Have an adventure. Take a
chance.
NO, BlueHeart. Anything that gives you a
feeling that might be dread is best
avoided. Have a different adventure.

1 share
13 comments

Results:
Yes: 96%
No: 4%

■ ■ ■ ■ ■

PART FIVE:
MAY 2018
ONE KISS

■ ■ ■ ■ ■

It hasn't been a bad morning's shopping for Ailsa's down-a-dress-size wardrobe. She has bought black jeans, blue leggings, and a skirt the purple-pink of a raspberry and banana smoothie. She now has navy brogues with turquoise laces and a couple of round-necked tops that sit high enough to hide her scar without making her look like a school-marm. It's not as livid as it was, pink rather than red, the puckering of skin not so obvi-ous — but it's still not something that she wants the world to be able to gawp at — or not bother to notice. She and Apple know the meaning of it. It's theirs. Her mother picked out a blouse with a narrow purple pinstripe, which is perfect except for the fact that the top of her scar shows. Hayley offered to put a press-stud on it ('By which I mean, persuade Tamsin to put a press-stud on it').

And Ailsa is not as thrilled with it all as

she thought she would be. It's not the shopping. It's the feelings. The mirrors in the shop changing rooms aren't quite as flattering as the one at home, on the back of the wardrobe door. They let Ailsa see all of her body, the places where she has little rolls of fat and the cellulite on the backs of her thighs.

She knows that she is more than the outside of her body, and that fitness is more than appearance, of course she does. But still, looking at her strip-lit self, the scar her eyes usually slide over and the backside she doesn't normally see, have leeched the confidence out of her. It's not what she needs when she's going to London tomorrow, staying in a stranger's flat, spending almost two weeks with someone who is, the more she thinks about it, as good as a stranger. She has a curdling feeling in her gut, which is nothing to do with her drug regime, or her diet.

Hayley is on edge, too. Even though talking with Tamsin helped — and so did making a plan, because at least they don't have to try to work anything else out for now — they can't seem to properly relax around each other. Like Tamsin said, they aren't a normal mother and daughter, and anything they try to do is going to be loaded. Ailsa had offered to move out instead, but Hayley insisted that it wasn't that that was the issue — 'This flat belongs tae both of us, and it's been your home as long as it's been mine'. It's just, it seems, the letting go.

Moving is stressful even under normal circumstances, Ailsa reminds herself. When she gets back from London, it will be over, and they can relax into something more normal. How many twenty-eight-year-olds have lived with their parents all of their lives? Only the ill ones. She's not ill anymore. And she'll be starting her new job. She couldn't quite believe it, when the call came. Christa says she'll be amazed at how quickly she'll get used to working at Full of Beans, but Ailsa doesn't want to get used to this feeling. She did it. She got a job. For the first time in her life she will be going to work, and Hayley had been pleased for her, she could see it in her face, but that hadn't stopped her from saying things like, 'You'll need to be sure they have a proper hand sanitiser at work.'

'I think we need to go and get you a new bra. You must have gone down a size in that, as well,' Hayley says. She adds, 'Because, of course, you lose weight from the top down,' as though this is a known and accepted fact of life. Ailsa doesn't remember reading this anywhere, even though she must have read that 'the first five pounds you lose is water' hundreds of times. But maybe it is true. If the next half stone goes from her middle, she'll be happy. She is happy. She is, she is.

Apart from the thought of exposing, explaining, the scar to a bra-fitter. She's not sure she's ready for that. But Hayley doesn't seem to think that bra-buying is up for discussion. They are in the lingerie section of Jenners department store before you can say 'underwired balconette'.

Hayley drops herself into a seat outside the changing rooms, and does what she always does when she's waiting: she takes off her scarf, folds it, smooths it, unfolds it, and wraps it around her neck again. Today she's wearing a fine silk scarf, moon-silver with heavy navy tassels that make it wrap tightly around her throat, so her skin seems to shine. It's not Ailsa's favourite, but when she commented on it this morning, Hayley said, 'I've only a few here, because the rest are already at Tamsin's, so you'll have to grin and bear it.'

Ailsa, in the changing room, takes off her T-shirt and stands in her jeans and her old bra while Shona, the bra-fitter, stands back and scrutinises her. 'We need to get you down a cup size and a back size, by the look of it,' she says, then adds, 'I see all sorts in here: mastectomies, reconstructions, implants. The messes some poor women are in beggars belief. Just young lasses, too, a lot of them, like you. But whoever did this has done a smashing job for you.'

'Thanks,' Ailsa says, although she shouldn't really be taking credit; she stores the compliment away for the next time she sees Mr Mokbel. If ever she does see him. The last check-up was with one of his interns. Presumably he's too busy with the ill to spend time with the heart-bearers he's fixed.

After trying on bras that seem to make her look all shapes and sizes, Ailsa chooses two, one black, one ice-blue, both the same style, a cup-size and back-size smaller than her old one. She feels herself stand straighter in them. She's looking at the lace, the straps, and the fact that she has a really nice bust with a perfectly formed heart beating behind it, rather than her scar or the fat around her middle.

When she leaves the changing room, dressed again but wearing the ice-blue one, Shona having snipped off the label and taken it to the till, Hayley smiles and says, 'Aye, that's grand. Feel better?'

'I do,' Ailsa says. 'You were right, I did

241

need a new bra.'

'Well,' Hayley says, 'you deserve to walk tall.'

The dresses she tries on afterwards seem to hang better, look better, than anything she'd worn in the morning. The one she decides on is all-over yellow roses on a navy background, round-necked, three-quarter-length sleeved, flared a little at the hem and sitting above her knee. The woman in the mirror, this time, is healthy and happy, confident.

And that's it for her budget. Ailsa was eligible for Disability Living Allowance as a child; she probably would have been as an adult, but she and Hayley had talked and thought and decided that they wouldn't apply. Though they wouldn't be means-tested, they agreed that the assessment process was something they didn't need in their lives then. And with a paid-off mortgage ('Thanks to your biological father, though not in the "thankful" sense of the word') and a reasonably sensible approach to living, they could manage. So they did.

Ailsa took student loans and has an allowance from her mother, but she's well now, and too old for being kept anyway, especially with Hayley moving out. They agreed, with Tamsin's help, that Hayley will continue to pay the bills for six months, and Ailsa, in that time, will find a job and decide what she's going to do in the longer term. Tamsin won't charge Hayley rent for that time. Then they'll reassess.

So today's shop will do her just fine for the foreseeable future. (How odd to count it in months and years.) Sure, some of her old clothes are too big, but some of them look great now she's got some weight off. Emily and Pritti were always big charity shop fans; she can see if they fancy an afternoon of raking around for bargains sometime.

'I'm done,' she says, when she's paid for the dress. It's almost two.

'Let's get a quick sandwich before we head back,' Hayley says.

'Good idea.' They don't talk so much, when they're in the flat, these days. No one is sulking, exactly, it's just that they don't know how to manage the transition. It will all be fine once it's done. Absolutely it will. There is barely any question in Ailsa's mind about it all.

They make their way to Rose Street and the cafe that they've liked since they used to come for strawberry milkshakes after hospital check-ups. They have the same routine everywhere they eat or drink: find a table, take it in turns to go to the toilets and wash their hands, order, relax. Ailsa chooses black coffee and a mushroom omelette, Hayley a cheese and ham panini and a cappuccino, which she stirs, even though, to Ailsa, this defeats the object. But they've had the cappuccino/latte conversation often enough over the years. Sometimes Ailsa thinks the reason things are quieter is simply the fact that she and her mother have had every single conversation that's possible between the two of them often enough to know them by heart.

'Happy with what you've got?' Hayley asks.

'Yes,' Ailsa says, 'I think so.' Her earlier feelings of too-fat have dissipated. She's getting healthier. That's what matters.

'You didnae want to treat yourself to a new bag?'

'Not today.' Ailsa loves her battered old satchel, and she doesn't care what anyone thinks.

'Worth a try,' Hayley says, with a smile. Then, 'It's all different, isn't it? Even the things we never thought were affected by your heart. They were.'

Ailsa nods, puts her hand on her mother's arm, just a touch, in thanks. 'Are we going to be all right?' she asks.

That pinched mouth again. 'It's a bit late for that now, isn't it? You were very sure in front of your Auntie Tamsin.'

'I know. I am. It's just —' She takes a breath and feels Apple press the words up to her mouth. 'Just because I want this doesn't mean I don't love you.'

Hayley sighs. 'And I love you. Right down tae our bones. We'll be all right, hen. I know we're doing it the other way around, and I don't know a mother who wouldn't be upset at her daughter moving away. But — the alternative is worse, aye?'

Ailsa nods, but she hates that they still feel that they aren't allowed to be sad about anything, on the grounds that she is Not Dead. She thinks of Seb and his story about Tom Foster, almost tells it to her mother, but decides against.

'I want to come and see you. Every week.'

Hayley nods. She reaches across the table, touches the side of Ailsa's face, and Ailsa bites back the impulse to make a joke about her beard being nearly gone, and lets herself be loved.

'If you can get in.' Tamsin, who deals in what she calls 'vintage collectibles' and what Hayley cheerfully refers to as 'tat', is notorious for mess and chaos, and her flat is crowded with furniture, paintings, small and pointless tables stacked with books and magazines.

'You might find that lodger she had when you clear out the wardrobe. He could be trapped in there.'

'I wouldnae be surprised,' Hayley says. Then, 'I wish you'd wear red again. You'd look lovely. It's a good colour for you. Your hair.'

Ailsa nods. When she used to wear red, the colour would pick out the gold of her otherwise dull blondish hair. It did something to her skin, too, warming it, neutralising the blue. It would probably work wonders now.

'I can't,' she says.

'I know,' Hayley says, 'not yet. But one day.'

'Yes.' Ailsa knows she has to agree, because now there are so many days. Anything could happen. But she thinks: no. If it's a decision she feels right about — taking part in *Romeo and Juliet,* or not wearing red — then it's a decision made. If not —

'I've been wanting to talk to you, about your blog.'

'What about it?'

'I'm just a wee bit concerned about this jaunt of yours. I'm not so sure it's wise.'

'You were the four per cent that voted

246

against, were you?'

Hayley laughs, stirs her coffee again, takes a sip. 'I don't vote. I'll not speak for Tamsin, though.'

Ailsa takes a breath, thinks this through. Her coffee is cool enough to drink now, so she sips, and then her omelette arrives. It's huge, spilling off the side of the plate, and it looks, and smells, like no omelette Ailsa could ever make. Hers end up like scrambled eggs whatever she does. Hayley says she doesn't have her pan hot enough and she needs to hold her nerve. Ailsa says that's what you need to do for pancakes. She'll soon be on her own in the kitchen, though.

'Is it the voting, or is it the going to London?'

Hayley sighs and looks away, before responding, 'You know I've never liked the voting. And some of it seems daft to me. Why does your heart need a name? It's yours. But this London thing — it doesn't smell right.'

'Why not?' Ailsa puts her hand to her chest, to quell Apple's outraged bumping against her ribcage. Her heart has yet to learn that her mother's not one for anything she considers whimsical or impractical.

'You can't tell me that this — *Seb*' — she says it as though it's in inverted commas, as though it's not really a name, or he's not really a person — 'has no one else who can help him with this?'

'Not for the length of time he needs,' Ailsa says, 'and he doesn't want actors, because they'll act. He just wants someone to help him learn.'

'And not be paid.'

'He's paying my expenses.' Ailsa knows she sounds defensive.

'Have you not heard of women's liberation, Ailsa? Do you not know that this kind of thing is not OK? Some people might call it exploitation. And when you've a job waiting . . .'

Hayley's voice is mild but Ailsa knows to tread carefully. 'He's a friend, Mum. That's why I'm doing it. It's the only reason. Well, that and — and getting away. We'll go out. I'll do some sightseeing. I'll be — normal. And we have friends who've done an awful lot for us. It's nice to be the friend who's doing the helping, for once.'

Hayley sighs, and Ailsa knows she's thinking of Mrs Owens, who used to live downstairs and would always babysit if Hayley was working, and all of the parents who made Ailsa welcome after school, because Hayley was anxious about her being in the house on her own. 'You havnae been friends for very long, for him to be asking such a favour of you. Even if you do get to do a bit of sightseeing.'

'I'll have my own place to stay,' Ailsa says.

'You've only his word for that.'

'Oh, come on, Mum. You're not really thinking he's going to murder me. If he is he's gone a stupid way about it.'

'No,' Hayley says, 'but he might — take advantage. You're not exactly . . .'

'Seb's not so short of offers that he needs to lure me from Edinburgh. And anyway — I'm not exactly what?' Ailsa's appetite has gone. She's barely eaten half of what was on her plate. She doesn't know if she's full, or if this conversation is doing something to her body. Cold omelettes are no good, anyway. She pushes the plate aside.

'Experienced. Worldly.'

Ailsa laughs. Her mother knows about Lennox, of course. And about Jacob, who she met in the kitchen one morning when he was making tea and wearing Ailsa's dressing gown. She doesn't know about the American exchange student she gave directions to on a Friday morning, who spent Friday night, most of Saturday in her bed. (Robbie? Randy? No, if he was called Randy that would have stuck in her mind.) Or the night of the Student Union's firework party,

when she and that guy who was studying
Ancient Civilisations were the only ones to
duck inside out of the cold. Or —

'Mum. I haven't told you everything, you
know.'

'I know, hen,' Hayley says, 'and I'd like to
think you — made the most of things.
That's not what I mean. I mean, you've
been quite sheltered. People treat you differently, whether you know it or not. You
didnae get to grow up and make the mistakes that other people learn from. You were
too — precious.'

'I'm trying not to be.'

Hayley replaces cup into saucer, takes a
deep breath. 'What I'm trying to say is that
you're maybe a bit naive about things. Men.'

'Please, Mum,' Ailsa says, and she's tired
now, not just because of the time she's spent
on her feet today, but also because she
doesn't need to hum along to this tune,
again. 'I know you think all men are bastards. I know where you're coming from. I
know my biological father let you down, and
you haven't given anyone else a chance since
—' She stops, because that's too far, even
for someone with all the get-out-of-jail-free
cards she has. Used to have. But Hayley
doesn't shout, or walk out. She just looks
her daughter straight in the eye, the way she

250

did that night in the hospital last year when finally she told Ailsa the full story about her father, and how he got cold feet before she was born.

'Ailsa . . .' She's almost wistful, and there's something between them now — the possibility of a different truth, perhaps, or at least a different way of living this new life.

'What? Talk to me, Mum. Tell me,' she's pleading. She can hear it. But Hayley looks away, out of the window again, the way she used to look towards the door of Ailsa's hospital room all the time, waiting for someone to come and save them. She doesn't have that excuse now.

'You're right. I don't know what your life is. But do you think it's easy maintaining any relationship outside of having a sick child? Do you think anyone's going to be up for a partner who spends every fucking minute of every fucking day praying for someone else to die so that her kid gets a heart? Do you think that's nice to be around?'

'No. I don't.' The words have found their target; even though Apple doesn't know Ailsa and Hayley's history, she still buckles, and tears are hot in the corners of Ailsa's eyes. She and Lennox always thought they were careful with their parents, protective of

251

them. She remembers sitting with him in his last days, holding his hand, talking about being frightened, and then Ruthie would arrive, ask how he was, and Lennox would raise a hand and smile, as though drifting past on a boat on a sunny day. With Ailsa, he cried. She could never tell anyone that now, because his history is written: Lennox Was Brave. But, of course, their parents weren't protected. Not really.

'I'm sorry. I really am, Mum. I can see that I've — stolen — your life.'

Hayley looks at her, a long look, as though she's deciding. She shakes her head. 'I just — I didnae get you this far for you to become a fucking — WAG.'

Although Hayley said it gently, this is so startlingly unfair that Ailsa could cry. But she won't. 'Seriously? That's what you think of me? And anyway — you can't say in one breath that I shouldn't let the blog make decisions for me, and then in the next that I can't be a WAG. Because that's you making decisions for me. Like making it hard for me to find my father.'

'Don't be clever with me, Ailsa.'

'Why not? I thought you wanted me to be clever? And you see what you just did? I mention my father, it's like I haven't spoken. You did the same thing just now.'

People are starting to look around. 'Aye, well, you've got Emily to talk to about that, haven't you? I've nothing else to say about him.'

'I've nothing else to say about my blog.'

There's a breath, a heartbeat, another. The waitress comes to clear their plates.

Hayley says, 'You're sure they said it's OK? At the clinic.'

'They said it was a terrible idea and I'd likely be dead within the week.'

'Sarcasm isn't pretty, Ailsa.'

'Oh, it's my life goal to be pretty, now?'

Hayley looks down at the remains of her coffee in the cup, looks up, straightening her shoulders. Her voice is deliberately gentle. 'I think we're both tired, aye?'

Ailsa takes a breath, nods. They are both tired, and they are both learning. She makes her mouth smile. 'I'll be careful, I promise.'

She remembers the morning of the transplant, and Hayley sitting quietly next to her bed, stroking her hand, saying, 'After today, your life will be your own.' She'd thought about those words as the anaesthetic pulled her under. It had seemed simple. It wasn't.

Hayley nods. 'I'll be all moved out when you get back. You'll have what you want, and we'll just have tae see how we get on.'

'Yes,' Ailsa says, and her words come out

right, for once: not an accusation, but a memory. 'I remember you saying that, after the transplant, my life would be my own.'

'And it is. As much as anyone's life is, hen. But this is still a big change. Things will never be the same. We need to be prepared for that.'

Ailsa thinks about how she's never lived on her own, and how she might not like it. How often, after Lennox died, she had made her way to her mother's bed in the middle of the night, and, without waking, Hayley's body made a space for Ailsa to fit into. Ailsa had been an injured bird, and her mother was the cupped hands that protected her. It might not be as easy as she thinks to fly.

18 May, 2018

Apple in the City

Apple and I really cannot thank you enough for sending us to London. We've done a whole ten thousand steps just inside the British Museum, and we've been to the theatre, because my friend here was horrified that when I used to be dying, I didn't put 'See *Les Miserables*' at the top of my to-do list, which apparently is what all right-minded dying people do. I said I had enough *Miserables* of my own going on, which was true, but I have to say, it would have been a shame to have died without seeing it. I've been on the London Eye, which was fun (and fulfilled my pre-Apple desire for queuing — we're over that now). And we've been on an open-topped bus, of course, though I think London is better on foot. We've been working very hard on The Thing most days. In the evenings we've meandered between restaurants and landmarks, parks and old streets, and I can see what he means. Above the street-level twenty-first-century stuff, there are gargoyles and fancy brickwork, hidden right in front of you. I think I'd got out of the habit of looking up.

It's like Edinburgh, but it's not: here things are more hodgepodge. I suppose Edinburgh has themes — sandstone, tallness, Georgian proportions, red-brick Victorian baronial architecture. London's more like: 'Oh, let's just leave this wee terrace here for now, next to a museum and a warehouse.'

London smells of exhaust fumes and lemonade. It's busy and bustling and you have to get busy and bustling too. But people smile if you smile, and there are wee bits of kindness everywhere, if you look for them. (I gave up my seat on the tube for a pregnant lady. She offered me a sherbet lemon.)

And I've a flat to myself while I'm here. This is my first time living on my own. The first night I was so shattered that I barely noticed. The second, I lay awake for hours and listened to the city noises — they are the same but different to home — and when morning came I got up, because I had a job to go to, and I thought: This is what people do. Get up, go to work. And I'm doing it. It's so exciting. (Apple was less impressed. I think she's maybe lived on her own, and had a job, before.)

When I get back to Edinburgh, I'll be home alone. It's a big deal. It's what I want — but it's a big change, too. This temporary home in London is showing me that. I'm having a practice at being in my own world. So far, I love it.

How do I manage this change?

You've got until I get home. Polls close Friday the 25th.

PLAN — make sure you always have things to do and places to go, and be prepared that this change is going to bring the sort of discomfort that these things always do.

PAINT — make the place your own. Decorate, move things around. A new era calls for new cushions. You might not have a lot of money but you walk past charity shops every day, and you know there's treasure to be had if you look for it.

PARTY — you've never had your own place. You might be a graduate but that doesn't make you old. Make the most of it.

3 shares
17 comments

Results:
PLAN   47%
PAINT 39%
PARTY 14%

24 MAY, 2018

Belsize Park

'Come up and see me,' Seb says, and the intercom buzzes. Ailsa waits for the click of the lock pulling back, pushes the door of the smart block of flats and takes the lift to the third floor. His flat door is open, and he's stepping back to let her in.

'Hey,' he says. He kisses her, one cheek then the other, and she is almost used to this, almost able to not be startled by the way he looks up close, the stubble on his cheek a shade darker than his hair, the slope of his temples. 'How are you this morning? And Apple?'

'I'm fine,' Ailsa says, 'and Apple's behaving nicely.' It's just shy of ten. Seb keeps the curtains half drawn, so his flat is cool and dusky.

' ". . . for my mind misgives. Some consequence, yet hanging in the stars",' she says.

' "Shall bitterly begin his fearful date",'

259

Seb adds, and they look at each other, smile.

'Twentieth time in a row. Nailed it,' Ailsa says. Their first stumbling point had been that line, Seb saying, 'fearfully begin his bitter fate'. They've practised, practised, practised it.

'Are you glad you came?'

She looks up, surprised. 'Of course. Why?' She thinks about her silences, the moments when she's been tired. She turned down going into town last night in favour of a takeaway and being back in her flat by nine. She thought he understood.

Now he's the one who's looking away, flicking through the post on the table near the door. 'Well, you only came because of the blog vote, didn't you?'

'If I'd known how it would be, I wouldn't even have asked.'

'Right.' Seb turns, looks at her, his face hard to read, or it could just be the way the shadows fall in the hallway. 'But if you knew what everything was going to be like before you decided whether to do it . . .' He shakes his head, steps past her into the kitchen, re-emerges a few seconds later. 'I picked you up a smoothie on my way back from the gym,' he says. 'Spinach, kiwi and almond milk. I turned down the spirulina because I didn't know whether it was an established

260

part of the caveman diet.'

Ailsa laughs, and takes the domed plastic cup, blue straw sticking out of the top. 'I'll have to consult my caveman book,' she says. 'I don't know what spirulina is.' But she thanks it for changing the subject. She doesn't need to have the conversations she has with her mother with Seb too.

'Me neither, but I didn't want to admit that and look stupid in front of you. I'll be honest, I didn't even know cavemen had access to smoothie makers. This diet of yours has really showed up my ignorance.'

'Thank you.' One of the lovely things about Seb — and in these eleven days, Ailsa has made quite a long list — is that he's very unselfconscious when it comes to talking about anything that relates to physical health. Ailsa is the same: years of checkups and meetings about what's starting to fail and what blood tests are telling her doctors have made her able to see her body, in almost every respect, as something that she cannot afford to be precious or embarrassed about. But she's noticed, in talking to others, those who have had more steady health, that this is not the norm. (After posting about gaining weight, she'd been amazed how many comments commended her bravery for saying so. She's been amused — it's not as though she could hide an extra thirty pounds. And being coy about it wasn't going to miraculously turn it into twenty pounds.) Whether it's because Seb is an actor, or whether he was like that anyway, she doesn't know. But he is as aware of the minutiae of his body as Ailsa is, listening to its clicks and whirrs, and trying to work out what they might mean. He's looking at her now. 'I think you've lost weight. Since you've been here.'

Ailsa nods. 'I think another couple of pounds. From here.' She puts her hands at the top of her waist, above her ribs. It is good, to feel a waist emerging. But not a patch on the joy it is to have a body that can walk, easily; breath and strength and beating heart and balance, all together. It's as though she used to be a flicker and now she's a flame.

'Yes,' Seb says, 'that's what I thought. You're getting more . . . hourglass.' He's turned away as he's said it, checking his phone and then switching it to silent, so he misses the blush.

She says to herself: Hourglass is not a compliment; it's an observation, Ailsa, for heaven's sake. Although she appreciates that he's gone for 'more hourglass' rather than 'less round'.

He puts down his phone, looks up at her again. 'And your glasses are getting bigger. Or your face is smaller. Not sure which.'

'Ah, I always wear my bigger glasses on a Thursday. It's a Scottish thing.'

Seb laughs and stretches his arms upwards, lets them drop, shakes them. 'OK. Let's get going.'

'Good idea. Romeo wasn't built in a day.'

'Still not funny,' Seb says.

'Still beg to differ.' And they laugh, and then they begin.

Here's how it works. Ailsa sits in the armchair near the floor-to-ceiling windows that form the front of the flat, trusty turquoise satchel on the floor, notebook, pen and play text on her lap, feet tucked around to her side, and reads the couplet before Romeo's line. Seb recites Romeo's speech. Ailsa waits until he either gets stuck or gets to the end of it, or they get to the end of the scene, and then, when he looks at her, waiting, she tells him what he's missed or goes over where he's stumbled. He is mobile as they work, sometimes sitting on the sofa at right angles to her, sometimes pacing, clicking his fingers, sometimes — her favourite — sitting on the floor with his back against the arm of her chair. Close enough to touch. Not touching.

It was arm-chewingly embarrassing at first, but now it feels normal, in the way that Ailsa had thought that waking up without a heaviness in her chest and an ache in her arms would feel normal. It doesn't, yet. Neither does a pink skin or the way a rosy lipstick looks on her mouth. But a grid in a notebook, with scenes and speeches written down the left side, dates across the top, circles for having practised, a tick for every perfect run-through — this she is used to.

They begin with the scenes that Seb already knows; he chatters through them, words as train-trucks, rapid and rattling, and Ailsa struggles to keep up on the page, although the lines are becoming familiar to her, too, and it's her ear rather than her eye that tells him when he misspeaks.

Ailsa consults her list. 'Right,' she says, 'let's start with the nurse coming to see you. Ready? "I pray you, sir, what saucy merchant was this that was so full of his ropery?" '

Seb sighs. They've struggled with the prose: the rhythm of the pentameter gives footholds, stepping stones, but the prose is — well, it's unmeasured. It's the difference, Ailsa thinks, between the routine of hospital life, and waking up in your own bed and having a day full of your own choices ahead of you. The one that looks as though it's easiest isn't.

He squares his shoulders, closes his eyes, opens them, looks at her and beyond her. ' "A gentleman, Nurse, that loves to hear himself talk and will speak more in a minute than he will stand to in a month." '

They work for three hours, then break for lunch. This afternoon, they're going to tackle Romeo and Juliet's parting. As usual, Seb has shopped at the deli on the way back from the gym, and brought in salads and cold meat for them to share, bread and cheese for him, fresh fruit and nut-stuffed dates for her. He lays them out on the kitchen island, along with the hand sanitiser Ailsa brought to leave here. They sit on high stools at either side of the island and eat. Their mealtimes have been quiet, and this last lunch is no different. Ailsa checks her blog stats and emails, Seb keeps an eye on his messages, on Facebook and Twitter. Then he makes phone calls while Ailsa takes a walk, twenty minutes or so around the leafy streets of Belsize Park. They are broader than home and quieter, the houses just as grand as those in Edinburgh, but squat-seeming rather than stretching for the sky. The air is heavy with May, the sky always soothing, whether it's blue or grey, close to her or high above. Ailsa brings coffee back in with her — an iced latte for Seb and a black Americano for her — and they work for another three hours or so in the afternoon.

Seb sits on the floor at Ailsa's feet, looks into her eyes; she reminds herself that he's not looking at her. He's looking at Juliet, or rather, Meredith Katz.

'You're going to have to read all the speeches,' he says, after another stumble. When they're running through a scene, Ailsa usually reads the first two lines of a speech, rolls her hand, reads the last two.

'Oh, no,' Ailsa says, 'there was nothing about acting in the contract.' She half laughs but she's squirming inside; it's school play and waiting-room, all in one, and no way to look away, because when she drops her chin, Seb reaches out and tilts her face towards him, smiles.

'I know,' he says, 'but honestly, I don't want you to act it. I just need to hear it.'

'OK,' Ailsa says. Act three, scene five is short — or at least Romeo's part in it is — but Juliet has more lines than her hero, and so Ailsa hears her voice quaver and stumble, while Seb's gains confidence. They do it

266

again, again, again. On the fourth time, or maybe the fifth, Ailsa puts down her pencil, stops making the marks where a correction needs to be made, and finds that Seb takes her hand. His memory stutters again and again over 'vaulty heaven', so when finally he gets it — ' "Nor that is not the lark whose notes do beat./The vaulty heaven so high above our heads:/I have more care to stay than will to go" ' — they look at each other, delighted, and then Seb is kneeling up and his arms are around her, bear-hugging. He sits back on his heels.

'We did it,' he says. 'I think I get a tick.'

'You do. But you need to run over it again, tomorrow. Just to make sure.' Ailsa's hand is warm where he has been holding it for so long. She can't believe she's even noticing. Seb jokes about the women who stop him in the street, squeal and squeak and take photos. Inside, she's squeaking. She hopes he can't tell.

Seb laughs. 'I'll go with you to the station and we can do it in the cab,' he says. And then, 'I thought a lot of the speeches would come back. From when I did *Wherefore Art Thou?*. But they've gone.'

Ailsa nods. She'd downloaded the final of the show the night before she left, and watched it on the train on the way to

London. Seb was skinnier then — not that he's fat now, but he's muscled, broader. His hair was longer, too, his face more open, so that every feeling of tension and fear, panic and hope, passed across it like the shadows of clouds on a hillside. At the moment when the winner was announced, the camera moved quickly from the air-punching, whooping victor to Seb, disconsolate, tears on his face.

She stands, stretches, moving her weight cautiously from foot to foot, dispelling the beginning of pins and needles in her calves because she has sat unmoving for too long. It's almost five thirty, and outside the window the purr and chatter of the rush hour is beginning.

Seb stretches too, shakes out his shoulders, fingers, feet. He looks like an actor, a dancer, at these moments. He's completely in command of his body, in a way that Ailsa will never be in charge of hers. Another deep breath, and then he opens his eyes, looks at her, before he puts his sunglasses on.

'Do you fancy going dancing?' he asks. 'I know a place you might like. There's a live band. A milonga. It's fun. And it's dark. I can actually take my sunglasses off.' Even in the flat, with the light low, he still can't

268

tolerate more than an hour before his eyes start to ache, and he tries to rub at his lids, usually stopping himself just in time.

Oh, she does. Tango has danced its way into her blood; alone in Yusef's kitchen she's been practising her ochos, hands either side of the door frame as she steps her feet across each other, hips twisting, opposite an imaginary partner.

But a club, with Seb, who can really dance — that's something else. 'You know I haven't had much practice,' Ailsa says. She thinks of his fluidity, his confidence. 'I don't know if I'm good enough. And I don't have my shoes.'

Seb pushes the coffee table to one side, holds out his arms. 'Let's have a go,' he says.

It's as though Apple propels her. She steps forward, puts her left hand on his shoulder, near his collarbone, lets her forearm touch, but not rest along, his upper arm, as Guy has shown her. He takes her right hand in his left, breathes in and out, slowly, and then starts to rock her from side to side, gently.

'I'm just getting the sense of where your weight is . . .'

And then his leg comes forward so that hers can only go back, and all they are doing is walking, but still, somehow it's more than that.

Seb comes to a stop. 'OK.'

'Yes,' Ailsa says. And oh, she is.

'Right.' Seb tilts his upper body back a little, looks at her, comes close again. 'Let's see what I can remember. We were practising the tango the week my eye went to hell, so I didn't get that far with it. Roz is sorting lessons for the cast but they won't start until rehearsals. Ready to go again?'

'It's tango. I'll just do as I'm told,' Ailsa says. Although she's not looking at him she can feel that he's grinning; it's as though the muscles in his jaw have twitched the air. She wonders if he can feel her smile.

Unexpectedly, he starts to sing, just below his breath-line, a soft *bom-bom-bom* that he then moves in time to. Before she knows it, her feet are in position five — her left foot in front of her right, her weight all in her right leg, a deliberate effort of keeping her body strong, hips straight, stomach taut, muscles working to keep her in balance. And then Seb steps back, *bom-bom-bom,* and twists his trunk, and she's pivoting, as best she can barefoot, moving towards him as he walks away. Step-pivot-close, step-pivot-close. There's something about the way Seb is moving, pressing on her hand to give her something to work against, that makes this easier than it's ever been.

He stops, laughs, drops his hands.

'What?' Ailsa's mind bounces an image of Seb and Fenella forward: everything about their movements sharp and precise. (She watched a bit of *StarDance* on the train, too.) Fenella's ochos would make her attempts look like a cow in wellies.

'Nothing,' he says, 'just — it feels good to be dancing. Doesn't it?' He touches her hand.

'Yes,' she says. And, cow-wellies notwithstanding, it's true.

'What size are your feet?'

'Five and a half.'

'Right.' Seb goes into his bedroom and returns a moment later, holding a pair of shoes by the straps. 'I. Am. The. King. Guess what size these are.'

'Five and a half?' Ailsa says.

'No, five, but you're supposed to go down half a size in dance shoes. Here you go.' The shoes are black and gold, higher than anything Ailsa has ever tried to dance, or even walk, in — although that's not saying much — and there's the imprint of the ball of a foot inside them. Something about dead men's shoes pops into her mind, makes her quell her impulse to reach out and take them from Seb's hand.

'I can't wear someone else's shoes.'

'Fenella won't mind.' Nothing that Seb has told her about Fenella makes Ailsa believe this. 'And anyway, they've been here for six months. It's not like she needs them. She'll have forgotten she ever had them.' He thrusts the shoes at her. 'At least try them on. They're your size! What are the chances of that?'

There's an excitement in him that makes her sit down and worry her toes into the pointed black patent leather. They are beautiful shoes, sharp and clean-lined, the way a tango ought to be danced. She fiddles with the fastening, which is set for a slimmer ankle, but once she has them on, they feel just right.

'Well?' Seb says, and he reaches out a hand. He's grinning; she sees the TV star in him shining through, the man with all his feelings on the outside, touchable, reachable. And also, to her, further away.

She takes his hands and stands, wobbles, finds her balance. When he takes her into hold she's tall enough to be looking at his ear, rather than his shoulder.

'Are you sure she won't mind?'

'She won't know,' Seb says, and then they are dancing again, Ailsa half pushed, half guided from move to move. Her balance is in a different place, and now she's standing she realises that the shoes don't fit quite as well as they seemed to when she was sitting down. Her big toes are pinching already.

But they are dancing, even in this small space, with their steps small to match it. Seb's arms are taut and she can see the muscles moving in his chest underneath his T-shirt. She remembers what Eliza says ('Are we using our bottoms to their full potential?') and extends her legs fully backwards, from the hip, feeling her own muscles move under her skin. When Seb turns her she overbalances, leans into him, and he holds her for a moment before letting go. Then he tips his sunglasses up to the top of his head, looks at her, green meeting blue.

'Up for it?' he asks, and Ailsa can do nothing but nod. 'OK. I need to change first. There's a restaurant upstairs: we can eat there. Steak and salad, as I remember.'

'Caveman staples,' Ailsa says.

Seb laughs. 'Do you want to change? We can go via yours if you do.'

'Yes,' Ailsa says, 'I brought a dress.'

'Two minutes.' Seb pulls off his T-shirt and walks, bare-torsoed, through the kitchen, dropping his T-shirt on the floor next to the washing machine as he passes it. Ailsa thinks of how easy it must be, to be so unmarked. Since leaving hospital, she has loved her physical privacy. She no longer needs to spend days knowing that any passing medic might stop and assess the scar that they would pronounce to be, depending on personality, 'beautiful' or 'healing nicely' or 'tip top'.

Seb's bedroom door closes behind him, Ailsa stands at the window, watching the North London street get on with its early evening: a father ushers three children on scooters across the road; a young woman picks up after a fat, furry dog; a BMW with its windows down parallel-parks in a space between a bright red Fiat 500 and a white van with a loft-conversion logo on the side.

Ailsa inhales the petrol-fumes-and-bougainvillea air, exhales as fully as she can, now that she's sure the stitches won't burst and her heart abscond. She wonders whether it had ever occurred to anyone in hospital that she might be self-conscious about exposing herself. Presumably part of medical training is about not looking at the nipples, or maybe to her doctors her body was nothing more than the cage for a transplanted heart, the thing that must not become infected, or be allowed to do anything to jeopardise all that time and work and careful stitching, and — not least —

waste the possibility of life not just for her but for the next faulty heart on the transplant list.

She still examines her scar in the mirror every morning. She can see (partly thanks to Shona, who fitted her bra) that it's neat, especially now it's lost the furious scarlet puckering that marked its first weeks. She imagines pulling off her top, in front of — well, let's say Seb, for argument's sake — and having a moment where his face falls and rearranges, or, worse (better?), remains studiously still, as though every naked woman he's ever seen has an unmissable scar. Either that or having to have a grim, unromantic chat beforehand: 'When you see me naked you'll notice something unusual . . .' Maybe she could roll it in with the contraception conversation. Hypothetically. With whichever man it might be.

'Right,' Seb says, and Ailsa turns around and sees him, and — 'What?'

Ailsa shakes her head, 'Nothing.'

'I might still be half blind but I'm not stupid,' Seb says. 'What is it? Have I spilled something on myself?' He's looking down at his shirt front, examining his sleeves.

Ailsa sighs, because there's no way out of this now except to show how ridiculous she's being. 'I don't like red. It makes me anxious.'

There's a beat, Seb looking at her, turning to look at himself in the mirror over the fireplace, turning back. A smile, but gentle.

'Yeah, I can see why you wouldn't like this shirt, then.' It's a tango shirt, for sure, the red of a seducing smile, bright and bold, with a sheen to the fabric that makes the colour glow.

'It's a lovely shirt,' Ailsa says, 'it's just that — well — there was a time when every time I heard bad news, I was wearing red. Both times I missed out on a transplant I had red striped pyjamas on when they told me, and the same ones when — something else horrible happened. Whenever I had bad test results I seemed to be wearing red. Plus — all the blood. All the time. All the tests, you're always looking at someone taking blood into a phial. Red makes me nervous. I know it's stupid.' She's looking at her toes, the nails painted a bright coral pink, peeping out from the black-and-gold shoes.

She waits for what's coming. She's had this conversation before. How many pairs of pyjamas did she have? Two? Then there was a fifty-fifty chance of getting bad news when she was wearing them. Plus, if she had red pyjamas, that suggested that she likes red, so there was a good chance that a lot of what she owned was red. She is an intelligent person. She knows that there's no logic to this. She knows, too, that she looks for things to confirm her bias. The fact that nothing of hers is red isn't what's making her life go well. Having a new heart is what is making her well. Correlation is not causation.

'I've got a black one,' Seb says, then, 'I'm wearing red pants though. Is that OK?'

She looks at him to see if he's teasing. Sunglasses: impossible to tell, even now they are better acquainted. 'Are you teasing me?'

Then, the most unexpected thing. He steps towards her, takes her hands; then steps back as she flinches away, not at the touch but at the unexpectedness of it, but there's no way to understand, to articulate that in time.

'Sorry. No, I wasn't teasing. I was serious. I wore the same pair of socks for every broadcast of *Wherefore Art Thou?*. Thought they were my lucky charm until I lost. I'll go and change. I won't be a minute.'

Seb, skin pale, blond hair blonder against his black shirt, waits while she changes. The dress is looser around her torso than when she bought it. He was right about the weight loss around her middle. She puts on black

277

tights, navy patent pumps, and takes the papers and notebook out of her satchel — she hadn't thought to bring a different bag for evenings.

She walks into the room where he's waiting. 'Do I look OK? For the place we're going?'

Seb takes off his sunglasses, gives her a long look, and smiles — or at least his mouth does. His eyes are serious and calm. It's a Lennox look. She hardly dares inhale, for fear of Driftwood in the air.

'You look as though you've dropped out of vaulty heaven.' He opens the door.

On the street outside, she stumbles on the step, and so it seems natural to take his arm. When he helps her from the cab, he keeps hold of her hand as they walk the hundred yards or so to the restaurant. They take a booth in a corner. Seb takes off his glasses, and suddenly the ground shifts and they can see — Ailsa can see, anyway, or admit — that they are bound now by more than understanding the oddness of having a bit of a dead person's body stitched into your own.

These London days have been a bit like making friends in the day room of a hospital, knowledge making intimacy until — well, that's where it deviated. In a hospital, when you got close enough to someone, you became part of their circle, someone to be updated, someone to share the everyday grimness with. With Seb, knowledge has made intimacy until the obvious thing is to sit in a dark restaurant, drinking deep plummy wine, feeling eye contact go on for just a little longer than it ought to.

And then something happens to remind Ailsa that it isn't a date. The waitress, whose eyes were drawn to Seb from the minute they walked in, who lingered when she took their order and brought their food, brings a phone to the table with their bill and asks, 'Could I get a picture with you? My friends will never believe how much more handsome you are in real life.'

Seb says, 'Sure,' and the waitress hands Ailsa her phone, as though Ailsa's entire purpose in being there is to take this photograph, and tucks herself in next to Seb, her head tilted towards him, their smiles white and bright. 'Thank you,' she says to him afterwards, and she kisses his cheek, right at the corner of his mouth. She takes the phone from Ailsa without looking at her.

Seb waits until she's gone, says, 'Sorry about that,' and then goes back to his story of Fenella and the cat she never remembered to feed, as though such interruptions are usual. Because, of course, they are, to him.

'Were you and Fenella a couple?'

Seb hesitates, wineglass halfway to his mouth, and says, 'Why do you ask?'

Ailsa shrugs. 'Just making conversation.'

'Not really. We had a thing, for a bit, but you pretty much have to, on *StarDance*, if you're both single. If you're not, it's optional. It's hard to spend that much time wrapped around someone else's body without at least' — he pauses — 'giving it a thought.'

Ailsa nods. It's the same in a hospital room. Even if you are both wrecks, physical proximity makes you think of what's possible, that there are better uses for hands and tongues than taking temperatures and swallowing medication. 'I can imagine.'

'I haven't ever had a proper relationship. Long-term. It's never — appealed. I like change,' Seb adds, and then he puts down his glass, gets to his feet, and says, 'Let's have some fun, shall we, Juliet?'

He takes her hand and leads her downstairs to a candlelit room, where a band is playing a warm, melodic rhythm. She hesitates, and he stops, steps back towards her.

'OK?'

'Yes,' she says, 'it's just — this is the first

280

time I've heard live tango music.' It's more sensual than she would have expected, spilling from the instruments and sliding through the air, making her skin pay attention to the feel of her dress, the touch of Seb's hand holding hers.

A few couples are making their way around a dance floor that's smaller than the one upstairs at the Dragon's Nest. They find a table, put down their bags and jackets, and Ailsa changes her flat shoes for the spiky dancing heels.

Seb put his mouth to her ear and says, 'You know that in tango, you don't ask people to dance in words. You have to look at them?'

She nods. And he looks her a look to which her wordless answer is: Yes. Anything. Anywhere.

Their steps soon match each other; the closeness of Seb's body becomes both natural and exciting, as Ailsa's learns how to move against him.

'Lean on me,' he says in her ear, and when she lets herself tilt forward a little, it becomes even easier to read what he wants her to do next in the pressure of his hands, the twist of his chest. She feels him smile. His mouth, at her ear, in a break between dances: 'I love that in the tango; your heart

281

always wants to be next to your partner's heart.' Apple, shiveringly, agrees, and Ailsa nods. The place is filling around them. More couples on the floor means that they are even closer, and there are times when it feels that all they do is sway against each other. The music weaves around them, sometimes fast, sometimes slow, but always, somehow, in time with the beat of her blood.

Oh, but she is tired before she wants to be. Yet Seb seems to know that, in the same way that his palm's pressure on hers knows how to tell her which way he'll take her next. At the next break in the music, he jerks his head towards the stairs, a question. Her nod, his grin, the clasp of his hand, leads to a squeeze through the dancers and the watchers to the bottom of the stairs, a trot to the top while others wait to come down. Ailsa does a quick shoe-change: her big toes are begging for release.

The music fades as they walk along the pavement; warm, gentle rain falls.

'Do you feel at home now? With the rain?'

'The rain would not get this warm in Edinburgh,' Ailsa laughs, 'or if it did, we'd all think the apocalypse was here.'

Seb magics a cab to the kerb, stands back for her to get in. She fumbles with the seat-belt, hands damp from the rain, and Seb helps, clicking the tab into the slot and then resting his hands on her waist for a minute, laughing, asking if she feels secure enough or would she like a safety helmet too. Ailsa watches London speed by: it's all lights and blur, and the clearest thing to see is the raindrops on the window. Funny how they travel up the glass when the cab is moving. Her hand is warm in Seb's. They're quiet.

The steps up to the building where Yusef lives feel like too much.

Ailsa's muscles realise, having had the chance to rest, how hard they've worked, and her feet are no longer letting her ignore their blisters and rubbed-away skin. She stops to give her body just a second or two of recovery time, rummaging for keys as a pretext.

Seb stands next to her, waiting, and it doesn't occur to her that on previous evenings, he's dropped her off and had the cab take him the rest of the way down Haverstock Hill to his home.

And then she pulls out the keys and goes up the first of the dozen steps to the flats, and he's standing on the pavement behind her, and he says her name, and she turns, and they are face-to-face, and he kisses her. She tastes hot wine, the salt of sweat; feels dizzied, violently awake.

The kiss is soft, almost gentle, but — like stepping onto a dance floor — full of possibility. When it ends their foreheads touch, nose tips resting against each other.

'I'm glad I suggested the dancing,' Seb says.

'Me too.'

A pause, a moment. Another kiss, gentle again at first, then becoming firmer, more intent. Seb's hands, which had held her at the waist, draw her towards him; one slides up her spine, pulling her body even closer. Or perhaps she's the one who's moving, trying to rid them of the space between them. Certainly every cell of hers is alive, alert to him —

Then his voice, just a notch above his breath, as though he's telling her a secret, 'Shall I come up? I changed my pants too. They're blue.'

If the kiss had woken Ailsa's senses, then the words dampen them down, and engage her brain, fast. Her mind fast-forwards to what happens next: switching on the lights in the flat, taking him into the bedroom, where her clothes from earlier are abandoned on the bedroom floor, her open make-up bag spewing the lipsticks she had tried and wiped away. And, more importantly than any of this, the fact that it has been so long. And that the last man who kissed her with intent was Lennox. Apple stills in the cooling night, breathless, waiting to see what Ailsa will do.

She is standing on a step in London, aching and elated with dancing, looking into the face of a man with a half-unpicked star in one eye. She is being offered the chance to reclaim the part of her that loves, and longs, and can feel the possibilities of what the body can give and take.

And she wants to take it, she does.

But then she thinks about her scar, ugly and bright against her clammy skin.

Oh, for the chance to write a quick blog post, and give herself five hundred words to talk some kind of sense into herself. Or let the universe decide.

Seb's hands are at her waist again; at first they pulled her close so he could kiss the part of her neck that shows above her coat, but now they are holding her a little away, so that he can see into her face, a question.

She knows what the waitress in the restaurant would do: lead him upstairs, run a bath or invite him into the shower with her. It would only take a moment to heap the clothes she discarded into her suitcase and close it, light a candle so the room was kind and soft.

But Ailsa is not the waitress. She isn't even the woman who had looked at Seb on the dance floor, said: Yes. And meant: Anything.

The longer they stand there, the worse it gets.

Three hours later, Ailsa is still awake. Her feet ache, but most of the hurt is elsewhere. It's in the centre-of-me heart, the I-didn't-know-how-lonely-I-was-until-tonight heart. Apple is, it seems, catching up.

Even closing her eyes is difficult, because as soon as she does, the images she has stored today are focussed, bright: Seb, close up, intense, smiling, leaning closer, laughing, kissing. The words that weren't theirs, written for star-crossed lovers, making a way for them to look at each other, to hold hands, to feel. The step-and-slide of the dance, the sound of the music running through her body, the fact that the only way to make the movements work were to trust Seb, to listen to what his body was telling hers to do, as she stepped into the spaces he made for her, pulling the sole of her shoe across the floor the way she'd been taught, keeping her heart close to his.

At four, Ailsa puts on the light and trails the duvet to the sofa. She rummages in her satchel for her notebook, wondering if writing something, anything, down will help, or whether it will make it worse — but her copy of *Romeo and Juliet* comes to hand first, pages turned down at the places where she and Seb have worked. She flicks through, and starts to read the rest.

Landing on the scene with Juliet waiting for Romeo to come to her for their wedding night, she reads: ' "When I shall die,/ Take him and cut him out in little stars,/And he will make the face of heaven so fine/That all the world will be in love with night.' " She wonders if Juliet would have been quite so attached to the idea of death if she had seen it stalk Romeo every day, turning him yellow, making him weak, his room full of the smell of dead lilies, even though there were no flowers in there, and only the occasional breath of Driftwood to remind her that he was still himself.

Ailsa goes to the window. The light pollution makes it hard to see the stars, but the rainclouds have cleared and some are visible, the brightest: she sees Orion, and, if she slides up the sash and cranes her head around a little, the Plough. She tries to be in love with night. But there is no comfort in the distant cold of the dead stars in the sky.

24 MAY, 2017

This Time Last Year

'It's a beautiful night,' Dennis says. 'You feel that you could touch the stars, if you wanted.'

'That's nice.' There was a time when Ailsa would have happily spent an hour in the hospital garden, craning upwards as Lennox tried to make her see the stories in the stars, but she has no will for it now.

'It is, but it doesnae look like you're in the mood for stargazing.'

'It's been a long day,' Ailsa says, half word half wheeze. They're all long now, and getting longer. Ailsa's failing three-chambered heart is running out of time. All the ingenious ways that consultants have fixed and helped and patched it over the years are coming to the end of their usefulness. She supposes — because her earliest memories are of not being able to keep up with games at school — that breathing has never come easily to her, but for the first time, every damn thing she wants to do, however small, is an effort. Words cost her. Her hands tingle, her legs ache. Her death is creeping up, beginning at fingers and toes. She's spending more and more time on the cardio-thoracic unit, on drips to keep her heart muscle working, on oxygen to help her lungs to do their job, and the only person who would understand every lousy beat of what she's going through isn't here. Since the morning of Lennox's death, Dennis has been a regular visitor. It's as though he and Ruthie have transferred their hope to Ailsa.

'I bet,' Dennis says. Then, 'Can you believe it's been five weeks?'

'I don't think I even believe he's gone.'

She prepares herself for Dennis to cry, but he doesn't. He takes her hand and says, 'I suppose we'll be saying the same thing a year from now. And five years on. I don't think it ever goes away.'

She's too bone-tired to talk, or cry, so she squeezes his hand, and he looks up. 'Lennox said you'd never had a dad and I should be yours. It's an honour, Ailsa, but I can't lose you as well. Remember that, aye?'

'I'll try,' she says. Don't make promises you can't keep. And she resolves that, when

Hayley gets back, she'll make her tell her the whole story of her father. She's not going to her grave with 'ah, you don't want to hear about him, hen' as all she knows.

From: Seb
Sent: 28 May, 2018
To: Ailsa
Subject: You've gone

Hi Ailsa,

Thank you for everything you did to help me with my lines. I really enjoyed spending time with you.

Sorry I misjudged things on our last night. I should have remembered you were there because of the great voting public. And sorry I missed seeing you off. It probably looked like I was being petty. I wasn't. My neighbour got back at the same time as I did and we ended up having a whisky, and then another one. Or two. It was 4 a.m. when I hit the sack. So I overslept. I hope you didn't. Did you get my text?

See you when I'm next up? (Maybe the photoshoot? You weren't kidding about how organised Libby is. My agent doesn't know whether to block her or employ her.)

Keep foraging.

Seb

From: Ailsa
To: Seb

Dear Seb,
I enjoyed spending time with you too. I did get your text. It said, 'Apron I nodded up, see', which I think might be autocorrect for something, or maybe a bit from the Nurse?

I was really glad that the vote went the way it did, for what it's worth.

The Internet tells me that cavemen were very fond of cakes involving eggs, chestnut puree and 80 per cent dark chocolate, so that's good news. I'll be in the kitchen this afternoon. I might go mad and have a trip on a tram later.

See you soon, and take care.

Ailsa

From: Seb
To: Ailsa

I was probably going for 'Sorry I missed you, Seb'. Or even 'I am never, ever drinking whisky again, as long as I live.'

You too. More stitches out later. Instead of zig-zags I'll have Ws around the edge of my eye. I'm not sure whether knowing what's coming makes it better or worse.

I look forward to the cake report. It sounds a bit worthy. Like carpets made out of — whatever it is. Hemp. String.

S

From: Ailsa
To: Seb

Worse — that's what I always found with medical procedures, anyway. Do you want me to explain the heart-biopsy-via-nasal-passage thing, seeing as you nearly blacked out when we were talking about it in the restaurant on my first night? Plus, they always explain what they're about to do, so you think you can feel it, even if you can't. My favourite phlebotomist never did the whole 'I'm just doing this, and then that' bit. She'd just lean in and whisper, 'cat's claw'. Or sometimes, 'bee sting'.

Good luck. Ws are better than zig-zags. Before you know it, they will be Vs.

The cake's in the oven. It smells good.

I don't think I've ever knowingly walked on a hemp carpet.

I should have said, I'm sorry too.

Ailsa

From: Seb
To: Ailsa

I blacked out again reading that. NO.

If there's ever a serial killer at large in that hospital, I think we'll know where to look.

If you go to events in marquees, they've usually put some sort of weird matting down. Not carpet exactly. They do it in soggy places too. I can't believe you haven't come across one in Embra.

I don't think you've got anything to be sorry about.

What are you up to this week? How's your flat without your mother in it?

S x

From: Ailsa
To: Seb

I think you mean hessian. I went to a wedding where 40 per cent of the women either fell over backwards or lost a shoe (or both) when their heels sunk down the holes. I was a lot more stable (onesie and wellies).

I'm doing some research this week. Way back I thought about studying law but it just seemed stupid given the length of time it takes and the length of time I thought I had. In the end I went for history because I was really interested in it and if you're dying, there's not a lot else to do than please yourself, really.

But when I put it on the blog, I had a bit of an 'aha' moment. I thought I'd lay out my options as I see them, because I've never thought much beyond the heart/not heart scenario, but after I'd put that post up, the law was the thing that I kept wondering about. When you're in hospital you meet all sorts and it makes you realise how lucky you are to be educated. There are people I would have liked to help. There are things that need to change. I'm trying to work out how I could qualify, whether I could afford it, all that. Havering a bit. And trying not to get nervous about starting work next week.

It's a bit weird without Mum. Actually, it's pretty miserable. I'm being pathetic, I know. She said it would be a big change for us and I'm only just seeing what that means. I'm going over to visit her at the weekend.

How about you?

Ailsa

From: Seb
To: Ailsa

You wore a onesie to a wedding?

And you didn't take my suggestion seriously? There's a real shortage of professional unicorns.

You'd be an amazing lawyer. Lucky that option came out top, isn't it? A more suspicious mind than mine would suspect vote-rigging.

If you're bored on your own you could always pop back and put me through my paces 😜 Excitement alert — I'm sending this from a bus.

S x

From: Ailsa
To: Seb

Maybe I wore a onesie to a wedding. Maybe I didn't. (OK, I didn't. I'm not insane. Do you know how hot a marquee gets, even in Edinburgh? And if you're wearing a onesie, you've nowhere to go, in terms of layers.)

Ah, so YOU'RE LondonRomeo? Never would have seen through that pseudonym without the clue. (That's sarcasm.)

I'm ignoring your allegation of foul

play until I'm qualified. Then you'll feel the cold hand of the law.

Tango was fun (and funny) this week. Everyone's concentrating a lot more now we're going to be In A Show. Eliza says she's going to start touting us around for panto if this is what we do when we're going to be on a stage.

Ring the bell for me. Though I might be getting over buses. Someone sitting behind me sneezed yesterday, and I could feel drops of wetness landing in my hair.

Ailsa

From: Seb
To: Ailsa

Will do. Here's a pic of the bell.

See you at the photoshoot. I'll let you know when I know my travel plans. Maybe we can meet up?

S

From: Ailsa
To: Seb

Great. See you then.

Here's a pic of my hessian cake. (It is

basically hessian.)

Ailsa x

From: Seb
To: Ailsa

OK, that should have been: 'you'll hear from me in a couple of hours'. You must be sick of me. Just wanted to let you know that I've had a call from my agent and we're going to be in The Sun on Saturday. That bloody waitress. She slipped me her number, she's obviously realised I'm not going to call. Call me when you see it, or not. I'm really sorry. The tabloids are bastards.

Seb x

The Sun

2 June, 2018

Who's That Girl?

Sexy Seb Morley has kept himself out of the spotlight since he opened up about his eye op earlier this year.

But we can exclusively reveal that it looks as though he's made a full recovery! He's been spotted dancing a steamy tango at Stephano's in trendy Shoreditch. He only had eyes for his new girl, and the two had a long, intimate chat before getting up close on the dance floor.

Who is that girl? We don't know — but she's not Seb's usual type. There's a lot more to this curvy lass than his usual models and actresses. But Morley didn't take his eyes off his pear-shaped partner all night, and they left early, hand in hand.

2 JUNE, 2018

'Have you stayed off the Internet like you promised?' Emily was the only person to call for this particular crisis and she's been fantastic, cancelling her Saturday-morning gym class so that she can arrive early with the paper, coffee and, by the looks of it, most of a bakery. Emily is to Ailsa as Tamsin is to Hayley. Ailsa cannot imagine life without her friend. And one of the best things about them is that — like with Seb — it's a two-way street. When Emily got herself into credit-card debt in her second year at university, Ailsa helped her to plan her way out of it. When Emily was elected as social secretary for the student union, Ailsa was her sounding-board and general right-hand woman. Emily has never made Ailsa feel more ill than she is.

'Yes. Apart from the blog, and that doesn't count. And emails.'

'The real world's more interesting. Have

you got plates?'

'Emily. Can we please get it over with? And I could have made coffee, you know.'

'I know you could, lovely. But I brought it. You'll have had enough of making coffee by the time you've put your first week in.'

Ailsa laughs and goes for the paper, but Emily is faster, taking it out of reach. 'Coffee first, and a croissant or two. We'll look when we're fortified.'

And of course Emily's right. Twenty minutes of chat — Jacob's upcoming wedding, Emily's job, Ailsa's London trip, though she can't bring herself to go into The Kiss — and the world feels bigger and less important than anything that *The Sun* might have to say.

'Here we go, then,' Emily says, and starts to turn the pages over. Ailsa, next to her on the sofa, feels Apple speeding up, sending a tremble to her fingertips. There's nothing on pages two and three, four and five, six and seven. Maybe Seb got it wrong, or the story — because there isn't a story — is too uninteresting to print.

It's on page eight. A photograph — grainy, hard to make out the fine detail of it at first — of Seb and her on the dance floor. It's taken from behind her, so Seb's face is clear: he's concentrating, square-shouldered, his

301

extended arm moving towards the camera as he guides Ailsa back. He's looking at her face. She's turning her head towards the right, but only her forehead is visible.

She sits and looks at the photograph for a long time. She can't bear to turn to the words yet.

That dress, with the yellow flowers, the one that made her feel so bright and beautiful: it's stretched across her shoulders, tight, showing the rolls of soft fat over the top of her bra-band. Her back looks thick, her backside broad, her calves almost comically exaggerated ovals. Her arms seem triangular, widening and widening from wrist to shoulder.

Emily is reading, her arm around Ailsa's shoulder; she's muttering to herself about spite and kindness costing nothing. Even before the words Ailsa feels sick, teary, and then ridiculous for being upset at this — at what is nothing more, actually, than a photo of herself. She looks at it again, and then closes her eyes, and remembers how she felt that night. Her body had seemed liquid, graceful in Seb's arms, moving from step to step, her heart opposite his heart. When they'd left she'd looked at the other dancers — women slimmer than her, bare-armed, narrow-hipped, some smiling, some thin-

302

lipped with concentration, some confident, some stop-starting, tentative. And she had felt as though she was one of them. When really she was the mismatched partner of the handsome man, the one that they would all go home and comment on, wonder about. She had been starting to love her body, its growing strength and ability to do most of the things that she wanted it to. But right now, although she knows that love must be there somewhere, she can't find it.

And then she reads the words of the article. They are no worse than the words she's just said to herself, but they hurt. She tells herself that to judge by appearances is shallow, wrong, and tries to become outraged on behalf of herself, of women. And she is, hypothetically. But mostly she feels fat, ugly, disappointed in herself for believing that being less overweight than she used to be was special. The sure knowledge that she is more than how she looks — the knowledge that replaced her fierce conviction that she was more than her illness — has deserted her.

'Are you OK?'

'Not really,' Ailsa says.

Emily pulls her closer and says, 'You know that this isn't true, don't you? Not just that it's awful about you, but everything it's built on. He's not better than you because he's famous. You're not unworthy because you're not a stick. There's just — there's nothing here.'

'I know.' Emily's quiet anger is comforting; so is the fact that she understands it all. 'Thanks, Em.'

'Are you going to blog about it?'

'No.' Ailsa chewed this over at 3 a.m., torn between saying her piece and prolonging the agony. 'I'm going with dignified silence.'

'Good. Oh, Ailsa.' The hug is hard and full of everything they've been through. Ailsa closes her eyes. It's almost like being with her mother, in the old days, before she had Apple. She squeezes her eyes closed, tight, and breathes in Emily's perfume, Black Opium, vanilla and sweet, the scent that her friend has worn for as long as Ailsa has known her. Then Emily sighs, holds her at arm's length and looks her over, as though she's checking for anything she's missed.

'I'm OK. Well, I will be.' Yes, she will. In the scheme of things, and all.

'Good. Screw the lot of them. Not literally. How about we go and get some paint samples? I've got all day.'

'Sounds lovely,' she says, and then her

phone rings. It's Hayley.

Her mother's voice sounds careful, picking its way down the line. 'I'm at work today. Eight o'clock start. They have all the papers in the staff room. I had a look through.'

'Yes?' If she pretends she hasn't seen the article, Hayley will feel as though she ought to tell her, on the grounds that it's better to come from her than someone else. May as well get this over with. 'Did you see the thing about — about Seb and me?'

'I did,' Hayley says. 'I was worried for you. Are you all right?'

'Sort of. No. Yes,' Ailsa says.

Hayley laughs, a sympathetic sound that makes Ailsa homesick even though she's at home. 'I think that's how I'd feel.'

Ailsa lets herself exhale, closes her eyes, rests her head back on the sofa. 'I am now. Emily's here.'

A pause. 'Good,' Hayley says. 'Tell her thank you, aye?' Ailsa hates this, but lets it go. She knows how her mother, Tamsin, Emily, Ruthie and Dennis have played a sort of looking-after-Ailsa tag for the last eighteen months, and it will be a while before it stops all together.

'You've a right to be upset,' Hayley says. 'They're bastards.'

'That's what Seb said.'

A beat of a pause from the other end of the line. 'You've spoken to him?'

'He warned me about it,' Ailsa says. 'His agent got a call.'

'Well, I hope he's ashamed of himself,' Hayley says.

'I don't think it's his fault. He can't help these things. He's in the public eye. People are interested in him.' Apple gives the tiniest twitch, in confirmation: *We are interested in him, Ailsa, you and I.*

Hayley sighs. 'It's all good publicity for him, though. And I notice they didn't comment about his shirt being open so far down. Or that he could have done with a shave. A cynic might think that he has friends at that paper.'

'It's not like that, Mum.' The peevishness in her voice surprises her. It's no wonder that Hayley sounds crisp in return.

'Oh aye? And how do you know? This won't just be keeping him in people's minds? At your expense?'

'Nobody knows who I am,' Ailsa says, trying to sound matter-of-fact. It's a bit strained but it's better than making her mother think she's annoyed with her. 'There was a waitress. She had her photo taken

306

with him. She obviously fancied him. It was her.'

Gently now, Hayley replies, 'Even so. I don't like it, Ailsa. I don't like to see you being talked about in that way. And it's a lovely dress.'

'Thanks,' Ailsa says. She means it. She hopes she sounds as though she does.

From: Seb
Sent: 2 June, 2018
To: Ailsa
Subject: Bloody Sun

Hi Ailsa,
I don't know if you got my text. I checked it before I sent it. It does actually say, 'Page 8. Call me when you've seen it if you want to talk'. As opposed to 'Paint cart Mohawk see see yodel' or whatever.

Anyway. I'm around, until about three. Then my sister's coming over to criticise my lifestyle and dress sense (probably) but she's bringing my little nieces, and usually cake, not made of nuts and mammoth-fur, so I'll put up with her.

Sorry, again.

Seb x

From: Ailsa
To: Seb

Dear Seb,
Yes, I've seen it. It fair put me off my croissant.

It's not your fault.

Ailsa

From: Seb
To: Ailsa

Cavemen had access to a patisserie? I need to have a word with my history teacher. I was taught all the wrong things. Or wasn't listening. Yeah, probably not listening.

You didn't say if you're OK. Are you OK?

It's really shit when that sort of thing happens. You do get used to it, but the first few times are hard. I've had a few months off — not interesting enough, once the eye stuff had died down — but now R&J is happening it looks like I'm fair game again. I'm so sorry.

After the episode of Wherefore Art Thou? where we had to do a dance routine from West Side Story (Roz had to explain why to me), *The Sun* published a picture of my head on a Thunderbird's body. And not even one of the cool Thunderbirds. Like I say, they really are bastards. (Journalists, not Thunderbirds).

S x

P.S. As you like old films I thought you might know what Thunderbirds are.

From: Ailsa
To: Seb

You're right. I didn't say if I'm OK. Honestly, I'm not sure. I felt quite shaken and tearful, and that's not like me. It's just a photo of me. I know I'm overweight. And I don't want to be whatever The Sun thinks is an acceptable shape for a woman, because if I was, there would be nowhere to keep my organs. So I've really got nothing to be upset about.

I suppose I could see that I looked awful in that photo and having to read the article pointing it out makes me feel — bullied. And I'm trying to get fit, and I feel the best I have done, literally, ever. I'm — oh, I don't know — I'm supposed to be above all this. If I'm happy with myself, I should be happy. If I'm not, I should be doing something about it (like not backsliding on the croissant front). What's in the papers should be irrelevant.

So, I'm not OK, but I guess I will be. I'm — let's say fine-ish (autocorrect just tried to make that 'fiendish').

I do know who Thunderbirds are/were (do puppets die? Maybe they get recycled into puppet transplants?). I'd say you dance way better than that.

From: Seb
To: Ailsa

Well, my fine-ish fiend, I'm still sorry.

And it was a terrible photo. You look much lovelier in real life. And you dance sort of — poetically. With your whole heart. You look great in that dress as well. I don't know if I said it but I thought you looked beautiful. Skinny-jeans waitresses with straight hair and big eyelashes all look the same. You look like you.

Am I making it better or worse?

Fenella thought the Thunderbird thing in the paper was hilarious. She didn't have much of a sense of humour, but she liked that. She always liked it when I fell over or anything where I made a tit of myself. She was nicer to other people. I'm not sure if it was a teaching strategy. It probably was.

I missed you when you went back to the land of the heatless sky. Once I'd got over the hangover. I brought you back a smoothie from the gym on Sunday morning and felt like an idiot. It was quite nice though. Spinach, orange, apple and avocado. I could have done without the spinach.

We've got the photoshoot/calendar thing a week on Saturday. Shall we go to dinner, or something, afterwards? (Do I have to say tea?) I've booked myself into a hotel for the night, and Roz has got me doing something with her on Sunday. She didn't say what. I'll do as I'm told. She's a slave driver. Worse than you. (Kidding.)

S xx

From: Ailsa
To: Seb

I think you're making it better, but I don't want to think/write about it anymore, if that's OK.

We Scots have to be bilingual because English folk never bother. So — it would be nice to have dinner after the photoshoot. I'll see you there.

Ailsa

312

■ ■ ■ ■

PART SIX:
JUNE 2018
THOU NEEDEST
NOT BE GONE

■ ■ ■ ■

1 June, 2018

Choosing a Word

I've got a funny request for you today, not least because I can't tell you why I'm asking. I need to choose a word that sums up how I feel about being a transplanted organ recipient.

I want to get away from gratitude. Not because (as I hope you know) I'm not grateful, but because it's a bit more complicated than that.

And — I've been spending a bit of time lately reading *Romeo and Juliet.*

So I've chosen three words from the play that I think are appropriate to life-after-transplant:

Torchbearer: I'm one of the first generation to survive Hypoplastic Left Heart Syndrome (HLHS to its friends). If I'd been born a few years earlier, then my mother would have watched me die. There were no other options. I'm a symbol. I'm a sign of what's possible. I'm lighting the way, not by anything I'm doing, just by the fact of my continued existence. I'm walking forward into the dark.

Cherishing: This is a great word, is it not? Sometimes I wake up in the morning and I lie there for a minute and I think of Apple, as though she's a treasure I've been given, and I've wrapped her up and put her in the safest place I can. (As anyone who's had their ribcage opened will tell you, it's really not designed for that. It tells you so, afterwards, in no uncertain terms.)

Fortune: You know the reason for this one. I'm not alive because I deserve to be or because I've passed a test or because there's some divine something looking out for me. (Feel free to think that there is, if that suits you. I prefer to think I'm here because of a fluke to some all-powerful being choosing me over someone else.) I'm alive because of a happy-for-me co-incidence of blood group, ill-enough-but-not-too-ill, and someone else's death. Each of those three factors has so many variables. Luck/chance/fortune: it's the reason for the blood being pumped around my body right now.

Here's the vote. I'm going to give you until Wednesday.

TORCHBEARER
CHERISHING
FORTUNE

5 shares
15 comments

Results:
TORCHBEARER 65%
CHERISHING 25%
FORTUNE 10%

1 JUNE, 2017

This Time Last Year

'Could you begin by telling me why you're here, Ailsa?'

'My mum thought it would be a good idea.'

'Is that the only reason?'

'Yes. No.' Being talked into going to a counsellor has brought out Ailsa's inner fifteen-year-old — the one she was never really allowed to be, because she always had to be looking after her heart. 'I'm not coping very well.'

'With what?'

A shrug. 'I don't know. Waiting for a heart. Missing someone.'

A nod, a soft smile that makes Ailsa feel as though she's already given one of the correct answers. Oh, how she doesn't want to be here.

'Who is it that you miss, Ailsa?'

Ailsa looks at the woman sitting across

from her — kind-faced, calm and ready to help — and she wants to try. But there seems to be no way to talk about Lennox now. After the first flurry of desperate sharing, the memories and the talking about him, as though she and his family had to create him and preserve them in their words, Ailsa feels as though just saying his name will break her in two. And what will be exposed, then, is uglier than her failing malformed heart: a tarred clump of sadness and frustration that he's not there; fury with him for leaving her to face his death, her death alone; the sick, black envy that it's all over for him now, and that he's cheated her by leaving her behind. She cannot let this out of her. Not yet.

'I can't,' she gets out, something strangled-sounding, but the counsellor seems to understand.

'If you don't feel up to talking,' she says, 'I'm going to suggest that maybe you write something down. A letter to yourself. Say, Ailsa this time next year — what would she say to you? Or what would you say to that Ailsa?'

Ailsa takes the paper and pen. To start with, looking at the blankness is just as bad as looking at her mother's anxious face. A year from now isn't really something she can think about — she'll be either dead, or a version of herself that's inconceivable now — but she could perhaps help tomorrow's Ailsa out. It's not what she's supposed to do, but as her mother says, she's done with giving a fuck.

Dear Ailsa,
Remember, if you die, at least it will stop hurting. At least it will stop.

Love,
Ailsa

9 JUNE, 2018

It's photoshoot day.

Which means it's three weeks since she saw Seb, a fortnight since the article that made her lie awake hating her body, even though to do so was a betrayal of her heart.

Three days ago, Ailsa received an email from Libby, asking her to arrive before three with freshly washed hair and without makeup, and instructing her to bring clothes that were neither black nor 'excessively patterned'. She would be made up, photographed, then interviewed, providing material in readiness for the launch of the calendar and campaign. She'd had a week's notice of the questions for the interview; she'd practised her answers with Hayley last weekend. Living apart from each other is hard, and they're adapting. That's what Emily says they're doing, anyway. To Ailsa it feels like non-stop wrong-footedness: she's always waiting for her mother to come home. It's a kind of diluted grief. Which it shouldn't be, because she's got what she wants.

Lucy answers the door and leads Ailsa through the house, stage-whisper voice trailing over her shoulder as she goes. 'Mum thought this might be a bit much for her, so she and Dad have taken Louisa to the zoo. We're doing OK. Libby's finishing off the interview with the liver. Come and meet Jules; she's waiting to do the kidney. You're after that.'

The shoot is taking place next to Lennox's tree, which is flanked by reflectors; there's a tripod in front of it, unattended for the moment, ungainly and purposeless on the lawn. The photographer is standing with her back to them, hunched, apparently headless. When she hears Lucy and Ailsa, she turns, smiles, holds up the camera she's been looking at.

'We've got some nice shots here.' Then, registering that she's looking at Lucy and not Libby, 'Oh, sorry.'

'No problem,' Lucy says. 'This is Ailsa. The heart.'

'Hi,' Ailsa says. 'The rest of me is my own.'

'Hello!' One stride, two, a handshake, and then Ailsa is being scrutinised. 'I'm Jules. You've great skin. We won't have any problems with you. What did you bring to wear?'

'These,' Ailsa says, opening the bag she's folded her clothes into. Libby's guidelines had ruled out her new dress. (She's become perversely fond of the yellow roses.) Instead, she's wearing jeans and a T-shirt with a heart-shaped cloud motif on it. In her bag she has a Breton-striped sweater that's a bit too big now — but if she has to hold up her word in front of her it won't matter — and the purple-striped blouse that Hayley chose for her before they went to London. Tamsin had not only sewn on a press-stud to make sure that the top of Ailsa's scar was covered, but also replaced the original white buttons with vintage pewter ones, in the shapes of tiny butterflies and hearts.

Jules looks her over, noticing her earrings, which are blue ceramic heart studs. 'I like those — very witty.'

'Thanks,' Ailsa says. Jules must have read her blog, to understand the significance. She feels herself relax, a bit.

'Do you want to keep your glasses on?'

'Why?'

'No reason,' Jules says, 'except that some people don't. It depends on if you think of them as you. They're great.'

'Thanks,' Ailsa says, and then, 'yes, I think they're me.'

'Fine. Let's go with this,' Jules says, holding up the striped shirt, 'and tell Pip — ah, no, I'll tell her myself.' Jules heads for the house, Lucy and Ailsa behind her. An anxious-looking man in a dark grey shirt smiles shyly at Ailsa as they pass in the kitchen. Lucy tells him it's time for his photographs and takes him out to the garden.

The dining table is covered with make-up, pots and pots of colours, each one working through every version of itself: blues from navy to the transparent tint of a drop of rain, pinks that start at blazing sunset and move to the memory of a blush. An older woman — bare-faced, big-smiled, hair tied back behind a purple bandanna — is waiting.

'Here's Ailsa,' Jules says. 'I'd like her really natural, very little around the eyes, lips something around' — she scans the table in front of her, picks a lipstick — 'this. Hair down. She's wearing her glasses.'

'Your wish is my command,' Pip says, making a kiss with her mouth. Jules laughs, and Ailsa thinks: Everyone has someone. Except me. And my mother, who doesn't want anyone.

Having her hair and make-up done is an intimate-not-intimate feeling, like a medical examination: touch with concentration, without eye-contact, without feeling. Breathe. The room is quiet, the heat from the rollers and the steam from the iron, where Lucy is pressing her shirt, reassuring.

Propped on the sideboard is a piece of board, about three feet by fifteen inches, the word 'torchbearer' scribed on it in a bold lower-case script, the vertical strokes thick and strong, the curves moving from fine to broad and back again, like the beginnings and endings of gusts of wind. Just looking at it makes Apple beat louder, and Ailsa feel like crying. She thinks about Juliet's words, as she prepares to part from Romeo after their wedding night, denying that the sun is the sun: 'It is some meteor that the sun exhales/To be to thee this night a torchbearer'. When she'd blogged about this she'd struggled to express how it made her feel, and ended up with something half right, half true. She is not brave or blessed, just the person who happens to be showing the way.

Twenty minutes later, Ailsa is made up and outside, in front of the camera. It would feel odd, but she has her word for protection, and Lennox's tree makes a safe shelter. So she can manage. She can. If Apple does her bit, she can take care of the rest.

Jules doesn't ask her to pose, apart from directing her in the way she holds the word: 'It's not a shield. Drop your arms a bit, that's it, and don't hold it tight, just balance the bottom corners between your fingers. Let your shoulders take the weight, let them be pulled down.' Once she's comfortable, Jules keeps her moving: 'Do you see there's an apple coming, just above you? Can you look towards the kitchen window, lovely? Now can you take a look at the toes of my boots? Grand. And over my left shoulder?'

She's just starting to feel cold in her feet and tired in her arms, when Seb appears on the back step, sunglasses on, a trilby on his head. He holds up his word — 'Revived' — and Ailsa recognises it as belonging to Romeo, although she's not sure where from. He kisses his fingers, waves them at her, and she laughs at the sight of him, at how foolish she has been to be churning over all that didn't happen that night after the tango club. Seb is just Seb. She is just Ailsa. She's been thinking about the five seconds where it went wrong, and had forgotten everything else. Although she hasn't forgotten Lennox; can't. She loses her balance, puts her hand out to the trunk to steady herself.

Jules says, 'I think we're done. Here, look.' Ailsa braces herself for the photos, but she didn't brace hard enough. Jules scrolls through the images she's taken — laughing, looking up, looking away — and Ailsa feels a rush and glut of anxiety. She didn't realise the lipstick was red. And not any red: the carmine of transfusing blood, on a day when there's nothing to do but watch it flow, and hope, even though there's hardly any point in hoping anymore. Oh, Lennox.

'I look really different,' she gets out.

Jules's hand is on her back. 'OK? This has got to be a bit emotional.'

She nods and excuses herself, goes to the downstairs loo and scrubs her mouth clean, before she goes to do her filmed interview. If Libby notices that her lipstick has gone, she doesn't comment.

9 JUNE, 2018

Ailsa's hair smells unfamiliar to her, hairspray-scent in her nostrils when she moves her head. Seb turned up to the photoshoot in a plum, peach and silver-grey paisley-patterned shirt, in glorious disregard of Libby's rules, and even though he does, presumably, have other clothes in the overnight bag at his feet, no one asked him to change. They are eating olives, waiting for salads. Looking at each other. The Northbridge Brasserie has, it seems, become their bar.

There's a bottle of wine on the table. Seb ordered it — it's Sancerre, his favourite wine and something that Ailsa has developed a taste for. Water first, though.

'What's new?' Seb asks.

'Well, we did ganchos at tango this week,' she says. 'That was fun.'

Seb winces. 'In theory. It's a bit nerveracking when you've got a three-inch stiletto flying at your crotch.'

'Like I said . . .' They look at each other, properly, for a moment; even with the sunglasses, Ailsa feels the intensity of the look. She's back in the bar on their last night in London, stepping out onto the dance floor, feeling Seb's hand on the small of her back. She wouldn't say she's smiling at the memory. It's more that the corner of her mouth is moving upwards at the taste of lust and shared memories.

Seb laughs. 'We'll agree to differ,' he says. 'I like your hair.'

'Oh, Pip did it,' Ailsa says. She'd thought it might have been straightened for the shoot. Its natural wave is neither curl nor straight, and means if it's not tied back it looks as though she doesn't care what she looks like. But heated rollers have made soft, deliberate waves.

'It's nice,' Seb says. 'I hate how everyone straightens their hair. They all look the same.'

'I can't tell men with beards apart, either.'

Seb laughs. 'And this is why I miss you,' he says. 'You're like a moral compass. But fun. I did not mean that all women look the same. I meant to say that — like men with beards — it's like a uniform. Which is unhelpful. In telling people apart.'

330

The thought of Seb missing her gave her a flare of happiness; being a moral compass extinguished it. Plus, she's annoyed with herself for caring. She has more important things to think about.

'So, I can make a decent espresso, according to my manager,' she says. 'It's not as easy as it looks.'

Seb laughs. 'I've drunk some awful coffee. I believe you. Are you enjoying it?'

'I think so. I like being with people and — I've never earned money before.' She offers the heel of her left hand for inspection. There's a welt where she caught it in the steam, when she was making tea. He takes her hand in both of his, inspects, and for a moment it seems that he will kiss it. Ailsa holds her breath and at the same time tells herself off. If she didn't know otherwise she'd think Apple's last owner was fifteen.

'Ouch,' he says, and lets go.

'I know,' Ailsa says. 'I won't show you my blisters.' It's tiring, being on her feet, of course, but the time flies past, and the steps rack up — an easy three thousand an hour. Getting home, taking a bath, she feels as though she's achieved something. And she's sleeping better. She used to be afraid that she was depressed. Now she thinks she might have been bored.

'You look well on it, though. Are they new glasses?'

'No, same ones.'

'Thinner face, then.'

Ailsa still likes this non-judgemental way Seb has, of talking about the physical.

'I'm getting there,' she says. 'It was good of you to come up.'

He shrugs. 'I wanted to see you. And to help with this calendar thing. And I told Roz I was coming up, so we're meeting Juliet tomorrow.'

'Three birds with one stone.'

Seb laughs. 'Meredith is flying back from somewhere in Europe. She's been filming some — I'm saying perfume ads, not with much conviction — some sort of ads. Roz talked her into flying into Edinburgh. We're meeting her for lunch then she and I are taking the train back to London.'

'Right.' Roz, Ailsa thinks, would be a good person to be shipwrecked with.

Seb adds, 'Meredith used to be in a TV show . . .'

'I know who she is,' Ailsa says.

Seb grins. 'Really? That's offensive. If you didn't know who I was — you should be consistent.' And then he opens the overnight bag that he tucked between his chair and the wall when they came in. 'I brought you something.' He pulls out a parcel, in silver paper with gold and purple ribbon hanging from it, big enough to be held in both hands. He puts it on his lap, pulls at the ribbon in a way that reminds Ailsa of Pip, teasing out her hair when the rollers were removed. 'It's all got a bit squashed. I had it wrapped in the shop. The ribbon was,' groping for the word, 'ringlets. A sort of waterfall of ringlets. Camp as you like.' He hands it across to her.

'Wow,' Ailsa says, 'that is a lot of ribbon.' She's not used to receiving gifts, unless they are of the basket-of-fruit or get-well-chocolate variety. She balances this one at the space to the right of her cutlery, but Seb flinches.

'Not on the table,' he says. Then, 'You'll see.'

Ailsa pushes back her chair so there's room on her lap for the box: it's shoebox-sized.

The ribbons are tight and the edges of the paper taped down with precision and force. In the end, Seb takes a Swiss army knife from his pocket and runs the blade around the slackening waist of paper where the lid fits the box beneath.

'There you go,' he says.

Ailsa takes off the lid. Black tissue paper,

333

and inside it, tango shoes. They are patent, black with an ankle strap, a closed toe, tiny silver buckles, silver-coloured crystals scattered across the top of the foot. She turns them over. Smooth leather sole. Heels maybe a half inch lower than Fenella's. Ailsa has never been much of a shoe person, but these she can appreciate.

'Well?' Seb says. 'What do you think?'

Ailsa exhales slowly, looks over at him. 'They're lovely.'

He smiles. 'Just don't gancho some poor bastard with them. They should fit — I took Fenella's to the shop, said I thought you'd want something not so high, and a bit wider. I saw the look of relief on your face when you took them off.'

'I know what tango shoes cost, Seb. I've been looking. I can't accept these. It's too much.' Since she's left London she's been telling herself that she and Seb are just — passing. He's like the best kind of doctor, the one that makes you feel that you, Ailsa, and your trying, failing heart, are the only reason she/he went through years of training. Of all the hearts that they will ever see in their career, their consultations seem to suggest, yours is the most interesting, the most important. And then, when that doctor moves on, to a new rotation or a different post, or another hospital, your sense of loss is out of all proportion because you thought you were special. And some other ailing patient is feeling that theirs is the broken heart that this doctor has been searching for all of their professional life.

'Try them on,' he says, as though she hadn't spoken. This ought to be annoying. Actually, it is.

'I've got trainers on,' she says.

Seb's eyebrows arch, and he says, 'I'm rolling my eyes behind here. I didn't think you were barefoot. Try them! No one's looking.'

Ailsa is minded to refuse — no one gets to tell her what to do with her feet — but there's a naughtiness to Seb's suggestion that reminds her of her and Lennox in the hospital garden in the dark, when visiting hours were technically over and he should have been in bed. She pushes her left trainer off, from the heel, with the toe of the right one. She slips off her sock, puts the shoebox on the floor and pulls out the left shoe. She's afraid her feet might stick, but actually —

'Does it fit?'

Ailsa smiles and raises a leg so he can see it. 'Like a glove. For feet.' She takes the shoe off and rewraps it in the tissue. She's about to pick the box up, then remembering, asks, 'Why not on the table?'

'Shoes on the table is bad luck,' Seb says, matter-of-factly. And then, 'This is a thank-you. If it makes you feel better, the ladies at the dance shop I go to do me all sorts of deals, because I got my *StarDance* kit from there, and I did selfies with them and generally bigged them up all over social media.'

'Did they wrap them up for you?'

'They did,' Seb says, 'though I resent your implication that I couldn't have made my own ribbon ringlet waterfall, if I'd wanted to.'

Ailsa laughs. 'I would not doubt that for a minute. Thank you.'

'No worries,' Seb says. Then, 'You're great to dance with. Plus, with the show coming up, I can't have your footwear making me look bad.' The sexy-cute-flirtiness of his smile is so deliberate that Ailsa feels sick at the thought she has ever lost sleep over Seb. He's impulse-bought some tango shoes and sent a couple of emails. She needs to get a grip. 'How's it going, anyway?' he asks. 'The tango classes, I mean? Apart from the ganchos?'

'It's good. And at the beginning of dance class every week we make a circle and Edie says, "What is this about?" and we shout,

336

"Make Sebastian Morley look great!" and we all clap and cheer.'

'Really?'

'No. Idiot.'

'I knew that,' Seb says, 'you just couldn't see my eyes. Look.' He pulls up the sunglasses, pulls a face. He's OK, when he's not acting.

Here's the food: two chicken salads, a side of chunky chips to share. Ailsa picks out the croutons and lies them on the side of her plate. She can't be bothered to remove the flakes of parmesan, and, not having eaten it for so long, the tang on her tongue is sharp, salty, sweet, too good to exclude. Her fridge-freezer these days is a virtuous place, full of nut milks and vegetables, dark chocolate that she has broken into chunks and wrapped, individually, in cling film. She has frozen spinach and berries for smoothies, avocados to make lunchtimes interesting.

Ah, but this cheese. There's not a lot of it and it's worth the extra thousand steps she's going to walk tomorrow to compensate for eating it.

'I liked your word,' Seb says.

'Sorry?' She was miles away, as her mother would say. In a place where looking at a photograph of herself wouldn't make her blink and wonder if that's what she really looks like. Or where the sight of red lipstick, bright and beautiful on her pink-cream skin, bringing out the blue of her eyes and the gold in her hair, wouldn't make her shaky.

'I liked your word. Torchbearer. To light me on my way to Mantua.'

'I liked yours. I knew it was Romeo, but I couldn't place it.'

' "I dreamt my lady came and found me dead — /Strange dream to give a dead man leave to think!" '

Ailsa nods. 'Of course. "And breathed such life with kisses in my lips,/That I revived and was an emperor." '

'Precisely,' Seb says. 'I'm glad you like it. It took me ages to find something.' A pause. 'I chose it myself,' he adds.

'I chose my options,' she says. 'I picked three I would be happy with.'

'Fair point,' and his face goes from serious, to smiling, to serious again, 'I suppose. But — don't you think it's a bit weird?'

'What?'

'Not making your own decisions? And doesn't it make your "torchbearer" not so . . . not so meaningful?'

'Have you been talking to my mother? You sound just like her.'

Seb laughs. 'I know what you're saying.

It's none of my business.'

He sounds so un-offended that she says more. 'I feel a little bit adrift, sometimes. I like the wisdom of strangers.'

'But no one knows you as well as you, surely?'

Ailsa thinks about the feeling of being a body out of time and place, an uncertain host. It's insignificant to doctors and would be puzzling to the people who love her and thought they might lose her. She's well. And she must never say anything to suggest that she isn't Lucky. Capital L.

'Honestly? Not this me. I knew ill me pretty well.'

Seb nods. 'I suppose it's like getting famous. Before and after.'

'Yes,' Ailsa says, 'before and after.'

Seb says, 'I was thinking about us on the way up. Radio, tango, photo. All the Os. We've made a Venn diagram for ourselves. Of ourselves.'

'You're very philosophical tonight,' Ailsa says. She's thinking of the two of them, circled and circled and circled.

'It must be all the Shakespeare.'

The waitress clears the plates. Seb might be watching the waitress walk away. There's no reason why he shouldn't. When she's gone, he asks, 'Are you OK? Really?'

'Yes,' Ailsa says, because for so many years, being like this — sitting in a bar, not too tired, not ill — was her living definition of OK. But then she thinks of all the things that are making her not OK. A moment passes, another. Seb is checking his phone.

'No. Not really.'

'Not really what?'

'Not really OK.'

Seb nods, takes a drink. The lights are lower — it's just passed seven o'clock, so it must officially be evening — and he takes off his sunglasses, blinks cautiously once, twice, lays them on the table. 'Why not? What's wrong? Is it still that *Sun* business?'

'No, it isn't. Well . . .' Ailsa thinks about how often she thinks about it. Which is every time she goes to the fridge, where she's stuck the article to curb her appetite. 'No. It's not that. I mean — it's been on my mind more than I'd like to admit. But — no.'

She thinks about all that's not wrong, exactly, but unsettling. The memory of Lennox, made greater by being around the people who will never be able to put his loss behind them. The things that only she knew, and that she can never speak about: Lennox crying, late one night, when he knew that it was too late for a transplant and all there was to do now was die, and how they'd talked about suicide and how they could contrive it.

Then there's the retrospective stress of the photoshoot: how tired she is now, by all of the attention, the pushed-and-pulled feeling of it. The lipstick. Having to give ninety-second answers to questions like: 'What does your transplant mean to you?' and 'What's your message to anyone who isn't on the donor register?'. Plus, she's thinking about the last time she saw Seb, and the way it felt to dance with him: the solid heft of what happened/didn't happen afterwards is buckled around her, biting into the skin at her waist. She's not sure what she wants to tell him or where to start with it all.

But New Ailsa, with her coffee-shop job and her possible legal career and her bravely beating heart, needs to say something, because shutting herself off isn't the life she is planning to have. She thinks about one of those consultants who made her feel that her heart was the beating/failing heart of the universe. He would come into her room, sit down on the end of her bed (he was the only one who did that, and it was against the rules, but he didn't seem to care and neither did she) and simply say, 'OK. Start anywhere, Ailsa.'

Start anywhere.

'You know Lennox and I were close?' she says.

'I'd gathered that,' Seb says. 'I assumed you were a couple?'

'Yes. No. He was my first boyfriend. We split up not long after we went to uni. We kept in touch. Then when he was back here, and ill, and I was ill, we sort of got together again. But not — not physically.'

He is looking at her, waiting, face serious. Start anywhere. Start somewhere else, maybe.

'When Lennox died it was the most horrible time of my life. I'd have died if I could. It was — I was crushed by it. I was really ill. But I didn't know which pain was which — grief or my body shutting down.' Just remembering brings back an echo of the pain, a shadow through her body, Apple turning her volume down in respect. 'Then I had my heart transplant. I've got — I've got scars, a big cut down my chest.' She puts her finger at the top of it, an inch below her clavicle, just below where the first button covers the press-stud at the top of her shirt. Her other hand goes to the bottom of the scar, three inches above her navel, although it's hidden from Seb's view by the table. 'And no one's ever seen the — the damage.

From the transplant. Except — except doctors. Nurses. My mother.'

'You're telling me that you haven't —'

'Yes. So that night when we went out, and you sort of — assumed — and I could see why you would, but I just — I panicked.' Ailsa thinks of all the people, everywhere, having sex and fucking, making love and shagging, without thought or analysis, — or conversations like this. She knows she's not the only person carrying a scar, of course. 'I'm being ridiculous.'

But now Seb's hand is reaching for hers across the table. She slides her palm against his and their fingers interlace. 'It's not ridiculous, Ailsa. Not at all.'

She looks at him, waiting. She can tell that he's thinking, recognising his expression from their two weeks of line-learning. The closeness in the memory seems to change something in the air between them, because he squeezes her hand and smiles before he speaks.

'I want to make sure that I'm clear. You're telling me that you haven't had sex in' — he tilts his head at her, an invitation to put a number on it, months, or years, but she decides not to — 'a while, and so when it seemed to be on the agenda, and I can tell you you were right, it was very high on my agenda, you . . .' The hand that isn't joined with hers holds the palm up, an explain-to-me gesture, and maybe it's the fact that it's him, or that after this afternoon, stand-ing under the apple tree, thinking-not-thinking of Lennox and wearing red lipstick, anything is easy, but she opens her mouth and this time the words are all there, unedited and ready, and they spill into the air.

'I wanted to, but I — I don't know, I re-alised I didn't know the rules, or whether I should say anything, and I didn't know what you were expecting from me, and,' she laughs, but the sound that comes out is too high for her, the sort of laugh that would make her mother put an arm around her and say, steady on, hen, 'if I'm honest, you know' — she gestures up and down with her free hand, taking him in — 'you. I know I didn't know who you were to start with, but I googled you, and there it all is, arse of the century, and all your models and what have you, and — well, I couldn't see how it wouldn't go really, really wrong. It seemed — ambitious. For the first time in — a while. Like having your first riding lesson on a — a racehorse.' Seb's face is a picture: amusement, bemusement, an attempt at seriousness, something like horror. Ailsa takes her hand back from his and lets her temples rest, heavy, on the bases of her thumbs. Her hair falls forward, spilling that hairspray scent again. 'I'm going to stop talking now,' she says. 'Make me stop. Please make me stop.'

Seb laughs, low and warm. 'Wow. OK. Just — you're going to have to give me a minute. Here, have a drink.' He's waving her glass of wine around under her nose. 'Drink me, Ailsa, drink me.'

She laughs too, a calmer sound now, takes the glass, takes a sip. Well, it's more of a gulp, but who's measuring, under the circumstances. She looks at him, waits. He puts his glass down, sets his palms flat on the table, rocks back on his chair, something that must take a bit of effort because these chairs are solid velvet buckets of things, not light. He looks straight at her.

'Well, first of all, it was Rear of the Year, and that was in 2014, and it's all gone to hell back there since, anyway. Second, you shouldn't believe all you read in the papers, about models and whatever. People think because you're in the same photo, you're sharing a bed, and it's just not true, most of the time. Third, as we're going to be spending a bit of time together come August, I think it best that I take the racehorse thing as a compliment. Especially from a unicorn.'

'Thank you.'

'Don't mention it.' Seb returns all four legs of his chair to the ground and leans over the table, beckons, smiling. Ailsa leans in, close enough to smell wine, something musky on his skin that makes her think of his bathroom in London, the line of Molten Brown bottles at the edge of the bath. He kisses her, gently, on the forehead, then he takes her glasses off, presses a kiss to the bridge of her nose, and puts her glasses on again. Then he sits back.

'How long since Lennox died?'

'Just over a year.'

'And how long were the two of you' — he considers — 'together-not-together?'

'About a year before that.'

'And how long —'

Ailsa can't stand it anymore. 'It's two and a half years since I had sex, OK?' And that had been a bit of a write-off, an exercise in proving to herself that she wasn't too unwell or too tired. It had been Marcus, who she had studied with sometimes, mainly because the two of them were taking all of the same courses. He was back in Edinburgh for a friend's wedding and had sent her a message, they'd gone for a drink, he'd walked her home, she'd asked him in and, well, hadn't exactly thrown herself at him, but not far off. When she'd woken in the morning he was gone. And there had been an eight-month dry spell before that. Seb doesn't need to know these things. He's looking incredulous as it is.

'OK.' Seb rocks back again. 'Jesus.' He looks into his lap, as though he's discussing the prospect of no sex for two-and-a-half years with his genitals. Looks up. 'Little Seb and I are having a bit of trouble computing that.'

A blush hurtles up Ailsa's neck, across her cheeks. Seb laughs. 'Arse,' she says.

'I'm sorry,' he says.

'You're not sorry,' she says.

'No. Not really. But you shouldn't believe all you read about — people like me. My last thing was with Fenella, and shagging your partner is more or less mandatory on *StarDance*. It wasn't serious.'

'Um — thanks.' Ailsa picks through his words, trying to work out whether this was meant to make her feel better and, if so, how.

'No worries.' They look at each other across the table. There's a directness here, an honesty; Ailsa hasn't felt it since she and Lennox used to talk about everything, their real lives and their hypothetical ones. Maybe this is just normal for relationships.

'Something springs to mind,' Seb says, and as she looks at him she sees what's coming, feels it in her belly, at the back of her throat, 'and that is — you've got a bit of catching up to do. And if the reasons you sent me home that night were really what you say . . .'

'They were,' she says. 'I'm not going to admit to something that embarrassing otherwise, am I? If there was any other explanation, believe me, I'd have told you.'

'Fair point. So, as I've understood things correctly, you would have invited me to come up, if it wasn't for the scar. I mean, it wasn't me.'

'No, Seb. It wasn't you.'

'Don't roll your eyes. Even former rears of the year have feelings, you know.'

'I'm sorry.' Ailsa makes her face a parody of seriousness, lips pursed, eyebrows low, and he laughs. 'It wasn't you.' Now that she knows where this conversation is going, she's desperate for them to say it: to make it real.

'In that case, would you like to — have another go? We could go back to your place, I could ask if I could come in, and you could say yes, and we could see how it went?'

'Yes,' Ailsa says. Her mouth has gone dry.

'We can just — take it easy,' Seb says, 'see what happens.'

'Yes.' A bit clearer, more confident, this time.

He smiles. 'Unfold the imagined happiness,' he says.

From: Seb
Sent: 10 June, 2018
To: Ailsa
Subject: Morning After

Hey BlueHeart,
I might need to call you PinkCheeks from now on. You're very pretty when you're . . . happy.
Thanks for a fun night. See you soon. Take care

Seb x

From: Ailsa
To: Seb

Hello,
Thank you for a fun night too. And thank you for my shoes. I tried them on properly after you left this morning, and did a bit of solo pivoting. They really are perfect.
How was Juliet? Shouldn't you be with her now?

Ailsa

From: Seb
To: Ailsa

Solo pivoting? You're insatiable.

350

Juliet/Meredith is asleep on the train. See pic. Or maybe feigning sleep, but that's the trouble with actors. You can't trust them. She is snoring, though, and it sounds pretty authentic.

She didn't give me a lot to work with during the reading we did, and was quite quiet over lunch, but Roz never stops talking so I was probably quiet as well. I think we were supposed to chat/bond on the way back to London, but she was asleep before we crossed the border.

Roz gave me a thumbs-up at the end of the reading, so I think we'll call that a result. She doesn't get her thumbs out for just anyone. I think I managed to look like I was reading. Just focussing on the page numbers kills my eyes. You saved me. We did a bit of vaulty heavens and I aced it. Not faulty, not vaulted. Praise me.

S x

From: Ailsa
To: Seb

Well Done You.

I expect Juliet was disappointed with your rear. It's all gone a bit downhill since you won that award, hasn't it? Did she get the thumbs? If not, she might be offended.

Seriously, the sunglasses thing is a little bit off-putting at first. Even when you know the reason for it — it's really hard to have a meaningful conversation with someone when you can't see their eyes. I know you know that, but I think you're maybe so used to wearing your shades now that you forget that other people are having to deal with them.

Ailsa

P.S. It's very rude to take photos of people while they're sleeping. Although Juliet looks like a (snoring) goddess, so she probably won't mind.

From: Seb
To: Ailsa

We both got thumbs. I was trying to impress you by leaving Juliet's thumbs out. I'm a terrible person.

You're right about the glasses. Our evening definitely picked up when I took them off.

Now I come to think of it, Meredith went quiet after Roz got into how we were really too old for the parts, with

Romeo and Juliet being teenagers. Not that teenagers were invented. But she talked a bit about 'recapturing gaucheness'. I don't think Meredith liked it much. She must be twenty-five or twenty-six, which is as good as dead for a lot of pretty actors/actresses. Roz says we need to reconnect with our younger selves. When I was sixteen I caught genital warts at a bus stop. I don't think I'm prepared to go that far.

From: Ailsa
To: Seb

Well, I've never got thumbs from Roz, so I'm still impressed. I've never caught genital warts at a bus stop either.

You're talking to the wrong person if you want sympathy because you're getting older . . . I've been as good as dead for most of my life. Bring on the being too old for things, I say.

From: Seb
To: Ailsa

Oh, God, Ailsa, I'm sorry. That was tactless.

Have I upset you? I really didn't mean to.

From: Ailsa
To: Seb

If I had a pound for every time I was asked to join in a general moan about being old, I'd have an awful lot of pounds. I'm not offended at all. I was trying to be jokey. I forget that if you haven't spent a lot of time around hopeful transplantees you develop a sense of humour that might look macabre to The Normals.

At ease.

From: Seb
To: Ailsa

Thank you.

We need a safe word. As in — this is a joke. For email purposes. (Vegan unicorn?)

You seem so well to me. When I think about you, I think of dancing and the way you always have almonds in your bag. And blue eyes. And cleverness. The way you say arse. Nothing to do with dying.

From: Ailsa
To: Seb

That's lovely. Thank you.
  I'm to Glasgow now to see my mother.
Take care.

A

Edinburgh Journal

14 June, 2018

Edinburgh Dancers Take Centre Stage

Well-known Edinburgh dancers Edie and Eliza Gardiner — known as 'The Tango Sisters' — are adding to their showbiz CV at the Edinburgh Festival Fringe this year.

The dancers run tango classes and events throughout the region, and have also appeared in films and TV shows with their dance partners Guy Peart and Simeon Graveney. They've made a point of remaining in Edinburgh, though, saying it's the city that supported them through their early career.

This year, in a new direction for them, they will be providing supporting cast for the production of *Romeo and Juliet,* starring Sebastian Morley and Meredith Katz, already hotly tipped as a Festival Fringe highlight.

'We're really excited,' Eliza says. 'We're always looking for opportunities to introduce tango to a wider world. We didn't get to see Seb tango on *StarDance* last year but we're going to see it now!'

The supporting cast will be made up of

regular learners from classes in Edinburgh, who range in age from their early twenties to mid-seventies.

The show, at the Dragon's Nest pub in Minto Street in Newington, is expected to sell out, not least because members of the cast will join audience members for an informal tango session after the show. Only dancers already registered with The Tango Sisters will be eligible to take part in the production.

From: Seb
Sent: 14 June, 2018
To: Ailsa
Subject: Embra

Hello, BlueHeart,

Well, we made the Edinburgh Journal! I was going to pretend Roz sent me the cutting but I've got a Google alert set on my name. (I feel as though we should have ultimate honesty now that we've — you know. Read Romeo and Juliet together.)

What's new in your world? Are you onto macchiato yet? If not, don't worry about it. It's a stupid drink. Have a coffee or have a hot chocolate. Or have both, one after the other.

What else is going on?

I'm coming up next weekend. We're having a read-through. Meredith is in Edinburgh doing something the day before, so Roz is taking advantage and introducing everyone. Then Roz is coming down to London to do some intensive work with me and Meredith. Do you want to meet up? I'd love to see you. I can book a hotel.

Seb x

From: Ailsa
To: Seb

Hello, Seb,
It makes it all seem very close, doesn't it?

What's new? Not a lot. Except I know the difference between a mochaccino and a macchiato. (Vegan unicorn.) Everything's pretty quiet. I've made a couple of appointments to find out more about the legal conversion course I've been looking at. The more I think about it, the more I want to do it. We're all supposed to accept that life's not fair but I think I could do something to make it fairer. Apple might have come from someone who worked with the law — she seems pretty keen, and jumps up and down in my chest every time I think about the people who need someone to be on their side, especially when it comes to health. Organ donation, living wills, assisted suicide — they are all places where people need advocacy.

My doctors are happy. We're tweaking the medication down another notch. So it's all good, I suppose, in an everyday sort of way.

It's still a bit weird with my mother

not here. I really miss her sometimes, and then I see her and we end up bickering. I got annoyed with her for calling you 'This Seb', as in: 'I see This Seb is going to be in Edinburgh'. Afterwards I thought, I should have just left it.

I thought (if I'd thought) that if you were rehearsing, you'd just all do it together, for a few weeks beforehand. Still, I also used to think coffee was coffee, and dancing was dancing.

I'm off next Saturday. It would be lovely to catch up — let me know what time your train gets in and I can meet you. And you're welcome to stay. But thank you for not assuming.

Ailsa x

From: Seb
To: Ailsa

You get more ordinary as the days go by, BlueHeart. Congratulations. I'm really pleased for you.

I can see you standing up for people. You were fierce with me when I was slacking. One day what I'll be most famous for is knowing you. I'll sell these emails for millions.

If you're being paid to do an acting

job, yeah, it's usually all in one go, and you do as you're told. If you're not — it's a bit more like the director is Bulgaria, and the actors are — well, all countries with more influence than Bulgaria. The stars can choose to behave like Russia if they want to. Roz is doing the best she can with people's free time. I'm doing my best to fit in.

From: Ailsa
To: Seb

Say no more. I'll see you on Saturday. X

23 June, 2018

'Well hello, BlueHeart.' Seb is one of the first travellers off the train on this fine June day. Once he spots her it seems that he's next to her in two strides. He puts down his bag and pulls her in to him, his arms around her waist, his nose in her hair. She's put her hands around his neck, her face against his chest. He's in the denim jacket he wore for *Hello Saturday;* the button presses into her cheek, and her glasses squash the side of her face, but she doesn't care.

Ailsa had wondered, as she walked to the station, quite how things would be when she saw Seb again. He's been upfront about the sex in their emails, so it wasn't as though they were pretending it hadn't happened, or that it had been a mistake. But there had also been nothing to suggest that it was more than a one-off. Although even if it was, it was worth it, just for the moment when he took a look at the scar, ran his

362

finger over it, said, 'I've seen worse tattoos, if I'm honest, BlueHeart.' And then kissed it, from top to bottom and back to the top again.

And then he kisses her forehead, and then her cheeks, the way celebrities kiss each other on chat shows, and then the tips of their noses touch, pivot, and then — yes, there's his mouth, on hers. Although Ailsa had thought she remembers everything about that night, there's a sudden hot pulse of visceral memory, and the bump of Apple in her chest. Thinking about Seb and being with Seb is the difference between thinking about the sea and standing on the tide line.

He looks around, up and behind him. 'This place has too many exits. Lead the way.'

'Right.' And they're off, heading through pedestrians, up the escalator and across the walkway.

He stops at the Sir Walter Scott quotes on the glass panels that decorate this part of the station, smiles and puts his arm around her shoulder. 'Romantic soul, wasn't he?'

The panel he is looking at reads: 'Scarce one person out of twenty marries his first love, and scarce one out of twenty of the remainder has cause to rejoice at doing so.'

'Well, Romeo and Juliet wouldn't argue,'

Ailsa says.

Seb turns to the next panel and reads, ' "To enjoy leisure it is absolutely necessary it should be preceded by occupation." '

'That's true enough.' Ailsa thinks of how good it feels to get into bed when she's worked all day; how much she looks forward to seeing Emily when she's spent the previous four hours being polite to strangers. 'And look at this.' She turns around and leads Seb to the other side of the walkway. They dodge a couple (another couple?) and stand in front of a decorated panel that reads: 'Life is dear even to those who feel it as a burden.'

'Having a picture of a heart on it doesn't make it cheerful,' Seb says.

'You weren't kidding about the temperature,' Seb says. He pulls a hat from his bag, pulls it onto his head, down over his ears.

Ailsa laughs. 'I did warn you. June in Edinburgh equals March in Highgate.'

Seb puts an arm across her shoulders in a way that is beginning to feel normal. 'I know you did. But — I'm an optimist. And anyway, I've got an excuse to get close. Leech the warmth from you.'

'Leech away,' she says.

They travel all the way around the open-top bus route, Waverley to Waverley, without getting off. Seb twitches an eyebrow at her when Burke and Hare are mentioned as they look down into the graveyards of St John's and St Cuthbert's churches. ('I'm guessing you're a fan,' he says, and she shoves him with her elbow and says, 'Not of the murdering'.) He wipes away an imaginary tear when they hear about Greyfriars Bobby; Ailsa hands him an imaginary handkerchief.

'All these bridges that are streets,' he says as they disembark, 'it's weird.'

'Or a good use of space.'

'Easier than moving a rock, I guess.'

The tour guide recognises him and he stops for a photo, in front of the bus, sunglasses on, thumbs up — Ailsa declines to be included — and now, here they are, back on the pavement. It's nearly five o'clock.

Ailsa's about to suggest they go home when Seb says, 'Right. I'd say coffee, but are you sick of it? Maybe tea? Really just somewhere to be warm.'

'Should we not be going to buy you a jumper?'

'My fingers are too cold. Where's good? Do you want to show me where you work?

Or are you sick of the sight of the place?'

Ailsa laughs. 'Not yet. I love it. But we're the wrong side of the city.'

She takes him to the food hall in Jenners, because they're almost on top of it where they get off the bus. It's odd to be there with him. She's only ever been here with her mother, when they've been shopping, or have fancied a change from their usual Rose Street haunt.

'What's up?' Seb asks.

'I was just thinking about having tea,' Ailsa says, 'and how it never used to be — an end in itself. Just something you did while you were doing something else. Like read a book or wait for an appointment.'

'It is something you do while you're doing something else,' Seb says, 'like talking to me. C'mon, Ailsa,' he says, and her name is different in an English mouth, sharp at the beginning and end — not bad, just different enough to make her notice when he says it, as though she's getting the smallest of static shocks. 'I know you well enough by now. You're not your usual self. Have you got scurvy?'

'Scurvy?'

'I don't mean scurvy, do I? What is it you get when you don't have enough carbohydrate?'

Ailsa laughs. 'Thinner? Scurvy's what you get without vitamin C. I've plenty of that, believe you me.'

'Rickets, then? Lack of calcium?'

'I don't think I've got rickets. Not yet.'

'Well, good. But there's something wrong, isn't there? I'm not as green as a cabbage, as you would say.'

'You're not as green as you're cabbage-looking.'

'That's what I said.'

Ailsa sits back and takes her cup in her hands. She wonders if she can explain how she's feeling — unstable, adrift, knowing everything she isn't but unsure of what she is.

Seb is waiting. Not in a finger-tapping way, just pouring his tea, sitting back. He takes off his sunglasses. Even though the light at their table, away from the window, is muted, he would have kept the shades on a month ago. His eye is healing, bit by bit, the way her body is strengthening, her life expanding.

She says, 'I'm not going to fall down dead any minute, anymore. And that changes things. I mean, my mother's been amazing through my whole life, but for most of that I've needed protecting. Now . . .'

'Even with only one fully functioning eye,

I see a but,' Seb says.

Ailsa sighs. 'You know I went over to see her? Things were a wee bit tense. I can't make her see that there are things I want to do now, and they don't mean I love her any less, they're just . . . they are important to me. I've long enough in my life now to find out for myself.'

'Find out what?'

'I want to find out about my biological father. But just the mention of him and she shuts the conversation down. Actually, she cried, and then she went outside to have a cigarette, and when she came back in she said, "I just cannae, Ailsa. I'm sorry, I cannae talk about him." ' Ailsa had said that she understood, because she did, in that moment, with the distress coming off her mother like the smell of Marlboro. 'There's only once in my life that she's told me about him, properly, and that was when I was ill enough that people have to give you what you want.'

Seb nods. 'Why is she so anti-him?'

'He's never been around. I don't think it's him specifically, I think it's more that he left us and he's never been around and she doesn't see why I should want to meet him now.'

'Because she's done all the work and now

he's going to turn up for the fun part? I can see her point.'

'Something like that. She thinks I've better things to be thinking about, than my father and This Seb.' She'll spare him the WAG comments.

'Well, she wouldn't be the first mother to be opposed to me. Isn't she impressed with your unicorn barrister plan?'

'She doesn't know. I was going to talk to her about it but — well, we got on to my father first. And then' — how to be fair, about this — 'she's not — all men are bastards. She just hasn't had a lot of luck with relationships. Or time for them. So mentioning my father didn't go down well. She wanted to know why. It's hard to explain that it's just for — for —' She thinks for a minute. 'for completeness.' Yes, that's it. If you have a four-chambered heart, there are things that go with it. A job. A plan. Knowing who your parents are, or were, even if they aren't together. Making choices about all of these things.

He touches the back of her hand across the table, smiles a gentle just-for-you smile. 'But she's not going to be up for a family reunion? No letting bygones be bygones?'

Ailsa laughs at the thought of her mother and father meeting, her mother tolerating a kiss on the cheek, saying, 'It's all in the past'. 'I don't think my mother would know a bygone if it hit her on the backside.'

'On the what?'

She's about to repeat herself when she notices his smile, lets it finds hers. 'On the arse.'

'I love the way you say that. So, what are you going to do?'

'Well, I've written a blog post,' she says. 'I can show you, when we get back. Maybe you can tell me what you think?'

Seb nods. 'Of course.' Then he smiles, a suggestive curl to his lip, an unmistakable glint in his eye. She feels naked under it. 'I'm staying at yours, then?'

Style it out, Ailsa, style it out. 'Did I not say in my emails? I thought I'd cook.' When they go out Seb always insists on paying and that just doesn't feel right. Plus, now that she's working she's all the more aware of what everything costs. Her lunchtime soup and sparkling water, at the Northbridge Brasserie before they got on the bus, was the equivalent of two hours of coffee-making. She needs to be more mindful of money. And she doesn't want Seb to be recognised again, and her to be photo-graphed, published. The bus people didn't have to ask; they could have just taken a quiet photo, and then Ailsa might have been in it.

Seb looks as though she's given him a BAFTA. 'Really?'

'Don't get excited, I'm no Masterchef,' Ailsa says, 'and we could go out, if you'd rather, but . . .'

'You're kidding,' Seb says. 'I don't know anyone who cooks. Except Yusef, and I haven't seen him since February.'

Ailsa says, 'No, you're kidding. You don't know anyone who cooks?'

'Well,' Seb says, 'bacon sandwiches, scrambled eggs, that sort of thing. My sister makes nice pasta things. Not making her own pasta. But other than that it's takeaways or stuff from Waitrose.'

Ailsa laughs. 'I don't know anyone who makes their own pasta.' Ah. But Lennox said he'd learned, at university, from a flatmate. He'd told her about it, one day, when she was sitting at his bedside — how he'd been amazed by how simple it is. She feels caught in a lie. How easily it is to change someone, once they're dead. She wonders what misremembrances there would be of her, now, if things had been different.

'Yusef does,' Seb says. 'I'll introduce you when he comes back.'

Ailsa can't process the long-term relation-

371

ship, or at least the future visits to London, it implies. Not that Seb means being a couple. Just — knowing each other. He seems to be friends with a lot of people he's slept with. Or it could be that he sleeps with most of his friends. Emily says what Seb might want is one thing, but what Ailsa wants is the other half of the equation. But Ailsa has no idea. That is, she loves the thought of spending time with Seb, of looking forward and seeing him there. But she doesn't know how to look forward. Not properly, anyway, not yet. Apple seems to think it will be fine. But Ailsa has only ever been in love when one of them is dying.

Back to safe territory. 'It sounds like your standards for home-cooked food are good and low, then.'

'Low standards never let you down,' Seb says. 'Do we have to go and spear a sabre-toothed tiger first?'

'We could,' Ailsa says, 'or we could go to the supermarket on our way back. You decide.'

'Supermarket,' he says. 'I didn't bring my spear.'

So that's what they do. It's almost like they're a couple.

It's odd, though, having someone else in

the flat. Odd, too, how quickly Ailsa has got used to Hayley's absence. Just the sound of Seb moving around, flushing the loo, throwing himself down on the sofa, makes Ailsa stop and listen as she stands in the kitchen. She's dismissed Seb from helping — 'I don't want you cutting your thumb off; Roz will kill me' — and chops vegetables for the ratatouille contentedly. She'll give it an hour in the oven, then grill the pork chops. Easy. Seb seems determined to be impressed/excited, though, so she lets him.

He closes the blinds and takes off his sunglasses, attempts to read the paper, gives up, has a look through Ailsa's law brochure, gives up faster.

'Put the TV on if you like,' Ailsa says. 'I'll come and join you shortly.'

'Was there something you wanted me to read? About your dad?'

She had been going to leave it until later, but this might be as good a time as any. 'My biological father,' she says, 'if you don't mind. Dad means riding bikes and helping with your homework. Father is . . .'

'I get it,' Seb says. 'Sperm. Sorry.'

'That's OK. Paper or screen?' Ailsa loves how easy this is.

'Paper, please. Nice big font size.'

She opens her laptop, puts the printer on,

opens the document, enlarges the text size, and sends it to print.

She goes back into the kitchen and tries not to think about Seb, sitting in the next room reading the story of the beginning of her life.

The lid goes on the dish, the dish goes into the oven and Ailsa sets the timer so she doesn't forget the half-an-hour stir point. She washes up the knife and chopping board, and puts the thyme away in the cupboard; then there's really nothing else to be done in the kitchen. Nothing for it but to go and see what Seb has to say.

Deep breath. Four-four time heart.

www.mybluebluehreart.blogspot.co.uk

(DRAFT — UNPUBLISHED)

A Big Decision

Advisory: swearing (you know I don't generally swear) and the kind of behaviour that might make you spit teeth.

I'm stuck on something and I need you to help me with it.

I can't ask you to make this decision cold. You need some backstory.

It's the story of how my parents met.

My father lived in the flat below the one my mother stayed in with her mates when they left university and were finding their feet in the city, working their first jobs. My father lived on his own and worked in a bank; Mum, Tamsin and Una could set the clock by his coming and going. They laughed at him because he looked so boring and ordinary, the way they were determined not to be. But at the weekends he played Usher, loud, and he opened all the windows and he baked — not cooking, baking, cakes and biscuits and all sorts, and the three women upstairs would always be hungover from Friday night, and too disorganised to ever have done any

375

shopping in the week. And there was this Saturday-morning smell of baking. My mother would lie in the bath, listening to the music coming up through the floor and smelling vanilla and chocolate. And one Saturday afternoon, when Tamsin and Una were away, Mum knocked on my father-to-be's door and said, 'If you're going to bake with the windows open, then you need to share. It's fucking torture otherwise.'

And he said, 'If you're going to laugh like that until two a.m., then you need to tell your neighbours what the joke is. It's fucking rude not to.'

He was tall and skinny, with blue eyes and straight brown hair cut 'like a schoolteacher' (whatever that means) and my mother thought: I like you. And before you could say 'Dundee cake', they were a couple. He was nice. He seemed like an adult to her, and she still felt like a wain, even though she was working, and paying rent, and her friends were getting married. My grandma was still sending food parcels from Inverness, and my grandparents used to come down for weekends and help Mum rub down awful old bits of furniture she'd found in second-hand shops and repaint them, so she'd have something to go in the hypothetical flat she was saving a deposit for.

When Mum introduced my father to her parents, he shook hands with them and they talked about house prices and she thought: I've grown up. This is real life.

I asked Mum once if she had loved him and she thought for a long time and said, 'I think so. It's hard to tell now.'

Over the next year she saved up half of a deposit on a flat, and my grandparents gave her the other half. She got a mortgage, and the only place she could afford to buy is now my home. Though it's in a positively desirable spot these days, in the nineties it was the sort of place where you took your life in your hands every time you went out of the front door.

My father helped her to do it up.

And then my mum got pregnant.

If they talked about abortion she hasn't said so. They decided that she would move in with him, and they would finish doing up her place and rent it out. Mum thought — she laughs when she talks about this, but not in a funny way — she couldn't have found anyone steadier.

Foetus-me grew, and so did Mum, and my father cooked and generally took care of his pregnant girlfriend.

They made a shortlist of names. If I'd been a boy, my father wanted Liam, but Mum thought he was joking and laughed herself stupid when he suggested it. She says it was the only time he was ever really offended. She wanted to call boy-me Hal. She wanted my name to be something no one could shorten. (People do try, with Ailsa, but it's not very successful. 'Ails' is actually harder to say than 'Ailsa', because your mouth doesn't want to stop at the s. Try it, you'll see what I mean.)

And then one day, out of nowhere, my father came home and said he'd been offered a promotion, his own bank branch to manage, but he'd need to move to Guildford. She said OK. It's not like her life was going to much of a plan, and she thought she could raise me as well in Guildford as Edinburgh. But my father looked away and said he thought it was best that he went on his own. He spun her a line about needing to get settled, and sending for her, but she called him on it — according to her she said, 'You're not a pioneer, and I'm not a fucking army wife, so either I come with you or you have the balls to say you've changed your mind.'

He said he'd changed his mind.

And that was that.

He went to Guildford.

He's never seen me, or asked after me, as far as I know. He has paid maintenance.

When life was short, it was too short to care about people who couldn't be bothered.

Now that there's a bit more room to breathe in this life of mine, I've got curious.

I'm resigned to not knowing much about where Apple is from. The provenance of my heart is her own business: the people who agreed to give her to me did not expect to be tracked down.

But now that I've a longer life ahead, not knowing where half of my chromosomes come from feels like too much missing information.

I don't think the man who didn't bother to wait to see me born can be curious. I still live in the flat my mother bought just before she got pregnant. There have been no letters or birthday cards.

But my parents were twenty-four when I was born. I'm twenty-eight and I can't even organise my washing so I've always got a clean pair of jeans.

Will I look back on the decisions I'm making now and think I've done everything right? Or will I look back and wish I'd done some things differently?

Here's the question. And I really don't know the answer to it. I can line up all the arguments, one way and then the other. But Apple has no idea which way to jump.

Do I find my biological father?

To vote YES click *here.*
To vote NO click *here.*

I'm giving you a week.

'It's in,' Ailsa says, and then, looking at the clock, calculating, building in a bit of slippage in case she's sliced the aubergines too thickly, 'it should be ready at about eight. Do you want another beer?' She'd insisted on buying the food, but Seb had taken his own basket and filled it with wine, cider and beer. There's now more alcohol in Ailsa's flat than she can ever remember there being. She'd said as much. Seb had said, 'Well, I wasn't thinking we'd drink it all tonight.'

'I'm OK for now,' he says.

'Right you are.' She sits down next to him; he pulls her in, like he did on the top deck of the bus.

'I read what you wrote,' Seb says. 'I can see why you're thinking about it.' He rests

380

his cheek against the top of her head for a moment, squeezes her shoulder, and then, 'You're not going to put this on your blog, though, are you?'

'I haven't decided yet.'

'Really?'

'Really.' Ailsa's least favourite medics were the ones who tried to coax and coach her to what they thought were the right decisions: 'Do you think going home would be the right thing to do, given how poorly you've been this week?', or 'Is your mother going to agree, do you think?' She hopes Seb isn't about to become her least favourite sort-of boyfriend. She suspects that if Hayley was listening in on this conversation, he would be shooting up in her estimation.

She feels him shrug. 'It's up to you. But — you've been on the receiving end of other people writing about your life. You know what it's like.'

'I don't think any of this is private. Give my mother two glasses of wine and she'll tell you the story herself. With swearing.'

'You and me doing the tango wasn't private. We were in a public space.'

'I suppose.' She doesn't suppose — she knows. She was never going to publish this, however much she kidded herself that she would. She might not like the way Hayley

381

still wants to manage her life, but she wouldn't do this.

She sighs. He kisses the top of her head, and then there's a beat, a second of waiting, before he asks, 'Dinner at eight?'

'About that,' she says.

'And ratatouille doesn't spoil, right?'

'I thought you didn't cook,' Ailsa says.

'I don't. I've got a mate who's been in *Educating Rita,* though. You learn a lot from helping people learn their lines.'

'Don't you just,' she says, and she gets to her feet, takes his hand, and leads him to her bedroom. She switches the timer off on the way through the kitchen. The stirring, after all, is optional.

The ratatouille doesn't spoil. They eat at nine, with candlelight and music and a plenty-of-time-for-talking-later quietness.

And in the morning, the first thing she sees is his sleepy smile. He cups a palm over his bad eye, opens the other. 'BlueHeart. We don't have to get up yet, do we?'

'We need to leave at ten,' Ailsa says, sliding her body against his, 'ten fifteen at the latest.' She starts work at eleven, and he needs to be at the Dragon's Nest for eleven thirty. He could, if he wanted, come and have a coffee before he goes to join the cast for the read-through. She hasn't asked him, because she's not sure if she wants him to. At the moment, at work, she's Ailsa the ordinary. It's nice, not being BlueHeart, now that she's been there for long enough to get to know people a bit. If she brings Seb in she might become Ailsa Who Knows That Actor Who Was On *StarDance.*

'Are you straight back to London after the read-through?'

'I'm booked on the six o'clock train,' he says, 'so probably. There'll be drinks afterwards, I would think. Nearly everyone's from Edinburgh, or Glasgow. Roz isn't stupid. She's not paying to put people up for the run if she can help it. But we can go and have a drink at the station, if you like.'

'I don't finish work until six,' Ailsa says.

Seb, who has been starting to sit up, stretch, both eyes cautiously open now, while Ailsa lies beside him, stops mid-move, looks down at her. The angle makes him look like a hall-of-mirrors version of himself, all chin and nostrils. 'Can't you bunk off early?'

She laughs. 'Coffee doesn't make itself, you know.'

'But I thought you could come, towards the end, and we could show them how to tango.'

The laugh bursts out of her. 'Us? Tango? In front of everyone? I can't imagine anything worse.'

'Thanks,' Seb says. She has to check to see that he's not really offended — it's funny, how sex and sleeping can make you think you know someone — and she takes his hand. His fingers are warmer than hers.

'I mean — I'm not used to being on show. And I'm not that good. If you want to show them the tango, you need someone better than me to dance with.'

A squeeze to her hand. 'But we're great at tango. It feels — like something.'

'I know.' She thinks about his heart, her heart, always opposite each other, and the way he moves, making it so clear what her next step should be. And then she remembers the photo. 'It feels great, dancing with you. But I don't think I'm exactly demonstration standard. And I don't like people looking at me.'

'Ah, you'll soon get used to that,' Seb says. 'We could practise. Right now.' He straddles her, kneeling, runs his hands over her; his eyes watch his hands, or maybe her body beneath them, learning her. She watches his face, to see if his fingers or his gaze snag or falter on the scar, but they don't seem to.

She laughs and says, 'This isn't tango.'

'No,' Seb says, 'next best thing, though.'

It's ten thirty by the time they are dressing. Ailsa squeezes past him, to the wardrobe — this bedroom has only ever been arranged for one, even though there's a double bed in it — and he holds her by the waist, pulls her in.

'I know I said you were looking better and better, but I might need another look.'

His skin is damp, his hair, where he's towelled it dry, sticks up and makes him look a bit more like a man who hasn't just stepped off a screen. She's in her underwear and tights, is heading to the wardrobe for her purple skirt. She usually wears jeans to work but she didn't do her washing yesterday, didn't want damp clothes all over the radiators.

She sticks against his skin, stands there for a heartbeat before she moves past. 'I'll be late if I don't get a move on.'

He lets go of her. 'Are you sure you can't bunk off?'

'No, I can't.'

'Why not?' His tone is light — or rather, light-ish.

'Because it's my job.'

His brows draw together in what's presumably meant to be comic puzzlement.

'It's making coffee.'

'That's not the point. I need to earn.' Hayley's voice in her head: *I didn't bring you up to be a WAG.*

'It's only a day.'

'It's my job. It's all I've got, for now.' She zips up her skirt, pulls a top over her head and straightens it. Seb's still naked, apart from the towel slung across his shoulders. Well, if he's not ready, she'll just have to go without him.

'You've got me.' He's pouting. The sash windows give a rattle. It might be the last of the wind that blew all night, although right now, to Ailsa, it seems more likely to be Hayley's laughter coming all the way from Glasgow and trying to get in. He has to be joking.

She kisses him — it's so good, to be wanted like this, to want. But she is her own self now. 'I know. But we didn't really plan today. And anyway, what am I supposed to do? Sit downstairs in the bar? Bring the drinks?'

He pulls on his boxer shorts and jeans, and turns to her as he finishes buttoning his fly. She isn't quite ready to reach for him, touch him, now that he's half dressed. 'I thought you'd want to make the most of me being here.'

He sounds wounded. More wounded than he has any right to feel. She glances at the clock. 'I'd say we've made pretty good use of the time we've had.' She closes her hand around the hand he's held out, smiles at him. 'I really do need to leave in five minutes.'

And suddenly, it's all right. Well, sort of. The air in the room has changed from stern to smiling. He touches her cheek, looks into her face, close enough for her to see the broken zigzags of stitches. 'That all came out wrong. Sorry. It's just — it would be nice to spend the day together.'

'Yes, it would,' she says. It's on the tip of her tongue to say: Let's make it another day, let's get our diaries. But Apple breathes a warning into her blood. She's not sure of the rules. She's seen him when he's been recognised in the street, asked for selfies; as the women who've asked for photos walk away from him she can see that he's made them feel like the centre of his world, for the fifteen seconds that he's saying hello, smiling into their phone camera lens. She needs to be careful. And not just because her mother says so.

■ ■ ■ ■ ■

PART SEVEN:
EARLY JULY 2018
LET'S TALK

■ ■ ■ ■

2 July, 2018

A Big Decision

Well, my dear faithful readers, today's post is short and sweet.

I have a dilemma and no clue what to do about it.

It's an espresso of a post, short and sharp, because there's really no other way to serve it.

All the background I can give you is:

I've never known my biological father. I've never wanted to. But lately, I've been wondering about him.

Should I look for him? What do you think?

I'll give you until the 8th.

To vote YES, Ailsa, he's part of your history, click *here.*

To vote NO, Ailsa, you've managed without him so far, so you don't need him now, click *here.*

73 comments

Results:
YES   82%
NO   18%

1 July, 2018

Romeo and Juliet Hit the Town

American TV and theatre star Meredith Katz has been seen out and about in London this week with darling of British TV Sebastian Morley, who has made dark glasses his trademark look following a corneal transplant early this year. Morley and Katz are to star as Romeo and Juliet in a production of Shakespeare's play at the Edinburgh Festival Fringe in August. They were snapped attending a charity auction to raise funds for a children's hospital.

Seb was unsuccessful in his bid to win a helicopter flight over London, but Meredith outbid all opposition to claim a bespoke, made-to-measure shirt for her new leading man. 'He's going to have to up his game if he wants to be seen with me,' she quipped. 'I know all you Brits love Marks and Spencer, but I'm looking for something with a little more — oomph.'

Morley — who once featured in a Guess jeans advertising campaign, which won him the Rear of the Year award — laughed and responded, 'I tried to claim I couldn't see well enough to choose my best shirt for tonight but that excuse cut no ice with Meredith.' The pair then got into a taxi together and headed in the direction of Chelsea, where they were later spotted talking intimately over a bottle of wine.

2 JULY, 2018

Ailsa forgot to take her phone to work. When she gets home, just after three, she finds she has nine missed calls, two texts, both from Hayley. One says, simply, 'WTF', and another, twenty minutes after the first was sent: 'Finish work at 2, see you by 4'.

Six of the missed calls are from Hayley and three are from Tamsin. There are two voicemails. One is Hayley, muttering 'fuck's sake' under her breath and hanging up — she's not a lover of leaving messages — and the other, Hayley again, says, 'Call me when you get this, would you?', in a voice that's one part upset, three parts anger.

Oh, Christ. There's an obvious explanation for this. Ailsa opens her laptop and switches it on. While she's waiting for it to power up, Tamsin rings again.

'How are you, Auntie T? Is Mum OK? I went to work without my phone and I've just seen —'

'Your mother's on her way. I thought I'd best let you know. She's not happy.'

'I'd guessed that,' Ailsa says, and then asks the question, even though the website for her dashboard is now loading, and she can see exactly what the problem is. Shit, shit, shit. 'What's up?'

'Well, that blog post of yours. It was a bit much, don't you think? She's mad as hell with you. And upset, o'course.'

'I was going to call her this afternoon. Right now. And I didn't think I'd published it. I was going to warn her about it first . . .'

'Warn her? Not ask her?'

'I thought I'd set it up as scheduled for tonight but then I must have clicked publish by mistake — I've not as much time now I'm working, I did it in a rush . . .' Ailsa knows there is no point in going into this, but it feels like her only defence, the only way she has of hiding from what she's begun.

'Well, it's too late now.'

'Yes.'

'You should maybe have talked to her first, you know.'

'I've been thinking about posting it for a couple of weeks. It's not a sudden decision. And she just shuts me down. Every time. And' — Ailsa can hear what she's going to say, how ridiculous it sounds, how childish, but she can't stop it from coming out, and anyway, she knows that it's a real, adult feeling. Because she is a real adult, and all she's trying to do here is not be treated like a child — 'it's not fair.'

'Aye, well. You of all people should know that it's not always about fairness.'

Ailsa feels her eyes close. She is so, so tired of this. 'No. It's not. But it's not always about — her — either.'

'She's still the right to privacy. She might not want her life all over your damn blog. Eighty-two per cent of voters think you should see him, do you know that? Well, they don't know the half of it.'

'It's my life too.'

'Oh, heaven forbid that anything should be not about you, Ailsa. You're just one of us now, one of the normal people, and all the same rules apply to you as they do to the rest of us.'

There's a part of Ailsa that wants to cry. And she wants to tell Tamsin that she has a right to her history — that it's not the selfishness it looks like, really; that knowing her father is something her new long life might need. But she can't find words, or tears; all she can do is look at the bedraggled window boxes on the sill. Looking after them was something Hayley did.

Tamsin adds, 'I know it isn't easy. For either of you. But you don't know everything. And this is not the way.'

'I don't know what to do, Auntie T.'

Now Tamsin is silent on the line. Ailsa waits. Then, her aunt's voice, gentler, 'Well, she's on the way. Try to be kind, if you can. She's been through a lot for you. You know where I am if you need me.'

It's not the first time Ailsa has heard Tamsin say those words. In the last weeks before the transplant — which at the time were, potentially, the last weeks, period — Tamsin was often at the hospital. She'd try to persuade Hayley away, for fresh air, a change of scene or a hot meal, but Hayley was immovable. Tamsin would kiss Ailsa goodbye, then take Hayley by the shoulders, look her in the face, say, 'You know where I am if you need me.' This is not a memory Ailsa needs right now.

Hayley rings the doorbell at ten past four. Ailsa buzzes her in, then hears her footsteps, slow, on the stairs. Her mother smells of cigarette smoke and she has smudged mascara at the corner of one eye. She might have been mad as hell when she left Glasgow, but she's quiet now. Today's scarf is all blues and greens; you only realise the pattern is peacock feathers when you spread the fabric out. It's soft from long use. A nurse, seeing Hayley shaking out the scarf and folding it, told her that to bring peacock feathers inside was bad luck. Hayley had said, 'Well, if that's the case, this scarf is me putting two fingers up to luck.'

'Mum,' Ailsa says.

'Ailsa.' It's not an angry voice, it's deliberately neutral.

'I was going to call you before the post went up. I thought I'd scheduled it for tonight.'

Hayley has slipped off her shoes, an old habit of their home that Ailsa doesn't bother with anymore, and walks into the living room, sits on the sofa. Ailsa follows.

'It was a shock to see it, that's for sure,' Hayley says.

'I'm sorry. I really did want to warn you.'

'But you were going to do it anyway.' Hayley still sounds calm. This is no longer good. It's — unsettling. Ailsa has already managed to say the things she thought it might take half an hour to fit into the gaps of the furious monologue she was braced for.

'Well — yes,' Ailsa says, then, sitting down next to Hayley, turning towards her, 'I know you don't like the voting. Or the blog. But it's mine. And so is — so is he.'

'I've told you all you need to know about him.'

Ailsa takes a deep breath. Her lungs expand, wait; then Apple beats and sends oxygen around her body, as though she understands. 'That's not your decision, though. I don't want to be protected. He's not — he's not a virus. He's half of my genes.'

Hayley nods. 'I can see that. But — this — it's . . .' She looks tired, disappointed. Ailsa knows how this works. Any reference to her father is automatically deflected to how her mother feels. Even Seb did it, when he read her original post.

'It's up to me, Mum. I'm sorry you don't like it. But I need to — I didn't go through all that we went through to be — to be smothered.'

Hayley still seems calm. It's still unnerving. 'I'm used to protecting you. It's always been my job.'

'I know.' Ailsa half shrugs. 'But I don't need protecting anymore.'

'We all need protecting, Ailsa.'

'Who was protecting you? When you were twenty-three?'

A spark, at last, in Hayley's face, some fight in the way her jaw moves. 'No one. I thought I was an adult. Then look what happened.'

'Thanks. It's a bit late for me to apologise for being born.' Ailsa gets up; exasperation is itching through her, making her move away from her mother, distract herself by looking at anything except those tired eyes, that bad-luck scarf. She thinks about Eliza: 'Bring your feelings to the dance. Your strong feelings. That's what makes a strong tango.' Ailsa could dance up a storm right now.

'You could have just asked me. If you want to see him,' Hayley says.

Oh, no, no, no. She can't have this. 'I know I could,' she says. 'You would have said, "Where has he been all these years?" and "How great for him to be able to turn up now when all the fucking work is done" and "Actually, did you realise he could have found you any time, if he had bothered to remember the address?" I know you told me a bit about him, that time in hospital, but I still don't even know his second name. You would have made me feel as though I had to choose between you, and if I want to see him, then I would be letting you down . . .'

'Ailsa . . .' Hayley is standing, facing her, and her eyes are bright, and it might be tears but it might just as easily be exactly the kind of outrage her daughter would have expected.

'No,' Ailsa says, and her voice isn't shaking so much as vibrating. There's a hum at the edges of it as it meets the air. 'No. I'm sick of this. I know you suffered. I know it. I just had Tamsin on the phone telling me how hard it was for you. I understand. And don't tell me that I don't understand because I haven't watched someone I love dying, because I did. I watched Lennox. I know.'

She's crying, of course she is — she can't say 'Lennox' and 'dying' without the tears coming.

Hayley reaches for her, but she twitches away, a step back. She doesn't want comfort. She wants to get this out. 'But all that is over. Lennox is dead. I'm alive. And you don't get to tell me how much to drink or who to have sex with or whether or not I can look for my own father. You don't get to pull this on me anymore.'

'I'm trying to keep you alive,' Hayley says. 'I'm trying to keep you safe. Can you not see that? I'm on your side.'

Hayley puts her palm against the top of Ailsa's arm. Ailsa shakes it off. She uses the heel of her hand to wipe the tears away, across her cheek and into her hair. 'I know,' Ailsa says, 'but — but . . .' All she can think of to say right now is that it's not fair, and it isn't fair, but if there are two people in the world who know about unfairness, it's her and her mother.

'Make me a cup of tea,' Hayley says, with a sigh that seems to come from somewhere deeper than today, 'strong as you like, and I'll tell you everything you want to know.'

When Ailsa comes back with the tea, Hayley is sitting on the sofa again, papers in her hand. Ailsa puts the mug on the table and sits down. They aren't calm but they aren't at daggers drawn. Not for now, anyway. Just an ordinary day in Verona.

'This is interesting reading,' Hayley says.

'What is it? Oh.' It's the printout of the blog post she gave to Seb to read. 'I was never going to publish it.'

'But you wrote it.'

Hayley sounds interested, rather than angry. Maybe if Ailsa is honest — 'It was — a sort of a first draft. I showed it to Seb. He said it was a bit — he said I was telling your story and it was like being in the paper. Him and me. I think I showed him because I wasn't sure whether I should publish it.'

Hayley brings the green-blue mug to her

lips; Ailsa chose it to match her scarf. 'I suppose the one thing you can't ask your blog is whether or not to publish a blog post.'

Ailsa nods. 'True enough,' she says.

'What does the blog say?'

'Eighty per cent in favour while I was waiting for the kettle to boil,' Ailsa says.

Hayley sighs. 'Will you, then?'

'Looks like it.'

'I think maybe we need to talk about this a bit.' Hayley is scanning the printout that Seb read.

Ailsa takes the papers from Hayley's hands. 'Did I get anything wrong?'

Hayley shakes her head. 'No, hen. That's what I told you. That's the story. It's just — it's not everything. There — there's a bit more.'

'What?' Ailsa knows she didn't mishear, even if the blood is beating more loudly than usual through her ears. The things she's been told have been watered down, sops for a sick kid. 'That night. We thought I was dying. And you still lied to me?'

'You'd have lied to Lennox if you'd thought the truth would make his last days worse, Ailsa. You know you would. Being honest isn't as black and white as all that, sometimes.'

'It is,' Ailsa says, but she's wondering

whether she would have lied to Lennox to make him happy. She knows the answer.

Hayley says, 'Can I have a cigarette? Out of the window?'

'If you like.' Usually she asks Hayley to go outside to smoke, but right now she needs to hear the true story of her father too much to worry about getting rid of the smell. The sash window rattles as it rolls upwards. The windowsill is wide enough to perch on. When the weather is bad, Hayley says, 'I'm going to have a smoke on the balcony' and sits on the sill, her upper body angling away from the room when she exhales, the arm holding the cigarette outside.

'We went in for a scan. You were thirty-five weeks. You'd been lying breech, so they wanted to scan me to see if you'd moved, though I told them you hadn't.' Shrug, inhale, exhale. 'So your father arranged to go into work late, and we were at the hospital for nine o'clock sharp for our appointment, and it was all happy — happy chat, chat, chat, have you picked names and let's see what this wee one is up to, and then it all got — serious.'

'They saw the problem, then? Before I was born?' Ailsa knows that it's possible; a three-chambered heart is usually discernible before birth, though it might have been

405

missed in 1990, if it wasn't being looked for.

Hayley nods. 'The radiographer asked us to wait, and then someone else came in and had a look, and all the time I'm saying, "What's wrong?" and your father's holding my hand and they were saying' — Hayley gestures with the hand that isn't holding the cigarette — 'that shit they say when they know something's wrong but they don't want to tell you yet. "Irregularities", "closer look", all that.'

Ailsa knows these phrases. As her mother used to say, in their in-patient days, we all know 'we'll just wait until a consultant gets here' is code for 'you're basically fucked'.

'At that point,' Hayley says, 'it was the most frightening thing that had ever happened to me in my life. Everything's relative.' Ailsa has seen photographs of herself at days' old, wired and tubed and with dressings over her chest. She had already had one operation to keep her peach–stone-sized heart working.

'We had another scan and waited. Eventually we were called in to see Mrs Elliott. She was your first consultant. We'd been in the hospital for six hours. She explained what exactly was wrong with your heart. That it was missing a chamber and, until

406

recently, this had been a fatal condition, but there was now a technique that could be tried when you were born.' Hayley shakes her head. ' "There's a technique we could try." I thought I was going tae die just hearing that; I'd never felt pain like it, never in my life.' She pauses, a gathering of her feelings, and looks at Ailsa, who sees something in her mother that says: *The pain went on, and on, until your new heart came.* 'All the time she was talking I could feel you kicking, and it was like you saying, "Don't talk about me." She drew a diagram on a piece of paper, red lines for oxygenated blood and blue lines for deoxygenated. A normal heart versus your heart. I was trying to concentrate, but you were hammering away with your wee feet, underneath here.' Hayley puts her hand about her waist on her left side, winces as though there's a close-to-term baby kicking her right now. 'It was like you were objecting.'

Ailsa's hands are shaking. 'I didn't even know I was breech,' she says.

'Well, you sorted yourself out in that respect,' Hayley says, 'although you left it a bit late for my liking. I was in the bath. It was like watching a sheepdog try to turn around in a pillowcase.'

'Why have you not told me this before?

It's — I can't imagine it, Mum.'

Hayley stubs out her cigarette in the window box and pulls the window shut. She continues as though she hadn't heard the question. 'I was shaken as all hell. So was your father. We went home. He hardly said a word. I cried.'

'God, Mum.' Ailsa doesn't know why this version of her birth is worse than the one she's always believed. It's not as though there's anything warm and fluffy about thinking that your baby is healthy and finding out, the second she is born, that she's not.

'Aye, well,' Hayley says, 'it was the next night before we talked about it. Your father went to work the next day. I slept on and off until he came home. And when he did, it was like a light had gone out of him. We talked about you, and about everything they said at the hospital. I'd been through everything I remembered and tried to write it down. I asked him what he remembered. For everything hopeful I'd written down, he only remembered the opposite. He never started a conversation about you, after that. And when we did talk about you, he used to shake his head. All the time. When I said I wanted to call you Ailsa, for my mother's middle name and because I'd looked it up and it meant 'victory', he just said, "Call her whatever you please, Hayley." And I realised that despite everything the doctors had said, he thought you were going to die. Whereas I was frightened you'd die, but at the same time fucking determined that you wouldnae. I called him on it. He said I was burying my head in the sand and I said he'd given up on you. He said I was unrealistic, blinded by my hormones.' A laugh escapes Ailsa, at the thought of anyone saying that to her mother and getting away with it. 'Aye, you're right, that was an argument and a half.'

'It sounds . . .' Ailsa says. But there isn't immediately a word. Grim? Heartbreaking? Impossible?

'It was.' Hayley speaks as though she's heard Ailsa's thought. 'We went from being happy and excited to bickering all the time.'

'Oh, Mum.'

Hayley's face is pale and her eyes are bright, focussed somewhere outside of this room and this afternoon. She makes Ailsa think of someone else, but she can't place who.

'You were three days early. It was a lovely day. When I went into labour, it was eight in the morning, the sun was coming in the window, and David had just left for work. I sat at the kitchen table and thought: Well, baby, here we go. I wrote your name down, to see how it looked. I got myself through the morning, walking about and having a bath and all the things you're supposed to do. I took a taxi to the hospital in the afternoon. I almost didn't call David, because I thought he wouldn't want to be there, but I thought it was the right thing to do. He came.'

Quiet, again. Ailsa, watching, realises that her mother reminds her of Ruthie, on the day of Lennox's birthday, when she took them into his old bedroom. She waits.

'It sounds stupid, but we had a really nice time when I was in labour. Gas and air's like gin and tonic. Plus I was so scared for you that labour was a distraction. At least I couldn't think. David brought a wee picnic to the hospital — pork pies and oranges and chocolate cake — and he cut everything up into bites for me. He brought a crossword book and a hot water bottle that he held on my back. And he made me laugh. I remembered why I loved him.'

'Had he baked the chocolate cake?' As she says it she feels like an idiot. It's as though someone has set her to 'irrelevant'. But then again, if one of the only things you know about your father is that he bakes, then . . .

Hayley smiles. 'No, he hadn't. He spent quite a lot of time talking about how it wasn't as good as his. He said he thought I wouldn't have appreciated it if he'd nipped home to do a spot of baking.'

'Fair enough.'

'That's what I said,' Hayley says. 'It was a bit like none of the last month had happened and we were having the baby we thought we would have. I thought he'd come round. I think maybe he did as well.' She sighs. 'But then — I'm going to save you the screaming and swearing and the great big tear . . .'

Ailsa winces, and for a minute they're back on safe and steady ground, somewhere they both know. 'I don't need to know about the tear. Please don't say . . .'

'It's like a patchwork quilt down there? OK.' Hayley grins, wickedness and love. She's all Ailsa's for a heartbeat, and then she's gone again, back into wherever she has stored all of this.

'It was just before midnight when you were born and they whisked you off to the side of the room to have a look at you, and I was shouting, "Is she all right? Is she all right?" He went to look at you and came back. He said — he said —' For the first time in this truth-telling Hayley looks down

411

to her hands, so that Ailsa couldn't see her face if she wanted to. 'He said you looked "quite normal". Then they brought you over so I could see you, just for a second or two. I thought how beautiful you were, and how precious. I felt as though — I don't know — I felt drenched with love for you. You were the loveliest thing I had ever seen in my whole life. The best. And all he could say was that you looked quite normal. I should have sent him away then.'

Hayley is quiet for so long this time that Ailsa prompts her. Even though she already knows that there isn't going to be a happy ending, she's full of tension and foreboding. Her stomach has contracted and her jaw feels tight. Apple is getting breathless with the wait.

'And then?'

'And then they took you to the baby unit — they'd warned me they would do that, so you could be assessed and helped, which sounded lovely and reassuring. What they meant was, they would be doing their damnedest just to keep you alive. That first week was fucking awful. You had your first operation. I was in hospital with you and I couldnae stop crying. The nurses used to come and change my pillowcases because they were so wet. You looked like such a sad wee thing and there was nothing I could do to help you.'

'And — and him?'

Hayley sighs, half nods. 'To be fair — and it pains me to be fair — I think he tried. He was there most of the time. He came to the consultations. He held my hand and made the right noises. If I phoned him in the night, he always answered. He brought takeaway in to try and get me to eat, and he brought messages from my folks because he called them every evening. He sat with me when I sat with you, but he wasn't really sitting with you, if you catch my meaning?' Ailsa nods, mute. 'Whenever we could hold you he took photos. I think it was a way of not having to look at you.' Hayley looks as though she might cry. 'I didn't want you to have to hear all this,' she says.

Ailsa does something with her head — she wants to nod empathy with her mother, shake her head to show that she still, fundamentally, disagrees with the way she's been lied to, and so there's a little wobble as she tries to work it all through. 'I never thought about who was taking the photos,' she says. And then, as a pre-empt to the usual retort she'd expect from Hayley, 'I know I haven't thought about this the way you have.'

It's Hayley's turn for the nod-shake. 'Well, I didnae want you to have to. I know you think I'm wrong. But . . .'

'What happened next?' Ailsa asks. Her father being more of a bastard than she thought doesn't make Hayley keeping this to herself OK.

Her mother takes a breath, deep and jolting. 'When you were ten days old, we had a meeting with Mrs Elliott, and she said that the first operation had gone as well as could be expected. She talked about your future. There was a lot that we needed to be alert to and protect you from. Your father sat there with his hand over my hand, and even though the hospital was red hot, his fingertips were freezing. He was so cold that I swapped our hands over — I remember it — I put his hand under mine, so he would have the warmth of my leg and the warmth of my hand.' Breath, judder of an exhale. 'He kissed me goodbye, took my list of what I needed, and left. Tamsin came that night, with the things I had asked for, and said he had called her and said that he needed some sleep and would she bring my bag. And he never came back.'

It's too sudden a stop. 'That was it?' Ailsa was waiting for the row, and whatever came after it. If it hadn't been for Hayley's reaction when she said she wanted to find her father, she wouldn't have been surprised if the story ended with him at the bottom of the Forth, and her mother and Tamsin rehearsing alibis in case the police came knocking.

'That was the last time we saw him,' Hayley says. 'I couldn't think of a way to tell you that wasn't . . .'

'I can see that.' And, intellectually, Ailsa can. Why trouble a child with this when she could be given a slightly more palatable story? But Ailsa could have died with the wrong idea. 'Lennox thought — Lennox didn't know. I told him what I knew. I didn't tell him the truth.'

'I'm sorry, hen.' Hayley takes her tea, drinks. Ailsa watches, for want of something better to do. She's chilled with shock, and she can feel that somewhere, deep — deeper than Apple, though she feels it too — her world is rearranging.

'Is that tea not cold?'

'It's clay cold,' Hayley says. 'It doesnae matter.'

'So that was it?' Ailsa asks. 'He just — went?'

'Yes and no,' Hayley says. 'I never saw him again. I got a letter, a few days later. Tamsin was checking for post. She had my keys.'

'Have you got it?' Despite everything she's hearing, feeling — and it's just starting to well up in her, a great wave of all her mother has had to do, be, care about, on her own, all of these years, and he knew what she was going to be up against — she wants to see what his handwriting is like, and put her hand on the paper that he wrote on.

Hayley laughs. 'You have got to be joking.'

'What did it say?'

'It said —' Ailsa half expects her mother to recite the whole thing, because how would you not know a letter like that by heart? 'It said — well, it said that he couldn't cope. That he felt no bond with you and that he had realised that he had expected you to die. And although he didn't want that, he hadn't thought about how complicated your life was going to be. And it was better that he let us down now, rather than later. I think — I suppose — in his head it must have made sense.'

Ailsa hears herself laugh. 'I wasn't expecting you to defend him,' she says.

'Oh, I'm not defending him, Ailsa. He was a coward. He didnae find that out until you were born. Just like I didnae find out what I was like until I had you to care for.'

'So you didn't speak to him again?' The questions are crowding in now, and Ailsa is trying to pick the best, the most important, because she can see that she isn't going to be able to ask them all. Her mother's shoulders are slumping, her hands are tight around the mug, and she's not so much blinking as closing her eyes for two or three seconds at a time. It won't be long until Hayley slams this conversation shut, asks for wine or finds her appetite, and Ailsa doesn't know whether this is one-off openness or the first of many conversations.

Hayley makes a sound, a laugh with the amusement sucked from it. 'I didnae. But — oh, Ailsa, I wasnae dignified about it. I called him at work and I cried into his answering machine at home. You'd probably call it begging. He broke my heart, he really did. I knew he was struggling but I didnae think he'd leave me. Leave us. There was a payphone on wheels in the hospital. I had it in my room all the time I wasnae with you. In the end, Tamsin refused to bring me any more change. Then there was a night when you were proper, seriously blue, and I sat with you, on my own, and thought about all the ways I was going to protect you. In the morning I found I'd grown a spine and I stopped trying to contact him.'

Ailsa nods. She's had some nights like that. Everything seems different at 3 a.m.

Usually, it changes back with daylight, but every now and again, you are a new person in the morning.

'In the letter he said that he'd been talking to work and they'd arranged for him to move straight away. He said he would stay away until the end of October and he hoped that was enough time for me to get my things out of his place and get settled into mine. So I had to cancel my tenants, and go back to his flat and sort everything so you would have a home to come back to.' Hayley's hand traces a shape, a mirrored parabola of helplessness, complication, up, down. 'You were this weak thing in the hospital with three-quarters of a heart and I was trying to work out what the fuck was happening to my life. I was determined to be an adult about it all. My ma and da were coming down — I'd put them off for as long as I could — but you were nearly three weeks old and I think your gran thought you were going to outgrow some of the five hundred pairs of bootees she had knitted for you. So I thought I'd get everything sorted and done ready for them coming. New beginnings, and all that. You were going to come home while they were in Edinburgh, or at least I hoped you were. Then I walked into his flat and I saw all the things he had. There was a whole shelf of recipe books and all his shirts were hung up on the hangers from the dry-cleaners. I thought about all the ways that you and me were going to struggle. So Tamsin and me cleared everything out and took it to the charity shops.'

'You did not!'

'We did. Well, most of it. That Le Creuset of Tamsin's was your father's. And I took all of the stuff that wasnae going to last. I didnae want the thought of him hanging around forever. But I had no idea where my money was going to come from. I didnae know about benefits, or how much I'd be able to work, or any of that. I had no clue if you could put a child with a heart condition in a nursery, or if you'd need to be warmer than other babies, because of your circulation, and I'd have whopping heating bills.'

Ailsa imagines herself, given a sick baby to keep alive. She wouldn't know where to start. She wouldn't trust herself with a kitten. 'So what did you take?'

Hayley shrugs. 'All the food. Cleaning stuff. Loo rolls. Soap and shampoo. Printer paper. All that.'

This is the mother Ailsa recognises. Hayley is talking as though she's reminiscing about a holiday. 'There were a couple of weeks when I'd been discharged from the hospital and you hadnae. Tamsin would pick me up and we'd go and load the car with things from his flat. She'd drop me at the hospital to be with you and then she would drive around all the charity shops. She'd take a bag here, a bag there. Then she came back and said hello to you, and then we went back to my place and she made sure I wasnae going to have an overnight breakdown. We did that until his flat was empty.'

'Empty? Actually empty?'

'We left the furniture, because it was too much hassle to organise someone to move it. We left all the electrical things as well, the toaster and all that, because charity shops don't take them. We took all of his records to the British Heart Foundation. We were going to take the mattress, but we couldnae be arsed. We gave his pillows to Oxfam. He had some nice stuff, his parents had been well off, and I thought he'd be walking around the city when he got back, down from the station, and he'd be passing the charity shops, looking in the windows, thinking, oh, I have a suit like that one, that's really like my china . . .'

Ailsa is laughing now, proper, thorough, belly-up laughter, though she doesn't know how much of it is horror. 'What did he do?'

Hayley has been laughing, too, but she stops. 'Absolutely nothing. Not a word from him. He just — sucked it up. Which goes to show he knew he was wrong. I half expected him to turn up on my doorstep, but he didnae. I had a lot of fine things to say to him, about valuing his cake tins more than he cared about his own daughter, but — well, it could be that he knew what I'd say. He didnae have to knock on my door to hear it. I chucked his keys in a bin outside the hospital. I didnae want to be tempted to go round when he was back in Edinburgh. But I wanted him tae be worried that I might.'

There's a minute of silence, another. Into it, Ailsa says, 'Mum. You should have told me all this.' She almost adds: Because you didn't have to carry it all on your own, but she can see from Hayley's face, her soft, calm profile, that she doesn't need to.

'I know. But I didn't want you to think that — that you made it happen. Kids always think it's their fault, do they not, if their folks split up?'

'Oh, Mum.' Apple is quiet in her chest, as though she's listening for clues that tell her how she should be feeling; she's beating gently, slowly.

Hayley turns to look at her, touches her

chin. 'It's all water under the bridge, Ailsa. He got in touch via a solicitor to offer us money. I didn't want to take it but your grandparents talked me into it. They talked me into getting your Child Disability Living Allowance as well, though I didn't want to sign you up as disabled for anything because I didnae want you ever tae think of yourself as disadvantaged. I wanted you tae feel capable of anything. When you were two, his solicitor wrote to me again. The letter said he had sold his flat, and he thought it was right that I should have the proceeds from it, as a full and final settlement of his child support obligations. I was tempted to tell him to shove it, but thirty grand's thirty grand and it paid off the mortgage. The fact that you weren't even mentioned in the letter pissed me off so much I'd have had his eyeballs and gone back for the sockets if I could. He'd never asked to see you, or asked for a photo, or how you were.'

They both sigh, an accidental harmony.

'I'm sorry I've had to tell you about all this.'

Oh, no, no, that's the wrong thing to be sorry about. 'I think I deserved to know, Mum.'

'Aye, well. If we all got what we deserved it would be fine world.' Ailsa knows how this is meant — the gentlest of reprimands, a reminder of how complicated this is — but she hears it in a different way. No one deserved a transplant more than Lennox. That would have been fine for sure. Take a breath, Ailsa.

'You should have told me, Mum. But I'm sorry you went through all that. It must have been — I honestly cannot imagine.'

'I've always done my best,' Hayley says, and Ailsa takes her hand, squeezes it. All that they've been through is between them. There were times, in hospital, when Ailsa wondered whether the sheer force of her mother's determination was what brought her new heart to her. Now, she wonders if it was love. One thing's for sure: they can weather this.

'I know,' Ailsa says, 'and you know, whatever he's like, he's not ever going to be my dad.'

Hayley's fingertips go rigid; she blinks, quickquickquick, the way she always does when she's surprised. 'You're not taking that blog post down, then?'

'Well — no,' Ailsa says, 'I'm going to do what it says. That's how it works, Mum. You know that.'

She's said it as gently as she can, but for a second Ailsa thinks her mother is going to slap her. Hayley does a worse thing than that. She starts to cry. Then she rummages in her bag, pulls out a pen and her diary, writes something down and tears out the page. She hands it to Ailsa. There's a single word: 'Twelvetrees'.

'That's his surname. He shouldnae take much finding.'

'Mum . . .' She knows she should say she's sorry. She probably is, somewhere, in the eerie fog that's filling up the space where certainty used to be. She sits and waits for something to happen. If only Apple was her real heart. Then she'd know what was right.

From: Seb
Sent: 6 July, 2018
To: Ailsa
Subject: Hello?

Hey BlueHeart,
You've gone a bit quiet.
  As it's Wednesday I hope you're taking your blue heart dancing.

Take care,

Seb x

From: Ailsa
To: Seb

Hello Romeo,
I'm a bit down, if I'm honest. Don't tell anyone — if you've had a heart transplant it's not allowed.
  I basically go to work, go dancing and sleep. There's the weekly thrill of a hospital appointment and trying to get my head around law conversion degrees. Plus — the biological father stuff. I know you're busy with rehearsals so I didn't think you'd be waiting to hear from me.

Ailsa

From: Seb
To: Ailsa

Always waiting to hear from you, babe.

I saw your blog post about your biological father, and the result. I'm glad you toned it down. It was the right thing to do.

Call me any time. I'm in rehearsals this week (just me, Meredith and Roz, because Meredith isn't around for all of the Edinburgh rehearsals) but I'll always call you back.

From: Ailsa
To: Seb

My mother wasn't a fan of the post. But she came over and told me the actual truth about him, which is different to the version in the blog post you read. So I suppose that's something.

From: Seb
To: Ailsa

Well, I'm hoping it's good truth, but your tone isn't exactly cheerful. It's not going to turn out that Mel Gibson is your real father, is it?

From: Ailsa
To: Seb

Thank you, I just laughed for the first time in a week.

No, Mel Gibson isn't my real father. Neither is Sean Connery or anyone else you can think of who is either Scottish or has worn tartan in a film.

From: Seb
To: Ailsa

Actually, I was doing a clever thing. BraveHeart/BlueHeart.

From: Ailsa
To: Seb

Aha! Maybe Mel Gibson *is* my real father, then.

But just in case he isn't, I'm googling 'David Twelvetrees' for what is probably going to be the shortest search for a parent in history.

From: Seb
To: Ailsa

You don't have to get in touch with him

if you don't want to, you know. If you do, do. If you don't, don't. Your blog's amazing, but you're better.

From: Ailsa
To: Seb

I do.

From: Seb
To: Ailsa

Not my business. Understood.
 So, rehearsals start on 2 July. I hope we can see a bit of each other.

From: Ailsa
To: Seb

Won't Meredith need your attention? And the others? I mean — isn't it all intense and — actorish?

From: Seb
To: Ailsa

I think it will be/can be intense, yes, and it has to be, because you have to trust each other. Like a massively complicated tango. On ice.

But the rehearsals are going to be bitty, because Roz (Bulgaria) has to accommodate everyone trying to fit in day jobs, and even though Romeo is, obviously, the most important character in the play, she won't need me all the time. She's offered to put me up.

Meredith can look after herself. Roz offered her accommodation as well but I think she's staying in a hotel.

From: Ailsa
To: Seb

It would be nice to spend some time with you.

I might not be great company. I've never really fallen out with my mother before. Not seriously. But it's like things have frozen over between us.

And I didn't even ask about your eye.

From: Seb
To: Ailsa

It will be more than nice, BlueHeart, if last time is anything to go by.

I could stay over sometimes, if you wanted.

My eye is OK. More stitches out next

week. I think the light's getting a bit easier. When things change little by little it's hard to tell.

7 JULY, 2017

'I've got good news,' Hayley says with a grin, and then adds, quickly, 'not a heart.'

Ailsa has been dozing. She dozes a lot, at the moment, pretending to herself that it's the heat but knowing it's the creeping failure of her body that's turning her into someone who can barely face getting out of bed. She sits up, and Hayley is there straight away to adjust her pillows.

'What, then?' Ailsa cannot imagine any other good news.

'I've got you a weekend pass. We can take a trip.'

Ailsa's torn between wanting to go — the sky, seen from the hospital garden, isn't big or broad or uncluttered enough to satisfy her dying heart — and the sheer effort involved in standing upright, unhooking from drips and monitors, leaving the room. But her mother's face tells her she needs to

431

pretend. During his last week, Lennox had said, 'It's not about me anymore.' Ailsa knows what he means, now.

'Fantastic! Where do you fancy?'

'It's up to you, hen.'

Ailsa finds a laugh. 'Disney? I could meet Mickey Mouse.' She stops herself, just in time, from making a joke about that being what all the dying kids want to do. Lennox would have got it.

'I dinnae think we could afford the insurance.'

'OK,' Ailsa says, 'how about —' And then her breathing starts to speed up with panic, because she realises that what she's being asked to do, in all probability, is decide where she'll go on the last trip of her life. The more ill she gets, the more the likelihood of a heart arriving in time diminishes.

Hayley takes her hand. 'It's OK, Ailsa. Slow it down.'

'Where do you want to go, Mum?' But Hayley looks away, and Ailsa can see that she has the same weight of decision-making on her. Where is the last place you would choose to go with your daughter?

'We should ask your blog.'

Ailsa laughs. 'You don't approve of the blog, remember.'

'Aye, well,' light tone, but a pain in Hay-

432

ley's eyes that Ailsa can't bear to look at, 'I dinnae have the head space to decide either. This time next year, you won't be needing a blog to make your decisions.'

Lennox's voice, in Ailsa's head: That's true, either way.

From: David
Sent: 7 July, 2018
To: Ailsa
Subject: Good to hear from you

Dear Ailsa,

What a surprise to hear from you. A good surprise, that is. Before I replied I looked you up. I can't tell you how glad I am to see you looking so alive and well. I've read your blog from beginning to end. What a time you've had.

I don't know what your mother has told you but I won't start with the past. I'll start with the now. That seems best.

I'm 54 and I live in Leatherhead in Surrey. I work for a bank and I'm married to Gemma. We met when I moved to Guildford, around the time you were born — we worked in the same branch. We have two boys, George and Thomas, who are 17 and 15. George is very keen on his music and we are trying to persuade him to go to university, but all he really wants to do is play in his band. We have no idea where his talent comes from. Gemma and I are music fans but have no skill. Thomas is severely dyslexic and loves animals and consequently we have a real menagerie at home — mostly animals that he rescues, although he does have a Labrador of his own. He volunteers at an animal shelter at the weekends. Gemma has three older sisters and we have such a big extended family that we hire a church hall on Boxing Day so that we can all get together!

I've spoken to Gemma and she agrees that it is important that I come to see you. In case you are wondering, you have never been a secret from her.

Guildford to Edinburgh is something of a journey (six hours by train, with two changes!) but I am happy to do it. Our diaries are quite complicated, with the boys' activities and Gemma being in an am-dram group. I play golf too, though Gemma says it's just me making an excuse to get some peace! If you can let me know when is a good time for you I will try to get myself organised. It's probably best if you send me two or three options.

With my very best wishes,
David (Twelvetrees)

10 July, 2018

What Now?

Tomorrow, I'm going to tango. And I love tango, for so many reasons. I love the music, which has more of a pulse than a beat, because in tango music there is no drum. I love that all I have to do is put one foot in front of the other and listen to see what my partner is telling me with the way he or she moves their body. I love the concentration of it: there's no room for anything else to crowd my brain. So it's a sort of rest. And I love that Apple and I started learning at the same time. It feels as though we're equal. I feel like one person when I'm dancing.

And I don't often feel like one person.

This is what my head is (mostly like) — it's like there's a conversation going on in there, every damn minute, between IA (Inspirational Ailsa) and EA (Everyday Ailsa).

IA: Hey! Let's do a thing! Let's do a cool thing!

EA: I'm tired. I want some chocolate.

IA: You're not tired! You don't want chocolate! Let's make today worth something!

EA: OK, what shall we do?

IA: I don't know! But just think of all the medical research and effort that went into keeping you alive! All the people who helped!

EA: That makes me feel as if nothing I could do today is good enough.

IA: You have a dead person's heart!

EA: That doesn't help, either.

Apple: Yeah. That was really tactless, actually.

I have no idea whether this is normal. I think it probably is. I know I ought to go and talk to someone about it, but, well, I haven't, because I also know what the answer is. Because, somewhere in the mix is SA (Sensible Ailsa) and she says: Keep going. It's early days. It's going to take a while for everything to shake down. You were some sort of ill for most of twenty-eight years. Plus, your personal life has got a bit complicated. Give yourself a chance to get used to some sort of well. Be as gentle with yourself as you were when you only had three quarters of a heart. You're making progress, but you just can't see it.

So, right now, Ailsa and The Other Ailsas are going dancing. They need to get some practice in, because they're going to be taking part in a show. Oh yes they are.

Poll for today: what's the best way to spend time with someone — someone who might be important in your life — when you're meeting them for the first time, and you're not sure how you'll get on?

I'm giving you a week.

GO FOR A WALK: It will disguise any awkward silences and you don't have to look at each other.

HAVE A MEAL: At least you'll know for sure if you never want to see them again.

BRING A FRIEND: It will diffuse things and you can see each other in a setting where it's easier to be relaxed.

ASK THEM OVER: You'll feel more confident on your own territory and you can ask them to leave if it doesn't go well.

7 shares
39 comments

Results:
WALK   60%
MEAL   22%
FRIEND 18%
HOME   0%

■ ■ ■ ■

PART EIGHT:
JULY 2018
AN ILL-DIVINING
SOUL

■ ■ ■ ■

*   *   *   *

Part Eight
July 2018
Anglu-Dining
Sour

*   *   *   *

11 JULY 2018

The actors form a clutch of leaning-in attention on Roz in one corner of the room. Her bright blonde hair is shining under one of the spotlights in the ceiling, her hands working, making circles in the air, then pointing up, making an encircling gesture. Finally, she raises her voice to say something not quite audible to Ailsa, the actors all laugh, and the group breaks apart, standing and stretching, hoisting bags onto their shoulders, checking phones.

Today has been the first day of the acting company working with Edie and Eliza. Ailsa tries to see how it's gone, but she can't tell: the Tango Sisters are always smiling, and she can't imagine they'd ever slump, round their shoulders, no matter how many two-left-footed actors they had to train.

'Edie says they're invited to stay,' Venetia says, 'and about half of them said that they will.'

Ailsa nods. She knew this — the first bit, anyway, via a text from Seb earlier — but she doesn't say so. 'We need to start getting used to each other,' she says.

'We haven't got a lot of time to train them up, for sure,' Venetia says, with a wink, and Ailsa laughs at the thought that she might know more than — well, anyone — about tango. She recalls Seb's suggestion that the two of them dance at the end of the read-through: it seems as ludicrous now as it did a month ago, even if she has had four more classes and been to two milongas in the meantime.

Seb puts his arm around the shoulder of a stocky older man (Capulet? The Friar? Though some of them are doubling, so he could well be both) and says something that provokes a rumbling chortle. The older man slaps his palm against Seb's chest before disengaging and walking towards the exit; Ailsa finds herself wincing at the slap, her shoulders coming forward, and feels as though Apple moves backwards, towards her spine. A chest is a fragile place, still.

Seb speaks to Roz and then to Meredith, who is almost as tall as him, and has a sort of gangliness that doesn't come across in photographs, or maybe is converted to 'willowy' by camera angle and clothes that aren't leggings and a T-shirt. Her face is serious, concentrated, and so is Seb's as he speaks to her. Then the two of them are walking towards the top of the stairs down to the bar, and Ailsa ducks her head as they pass, because she's not sure what to do.

Jesus, Ailsa. Get a grip. She stands up just after they pass. 'Seb,' she says, 'welcome back.'

He turns, and Meredith with him; he smiles, kiss-kiss, a tiny rub of stubble. 'Hello you.'

'Hello.' He does what he always does in person — he is so himself that there's nothing to do but to trust him, and to be herself in return.

He holds her by the shoulders for a heartbeat/blink, and then, 'Meredith, this is Ailsa. She's my favourite blue-hearted bus fan.'

'Hello,' Meredith says with a smile, as though this is a normal way to introduce someone, or as though she wasn't listening. Ailsa, at work, is starting to perfect the art of communication that slides over her instead of going in — conversations about the rain, the tourists, sport — so she doesn't mind.

'Hi,' she says, 'it's good to meet you.'

Meredith nods, and turns back to Seb. 'I

need to go.'

'I'll walk you out,' Seb says. And then, to Ailsa, 'Don't go anywhere. I'll be back to take a good hard look at your ochos.'

12 July, 2018

A Question of Country

Hello, hello, my friends.

Oh, it's good to come to a blog post and say, sorry, this is a bit late, but I've been busy. Rather than sorry, this is a bit late, but I've been too ill to keep my eyes open for more than three seconds at a time.

I'm taking a very small part in an Edinburgh show this year, and it's having quite an impact on me. I'll be honest, for a while I was in two minds about taking part at all, because I thought I might not be good enough, and because I've never really put myself Out There on a stage before, and been myself, with people looking at me. (Doctors on ward rounds having a look at your scar doesn't count.) But — I'm doing it, and I'm not sure when or how I definitely decided, I just got a bit swept into it. Which, I suppose, is a normal life thing. And it's absolutely fantastic.

I've been practising my dancing. I've been going to rehearsals where I learn to shout. (Yes, there is a special way to do it, so you don't strain your voice.) And I've been part of a team for the first time in my life, I think. When I was ill I had a big team of people looking after me, but that's not the same. I like working towards something, with other people, and being just the tiniest part of a bigger thing. I like having things in common with others that are more than illness and the misery that comes with it. And anyway, being ill is lonely, even if someone else is being ill beside you.

So: life's good, and busy, and I think I might be feeling a bit — normal, but in a good way.

Apart from working, and dancing, I'm thinking seriously about my next career move (another nice, normal activity). And it's based on two things:

1. When you are ill, people protect you. They don't always tell you everything about things, because they don't want you to worry. They simplify the truth, because they want you to sleep at night. I've been finding out what the world is really like, now I am eligible for the full picture. Now that I'm not struggling, I can see the way that others have struggled.

2. The world's not fair and I know I'm sup-

posed to grow up and accept that at some point, but I don't think I ever will. People who know they are dying, and dying painfully, can't legally commit suicide (unless they can afford a trip to Switzerland). If you consent to transplant and your next of kin doesn't agree, your wishes aren't respected. Those are two things that need to be fair. That's before we get to sick people who don't have access to the medication they need, parents who don't take their responsibilities seriously . . .

Apple has given me the chance to look up and around and see the full picture, and I don't like what I see. I know that many people are good people, with good natures, but that isn't always enough. So I'm going to do something about it.

It turns out you can't get in to Superhero University if you're on immunosuppressants (too many radioactive superbugs about) so I'm going to take my as-well-as-can-be-expected body and donate it to the law, instead.

It's a long road. I have to do a conversion degree, and that's only the very beginning.

I'll be able to take out some loans, and

maybe get some grants. I'll have to support myself, too. I'm not complaining. But realistically, I need to study somewhere close to home. So I have two choices. I could study in-person and do a conversion that fits me to do (or at least learn to do) anything to do with Scottish law. Or I can do an Open University course that fits me for UK law. The question is which? I feel as though I should be able to do good anywhere. I think Scotland is my home. But that might only be because there's still an umbilical cord tethering me to the hospital, telling me that if I stray too far, then Apple will just switch herself off, or I won't remember to take my tablets, or — something will happen. Maybe this feeling will wear off, like the beard did. (Well, it was removed. But it doesn't grow back anymore.) Or maybe I like it here. I think I like it here.

Help me.

I'll give you a week.

CLAIM YOUR HERITAGE: Be Scottish. Trust your instincts. Study in real life with real people. You'll always find opportunities. Even if you move somewhere else you can still practise Scottish law. That's what the Internet is for.

BE BOLD: Take fresh new steps. Your horizons can be broader now. And if you study with the OU, then you've got more flexibility to work and earn. And it's not like you never meet people in real life anymore.

2 shares
11 comments

Results:
EDINBURGH 27%
OU   73%

'God, it's good to be here,' Seb says. 'I've missed the old place.'

Ailsa laughs. 'It must be all of ten days since we were here,' she says. They'd spent a long evening at the Northbridge Brasserie after that first joint tango night, with Roz and a couple of the local actors.

'Feels like longer,' Seb says. 'Theatre is hard. Good, but not like TV. There's not a lot of time sitting around while someone sets the lighting up. Not much of a buffet.'

'And it's only your second day off this week,' Ailsa says. She grins. He grins back. These moments — more and more of them, inconsequential, but not — are like a breathworth of flying.

'I'm not having a day off,' Seb says, 'I'm — reflecting. While the ladies do their mysterious lady acting. What? Why are you pointing your knife at me? That's rude.'

'In Scotland, it's a sign of affection. And I

feel as though I should pull you up on the mysterious-lady-acting thing,' Ailsa says, 'but I haven't worked out why.'

'Ah well,' his smile widens to wickedness, 'while you work it out, I'll just sit here, reflecting on my part.'

Ailsa laughs; she can't help it. 'You're terrible.'

'It's too easy to get a rise out of you.'

'That's my line,' she says.

'Ailsa Rae . . .' He laughs, and his foot finds her ankle under the table.

Seb staying at Roz's hasn't really worked out. He's a permanent fixture at Ailsa's. In public — apart from the dancing — they don't touch, except under tables, like this. In private it feels impossible not to be in contact. Ailsa isn't sure when they became a couple, or if she wants them to be one. Or rather, if it's a real relationship, or for-the-duration. They have an easy way of being, already, and sometimes it's as though he reads her —

'I like staying with you. Do you feel as though we've known each other forever?'

— mind.

'I was just thinking that.'

'It's funny,' Seb says, leaning in so that he can touch her knees under the table, run his fingers over the insides of them, 'I always thought living with someone would be boring, when the novelty wore off. But knowing someone better is — sexy. Don't you think?'

Ailsa can't help but laugh. 'Like I said. It's been ten days,' she says.

'Have you ever lived with anyone for ten days?'

She pulls her face into pretend-seriousness. 'Good point.'

'Me neither. You see.' He smiles and sits back. Her knees feel cold, in the place where his hands were.

'Is it going OK, though,' she asks, 'the play?'

'I've no idea.' He sounds neutral, matter-of-fact; if Ailsa was an actor, she supposes, she'd know what he meant. But she isn't, and she doesn't.

'Is that not — should you not know by now?' Two weeks until opening night. Sometimes she's so excited about the prospect of it that she can't stop smiling, but more and more Ailsa feels sick at the thought of it. And not dainty, mild butterfly-sickness, but serious post-operative nausea. Seb seems calm, but his sleep is twitchy, and he tutted at her this morning when she forgot to pick up her phone and had to go back for it.

'Roz says that you never know until you've

got an audience in front of you, and shame on you if you think anything different.'

'I can imagine her saying that,' Ailsa says. She can see the sense in it too. The difference between thinking that you can do something and doing it is the size of the mountain she thought, pre-transplant, that she would be climbing by now.

'Have you fixed a date with your father?' Seb asks.

'Next Monday.' There's one of those moments, increasingly frequent, when their feelings for each other make another presence between them, vivid, alive, blotting out everything else.

He nods. 'How are you feeling about it? Have you talked to your mother yet?'

'Nervous. Not really.' She's not going to get away with that. It's the equivalent of telling a doctor that you're fine. She tries harder. 'I don't know what to expect from him. And I know exactly what I'll get from her.' *You'll get what you deserve,* Apple says, and the look in Seb's eyes agrees. Great. They're ganging up on her.

He says, carefully, 'I can see why she might be upset. I can see why you want to see him, too.'

'Yes.' Except she doesn't, not really, but it's too late to say so, and anyway, the blog.

455

'Can we talk about something else? Please?' She touches her foot to the inside of his ankle, rubs it back and forth, to say, this is not rejection.

Seb smiles, and then leans forward, and Ailsa finds herself mirroring him. 'Do you want to know a secret? A good one. From Roz. I'm not supposed to say anything. Promise not to leak it to the press?'

Ailsa struggles for a straight face. 'Promise.'

'You know *Love's Labour's Lost*?'

'Not intimately.' Emily wrote an essay on it, mostly while keeping Ailsa company when she had flu in their second year; there was a lot of sighing and cursing. 'Not Shakespeare's most popular play, I'm told.'

'Well, it was all news to me,' Seb says, 'not that that's saying a lot. Apparently, it's one of those plays that's — of its time. Would have had Elizabethans rolling in the aisles. Modern audiences need a translator to explain why it's supposed to be funny. But Roz is directing it at the Wheat Warehouse in London next year. Spring. Six-week season to start with, maybe a tour, depending on how it goes. It's going to be a big deal. Proper pay. Serious theatre.'

'Why not do something more popular? Are you going to be in it?'

Seb laughs. 'The thing with Roz is, she could make toothache popular. And anyway, she's got a really strong — she's got this idea that the way we live now is too black and white. You click "like" or you don't. You vote yes or no. No one is allowed to be undecided. You can only be in public life if you've never shagged someone you shouldn't have, in case the papers find out. And the world's more complicated. Stuff gets hidden. We have unrealistic expecta- tions. We're divided. She thinks it's relevant, and she wants to do a — well, she's calling it a monochrome production. I don't know what that means. But she's excited.'

'And is she giving you a part?'

'Berowne,' Seb says, 'who has the longest speech in all of Shakespeare. We're going to be busy, you and me.'

'That's fantastic,' Ailsa says. 'Is that what your phone call was about?' Seb had been on the phone when she got out of the shower; it had sounded businesslike, his spine straight as he stood, looking out of the window as he talked.

'Yeah. Wilkie. He's not keen.'

'Why not?' Ailsa has always been under the impression that actors needed work, and there was never enough around. Seb's agent seems to have a different view.

'He thinks I'm wasting my beautiful years, if I spend them on the stage. There's plenty of time for Shakespeare when my TV Romeo days are over, according to him.'

Ailsa thinks, not for the first time, about how miserable life as an actor is. The first day Seb rehearsed his fight scene, he came back pale-faced and blooming blue bruises across his back and on his thigh, and Ailsa felt sick at the thought of all her mother must have felt, watching as she bruised and ached. Rejection, waiting, bruising. At least Ailsa didn't choose it. When she and her mother are having real conversations again, she'll mention it. She's doing her best to build bridges, but until she's seen her father, it's not going to be easy to move on.

'Don't you think — is that not a bit unfair? Being in this play and not knowing that you're being measured up for something else?' Seb's face changes, from serious to a smile, but Ailsa doesn't think she said anything funny. 'What?'

'Sorry, I thought for a minute you were suggesting someone else's life was unfair.'

Ailsa sits back, a sudden, sharp movement. 'That's —'

'What? Not fair?'

Green eyes meet blue for a second: this could go either way. A decision. Ailsa laughs. 'Bastard.'

'That came out wrong,' says Seb. 'It was meant to be — what's a word for light-hearted that doesn't have the word heart in it?'

'It's OK,' Ailsa says. She doesn't know where the time goes when they're together. If only her hospital days had passed as swiftly, and this — this joy — would slow down, dissolve softly, instead of fizzing the days away from them.

He leans back, signals for the bill. 'You did say you start work at one? Do you want to walk over together?'

'I'm not really like that, am I?'

Seb looks at her, seriously. 'No. But you have your moments.'

Ailsa nods. 'That is fair.'

The bill arrives and Seb glances at it, puts thirty pounds to pay for their brunch on the table, and takes his sunglasses from his pocket, ready for the outside world. He hardly ever wears them indoors these days. Before he puts them on he hesitates, reaches for Ailsa's hand, and looks into her eyes in a way that makes her forget to look for the familiar, well-spaced 'V's that show how he is healing.

'You're all right, you know,' he says.

If Ailsa isn't immediately sure what he

means, Apple is, lurching and contrating in her chest. 'Is that English for something too?'

Seb slips on his sunglasses, stands, and waits for her to stand and pick up her bag. He kisses the top of her head, a gesture somewhere between tenderness and a promise. 'You know it is,' he says, and he leads her out into the sunlight.

It's a short enough walk, ten minutes or so, fifteen if you dawdle, and it's dawdling weather. Seb is wearing his trilby as well as his shades, and maybe he feels disguised or maybe their unspoken public policy has been rewritten, because he wraps his arm around her shoulder and they find a pace that almost matches, hip to hip. Ailsa can take the walk up to the old town without a rest, these days, but she doesn't have a lot of breath for conversation; Seb is quiet too, looking around, looking up. Anyway, she's thinking about what he just said. She does know what it means. She's been telling herself that she's not ready to love yet/only having a fling. But Apple hasn't been listening. Ailsa's chest has an expanding, singing feeling that's almost enough to blot out how much she's missing her mother.

The walk, from North Bridge to Bank Street, is quick but it's through the busy heart of the city; the Royal Mile is always crowded with sightseers. Bagpipe music is drifting across from a busker; a serious-looking pair of tourists are poring over a map. Seb dodges them, stepping Ailsa onto the road and then back to the pavement.

'I suppose it will be busier,' he says, 'when the Fringe starts?'

'You've no idea,' Ailsa says. 'It's fun, though.' Last year, she was staggering from grief for Lennox to admitting that her own heart was failing, and the Fringe had been a sudden burst of colour in her grey world. The weather was beautiful. Her friends had got her out of hospital for a couple of hours here and there: Emily had taken her to some comedy, she and Christa had sat outside the World's End pub, drinking lemonade and watching the world go by. At the time she had thought these were her last good days.

When they turn down towards the coffee shop, she hesitates, and he turns back towards her. 'You're all right too, you know,' she says.

'I'm glad,' he says, and he tilts up her chin and kisses her, lightly, on her temple, the tip of her nose, her cheek, her lips, then holds her close. The last time he kissed her in the street doesn't bear thinking about: it was the night that they'd been dancing, in London, and she panicked and sent him away. How things change. She presses her cross-kissed face into his jacket, and feels the pressure of his arms around her increase in response.

'Can I come in for a coffee?' Seb asks. 'I'll be good, I promise. I'll sit quietly in the corner and read Shakespeare.'

'Sure,' Ailsa says. Now that novelty of Seb has worn off, none of her co-workers remark on him; plus, Full of Beans has become a regular haunt of a couple of novelists and a singer, so the staff is doing its best to take celebrity customers in its stride, trying for a blasé, oh-is-that-Sebastian-Morley-I-didn't-notice vibe.

And then she looks through the window and sees her mother, sitting at one of the corner tables, with a pencil in her hand and a folded newspaper in front of her. She'll be doing a crossword. It's a long time since they've done one together. It's strange, what you miss.

'My mother is here.'

Seb puts his hand against the glass, scans the cafe. 'Oh, I see her. In the corner, right? Yellow scarf? She looks like you. Well, you look like her.'

'It's the first time I've seen her since she

told me the whole story about my father.' They've spoken, texted, but neither has suggested a meeting.

'It's good that she's here, then?' says Seb.

'I suppose,' Ailsa says, takes a breath, and pushes the door open.

Hayley looks up at the sound of the door and gets to her feet. 'Ailsa.' They are standing two feet from each other. It seems they have forgotten how to embrace.

'I didn't know you were coming,' Ailsa says. 'I start work in ten minutes. I can't really —' She can't really complete the sentence. 'I can't really rerun the blog argument again with you or tell you how upset I am that you didn't tell me the truth or start to talk about how I miss you.'

'That's OK, hen,' Hayley says, and there's a look on her face that says she understands that Ailsa's hurt, even as she's hurting. It's enough for Ailsa to close the physical gap between them, at least, step into her mother's arms and feel the comfort of her familiar shape. 'Tamsin's over here, seeing a dealer, so I thought I'd come and say hello. I just wanted to see you. See that you're OK.' Hayley has stepped back now and Ailsa knows that she's checking her skin tone for blueness, the shape of her face for weight loss or gain. She ought to mind. She doesn't. This time next week, she'll have met her father, and she can call Hayley and they can start over. She ignores Apple's whispered suggestion that she could change all this right now.

'Seb's with me,' she says.

'Pleased to meet you, Ms Rae.' Ailsa glances up at him and sees he has the sense not to be wearing his hundred-watt smile. He looks serious, sober.

'Hello,' Hayley says.

'May I join you?'

'You're welcome to,' Hayley says, 'and you can call me Hayley. But I'll not be charmed.'

Seb takes off his shades and pulls out the other chair at the corner table. 'That's fine with me. I've no intention of charming you.'

Oh, well played, Seb, Ailsa thinks, and she reaches out to touch his arm, smiles at them both, then goes to put her apron on and start work.

464

22nd July 2018

The Real Romeo and Juliet?

Sharp-eyed *Sun* celeb-spotters spied sexy Sebastian Morley in Edinburgh last week, where he's rehearsing for his role as Romeo. But the lady who's captured his heart isn't his co-star, willowy Meredith Katz.

Seb was seen out and about with the curvy mystery dance partner we spotted him with earlier this year.

She might have lost a pound or two since then but she hasn't lost her hold on Seb's heart. The pair laughed as they left the Northbridge Brasserie with their arms around each other. They were later spotted kissing on a street corner. We've always thought Seb was a player — but maybe he's been looking for a girl who's larger-than-life.

Seb was thought to be dating his *Star-Dance* partner Fenella Albright before leaving the show last year. But the pair, who had steamy chemistry on the dance floor, haven't been seen in public together since shortly after his surgery. Could it be that Fenella needs to fatten up if she wants to catch Seb's eye?

22 JULY, 2017

This Time Last Year

Ailsa and Hayley go to the Scottish Borders, in the end, the blog vote being 43 per cent south, 23 per cent north and 34 per cent west. Although they had ruled out east because there wasn't anywhere new before you hit the sea, they still find that they can't really bear to travel far: it feels reckless, and Ailsa is so very tired that the thought of any journey further than a couple of hours feels unbearable. Tamsin drives them there, Emily will collect them after three days, and Hayley gets a briefing on drips and dressings that she puts up with even though she knows everything there is to know about her daughter's regime. The duty sister, waving them off the ward, tells them that this time next year they'll probably be in Tenerife. Ailsa, exhausted by the effort of getting up and dressed, can think of nothing worse. She'd already rather be back in bed.

But it's worth it. Oh, it's worth it. The hotel is a castle; they have a suite, in a turret, the light bright and strong but the curtains thick and heavily lined, so they both sleep better than they have in months.

They have room service, because they have had enough sympathetic and curious looks to last them a lifetime, even a long one. In the year's longest days, after slow walks around the grounds and lazy afternoons in the spa, they sit at the dining table in their turret window and eat meals that taste better than anything either of them has eaten in a long time.

On their last evening, they are looking out over the hills, heathery and muted, dotted with sheep, the roads crawling with slow white caravans as the rest of the world goes on holiday, and even though Ailsa has been determined to keep hoping, and looking forward, now that there's less and less future, her mind cannot help but go back. Lennox's death is still a raw bitter edge that catches every time her failing heart beats; she knows that this is what her mother is facing. And as for her —

'I'm frightened, Mum,' she says. She didn't realise the words were going to come out until she says them. Sometimes it seems that her heart has already resigned from her

468

body and doesn't bother telling her things she ought to know.

'I know, hen,' Hayley says, then, with the sound of put-aside tears in her voice, 'me too.'

'I don't know how we can do — this.' Ailsa isn't sure whether she means her death, or continuing to live this way. A new heart is feeling more and more hypothetical.

Hayley sighs, gets up from the table and opens the window, lights a cigarette. There are 'no smoking' signs, but the hotel seems to be turning a blind eye. 'I suppose I just think — look at this. We're OK now. We've got this view and air in our lungs, and we've just eaten better food than most of the people in the world will ever get to eat. Right this minute we're fine, and that will have to do.'

Ailsa smiles. 'Right now, we're fine,' she says.

Hayley blows smoke out of the window. 'Tamsin says I'd make a grand Buddhist.'

'You might have to give up the smoking, though. And the swearing.'

'Fuck that.'

And Ailsa almost lets the moment go, but she can't, because at some point she might need to know the answer to the question that fills her every time she looks at her mother. 'What will you do, Mum? If — if I don't get a heart in time?'

Hayley stubs out her cigarette on the stone windowsill, a slow-motion grinding. There's the smallest of shakes through her shoulders. When she turns back towards Ailsa, there are tears in her eyes. 'I'll take it a minute at a time, Ailsa.'

23 JULY, 2018

'You're nervous about this, aren't you?' Seb's looking at her the way he does, sometimes, half scrutiny half love, and she feels more naked than when she's naked.

'Maybe. Why do you say so?' It comes out more sharply than she intends, and she touches his arm in apology.

'That's the third time you've got changed this morning. That's saying something.'

Ailsa sighs, throws herself down on the sofa next to him. 'It's saying your eye's getting better?'

He laughs. 'That's more like it. But honestly, your blog isn't cleverer than you are. And you know best.'

'You sound like my mother.' Just the thought of Hayley still hurts. Ailsa used to think it was anger, at being lied to all of those years. Maybe it was. Maybe she's missing her. But if she thinks about that now it'll all come apart.

471

'Wilkie rang, while you were changing,' Seb says. 'Guess what?'

'You're the next James Bond? You're doing panto?'

He laughs. 'Well, make those into a Venn diagram and you've more or less got it. I'm doing *StarDance* again.'

'Wow. Congratulations!' And she means it, she really does, because the only way to be here, now, is to deal with future complications later.

'Thanks, BlueHeart,' he says, and then, 'it's funny. When I was first offered it last year, I thought it was all my Christmases come at once. Now I'm more excited about *Love's Labour's Lost.*'

'And Romeo,' she says.

'No, I'm petrified about that.'

She has to check his face in case he's joking, 'Seriously? You've not said. You don't seem scared.'

'It's not scared, exactly. It's — tension. Build-up. I always get it. I used to be sick before the live shows for *Wherefore Art Thou?.* And *StarDance.* It's OK when there isn't a live audience. If you mess up a recording, you just go again.'

'I always get nervous before the hospital. And the tango.'

Seb pulls her closer. 'The hospital, I can

see. But the tango? Because of the show, you mean?'

'Not the show,' Ailsa says, 'just the dancing. I'm all right once it starts. But the second before, I feel . . .' She stops, shakes her head. 'I don't know. It seems silly. It's only dancing. And I love it, once it's — once it's happening.'

Seb squeezes her hand. 'It's the unknown. You think you know what's going to happen. You've got the lines, the moves, whatever. But it could still all go wrong.'

'That's it.' Ailsa leans her head in to him. It's frightening/lovely that he should understand her so well.

'Do you want me to walk you there?' he asks.

She laughs. 'Would you be able to fit on the pavement? Next to my larger-than-life curviness?'

They've been joking about the latest article. Seb's right, it does get easier — and the fact that he's here, and they are just the two of them, together, makes the spite and stupidity of yesterday's newspaper story seem obvious. Not that it doesn't sting. But it's so obvious that the Seb in the press is not the Seb in her flat that she can joke about it with. And when she does, he does something like what he does now — grabs her, kisses her, says, 'You've captured my sexy playboy heart, Ailsa Rae.' She can cope with the tabloids, because what they say is just not true. 'Seriously, though,' he asks, 'will you be OK?'

'Yes.' And in this moment, she knows that she will be — can be — OK. And it's nothing to do with Apple, or having to be some kind of walking miracle all the damn time. She just knows that she's strong enough to meet whatever it is that David brings to her life. And to keep on building the bridge with Hayley that started in Full of Beans two days ago, when she talked to Seb, and hugged Ailsa when she left. Ailsa lets her shoulders relax, and her eyes close, leaning back against him.

Seb kisses the top of her head and says, 'I've said I don't want Fenella as a partner.'

David is unmistakable, because he's her: the breadth of his forehead, the colour of his eyes. Ailsa recognises the shape of his hand as he shakes her hand, rather awkwardly. She'd wondered if she'd be overcome when she saw him, cry or rush to hug him, but actually, an awkward handshake hits the mark.

'Hello,' she says. Her voice is steadier than she thinks it will be. Her heart is too, come to think of it. This man, on the other hand — half a head taller than her, broad-shouldered, paunchy, well-dressed — looks like anxiety personified.

'Ailsa.' He says it with the emphasis on the second syllable, as though she's a magic spell. 'Good to meet you.'

She'd proposed they meet at the floral clock, because everyone knows where that is, and it makes a walk the obvious thing to do. A sightseeing bus passes, and Ailsa can almost see herself and Seb on the back of the top deck. How far she's come since then, with her job and her career plan, and getting used to her solo home. She puts her hand on her chest, as though that will stop Apple from reaching out for Hayley.

'I always liked this clock,' David says. 'It's clever, isn't it?' His accent is a sort of characterless English, free of stresses.

'Yes.' The floral clock used to be a wonder to her. She and Hayley used to come and look at the time, after milkshakes at the Rose Street cafe.

David nods. 'They've used succulents, so there's not a lot of maintenance. Nice and practical.'

'If you wanted a practical clock, surely they wouldn't make it out of flowers to begin with?' Ailsa smiles to show that she isn't being argumentative. This is a bit like her first day at work, striving to make the right impression.

David nods. 'True enough.'

'I thought it would be good to take a walk, and I have to make sure I get enough exercise.' She's not going to brush Apple under the carpet, as it were.

They set off, the sharply rising bank to Princes Street on their right, where there's a mass of flowers in purples and yellows, silver and green foliage, thistles and heather and fern, all tumbled together in a sort of well-planned chaos. To their left, down the slope, are trees, more formal flowerbeds, and lawns peppered with people.

'This must take some maintaining,' David says.

'There are always gardeners around,' Ailsa replies. She looks at the path they are walking, a sort of pebbledash pavement, sees how one foot just keeps putting itself in front of another. She can do anything this way.

She looks at his shoes. They are dark grey, suede, the sort of shoes that are advertised in the back of the Sunday magazines she recycles at the ends of shifts. He's wearing jeans and a polo shirt and carrying a jacket. He looks — respectable. She eventually fixed on jeans, her silver plimsolls, the cloud-heart T-shirt and a cardigan that Tamsin gave her, royal blue and wrap-around, so almost a coat if it gets cool.

They make small talk: David's journey, Ailsa's job, the weather in Scotland (again), how distinctive the Edinburgh skyline is. Ailsa waits — wants — to feel something, the bond that she's owed, her genes remembering this connection. Something that will justify how much she's hurt her mother.

They pause at the war memorial to the Scottish dead of the Second World War. David reads the inscription aloud: 'If it be life that waits, I shall live forever unconquered. If death, I shall die at last, strong in my pride and free.' He stands for a moment, then glances at Ailsa — they aren't looking at each other, much, yet. 'Beautiful.'

'I'm not so sure,' Ailsa says. 'Death doesn't seem so glorious when you're looking it in the teeth.'

'True enough.' David seems to agree with everything. Ailsa thinks of Dennis, shaking his head and saying 'owt for peace' when Ruthie is trying to persuade him to do something. But when Dennis says it, it's a joke.

She's tired, all of a sudden, and sits on a bench. The plaque on the back commemorates Maisie Sietsema, nee Stirling, born in Edinburgh in 1919, died in Massachusetts in 1966. How far some people manage to go in their lives.

'I said pleased to meet you, but it should really be: pleased to meet you again,' David says when he's settled himself next to her, with something that might be a chuckle. Ailsa reminds herself that they are both nervous.

'I don't remember the last time,' she says.

'I do,' David says, shaking his head. 'Awful. Awful. Who'd have thought it, to look at you now?'

Ailsa bites back the obvious response — that clearly he didn't. She's here, so she'll make the best of it. 'I'm fine now,' she says. 'Better every day.'

'It's been a while since I've been to Edinburgh,' he says. Ailsa pushes her teeth together for a second to make sure she doesn't say something sarcastic. 'And it's a lovely day for Scotland,' he continues.

'Uh-huh,' Ailsa says. She gets up and sets off again, slowly, along the path. David follows.

'So you're well?' he asks.

Ailsa nods. 'As well as can be expected. I have a check-up every week. Things seem to be going to plan.'

'Good,' David says. He touches his hand to his chest. 'I had a bit of a scare this year with mine. Thank goodness for private health insurance. I had all the tests in a week.'

'So what's wrong?' Ailsa asks. Heart trouble isn't her favourite icebreaker but it will do in a pinch.

David gives a laugh. 'Well — funny story — it turns out it was indigestion! Terrible pain, though, right up my side, down my

479

arm. Sweating like a pig. I thought my number was up.'

'Indigestion?' Ah, here come the feelings. Ailsa suddenly, viscerally, would like to be anywhere else in the world than here. But most especially on the train to Glasgow, to her mother.

'I know.' David laughs again. No, actually it's a chortle. It's the sound of a man who always has someone to hand to laugh at his jokes. 'Gemma gave me such a going over. No more chilli con carne for me!'

Ailsa doesn't say anything. She really, truly cannot think of a single word to offer. She can hear Apple, though, loud and clear: *Seriously?*

David steers her to a halt in front of a flower bed. 'I've tried to grow these,' he says, indicating — well, something, Ailsa has no idea what, but they're yellow. 'I think the soil is wrong where we are. Too loamy. This will be peatier, I should think.'

'I'm not interested in gardening,' Ailsa says. Politeness seems pointless.

'You don't have a garden?'

'For a while back there,' Ailsa says, 'I would have fainted if I'd bent down, or stood up. But no, I don't have a garden. Don't you remember? I've a couple of window boxes.'

David looks straight into her face for the first time since the moment they met. 'You aren't still in that flat?'

'I am,' Ailsa says. 'It's a great flat. A great spot. And such a lot of memories for me and my mother.'

David makes a gesture of shoulder and eyebrow, a sort of, 'I don't agree but I won't argue', and Ailsa is horrified by both his easy dismissal of such an important place in her life and the fact that she recognises that gesture as her own. Or rather, one she's inherited, it seems. No wonder it's always irritated the hell out of her mother.

'We've nearly an acre,' he adds, 'but Gemma's keen, as well, so it's a hobby for us both.'

'That's nice,' Ailsa says, because she can't think of another response.

'I'm sorry,' David says, 'I'm not doing very well. I don't know what to say.'

'Why don't you tell me why you were never in touch?' Ailsa says. She's worked hard to expect nothing, yet she's disappointed by him. And envious — a real, ugly, pus-like feeling — of the younger son, with his rescued animals and all the support he needs to cope with dyslexia. Why was he different from Ailsa? Why did he get a puppy when she got distance and disinterest?

'Well . . .' David says, 'I suppose — I suppose I had assumed that you had — had not survived. Your chances weren't good.'

It's horrible to hear him so cold and clear about it, even though she has always insisted on an unsentimental approach herself. She's earned it. He hasn't.

'I know that,' Ailsa says. 'But I had a chance. I'm surprised you didn't want to know. And did you not think my mother would have told you?'

David sighs. 'She was angry with me. And,' he holds up a finger, as though Ailsa might have been about to interrupt, 'rightly so. I accept that. After what she did to my flat — I don't know how much she's told you . . .'

'She told me everything.' Ailsa is full of pride for Hayley, her bravery and her truth. The fact that she took so long to tell Ailsa everything doesn't seem to matter so much.

That half shrug again. 'Did she tell you it was my parents' le Creuset that she took?'

Ailsa almost laughs. Or cries. How she's messed things up. Why didn't she trust her mother, who's fought for her, whose judgement is almost always right?

'Well, I did want to know what had happened to you,' David says, with a rising inflection of defensiveness in his tone, 'but it never seemed to be the right time to ask. You know how it is.'

'Not really.' She's keeping her voice even, but her feelings aren't quite so serene. 'In my life, I've always had to do things when I could, because there might not be tomorrow.'

It's as though she hasn't spoken. 'I thought I would give your mother some time to — to calm herself down. I thought she might get in touch after I sold the flat and gave her the money from it. But she didn't. And then, once we had George . . .' David says. He fumbles in his pocket. Ailsa fears he's going to try to show her some family photographs. She's ignored a Facebook friend request from David until she met him. But he takes out a handkerchief, takes off his glasses, and polishes the lenses. He might be avoiding her scrutiny, but she has nothing to lose.

'You were too busy?'

'No, no,' he seems genuinely distressed, 'not at all! I often thought I should find out what had happened to you. I just never —'

'Never got around to it?'

He looks straight into her face. It's strange, how his eyes are her eyes. 'Even though I thought you probably hadn't survived, I didn't want to know for sure. I wasn't — I wasn't ready for that. I know that seems ridiculous. I do know how badly I let you and your mother down, Ailsa. I'm not proud.'

'I'm glad to hear that. I don't think you have any idea how badly you let us down, though. Not really.'

They walk on. Ailsa imagines him with Gemma and her three sisters, and their husbands and children, not the perfect family but a cauldron of disagreements and unresolved arguments.

He takes a breath. 'Ailsa, I've no excuse. I did badly by you and your mother, and you both deserved better. Then when your message came, well, I thought it was a chance. I was so glad that you were alive.'

'It hasn't been easy.'

'I do know that, Ailsa. Especially when I read your blog. You've been lucky.'

Oh, no, no. Ailsa already knows — and Apple is in perfect accord — that she never needs to see this man again, and needs to get away from him before he starts trying to include her in his sprawling family, the half sister/stepdaughter back from the dead. But that doesn't mean she's going to let him get away with that.

'Lucky and determined. It's been hard work. Plus, my mother has been amazing.

She never gave up.' The emphasis comes out on the 'she'. Ailsa doesn't care.

'Maybe lucky was a poor choice of word. I suppose I've always been risk averse by nature. Your mother pulled me out of that for a while. But when the chips were down — well, a leopard doesn't change its spots. I think you must understand that, though?'

'Why?' Ailsa asks. (*Yes. Why?* Apple echoes.) If she has sacrificed her relationship with her mother for this man, she will never forgive herself. Oh, she wants to cry, enough tears to flood her heart and wash her eyes away.

'Well, your blog. When I saw your polls, I thought: now that's my daughter. It's always good to canvass opinions, isn't it? Take a consensus. That's what Gemma and I like to do. There's no excuse for rashness in this day and age.'

Ailsa starts to walk more quickly, as though speed will lessen the impact of this body blow. She doesn't much care if David keeps pace with her, but he does.

'Ailsa?'

'I'm not so sure it is a good thing, actually,' she says. 'Sometimes you trust your gut, don't you? Or — or your heart. I mean — if you asked a hundred people whether you should abandon your child because she has a heart problem, I imagine a hundred per cent of the vote would say no, don't do that. But you did it.'

'I don't think that's entirely fair,' David says, 'and anyway ——'

'No,' she says. It's never too late, Ailsa. Say what you want to say. 'You said in your email I was never a secret from Gemma. Do your boys know about me?'

'Well . . .' He looks bewildered now. Ailsa imagines Gemma joking about having three children, not two, and drinking a lot. 'Gemma said we should see how this went. And then we could introduce you to the family. Slowly.'

'What, first I'm a friend, then I'm a cousin, and then, if everyone votes that they like me, I'm allowed to be your daughter? I'm sorry, David, this was a mistake. Have a safe journey home.' And she turns and walks away. She'd like to think she's dignified but there's a panicky half run to her pace.

It's an hour until rehearsal. She hopes that Hayley will answer her phone.

Voicemail. Ailsa never used to get her mother's voicemail. Another perk of being no longer dying. She's walking, walking, her breath fast and ragged, people looking at her. She heads for the graveyard of St Cuthbert's church, which adjoins the gar-

486

dens, and stops when her anger — at herself, at David, at the stupid, stupid world and how complicated it is, even when you're supposed to be normal — runs out.

She stops in a part of the graveyard where the palest of sunlight is picking its way through the trees. Sitting on a low wall, she notices how the Edinburgh skyline is hidden. She could be anywhere. Even the graves have their backs to her. She can hear voices as people walk nearby, but apart from a seagull glaring at her as though it knows how ungrateful she's been, she's on her own. Well, sort of. There's just her, and Apple, and the seagull, and all of the dead people.

Inhale. Exhale. She closes her eyes and tilts her head to the sky. When she opens her eyes again she sees that it has changed from grey-blue to blue-grey. It's a small change, but it matters.

She's about to call Hayley again — even if she doesn't answer, she'll hear her mother's voice on the message — when her phone rings.

'Ailsa?'

'Mum, it's me. I'm sorry,' she half says, half cries.

'Are you OK, hen? Breathe. Calm down. Is this about that thing in the papers?'

Hayley had called, to see that she was OK, after the story about her and Seb; Ailsa hadn't got around to calling back, or that's what she had told herself. She hadn't wanted to talk about David, hear the hurt in Hayley's voice.

'No. That's — that's OK. It's just that — I've just met him. It was today.'

'Who? Oh,' Hayley says, and Ailsa hears her shock, how her voice has a shake in it that's the shadow to the way her own voice sounds. 'David? Has it not gone well?'

'He's — I thought I'd feel something, but I just . . .' She's fumbling for a tissue in her satchel. A couple walks past, and the woman glances at her, concerned, but at least in a cemetery she has a good chance of being left alone to cry.

'Has he upset you? That fucking man. Honestly, Ailsa, if I'd known it was today I'd have —' Hayley's voice, furious, pauses, as they both imagine what she might have done.

'Yes. No. Only by being — by being the sort of person who would do what he did.'

A sigh, down the line, and the sound of what might be tears. 'Oh, Ailsa. I'm sorry. I wanted to protect you from all this. I just made you more curious.'

'It was my fault, Mum,' Ailsa says. 'I

should've . . .' But there's such a long list, and she doesn't know what she should have done. Taken her mother's word that he wasn't worth the bother? Not asked the question about him? Not asked the blog? Not gone with the vote? Trusted the love her mother's always shown against the curiosity Apple kindled in her, now she has the time to wonder?

'Well,' Hayley says, with a sniff/sob, 'we are where we are. Are you OK? What are you going to do now?'

Oh, yes. If in doubt, be practical. 'I've got rehearsal. Seb's staying. I'll be — I'll manage.'

'Are you sure?'

'I'm sure.' She isn't. Not really. But being not quite sure seems to be what a lot of normal life is about.

25 July, 2018

I'm Sorry

I've talked a lot, this year, about learning what it means to be normal. I'm sure you've laughed along as old Blue-Heart here has found out that some afternoons are long and doing your washing is boring. I like to imagine you chuckling at my discovery that how much you weigh is directly related to what you put in your mouth, and mountain climbing takes a bit of preparation and practice.

Here are some of the things I've discovered that being three heartbeats from death allows you to do, even though you can't get away with them (most days) in normal life:

Falling asleep during a conversation
Asking someone to make you a sandwich in the middle of the night (and them doing it)
Feeling sorry for yourself
Not thinking about/planning for the future
Having your wishes/needs treated as more urgent than everyone else's

Claiming that life's not fair and expecting
  sympathy.

In summary: generally behaving as though
you are more important than everyone
else.

   Well, I'm here to say, with you as my wit-
nesses, that I accept I have no excuse for
behaving badly anymore. I can't claim
tiredness/anxiety/impending death. I can't
even really claim drug imbalances now
that we seem to have got that right.

   So if I am rude, inconsiderate, or plain
disrespectful to someone that I love, I have
no get-out-of-jail-free card. Of course, I
never should have had one, or used one,
but — well, I did. When you're the one
that's dying, it's easiest to ignore the pain
of the person who's watching you die.

   This last few weeks, I've behaved unfor-
givably badly to my mother. I've been rude
and unkind, and I've chosen not to make
the effort to understand things that are not
black and white, though I've tried to make
them so.

   You'll also recall that I saw my birth
father. (Your suggestion of a walk for our
meeting was spot-on, by the way. I was
able to — literally — run away. Well, walk
fast, at least.) All you need to know is: I

won't be seeing him again.

I'm doing my best to patch things up with the only parent I've really ever had. It will take time.

I've got time.

But, as a start: I'm sorry, Mum. And I love you. You're right — some things are private. But sorriness and love don't need to be.

17 shares
72 comments

■ ■ ■ ■

PART NINE:
AUGUST 2018
UNPLEASING SHARPS

■ ■ ■ ■

30 JULY, 2018

Dress rehearsal. The show opens tomorrow.

The eight members of the cast, the three musicians and all of the dancers taking part are here — thirty-odd people in total. Eight members of the tango club will be in the audience every night.

Over the last few weeks these sessions have been jokey and relaxed. There's no sign of that tonight. It's as though they'd all forgotten what these rehearsals were actually about, until now.

The actors are wearing jeans and white shirts, with yellow sashes for Montague and green for Capulet. The dancers are in black — Ailsa's old dress fits again — and will have scarves tied around their throats or wrists; on performance nights, scarves on the back of chairs will reserve their seats, and masks will be concealed beneath. The scarves are red. Of course they are. Ailsa's scalp prickles. She sort-of wishes that she hadn't volunteered now. Or at least that she'd put it to the vote so these feelings wouldn't be her fault. *Did you notice that?* Apple asks. She's not sure when her heart became her emotional auditor. Maybe when she began to trust her.

The central dance floor has become a stage, thanks to blocks stacked at one end, arranged so that there's a stairway up one side, a shape that might be a doorway in the centre, a smaller half door at the other side. Other, loose, blocks are scattered around the edges of the dance floor. Ailsa thinks of Seb describing the balcony scene in rehearsals, Meredith asking that Roz walk through all of her moves first, to make sure that it was safe. She can see Meredith's point.

Roz steps forward, smiles. 'Welcome,' she says, 'all of you. This is our final time together before the show opens. I hope you're excited. You should be. We've worked hard and I'm proud of what we've done.'

There's a ripple of applause, led by Eliza. Roz holds up a hand. 'But this is not a school play. This is a professional production of a classic of the English language. It's a timely and thoughtful show. We have worked on it hard and we stake our reputations upon it. I am not standing here to ask you to go out there and enjoy yourselves.

496

I'm standing here telling you to find the best of you, the strongest and the bravest, and bring that to this space, every night of the production. Do justice to yourselves, to your fellow actors and dancers, to your teachers, to Shakespeare, and to your audiences.'

Eliza opens her hands, ready to applaud again; Edie puts her own hand out to stop her sister. All of the faces in the room — Ailsa's too, she suspects — have the same expression: serious, bright. And all of a sudden she could cry, just because she is here, part of this. She's not sitting on the sidelines, blue, waiting for Lennox to score a goal. She'll step forward.

She can.

Roz has let the silence thicken; she drops her voice now. 'You are not being paid. That does not make you amateurs. Please be on time, play as we've rehearsed, and do not let yourselves get slack. Every audience is a new audience. Every show deserves all of your love and your best mind and heart. Expect notes from me after every performance. And know that it's been an honour to work with you all. Those of you who have worked with me before will know that I don't make a habit of saying that.'

There's laughter, and a sudden sense of relaxation in the air. 'One more thing, before Edie gives you a briefing about this evening. Romeo here has got himself into the papers again, and any of you might be approached by the press for gossip. They tend not to declare themselves. If someone downstairs offers you a drink and asks you how it's going, by all means speak your own truth, but please do not speculate about the others in this room, or comment on things you know nothing about.'

Heads swing away from Roz to Seb, then to Ailsa. Seb looks at Roz. Ailsa looks at Seb, then down at her feet, and slows her breath.

'Meredith and Seb will give a few television interviews tomorrow afternoon. There will be some pieces in the Sunday papers with Meredith. We've made no arrangements with the tabloids, so anyone who approaches you claiming that they have is not telling the truth.'

'Imagine that,' says Seb, and there's a soft sound of laughter.

'Five minutes,' Roz says, and the enchanted circle breaks apart.

Ailsa looks at her feet again. She hopes they remember everything. They love to dance, but boy are they tired. When she looks up, Seb's standing in front of her.

'Hey,' he says. 'There's nothing like a Roz

pep talk to make me nervous as hell. I'm glad one of us will know what I'm supposed to say.'

She puts her hand up, touches the side of his face, smiles. And then someone calls his name and he turns away.

As Montagues and Capulets, Ailsa and her fellow dancers, sitting among the (for now, imaginary) audience, leap to their feet and howl support and derision as the arguments unfold. Ailsa can hardly bear to watch the fights, which seem like fights, nothing acted about them. The power of the words is the greater force, though.

She knows almost every line. Romeo's lines, and the ones either side of them, she could have written down, perfectly, from memory; most of Juliet's she knows, too. And the rest of the play has found its way into her, from watching the films, from reading the play, and from the snippets of gossip and explanations of rehearsal that Seb has given her. It's as though she's been taking in these words with her immunosuppressants every morning and evening. When she hears the words, the cells in her body all react, like daisies turning to the sun.

Romeo's speech, before the music that is the dancers' cue in the party scene, takes her back to Seb's flat, sitting in her chair, listening to him stumble over the last lines, Romeo's last words before he first sees Juliet. 'Bitterly begin his fearful date.' She had forgotten that this was poetry, and love, and life, because they were just lines to memorise.

Seb is word-perfect. And Ailsa knows that this new heart is really hers, because it feels the beat and fall of each syllable as she does, breathless, waiting:

'For my mind misgives
Some consequence, yet hanging in the
    stars,
Shall bitterly begin his fearful date
With this night's revels and expire the
    term
Of a despised life, closed in my breast,
By some vile forfeit of untimely death.
But he that hath the steerage of my
    course
Direct my sail! On, lusty gentlemen!'

And then the music begins. It's a sparse, traditional tune, slow, the sound of the bandoneon strong and steady, two violins crying and praying over the top of it. She steps forward, towards the stage, and Murray catches her eye, takes her hand. And even though she's had to tie the red bandanna around her wrist — this is not about her, she's not an amateur — every step works, every move feels true.

Perhaps the spell is broken.

31 July, 2018

When Seb calls, half an hour after he's left
for the theatre, Ailsa assumes that he's
forgotten something. She's due to go to
work but she's already thinking, as she
answers, of where she can meet him to pass
along whatever it is that he needs. But as
soon as she hears his voice she realises that's
not it —

'What's happened, Seb?'

'You haven't seen? No one's called you?'

'What? Seb, what?' All she can think is
that something's happened to Hayley,
although why Seb would know about it
before she did she can't imagine.

'The papers. There's something else —'

'Is that all? I know what my arse looks
like, I think I can —'

'No. It's Fenella. She's leaked something
to the press. It's online already. I'll send
you a link.'

'I thought you and Fenella were over —'

'We are. Were. I think she must have found out that I asked for her not to be my partner on *StarDance,* so she's getting her own back —'

'But —'

'Look, just watch it. I'm sorry. It looks bad. It is bad. But —' His name is being called in the background. 'I have to go. Ailsa, you know I love you, don't you?' There's something like pleading in his voice. And then he hangs up, before she has the chance to reply.

503

Rom-e-NO: Morley Puts His Fat Foot in It

Seb Morley fans will be shocked today when they see the sensational video Seb's former dance partner, Fenella Albright, has released.

The film was shot on Fenella's phone while the dancers waited to go on stage in the second show of *StarDance* last year. Her partner Seb is out of shot — but we can still hear every word he says.

Celebrity gardener Isabella Dun was dancing a rhumba with her partner Benjii Angelo. Seb scoffs, 'Well, he's never going to do a lift, is he? You'd need a man for each thigh.' He then adds, 'The thing is, she might be good, technically, but with someone her size it's never going to look right. Nobody's going to say it, but the real problem with fat girls dancing is they just look wrong.'

Isabella Dun, who was knocked out of the competition in the quarter-finals, has released a furious statement saying, 'Sebastian's comments are disappointing and ignorant, but nothing new. Women with curves, muscles and hard-working bodies are used to this sort of abuse. I hope that by doing as well as I did in the competition, I showed bigger women — and men — everywhere that regardless of your size you should feel free to do the things that you want to do. I'm not going to say that I'm not hurt, but this kind of name-calling reflects more on the person who is doing it than the target. I have no problem being a fat girl dancing. Though I feel the term "woman" would be less patronising. You'll notice that I have not called Mr Morley an ignorant boy.'

Morley is lying low today, but his agent says: 'I know that Seb is mortified to have some ill-judged remarks broadcast like this. All of us might say things we regret when we're nervous, excited, or in a competitive, high-pressure situation.'

Morley and Albright were a couple for a short time after the show, but have not been seen together in public since Morley left hospital after his eye op. He has sparked gossip after being spotted with a mystery plump pal. She'll have a thing or two to say to him.

Romeo and Juliet, in which Seb stars

opposite the new face of Chanel, Meredith
Katz, opens in Edinburgh tonight.

31 July, 2018

'Thanks for coming, Mum,' Ailsa says. She'd stumbled through her shift this morning, once she'd watched the video clip, three times, maybe four, just to make sure she'd heard it correctly. By then it was trending on Twitter — #fatgirldancing — and being written about everywhere, and there was no way it wasn't true. It nullified the happy answering shout that Apple gave when Seb said that he loved her. Love is not a get-out-of-jail-free card, any more than a faulty heart — or the replacement of it — is an excuse for bad behaviour.

Then Hayley had texted — *Seen the latest. Are you OK?* — and that had been enough to make her lock herself in the loo, take some deep breaths, and call her mother for help. Hayley wasn't working, so she could come straight away, and she did. She's waiting at the flat when Ailsa gets back.

Ailsa clings to her for a long time. 'Thank

507

you,' she gets out.

'No worries, hen. It's just like the old days. Without the' — Hayley steps back, waves her hands in the direction of her chest, fists clenched — 'paddles. Defibrillators.'

A shudder, radiating out from Apple: *Don't.*

It's been an unseasonably warm night, even for the end of July; the windows are open, and a warm breeze blows through the flat.

'Have you eaten?'

'I had a sandwich at work.'

'Bread? Things must be bad. And I can see you've been crying.' Hayley sits down on the sofa, waits for Ailsa to settle with her head in her lap, the way she used to when she was ill. 'Now, tell me all about it.'

'What's to tell? It's definitely him. He didn't deny it. He rang to warn me and sent me the video clip himself, and he left me a voicemail.' Just the thought of it starts her tears again. It's the indignity. She is the fat girl Seb danced with after he'd slagged off fat girls dancing, as though he was making a point, or taking a holiday while he was, briefly, less-than-perfect himself. When he's well, he'll go sparkling away with a new dance partner, tight-arsed and prancing like a — like a shiny unicorn — and even if he does think that he loves her, well, she doesn't want to be some sort of step down for him.

Hayley hands her a tissue. 'Come on, hen. We've got through worse than this. What did he say?'

Ailsa sits up, wipes her eyes and puts her hand to her chest: she has, appropriately enough, heartburn. The bread, probably. Though Apple feels cold and tired, her beat subdued. She takes a deep breath and waits for her breathing to come in waves rather than hailstones.

'He said he was stupid. Excited. He wasn't thinking. He said he felt like everyone else was better than him and it was his way of making himself feel better.'

Hayley says, 'Aye, well.'

'Aye, well? What does that mean?'

'Well,' Hayley says, 'everybody's an idiot once in a while.'

'What?' David wasn't what he might have been. Seb isn't what he pretended to be. Hayley can't do this to her too. 'Why aren't you telling me all men are bastards? Or that you told me so?'

'Would that help?'

Ailsa shakes her head, as though that might wake her up, or dislodge whatever it

509

is in her ear that's making her not hear things properly. 'That's what you do. And you said —'

'What I said,' Hayley says, 'was, dinnae be a WAG. And you're not. I should have known you knew better.' A pause. 'You're not the only one with a sorry to say.'

Ailsa nods and reaches out for her mother. 'But you were right. You said Seb was a charmer.'

'And he is. But, like you said, I'm not exactly a good judge of men.' There's a pointedness in Hayley's voice, but not a lot of it. It's not as sharp as it should be. 'And there's worse things to be than charming.'

'Like a man in a church hall in Guildford,' Ailsa says.

'Aye, well. To each his own.' Oh, God. Ailsa has broken her mother. Why isn't she raging? Looking at her daughter's face, Hayley says, 'Tamsin told me a thing or two. Including that I need tae turn down my lioness act.'

Ailsa nods, but then the tears start again. 'I like it when you're a lioness.'

'You'll like it better when you're a lioness for yourself, hen.'

'I don't feel like a lioness —' She pauses '— before I rang you that day, I ran away. From — David.'

'Did you? Or did you take control?' Hayley asks.

Ailsa shrugs. 'I don't know.' Then, 'What do I do about Seb?'

'Do you have to do anything?'

'No. Yes. I'll see him at the theatre later. All his stuff's here. He said he'd stay at Roz's tonight. He's coming to get his bag.'

'When?'

'He said he'd text a time —' Ailsa looks at her phone '— about half three. Half an hour.' Oh God, oh God, she can't face him. She's put the bag by the door already, but she's going to have to hand it over. 'I've got two missed calls from him. One from his agent. A couple from — papers, probably.' A sob, unexpected and forceful, breaks free from the place beneath her ribs where Ailsa is keeping her tears. 'I haven't spoken to anyone.'

'That's best, I should think.'

'What would I say?' Another sob, another, another, and Hayley holds her until she's calm. Maybe they're both remembering when a problem with her heart was life or death. 'Why aren't you saying all men are bastards? Because I'd agree with you.'

'He's been an idiot. That's a wee bit different.'

'I can't believe you're defending him.'

'I'm not defending him, Ailsa, I'm really not. He made an arse of himself before he met you. People do that. That's what they do. Other people forgive them. And you dinnae need me to tell you it's what's on the inside that counts. Because I really am a terrible mother if you do.'

'The most important thing on my inside isn't even mine.'

'Well, if you're talking about your heart, I don't know who else you think it belongs to.'

Ailsa puts her head in her hands. Her hair feels greasy at the roots. She wants a bath, sleep. She wants Seb. No, she doesn't. But she has to go tonight. She's committed. She's part of a team. She's not the star of the Failing Heart Show anymore.

'I'm not going to be treated like that.'

'No, you're not. What does your name mean?'

'Victory. Warrior.' It's hardly a war cry.

Hayley looks at her daughter, strokes her hair. 'Do you want some tea?'

Ailsa shakes her head. 'No. I'm going to have a bath.'

'Do you want me to run it for you?'

'Thanks, Mum. But — I'm not ill anymore.'

'No, but that's not to say your mother

cannae run you a bath now and then.'

And then the doorbell rings. Ailsa jumps, as though it's connected to her by electrodes, and goes to the window, looks out, steps back as though the air outside is charged enough to give her a shock too.

'It's him.'

'Do you want me to answer it?'

'I want him to go away.'

Hayley looks at her, a long look; the kind that she and Lennox used to get, in their teens, when they said they were going to her room to listen to music. 'I'll tell him that, then.'

'Thanks, Mum.' She'll be a lioness later, when she has to be in the same room with him, has to ignore the looks of everyone who's seen the video. Has to dance, because she is not an amateur, not in this show, not in this life, because she didn't go through all that she went through to go at it half-arsed.

Outside the venue, on the street, Ailsa breathes the city air and wills herself to strength and calmness. She touches the place where the top of her scar is with her left hand, the bottom of it with her right, and feels how well she can mend. And then she's through the bar, which is buzzing with theatre-goers who haven't made their way upstairs yet. There are still forty-five minutes until the show begins. She signs in with Eliza, changes her shoes, and takes one of the seats with a kerchief tied around the back. Guy, at a kerchief-marked chair on the other side of the stage, gives her a wave and she waves back.

Edie comes to speak to her, just a quiet, 'Hello, how are you?' and Ailsa feels her spine straighten, as it always does in response to one of the Gardiner sisters. She drops her shoulders, finds her centre, makes it solid and calm.

And then, because she can only be really calm if she does the right thing, she heads for the curtained-off area that's serving as wings and green room. There's time. She has an idea that she'll leave a note for Seb, but he's there, with Mercutio, deep in conversation. When he sees her, his eyes light, and he excuses himself.

'Ailsa.' He says it cautiously, as though the saying of it might make her disappear.

She shakes her head, quickly, as a way of saying, 'Don't talk to me about it now.'

'I don't want to — interrupt you,' she says, 'but I wanted to say' — she remembers just in time that she can't say good luck, because it's bad luck — 'may the unicorns be with you.'

He nods. 'Thank you. Ailsa, let me explain . . .'

There are tears waiting in her eyes. The shoes he gave her are on her feet. She can't, she can't, she can't talk to him about it, not now. She can barely stand next to him, smelling his skin, remembering how she's trusted him with her body, with Apple. She stands on tip-toe to kiss his cheek, and then she turns away, because to look into those eyes will hurt too much.

It begins exactly on time, as Roz had said it would. There's a street-fight in the first scene where the dancers stamp, beat the tables, bellow the names of Montague or Capulet. Ailsa makes the woman sitting next to her jump and put her hand to her chest, and she feels a small sense of victory. She hears another voice behind her — Tom, maybe — snarl, and she tries a snarl herself, adding it to his, remembering to constrict her throat as she bares her teeth. And when the scene is over — the peace made, after a fashion — here is Seb. Or rather, Romeo. But he's Seb, too, playing a part he's scared of because he doesn't have a choice now, making something real when it's the last thing he wants to do. And instead of her heart shrinking, as she thought it might, it expands.

Juliet isn't sure about being married. And then Romeo, Mercutio and Benvolio are heading for the party. Romeo has, he says, a soul of lead, while Mercutio has dancing shoes with nimble soles. Seb's eyes catch on Ailsa's as the audience laugh. And then the three actors sit, cross-legged, on three blocks they pull to the centre of the stage, so the audience cranes in to see, to hear.

Ailsa had been especially captivated by this scene at dress rehearsal the other night, the liveliness and intensity of it; it made her think of the Edinburgh parks in summer, students in twos and threes, deep in talk and laughter, barely noticing the day move to evening. And — though she hasn't seen a lot of theatre — she admires the way that Roz has put the three actors so they face away from everyone, excluding the audience, making them lean closer, wanting to know more. Seb sits in profile to her so she can see the shape of his forehead and nose against the light beyond, and looking at him hurts, but not as much as thinking about how heedlessly, how easily, he dismissed women like her, before he knew her. And though she knows life is more complicated than it looks from the sidelines, it still feels as though one of these Sebs is pretending.

Before she knows it, it's the cue for the dancers, and here she is, standing, moving, accepting Capulet's outstretched hand and remembering that all she has to do is walk, walk, walk. The lights are brighter and the music louder than she's used to; Apple shudders and dances within, pulsing with the beat of the music.

This is living, Apple sings to her. *This is what you do all of the other days for. Feel my life glow in you. You are not the audience anymore.*

From: Libby
Sent: 3 August, 2018
To: Ailsa
Subject: Calendar

Dear Ailsa,
I hope you are well.

I wanted to let you know that I've posted a calendar out to you. It looks great, and we're very proud of it. But I know (from when they arrived with me) that the cover, which is a montage of photographs of Lennox, is a bit of a shock if you're not prepared.

Anything you can do to help us promote it we'd be grateful for.

Very best,
Libby

From: Ailsa
Sent: 4 August, 2018
To: Libby
Subject: Re: Calendar

Dear Libby,
Thank you — for the calendar and the warning. You were right on both counts. The calendar is really lovely, and seeing Lennox in all those photos made me feel — well, all the things we feel when we

518

lose someone. I'll never forget him; not just because he was my first boyfriend, and for the time we spent together at the end, but because I don't think I'd be the person I am now without him. This time last year I was still so angry with him for dying, and for leaving me to face my own death alone. Now I'm grateful that I had him as part of my life.

I'll put a blog post up in the next couple of days, and I'm giving my copy of the calendar to my mum when I see her at the weekend.

Love to you and the family,

Ailsa x

4 August, 2018

Long Live Romeo and Juliet

'Sell a kidney if you have to, just get a ticket!' declared ecstatic Twitter user @shakespeareordie after the opening of Roz Derbyshire's eagerly awaited Fringe production of *Romeo and Juliet* at The Dragon's Nest in Newington last week. That tweet may have been a little extreme — but theatre critics and the public have been unanimous in their praise for the show, set in a Verona that's somewhere between a mafia hangout and a sultry Buenos Aries. This critic is no different.

The Edinburgh heatwave, which has actors and audience alike all aglow, probably helps, as does the simple staging of Derbyshire's production. The power of this so-often overdone tale of star-crossed lovers is here a tale told through touch and look, through eye and tongue. The actors are, to a man and woman, a pitch-perfect company, resisting melodrama for pathos, and in doing so they make this story into one about every one of us.

Cynics may have been forgiven for thinking that the leads, Sebastian Morley and Meredith Katz, were chosen more for their looks and their audience-pulling-power than they were for their acting skill. But both are sublime. Katz, who has a reputation for coldness both on and off set, is coltish and serious as a preoccupied Juliet, solemn and almost feverish in her love and the death-wish that comes with it. Morley, who was runner-up for the part in the TV reality show that launched his career, shows that the judges on *Wherefore Art Thou?* were correct when they considered him too young for the part. The intervening decade has given him a gravitas that audiences have not seen from him before. He is syllable perfect, in intonation and in depth, and he moves like a man weighed down already by what he seems to know is coming.

Both are supported by a cast of warm and considered performances. There's barely a wrong note, though some of the doubling is confusing, especially as this is so clearly a no-money, no-frills production, with the cast all wearing jeans and plain shirts throughout, with only a kerchief to mark them Montague or Capulet, a cross for the Friar and a sash for the Prince. The only variation is the scene of the revels at the Capulet house, when the cast don identical black eye-masks, and the women wear tango shoes.

And here we come to the other much-vaunted aspect of this show: the tango. Here the local Edinburgh Dance Club do the play proud, joining in the dance with confidence. They certainly aren't ready for *StarDance* but that isn't the point: the fact that there are slightly too many people on the stage, the noise of movement and the disrupted sightlines create a sense of reality rarely seen in a stage production. We can see how Romeo would need to dodge for a sight of Juliet how the Capulets struggle to make him out, and how he can manage to kiss Juliet unnoticed.

All in all, Derbyshire's confidence and verve shine bright.

11 AUGUST, 2018

'I've Lennox's calendar here,' Ailsa says.

'Ruthie mentioned that it was nearly ready when I saw her last,' Hayley says, rousing herself to a slightly more upright position from her sofa slouch. It's a hot Sunday, and they are taking it easy before Emily comes to join them, and then they'll all go to the show. The cotton scarf that Hayley has with her instead of a jacket is new, and has a cheerful yellow pompom trim. It makes Ailsa happy/sad that she's never seen it before today.

They sit side by side and examine the cover: so many Lennoxes. Ailsa has looked at it often since it arrived almost a week ago, but still gets a shock/stab when faced with such clear reminders of his life/death. She'd almost posted it to Hayley, but couldn't quite let it out of her possession, so she'd told herself it was best that they look at it together.

The marathon-finishing photo is here, and one from a gap year trek; here he is, cropped from a school photo, the mop-headed smiler Ailsa first met. Those bright blue eyes never faded, and his face stayed rounded into adulthood, even though as he grew older his body turned lean and taut with all of the sport he played and miles he ran. There's a photo of him holding baby Louisa, one of him graduating, one of him in a suit. It's hard to see so many versions of his face; harder to accept that there won't be any more. Impossible to admit that it's getting harder to carry the memory of how he looked, as time goes on.

'Aye,' Hayley says, shaking her head, 'he was a good lad. It's not right.'

And then she starts to turn over the pages. January is an older woman with a purple bob, whose sign says, 'GRATEFUL'. Ailsa is February. She looks happy and healthy, flesh-coloured flesh rather than blue-grey. The red lipstick that she wiped away afterwards looks lovely.

'Oh,' Hayley says when she sees it. 'Oh, Ailsa. You look — you look alive.'

Ailsa nods. It's strange, to be in Lennox's calendar, her face caught at the moment where Seb came out into the garden and blew a kiss to her. Whenever she looks at the photo, she feels — complicated, because what she is looking at is both true and not true. It's her, and it isn't. Or maybe it's a version of herself that she doesn't recognise, because it's not the one she thought she'd be, once Apple arrived with her promise of 100 per cent life. She keeps on turning the pages. Seb, in July, is laughing, bright, his trilby pushed back and the green of his eyes almost glowing against the background of his clear skin and the shadow cast by the tree behind him. Ailsa looks away.

'Have you talked to him?'

'Yes. No,' Ailsa says. 'I see him at the show.' When she's not with him she can almost talk herself into understanding how easily the whole thing came about. But when she sees him, his ridiculous hand-someness, the way he is a perfect match for Meredith, it makes sense that he would mock a fat girl dancing. On the nights when she's been scheduled to take part in the show, she's avoided looking in his direction when the dancers have got to their feet. There's always been an eagerness for Seb's hand, anyway. And Ailsa has brought her feelings to the dance each time, her tango sad and furious, hurting. Roz has praised her performance. If only she knew.

'Have you tried?'

'No.' He had come to collect his suitcase while she was out at work, the day after the story broke, and in the busyness of the show, there's never a moment to say what she needs to say. But she doesn't know what that should be, could be. How do people ever sort things out?

'Living is hard,' she says. It sounds pathetic but she doesn't care.

Hayley laughs. 'Death's worse, hen.'

'I know.' But does it always have to be this — you must always be grateful, because you're not dead? Maybe it is that simple. They sit, quietly, in something that is starting to be companionship again. They've talked about David once or twice, but there doesn't seem to be much more to say.

'How are you and Auntie T getting on?'

Hayley gets up and goes to the window; she perches on the sill, lights a cigarette and laughs. 'Well, the novelty isnae wearing off yet. We sit up half the night talking about nothing, half the time.'

'Do you like it?' Ailsa keeps wanting to ask this, but she's scared. Scared that the answer will be no. Or yes. Or that Hayley will ask the question back.

Her mother gives her a long look. 'I think I do. How do you like your independence?'

She smiles. 'Too early to say. I miss you.

But I think I like it.'

Hayley nods. 'That's as it should be. I'm starting tae think I'll maybe find a permanent job in Glasgow. I've done twenty-five years of locum work. Tamsin says that's long enough tae be a temp. And I could do with some paid holidays.'

'That sounds good,' Ailsa says, and it does. And different; another soft shift in her landscape. *But,* Apple chips in, *if you get to do what you like, then your mother does too.*

Hayley leans out of the window to stub out her cigarette, and Ailsa sees her body stiffen. 'Visitor for you, I think.'

'Who?'

'Who do you think?' Hayley comes towards her, and the smell of cigarette smoke and soap is something that even Apple understands now is one of the best smells that there is. 'Come on. He's come to talk to you.'

So she goes to the window. He is standing on the pavement two storeys below her, looking up.

'I got the calendar,' he calls. 'Wilkie sent it on.'

Ailsa pauses, absorbing the sound of his voice, reaching up to her. Then: 'What do you think of it?'

'I've emailed Libby and told her I'll do

527

anything she needs to promote it.' He's pale, tired-looking: his face is as white as the inside of her wrist. He rubs his hands across his forehead. She leans forward, craning out of the window to see him better. He takes a step forward. It would be so easy to ask him to come up. And, at the same time, impossible.

'That's good of you,' she says, and means it.

He nods. 'Your photo. You look perfect,' he calls up. 'Like — like yourself.'

She thinks of all the things she could say; for all she hasn't been talking to Seb in real life, she's had plenty to say to him as she's walked to work and back, watched him on the stage, thought about him as she's lain awake, high/tired after dancing. But she doesn't. Because it comes to her — or Apple, maybe — in a flash, that he doesn't have to be doing this — this ordinary, difficult thing of trying to put things right. He could be laughing with Meredith, flirting with — God, with anybody, he just needs to throw a stick and whoever it hits will probably be up for it. But he's here, standing on the pavement, looking up at her, hope and sadness on his face. If there was a tree, she thinks, he'd climb it.

'Thank you,' she says. She hopes he knows

she means it. She's leaning further forward, because the one thing she does know is that she wants there to be less space, less air, between them. She opens her mouth to speak, to invite him in, but then there's a smell, sudden and strong. Driftwood: beach and sky, love and sorrow. And it might be permission or it might be a warning, but it's enough to stay her tongue.

He spreads his hands. 'I don't know what to say. If I could change it, I would. I know I'm not Lennox, and I wouldn't try to be. But I'm trying to be a better me.'

Is her head nodding? She can't tell. 'Me too,' she gets out, even though her mouth is as dry as the bark of an apple tree.

'Don't let this be it,' he says, 'please. We're just getting started.'

She wants to say something, about how she knows she has to trust her heart but that feels too complicated, about how, maybe, however much he didn't mean it, there was the smallest glance of truth in what he said. But nothing will come.

She nods. Apple aches as only a healthy heart can. 'I'll see you later,' she says.

He nods, looks down, then up again, and takes off his sunglasses. She knows how it must hurt, this bright afternoon. And then he turns and walks away.

■ ■ ■ ■

Hayley suggests that she take a rest before they leave for the show, and though Ailsa doesn't think she'll sleep, she actually falls into something like unconsciousness, and when her mother wakes her, for just a second or two she's lost in time, and it's as though she has her old heart back in her body, feeble and afraid as it was this time last year, and she's frightened and panicky, and wraps her hands tight around her mother's forearms and sits up with a lurch.

'Easy,' Hayley says, and Ailsa nods, swallows, and feels Apple's steady beat. And knows what she has to do.

When she slips behind the green-room curtain before the show begins, a clutch of the actors is there, but there's no sign of Seb. They look around, nod, and go back to their conversation. Seb's jacket is on one of the pegs along the wall, along with his sash and the mask he'll wear during the party scene. She takes the unicorn headband from her bag and hangs it over the mask, so he can't miss it, and hopes he understands what she's trying to say: I know, now, that what we do is not always what we are.

Emily and Hayley are sitting with Ailsa, so it's hard to concentrate in the same way during the play; Ailsa wants to look at them, read their faces, whisper secrets. But she doesn't. She bellows and howls in the fight scene, the way she always does, and then she feels every one of Romeo's lines, in the filaments beneath her skin, in the second before he says them.

Soon they are at her favourite scene, the pre-party huddle of Romeo, Benvolio and Mercutio, and she is lulled along in the familiar rise-and-fall of it, the dynamic of the three actors, when something changes. Seb, instead of responding to Mercutio's teasing with a poke in the chest, gets up and turns away. Mercutio, after a heartbeat, turns too. Seb turns his back on his fellows and, looking at Ailsa — and only at her, she can see it, and so, it seems, can others, as they follow Seb's eyeline — says, 'Is love a tender thing? It is too rough / Too rude, too boisterous, and it pricks like thorn.'

Mercutio gets to his feet and cuffs Romeo around the head — it looks as though it's more than acting — pulling him back to the central huddle as he says his next line.

And then it's back to business as usual, Romeo lovelorn, Seb word-perfect and focussed on his fellows as he has been in every other performance. Until, as they stand and move, he mispronounces a line: 'Fearfully begins my bitter fate,' he says, and if the others notice, they don't flicker.

Ailsa notices.

Of all the lines in the play, he would never, ever get this one wrong.

Ailsa inhales, feels the perfect four-four beat of this gifted heart. She has made mistakes. She has hurt people she loves. She can walk away, or she can be brave.

Benvolio calls for the drum, the rest of the actors come from behind the archway, masks already covering their eyes, and Mercutio, Benvolio and Romeo disguise themselves too.

It's time.

Ailsa puts her own mask on. Guy is on his feet, opposite, stepping towards the stage, taking a delighted Nurse in his arms; behind her, Ailsa hears Venetia's chair scrape as she stands, and to her right, Eliza snakes her way towards Tybalt's beckoning. Ailsa stands, takes a breath, steps forward, remembering to smile, raise her chin ('You'll only look ridiculous,' Roz says, 'if you go half-cocked at it.').

And Seb is there: a bow, a smile, a question in his almost-perfect eyes and his arms ready for her. She puts her hand on his shoulder and feels where her thumb fits into his collarbone, the way his fingers spread across her back, strong and true. His other hand laces hers, and he pulls her closer. She waits for the nervousness but it isn't there. Not this time. Because all she needs to do is keep her heart opposite his heart.

■ ■ ■ ■

Part Ten:
October 2018
Sweet Division

■ ■ ■ ■

10 October, 2018

Happy Anniversary

This time last year, my mother and I were looking at each other and at the transplant coordinator, trying to work out if we'd just heard what we thought we'd heard.

The heart was a match. We needed to get my fading blue carcass down to theatre as quickly as we could, and prise my rib-cage open, and wait for the swap. Fingers crossed, I would wake up with a chance of seeing 2017 out. Fingers crossed, I would wake up.

There wasn't really time to be scared, or to think beyond the next eight hours. And anyway, that would have been a waste of thinking, because I had no idea of what it would be like, to be Ailsa instead of Blue-Heart. To be normal.

In a way it will never be over. I'll never stop taking the tablets. I'll never be un-scarred. That time I lost to hospital-waiting, hospital-hoping, it's all gone. I won't get it back.

But, here I am. I can dance, after a fashion. I've a job. I've a career plan. I've joined a hill-walking group (over and above the fact that anyone who lives in Edinburgh is, by definition, a member of a hill-walking group) because I will climb a mountain one day. My friend Jacob is getting married next year, which means I need a passport to get to the wedding in France.

Here's something I realised, this summer. Being ill for so long, waiting for a heart for so long, made me a permanent child. Today — a year on from transplant day — I'm going to admit it: I'm an adult.

And I'm going to be honest: I don't like it as much as I thought I would. It's not as thrilling as I'd hoped. In particular, this ordinariness business can be quite — ordinary. You might say dull. And the biggest bit of growing up I've had to do is admitting that there are times when I quite miss being blue. Not all of it. But the way it made me special.

I've forgotten, sometimes, that I was special like Juliet was special. She had death hanging over her from the start. That's no way to live. Everything tastes of ashes.

Here's what I've been mulling over, since the Festival left town and I sat down in my flat and did some serious planning. There's no such thing as ordinary, just like there's not really a normal. And there's no such thing as special, either. Or rather, we bring our own special. We make it. We make it when we dare and we make it when we ask for help. We make our lives special when we choose to forgive and move on, and not to make ourselves the centre of everything. We make specialness by trusting to the music and the dance.

I know blogging's been sparse these last few weeks. Life's been full on and I've needed a bit of time, so I've taken it.

I've been thinking.

I'm working more hours.

My hospital checks are going down to fortnightly.

I'm going to be working with the Lennox Life Trust (have you got your calendar yet? Click *here*) to set up a support and mentoring scheme for post-transplant patients.

I've applied for a passport.

I've asked my mother to come away on holiday with me for a week in January. We're going to go and get warm somewhere. I'm going to lie on a beach in a bikini and the world can look at my scar and the wobbly bit of tummy that's determined to stay, and it can judge if it wants to. What the world thinks of me is irrelevant.

I've decided I want to do a Scottish law conversion and I'm applying for that. I know you said OU, but I think working in Scottish law will suit me better. I'm grateful for your thoughts — but I trust Apple and I trust my gut, so I'm going with them.

I'm looking for some voluntary work to help me get a bit of legal understanding.

I'm getting on with my life. I have good days and bad ones. There are people that I miss and times when I think I didn't deserve this Apple of mine. Which is probably normal. Which makes me glad.

There are going to be some changes on the blog, too. I'm probably going to move it to a new site with a new name, and I'm going to move the focus away from me and towards the broader health and transplant world. (And I'm going to make that more exciting than that sounds.) The way I've done things has outlived its usefulness. It hurt people who were close to me for the sake of the ones who are far away. That's no way to live.

For now, I'm signing off until 2019.

Just one poll before I go. I'm going to leave it here for as long as I feel like it. You'll see why.

Is it time to stop using the blog polls to

make decisions that I need to take respon-
sibility for myself?

YES, BlueHeart. It was fun while it lasted
and it made your point, but things move
on.
YES, Ailsa. Listen to the people who love
you, but take control. Have confidence.

That's all for now, folks. Dance on.

Ailsa x

From: Seb
Sent: 11 October, 2018
To: Ailsa
Subject: Goodbye Blue Heart

Hey, BlueHeart,

I'm a bit sad that I'm never going to call you that again, but it seems like it's time to let it go. You'll be Ailsa from now on. Or CaveDancer. You choose.

I know we said we'd only talk once a week (I love the talking) and not overdo emails but that YES/YES should be marked. I hope Apple likes the flowers. They're definitely not for you. 😊

I am completely bloody knackered. Saskia is relentless. She's the dance partner equivalent of Roz. She says we can't rest on our laurels, just because we got through on Saturday, and she's written the 'hands like hams' comment that one of the judges made on the rehearsal-room mirror in lipstick. We're doing Viennese Waltz and it's horrible — it makes you dizzy and yesterday I threw up. Today she brought in a bucket so if I was sick again I wouldn't waste time running to the bathroom. I'm only 85% sure it was a joke.

No sickness today but we did have a

costume fitting so that gave me a break. I've got a coat with tails and it's powder-blue with silver lapels. I'm sending you a photo. My sister says I look like Ken (as in Barbie). I told Saskia. She says she wishes I could dance that well. That was definitely a joke. Her sister's on dialysis, and has been for three years. I think you'd like her (Saskia, I haven't met her sister).

Next week is tango week. If I get through you HAVE to come. Please? I want you to see Saskia laughing at me (she's much worse when the cameras are off). Tango is her thing so it's going to be carnage in rehearsal. Even if you could only come for the recording (I know you're busy) I'd love to see you, and for you to meet everyone. I wouldn't expect you to stay with me. Though of course you'd be welcome. Little Seb would love to spend some time with you. He says to tell you, in case you're wondering, that he's not seeing anyone else.

I saw Roz (briefly) yesterday. She says hi. She's meeting people about Love's Labour's Lost. Meredith's got a couple of film offers for next year. I don't know whether Roz was looking at her for LLL or not. She was bloody amazing in the show but I'm not sure that makes up for rehearsals. I've told Roz I think we should have open auditions. She said, Oh, yes, we could make a documentary about it. There's no escaping TV.

How's it going?

Am I allowed to say I miss you?

Seb x

From: Ailsa
To: Seb

Hello you,

I miss you. Especially when emails like that make me laugh. Saskia sounds like my mother. (My mother's here for a couple of days. She says hello.) A few of us from work are getting together to watch the show on Saturday night. Please send gossip. It's my currency.

Is your eye OK? Is it weird knowing that the last of the stitches are gone? I thought of you.

Thanks for being nice about the blog. I've been writing that post for three weeks. I still don't think it says every-thing, but it's as close as I could get. And the flowers are gorgeous.

It's going OK, I think. Mum has got a job in a place just outside Glasgow. She's taking over from a pharmacist who's retiring. She's got a three-month contract but if it goes well she can make it permanent. She says she likes that she's getting to know people. And that she doesn't work Sundays. She might have said something about going speed dating with Tamsin but I'm in denial about that. I've told her that if she does want to come back to live here, I'll move out. (I said it in a nice way, because I meant it in a nice way. It's getting easier, for sure.) But she and Tamsin seem to be having a ball. So I had Christa and her partner Kate over yesterday, to talk about them moving in when their lease is up (February). They're starting a business and they need to save money. I need to have some more income. Job done. Plus, they can cook.

I had an email from my biological father saying he'd like to have another go at getting to know me, and maybe I'd like to come to Guildford and meet everyone. I've said I'd need to bring my mother. That should put a stop to it.

This week I've mainly been trying to find some work experience in a law firm for next year. I thought offering to work for free would be enough to get me something easily but no, there are a thousand thousand other legal-profession hopefuls in the queue ahead of me. There's a woman who comes into the shop for her coffee (Ethiopian double espresso, pecan Danish, if we have any) and she's a barrister. I'm going to pluck up my courage and ask for advice.

Application deadline for the course is March but I'm going to try to get it in next week and then it's done. Libby's asked me to do a bit of work on the Lennox website so I'll get on to that.

I've been asked to work full-time for December so I might be able to sneak some time off in advance and come to London. I really want to see you. But I also really meant it when I said we should see how we felt after six months. August was so — full on. I know that's normal for you but it isn't for me. I want to trust how I feel before I see you. Sorry. It's all a muddle. I'm not explaining very well.

I hope you don't need the bucket today.

Ailsa x

P.S. I am ignoring your Little Seb reference in the hope you'll realise that the naming of parts isn't — oh I can't say that, can I? Because of Apple.

From: Seb
To: Ailsa

I nearly didn't mention you coming for the tango week show, but it seemed dishonest not to, because it's all I can think about. I understand if you feel it's not the right time.

Dress rehearsal today. Saskia said I wasn't terrible. I told her about your blog a couple of weeks ago. She sent the link to her sister and she's read it from end to end. I sent her a calendar too. They both say hi.

Did you watch the DVD of Love's Labour's Lost yet? I watched mine in bed on Friday night. I know. Rock and roll. Two things I noticed. One: Berowne is the best of them by miles. Two: at the end he says, 'Our wooing doth not end like some old play'. I thought about you and me. Last time I saw Roz, she said the happy ending was 'implicit' and in the final scene, when the women leave, they'll be wearing colour for the first time in the play.

547

Here's hoping.

Seb x

If you say 'my heart' instead of Apple I'll stop saying 'Little Seb'.

From: Ailsa
To: Seb

I did watch it. Berowne definitely has the best lines. And if the old play is R and J — all the better.

'Behold the window of mine heart, mine eye.'

Mine heart. My heart.

I think I might come to London. I've got some new red shoes and a matching bag. They need an adventure.

Ailsa x

15 OCTOBER, 2018

Dear Stranger,

I know I'm supposed to write to your family, but I can't bear to visualise them, the same way I can't imagine what would have happened to my mother, if I had died. I hope that when the transplant coordinator passes this letter on to them, they'll understand.

You're the one who registered as an organ donor, gave permission for your heart to be taken from you, and so you are the one who saved my life.

You did more than save it, in fact. You created it. Because what I had, up until then, was the best that medical science could do for a baby born with Hypoplastic Left Heart Syndrome in 1990. I'm grateful for the operations that I had and the check-ups that headed trouble off at the pass. Doctors found ways to keep me alive in the hope — and it is a hope,

549

even though that's a terrible thing to admit — that a heart would arrive and save me.

Thanks to you, I am not so much continuing my life, as living for the first time. Don't get me wrong, I did my best before: I started a degree there was no guarantee I would finish, and I went to all-night film screenings with my friends. I went to about half of the things I was invited to and stayed out as late as I could manage. I had a lovely boyfriend, a few great flings and one or two adventures that make me cringe when I remember them. I wrote about the things that happened to me so that someone who started a few months or years after me along the same road would have an idea of what was coming, and might cope better than I did.

But I was powerless. I felt, fundamentally, like a human-shaped object wrapped around a patched-together not-heart-shaped heart. And I waited, with all the strength I could find, for the double-six that is an available, matching heart when you're not too ill to embrace it. People call it bravery. It isn't. But I've come to understand that it's something.

You, my heart donor, were the double

six. The unlucky throw that you made became the best thing that's ever happened to me.

I cannot tell you how grateful I am. But I am. My mother is too. We are all each other has. We always have been. There are other people we love, and who love us, but for most of my life, if I was the failing heart, she was the hard-working, over-compensating lungs that kept me going.

I'll be honest. I haven't completely got a handle on your heart, yet. It's doing great things, pumping me up steps and getting all the blood to all the places so I can act like a real person.

I'm not yet the woman I hoped that I would be. But I'm working on that. Rome wasn't built in a day. I didn't think I would save the world. But I thought I would know where to start with making my life count. I didn't, then. I think I do now.

And the fact that I'm here, now, working on it at all, is down to you.

I'm sorry for all the things you didn't get to do, or be. I chose not to know anything about you, which I think is, if not exactly cowardice, the opposite of the thing that isn't bravery that kept me going until your heart came along. I think I was afraid of hearing something that I would never be able to forget. What I do know about you, whoever you are, is that there will be a small, tight circle of people grieving for you, every day, with every breath. Wider than that, there'll be others — colleagues, partners-of-siblings, friends from the gym or the pub — all suffering your loss in smaller ways.

I am trying hard to do justice to this perfectly functioning pump of ours. It seems really loud to me. I wonder if it seemed loud to you. Probably not. But I wonder if you ever thought about the noise it made, the way it moved. Sometimes I lie in bed at night and fall asleep by thinking about the happy pulse and thump of it. It's the sort of music you can dance to.

Thank you.

Ailsa x

ACKNOWLEDGEMENTS

It took me a long time to find my way into this book. Jackie Leach Scully, Monica Buckland and Lorraine gave me the key to unlocking Ailsa's story, and it wouldn't be what it is without them.

Professor Martin Elliott, MD FRCS FRSA lent his expertise and patience in helping me to find, then understand, Ailsa's heart condition. Kate Beales answered endless questions about my imaginary Edinburgh production. Toni Glitz shared Pam's story of corneal transplant. Julie Grey, Helen Dobson and Victoria Tremlett talked to me about different health aspects of this novel. Many others shared memories of Edinburgh, dancing, acting, press reporting, studying the law, parenting sick children, illness and recovery. Thank you all, in particular Katy Bromberg, Jane Buffham, Ian Burdon, Jacq Kelly, Virginia Moffatt, Ann Ogbomo and the people who spoke to me on condition that they weren't mentioned in the acknowledgements — you know who you are! Thank you too to Meredith Katz and Edie and Eliza Gardiner, who gave me permission to use their wonderful names.

I learned to tango as part of my research for this book, though Ailsa does it WAY better. Thank you to Angela and Andi of Tango on Tyne and the dancers at their weekly class, who were patient and helpful, and who showed me the wonder and excitement of this life-affirming dance.

Although much of writing is solitary, there's a lot of support that goes on around it. Thank you to my long-suffering family and friends, who put up with much for the sake of my career. Honourable mentions: Alan, Ned, Joy, Mum, Dad, Auntie Susan, Jude, Lou, Tom, Rebecca, Scarlet.

My fellow novelists Carys Bray, Sarah Franklin and Shelley Harris are always there with sage advice and/or silliness, as required, and I feel honoured to have their intelligence and friendship in my life. Shelley, thank you for all the times you've told me it's going to be all right.

My agent Oli Munson is steady and wise; my editor Eli Dryden eggs me on to better writing with insight and vision. And they are both great friends. My wider publishing team, at A. M. Heath and Bonnier Zaffre, are unfailingly hard-working, professional and creative, and working with them is a joy. Thank you all.

My beta-readers were Joanne Baird, Kate Beales, Alan Butland, Jude Evans, Emily Medland, Tom Nelson, Jackie Leach Scully and Susan Young, and their comments were immensely helpful in shaping this book.

Emily Field is a real person, who generously bid to name a character as part of the #AuthorsForGrenfellTower auction. Real-life Emily is as wonderful as Ailsa's best friend Emily is, and they wear the same perfume.

ABOUT THE AUTHOR

Stephanie Butland lives with her family near the sea in the northeast of England. She writes in a studio at the bottom of her garden, and when she's not writing, she trains people to think more creatively. For fun, she reads, knits, sews, bakes, and spins. She is an occasional performance poet and the author of *The Lost for Words Bookshop.*

The employees of Thorndike Press hope you have enjoyed this Large Print book. All our Thorndike, Wheeler, and Kennebec Large Print titles are designed for easy reading, and all our books are made to last. Other Thorndike Press Large Print books are available at your library, through selected bookstores, or directly from us.

For information about titles, please call:
(800) 223-1244

or visit our website at:
gale.com/thorndike

To share your comments, please write:
Publisher
Thorndike Press
10 Water St., Suite 310
Waterville, ME 04901